Michael Jecks gave up a career in the computer industry to concentrate on writing and the study of medieval history, especially that of Devon and Cornwall. He is a regular speaker at library and literary events, was the Chairman of the Crime Writers' Association in 2004, and judges awards for the CWA and other literary groups.

All his novels featuring Sir Baldwin Furnshill and Bailiff Simon Puttock are available from Headline.

Michael lives with his wife, children and dogs in northern Dartmoor.

Acclaim for Michael Jecks' previous mysteries:

'This fascinating portrayal of medieval life and the corruption of the Church will not disappoint. With convincing characters whose treacherous acts perfectly combine with a devilishly masterful plot, Jecks transports readers back to this wicked world with ease' *Good Book Guide*

'A torturous and exciting plot . . . The construction of the story and the sense of period are excellent' *Shots*

'Captivating . . . If you care for a well-researched visit to medieval England, don't pass this series' *Historical Novels Review*

'Michael Jecks has a way of dipping into the past and giving it the immediacy of a present-day newspaper article . . . He writes . . . with such convincing charm that you expect to walk round a corner in Tavistock and meet some of the characters' *Oxford Times*

'Jecks' knowledge of mediev~~al~~ ~~his~~ used here to great effect' *Crim~~e~~*

Also by Michael Jecks and available from Headline

MICHAEL JECKS

Dispensation of Death

headline

First published in 2007
by HEADLINE PUBLISHING GROUP

First published in paperback in 2007
by HEADLINE PUBLISHING GROUP
1

Cataloguing in Publication Data is available from the British Library

ISBN 978 0 7553 3281 6

Typeset in Times by Avon DataSet Ltd,
Bidford-on-Avon, Warwickshire

Printed and bound in Great Britain by Clays Ltd, St Ives plc

Headline's policy is to use papers that are natural, renewable and
recyclable products and made from wood grown in sustainable
forests. The logging and manufacturing processes are expected to
conform to the environmental regulations of the country of origin.

HEADLINE PUBLISHING GROUP
An Hachette Livre UK Company
338 Euston Road
London NW1 3BH

www.headline.co.uk
www.hodderheadline.com

This book is for Quintin Jardine and Eileen.

The best company.

Cast of Characters

Sir Baldwin de Furnshill — the keeper of the King's Peace in Devon, and occasional investigator of crimes, Baldwin has become a Member of Parliament

Jeanne — Sir Baldwin's wife and only recently mother of his son

Simon Puttock — the first friend Sir Baldwin made when he returned to his old manor at Furnshill, Simon was Bailiff to the old Abbot of Tavistock

Margaret — Simon's wife

Rob — for the last few months Simon has been the Keeper of the Port of Dartmouth under the Abbot, and Rob is his servant from that town

In London

King Edward II
– the feeble and feckless King of England from 8 July 1307 to 20 January 1327

Queen Isabella
– wife to King Edward II

Peter of Oxford
– Chaplain to the Queen

Earl Edmund of Kent
– also known as Edmund of Woodstock, the Earl was the King's youngest half-brother

Piers de Wrotham
– Earl Edmund's adviser and spy

Sir Hugh le Despenser
– the King's best friend and reputed lover, Sir Hugh became a tyrant in all but name

Ellis Brooke
– Sir Hugh's most trusted henchman, Ellis has been with him for many years

William Pilk
– a loyal servant to Sir Hugh, William detests Ellis and looks forward to taking his post

Jack atte Hedge
– Jack has known Sir Hugh for many years and is now used as a specialist – an assassin

Lady Eleanor de Clare
– niece to King Edward II,

Eleanor is wife to the Despenser

Alicia – one of Lady Eleanor's companions, Alicia has become a lady-in-waiting to the Queen

Mabilla – sister to Ellis, Mabilla is one of the Queen's ladies-in-waiting

Richard Blaket – a known and trusted guard from inside the palace complex

Arch – the guard from the south-east corner of the palace walls

Bishop Walter de Stapledon – hated by much of the country, the Lord High Treasurer has long been a friend of Simon and Baldwin

Bishop John Drokensford – Bishop of Bath and Wells, John is one of many who is sure that the tyranny of Despenser must soon be ended – by any means

Bishop Roger Martival – the Bishop of Salisbury, and another important and powerful cleric in the politics of the day

Glossary

Alaunt — a form of hunting dog. There were many types, but some were noted for their unthinking ferocity. Quite large, similar generally to a greyhound (but much larger than modern ones), with strong, short jaws and squarer heads

Corrody — when a loyal servant wished to retire, sometimes his master would win him a pension, or 'corrody'

Familia — the term given to a household. In a religious household, it would mean all those who slept under the Bishop's roof i.e. all the clerics, the cook, the servants, etc

Gipon — a close-fitting tunic, reaching to the knees, with tight-fitting sleeves

Rounsey — a type of horse, popular for being strong and hardy, that was ideal for a richer man's general use

Author's Note

It is quite common for an author like me to begin his or her series in a specific location. After all, it makes life a lot easier generally, because the author only needs to research one area – be it a town or city – but there are also sound logistical reasons for doing so, because many types of book need the stability of the single location. They wouldn't work accurately over a broader sweep.

Modern police procedurals are a perfect example: if you have a detective working for Devon and Cornwall Constabulary, it's OK to have him working in Exeter and, at a pinch, migrate him to Plymouth. However, there are many practical and political problems about moving the same poor devil to the depths of Greater Manchester (where his life expectancy could also be significantly reduced).

For medieval stories there is a greater tendency to stick to a specific and well-bounded location – people didn't tend to travel far. The average freeman, for instance, would rarely travel farther than twenty miles from home. Many did indeed go on lengthy pilgrimages, but for a medieval murder writer like me, I have to bear in mind the strict boundaries of authority, from those between the

Church and secular world, from one Lord's manor to another's, from county to county, among many others. It is more realistic to stay in one area.

The trouble is, my characters are living in 'real time', for want of a better description. Each murder they investigate has been set in a specific month and year, and the two fellows and their wives are growing older year by year. And now historical events are beginning to overtake them. It is because I want to be able to explain the politics of the time that I have been forced to make poor Sir Baldwin a Member of Parliament, a post which is uniquely unsuited to him, bearing in mind that he is honest, decent, and a man of integrity.

It was necessary, though. Sir Baldwin has to be involved in the great debates of the time, and the first of these was the discussion about the French territories, King Edward II's requirement to pay homage to the French King, Charles IV, and the matter of who should be sent to negotiate with the French on Edward's behalf.

There were many eminent diplomats at this time, but for any of them to untangle the dreadful situation was asking rather too much. For those who are interested, there are many books on this period which go into the affairs in more detail, but for the majority who want a taster, here goes!

There were several spark-points. The first was that the French King was angling to take over the remaining English possessions in France.

This can be a little confusing, but suffice it to say that the English had retained some French assets. These areas operated under the English King's laws, and he was the supreme judge, so if there was a dispute, litigants could plead in his courts. However, they were French territories which were held by the English King under the rules of feudal law. That meant he must go to his master, the French King, and pay homage for them.

In 1325 King Edward II did not want to.

There were some pretty good reasons why he didn't. One was the journey. Travelling over the English Channel was not like climbing into a ferry and listening to massive diesels thundering deep below you and pushing you across. Men and women died on the crossings. When there was bad weather, or when the wind turned, a ship could be left bobbing about like a cork for days. And sometimes ships were thrown against rocks.

Now the King accepted his feudal duties, but even so, he had already paid homage several times during his reign – to the French King's father, Philip the Fair, and to his brothers (I think) Louis X and Philip V. It was not his fault that the French kings kept dying with monotonous regularity – and he did complain about having to go yet again. However, it's clear that much of his refusal was prevarication because he didn't really want to swear fealty. To do so could have imposed restrictions upon his powers, and would have forced him to accept his subservience to the French. That would have been insufferable.

His reluctance was not helped by the fact that King Charles had recently overrun and confiscated the English possessions. The reason for this, the War of Saint-Sardos, is fairly convoluted, but can be simply explained.

I mentioned that the English courts held sway in the English territories. Charles IV needed a pretext to invade. One line of attack was to undermine the English legal system. So petitioners dissatisfied with losing their cases before the English courts were persuaded to take their cases to the French courts for a more sympathetic hearing. And the French King took to telling his English vassal, King Edward II, to overturn decisions already declared in King Edward's courts. This was intolerable for the English, but didn't directly cause the war.

The second line was much more problematic. In Saint-Sardos there was a priory which was a dependent house of the Abbey of Sarlat. The enterprising Abbot of Sarlat was content that his dependency was an indivisible part of his Abbey, and as such it was responsible only to the French Crown. It couldn't be detached and held liable under any other laws. That was problematic, but then the Abbot decided to build a *bastide*, a fortified town, on his lands in Saint-Sardos, and the foundations were laid for the war.

It was clearly a deliberate provocation. To put up a castle in the midst of the King of England's duchy without permission was tweaking his nose unmercifully – but worse than that, the locals considered themselves to be English too, and didn't like the high-handed efforts of the Abbot. So the English reacted as they have done through centuries. A mob stormed the works, destroyed them, and when a French official remonstrated, he was hanged.

This was the 'riot' that caused the invasion of the Agenais. The town of Montpezat held out for some little while, as did La Réole, but soon it grew obvious that they couldn't survive, and King Edward II's brother, Edmund, who was in charge of the army for the King, was forced to surrender. Shortly afterwards the castle at Montpezat was razed to the ground in punishment for holding out.

And as all this was going on, the English King and his wife were going through what may charitably be described as 'a difficult time', owing to the fact that she was the French King's sister – oh, and the English King was having a homosexual affair with his chief adviser, Sir Hugh le Despenser, one of the most repellent and thieving politicians we have ever seen in our country.

Sir Hugh did not so much bend the rules as ignore them: he took what he wanted, by threatening the owners with murder if they refused; he stole from widows shortly after their men had died in the King's service; he used torture to extort lands from the recalcitrant. In an age when many nobles and knights were little better than felons (look at the Folvilles, the Coterells, and the deplorable Sir Gilbert Middleton) Sir Hugh le Despenser stands out as a particularly nasty piece of work.

There is one more aspect of research which has given me some headaches – the layout and use of Westminster's halls.

The Great Hall was already old by the time of this story. Built by the Conqueror's son, William Rufus, it is the largest surviving stone hall in Europe. Now it is the only relic of the ancient palaces of Westminster. The other buildings were destroyed by fire in the nineteenth century, which is why the current palace was built. However, the others must have been extraordinary.

South of the Great Hall was the Lesser Hall, which was

where early on the monarch performed his legal and administrative duties, as well as eating. Possibly built by Edward the Confessor, it would have been a single-storey hall until the time of Henry II, when a second was added. At the eastern wall was another hall, pointing towards the river. This was the Painted Hall, noted at the time for the magnificent quality of the pictures set about the walls, and also for its wooden ceiling with decorative *peterae*, flat panels with shields or rosettes carved into them. The chamber had to be redecorated after a fire in 1263, and in Baldwin and Simon's time, this was the state bedchamber.

However the whole of this palace complex was rambling. There are no maps to show exactly what the layout was in 1325, where corridors and passages may have led, nor even how the roof of the Great Hall was supported. There may have been one or two rows of columns holding it up – we have no way of telling. So, as usual, I have had to read through many descriptions, try to make sense of archaeological works, and when all else failed, guess!

For those who want to learn more of the history of Westminster and its buildings, I can recommend 'The Archaeology of Medieval London' by Christopher Thomas, Sutton 2002; 'Medieval London Houses' by John Schofield, Yale 1995 & 2003; 'Westminster Kings and the Medieval Palace of Westminster' by John Cherry and Neil Stratford, 'Occasional Paper 115' from the British Museum's Department of Medieval and Later Antiquities, 1995.

As usual with all my works, where there are any errors, they are my own. However, I have made some conscious decisions to make this work of fiction a little more comprehensible, such as moving much of the action to the Great Hall rather than confuse the reader with references to other chambers and simplifying the Queen's block.

I have invented the situations in this book. I have invented a murder – and put genuine historical figures in the frame. There's a certain sense of guilt at suggesting that these people could have been responsible for such a crime; however, I am confident that the main political leaders of the time were so uniquely venal, ruthless, and violent, that even were they to be watching me over my shoulder, I doubt that they would feel unduly hard done by.

Of course, if any of them come to haunt me for my presumption, I will be happy to apologise profusely.

Michael Jecks
North Dartmoor
October 2006

West London and Thorney Island

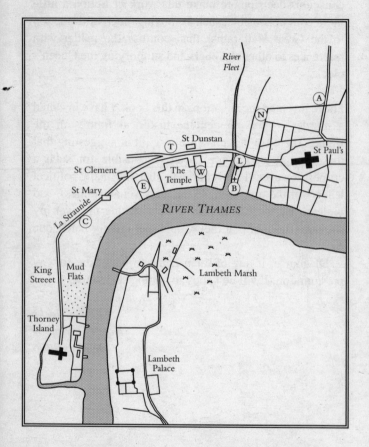

- **N** Newgate
- **A** Aldersgate
- **L** Ludgate
- **T** Temple Bar
- **E** Bishop of Exeter's House
- **C** Charing Cross
- **B** Black Friars
- **W** White Friars

Thorney Island 1325

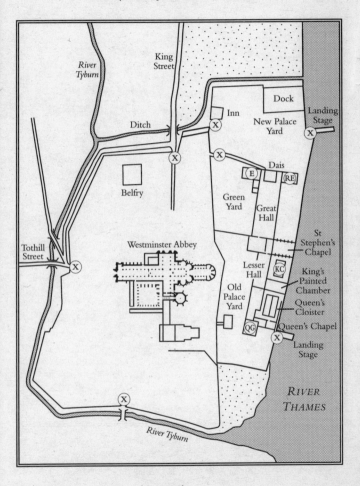

Chapter One

River Thames near Westminster

It was a grey, dank morning when the assassin floated quietly downriver to the house on the Straunde. He sat huddled in the back of the boat with his greasy, grey woollen hat pulled down low over his brow against the fine drizzle thrown against his face. With his chin resting on his breast, he was confident his face was hidden, but he still eyed the river traffic warily. Many craft passed up and down: barges and boats with gaily painted sheers flaunted wealth he could only imagine. Many stopped and pulled in to bump at private jetties, while above the noise of the oars and the wind, the shouts and curses of sailors came clear across the flat water.

It was alarming to a man devoted to remaining inconspicuous. There were officials here, fighting men with good vision, and if one of them caught sight of him now, that man might recognise him in the future. Best always

[1] 14 January 1325

to be still, silent, a shadow in the corner of a wall – never a person who could be spotted and brought to memory by a guard at the wrong moment.

It had taken two days of hard travelling to get here. Two days, and the man at the hall up there towards London must have been keen to have paid him in advance, just to get him here. Very keen indeed if the cost of the rounsey be added to the account. It was a magnificent black stallion, a fast, powerful beast, with a richly ornamented saddle and bridle, and he'd climbed onto it with trepidation, for a man like him didn't learn how to ride at an early age like a lord. He was born to a lower class. If he hadn't managed to be born illegitimate, he'd have been a serf. Fortunately a bastard had to be assumed to be free – the law refused to condemn a man to serfdom unless there was absolute proof that the father was a serf, no matter what the status of the mother.

Yes, with the amount of money already advanced, this must be a serious commission. That was good. But there was a double-edged quality to money – too little and a man like him had to reject it with disgust. He had some pride still. Not much, but some. Still, if there was too much money, that would mean that the task was inordinately dangerous. There was no profit in an early grave.

They were passing by the King's Great Hall now, and he allowed his eyes to study the Palace with the interest of a traveller, unaware that this was the place where he would die.

Westminster was a strange area. It was there at the bank of the river, almost an island, with the River Tyburn just to the south of it, the new mill turning gently with the tide. Then there were the main buildings. This was where the King's councils met, where he held his parliaments and met his people when he held court, but it wasn't purely designed for law-giving and law-making. This had become the King's home, too.

The boat swung into the river a little further to avoid the first of the landing stages, and looking down its length like an archer aiming down his arrow, he could see the chapel at the edge of the buildings. Then came a small block with pleasant lancet windows – the Queen's rooms, so he had heard. Behind the chapel's windows was a flickering light, and he thought how warm it must be in there, out of this chill wind.

Next was another two-storey building, the King's, and a little beyond was the new chapel. This one filled the gap between the Great Hall and the King's rooms, and was built on two levels as well. On the ground floor of the King's apartments were all the King's household, while the uppermost chamber was for Edward's family and closer friends.

Everyone knew who his 'closer friends' were now.

The man in the boat pulled his old russet-coloured cloak tighter about his shoulders, grunting to himself as he tried to knot his belly muscles to keep in a little warmth.

Yes. The money implied that the man he was going to be asked to kill was someone important. This would be no easy assassination: no quick dagger between the ribs in a tavern when all others were so drunk they wouldn't notice the corpse till morning; nor a thong whipped about an unsuspecting throat and the body allowed to slip into the river to float off downstream in the dark. This was more likely to be an attack that would risk his *own* neck.

And yet he could not afford to throw away such an opportunity. Oh, he could put bread on the table and wine in the cup when he wanted, but life without the little luxuries was empty. Women, choice meats, new clothes, perhaps a hawk again . . . there were so many little things he could desire.

A twinge made him shift his position. At eight and forty years, he was growing old. He had endured too many campaigns, too many cold nights sleeping rough on the damp ground, too many mornings waking with a sore head and a purse emptied by a whore's pimp. Perhaps one more kill could earn him enough to survive a little longer. Others he'd known were living rich lives with great houses and servants. He'd heard tell of a comrade who'd been made Sergeant of a castle for the King. Others were granted corrodies in convents, where they would live out their lives in relative comfort with a gallon of ale a day. Perhaps he could too.

They were past the Great Hall itself now, and soon they passed the last jetty and the dock, and all he could see on the bank was the low-lying lands which swept back and up to the roadway. Merchants and lawyers kept small houses out in the waste beyond the island, but there were few here, at the riverbank. The land was too soggy and prone to flood this close to the Thames. There was just a scattering of rough dwellings for some of the servants of the court and lay brothers of the Abbey. Through them all cut the King's Street, which headed northwards along the line of the Thames until it joined up with the Straunde and thence Fleet Street.

When he had been here last, maybe fifteen years ago, houses were thinner on the ground, but now he could see that the area was much more built up. It was natural enough. Since the Exchequer had moved here from Winchester, a lot more people needed access to the place. Now it looked as though all the spaces between here and London were gradually filling.

But after a scant eighth of a mile, the rough houses gave way to substantial properties. These were owned by the rich, the men who would rule the land, those with power residing in their armed men, and those who would command a man's heart and soul. He could remember these houses. That was the Archbishop of York's, and beyond it he could see the Savoy, the palace of the Duke of Lancaster, with its new wall and castellations – and then came the mansions: first the Bishop of Norwich's, then the Bishop of Durham's, the Bishop of Carlisle's, the Bishop of Bath and Wells's – and the Bishop of Exeter's. And then, last of all for him today, was this enormous place.

It was a strong site. Standing just west of the River Fleet, it lay behind a ditch and wall. From here on the river it was impossible to see much inside the precinct, but it didn't matter. He looked up at the walls as the water gate opened; and thought to himself that they were daunting. Entering here was like being pulled in through Traitor's Gate at the Tower; the idea made him shiver.

As the gate closed, he saw a flaming torch coming down steps slick with water; two men were approaching.

The boat stopped at the jetty and he sat for a moment, eyeing them with that expanding sensation in his belly he recognised so well: pure, simple fear. So often in his life he had known that feeling. It was in part a mark of his existence. There were always men about who wanted to kill him for what he had done, or for what he planned.

Not today, though. He stood, letting the old cloak fall away and looked about him.

'Jack atte Hedge? My Lord Despenser waits for you,' a man said.

Jack atte Hedge glanced at him. It was the second of them who had spoken, the one who didn't carry the torch. Probably thought carrying something like that was too menial for him. Jack ignored him. He looked out over the river, then upstream back towards Thorney Island where the King had his new palace.

'I said . . .' the man began again.

'Take me to him,' Jack said quietly, and followed them in through the gate.

The little short gate with the incised cross of the Knights Templar cut into the lintel.

New Temple, London

Jack atte Hedge gazed about him as they passed up the path from the river. There were orchards, gardens, a little pasture all between the river and the cloister, but everything was sadly dilapidated. They entered the cloister by a small door, and he was led up some stairs into a large, almost bare chamber.

'Sit here and wait,' the second man told him.

Jack stared at the man, who scowled back as he took

up position at the side of the door as though guarding his prisoner.

'What's your name?' Jack asked.

'What's it to you?'

'Nothing whatever.'

The man scowled, but as Jack turned away, he muttered, 'William Pilk.'

He was as thick-skinned as he was thick-headed, Jack decided. One of those employed more for his ability to break another's arms than for his skill at thinking. He had been told to bring Jack, so he assumed that Jack was in some kind of trouble and deserved to be beaten. He stood, and the man at the door stiffened as though preparing to defend it and stop Jack escaping. There were glazed windows at the northern side of the room, and he went to look out. In the courtyard he saw three men, all talking quietly together. He recognised two of them: Sir Hugh le Despenser and his henchman, Ellis Brooke. As he stood watching, they broke up. Ellis and his master walked towards the building from which Jack peered out, but the third man crossed to the other side of the courtyard. 'Who is that?' Jack asked.

Pilk walked to his side suspiciously, as though expecting him to try to knock him down if he lost concentration. He risked a quick look. 'Him? Don't know.'

Jack kept his eyes on the figure. Just for a moment the man turned before he walked through a doorway, and Jack saw a sallow face, a pointed chin, and black hair. Then the man was gone, slipping through and pulling the heavy door closed behind him.

Jack was always interested in strangers in this place. If

Sir Hugh le Despenser was talking to someone, it could only be because there was profit in it for him. He wasn't the sort of man to waste time with those who were of no use to him. Jack turned away from the window, wondering who the third man had been, barely aware of Pilk walking back to the doorway, where he stood glowering as before.

Before Jack could worry himself overmuch, he heard footsteps coming up the stairs; the door opened and Sir Hugh le Despenser walked in with Ellis.

'I am glad to see you again, Jack,' Despenser said.

'And I you,' he replied. But when he looked at Despenser, he was shocked by the change in the man.

Last time he saw him, Hugh le Despenser was a fit, tall young man in his early thirties, but the fellow before him now, although not yet forty years old, had the weight of the realm's troubles upon his shoulders. There was a tiredness in the set of his shoulders which Jack himself had not experienced in all his nearly fifty years. He could have felt some sympathy for the young politician – if he hadn't known how devious and untrustworthy the bastard was.

'You asked me to come,' he said.

'Yes, I did,' And Despenser moved into the room as though to embrace Jack.

That was too familiar, and Jack wanted none of it. He withdrew and glanced over Despenser's shoulder. Ellis leaned there against the door-frame, mouth twisted into a smile. Since a knife attack, a scar left the left side of his face permanently drawn down in an expression of disapproval. 'Jack. How goes it?' Ellis said smoothly.

Jack grunted. Near the door still was the guard, his eyes widened to see that Despenser trusted this tatty old man. 'That fellow Pilk can leave us,' he snapped.

Despenser shot the man a look as though surprised he was still there. 'You, Pilk – out!' He waited until the door was closed, then began, 'So, Jack, the reason I—'

But Jack had already soundlessly crossed the room and yanked the door open: William Pilk was standing less than two feet from it, looking guilty. Jack stood on the balls of his feet, staring at him. He heard a step, and felt a man at his side. He knew it was Ellis. Pilk glared at them both, then turned on his heel and left, stomping down the stairs. Jack glanced at Despenser, who nodded to Ellis. Ellis grunted assent and walked out, standing at the doorway to prevent any others from eavesdropping as Jack silently closed the door again.

He eyed his master. 'So – who do you want me to kill this time, my Lord?'

'Oh, it's just a small job, Jack. I want you to kill the Queen.'

Chapter Two

Lydford, Devon

Simon Puttock listened as the sound broke on the wind in the early morning. It was the sort of sound that a man who was used to the countryside would recognise from a great distance: a horse riding at a steady canter. Neither pounding along the roads with the urgency of a knight at the gallop, nor the steady plodding of a farmer with a packhorse, this was a man who had ridden some distance already, who had a need of haste, but who would have farther to ride, so was measuring his pace.

Simon was in his small hall when he heard it. A tall man, in his late thirties, with the broad shoulders of a farmer, and calm grey eyes set in a face that was sunburned even now in the winter, he was no coward, but he knew what the horse presaged.

Grabbing his staff, he ran out through the screens to the rear of his house. The stables were over on his right, and he made for them, his ear all the time cocked to the

---

[1] 17 January 1325

hooves pounding along the road. He had some time to escape, but not enough.

His wife, Meg, was gathering bundles of twigs and sticks to fire the copper ready to brew ale. There was a space behind the stalls which they always used as an overflow for their log pile, and as Simon came into the stables, he found her bent over, collecting some of the smaller twigs.

The temptation was too great. He grinned, and clapped a hand to her buttock, making her squeal, not entirely happily.

'It's not my fault,' he protested, 'such temptation . . .'

She eyed him coolly, a tall, blonde woman with her hair awry after her morning's exertions. 'It may be a period of rest for you, husband, but I still have a house to maintain and run.'

'Oh, Christ's pains!'

'What is it?'

In answer, Simon jerked his head. She was still for a moment, listening, but then her face cleared. 'The messenger?'

'It must be.'

'Would they have decided already?'

'Meg, John de Courtenay was furious when he saw that Robert was to be made Abbot of Tavistock. He told me that he would contest the election as soon as he had been defeated.'

'Yes, you told me,' she said.

'So – he will already have itemised all those aspects of the election which he feels may *look* as though something underhand has happened, and probably he has instructed a proctor. All he wants now is any other information on Robert. And I don't have anything *to* give him!'

If only he did! Simon was not convinced of the integrity of the new Abbot, any more than he was of many other men. His only certainty was that John de Courtenay was even more unfitted for the post of Abbot than Robert Busse. John was from wealthy stock, and his main interests struck Simon as being modern fashion and hunting, as well as his wine-cellar. Of course, as the son of Baron Courtenay, he could muster some influential friends, and Simon was unpleasantly aware that the other man could make his own life difficult, if he chose.

'But if he has his own proctor involved—' Meg began, but Simon cut her off.

'No! He has the support of two or three Brothers already, I suppose – John Fromund and Richard Mountori, certainly – but that's not the point. Even when he's put in his complaint, he'll try to mobilise as many people as possible within and without the monastery to aid him. And he looks on me as having influence.'

'Because your father used to be his father's servant,' Meg nodded.

'Yes. And because he set me to spy on Busse, and will seek me to work for him again. That is why I must hide from any Abbey messengers.'

'But it could be that it's Robert Busse who is sending for you.'

Simon groaned. 'In God's name, I pray it's not! For he's the man whom I spied on, and I still don't know what he has attempted in order to win the abbacy for himself. I trust neither of them, and whoever I offer support to, the other may win, and then destroy me. Our livelihoods depend upon the Abbot, whoever he may be, and to have to pick one now is a task I should much rather avoid. So if it's a messenger from the Abbey, keep him here, Meg, please. Just give me a few moments. Tell him I'm at the castle, love, and I'll bolt from the rear here.'

Meg shook her head in exasperation at the weakness of her husband. 'I'll try to, Simon, but some messengers can be most insistent.'

He looked at her, and she raised her eyebrows. '*What?*'

'Nothing.'

He grinned to himself as she walked back to the little lean-to building which contained the copper and brewing barrels, and then turned and fled.

Tower of London

The guard at the door snapped to attention as soon as he recognised the coat-of-arms. Only a fool would not show respect to this man.

Edmund of Woodstock, Earl of Kent, half-brother to the King, barely noticed him. The discipline of a prickle-witted guard was nothing to him.

Inside the large chamber he saw the man he was expecting. 'Well?'

'My Lord.'

The man rose and now bowed low for him. Edmund set his teeth, but he could not in all conscience insult him for displaying the correct deference. 'Yes, yes. Please, sit. Now, what can you tell me?'

Piers de Wrotham had been loyal to him even before

he had joined the Earl at the attack on Leeds Castle. Short, with a slim build and thick black hair that was greasy and stayed plastered to his brow when he swept off his cap, he was narrow-featured, and had the look of a clerk rather than an astute spy and information-gatherer. However, the Earl knew that he could collect news more efficiently than ten of the King's men. 'My Lord, there are many dangerous stories. However, I fear that nothing is good for you.'

Kent growled. He had expected such news, but it didn't make it any the more palatable. 'Since those bastards pulled the rug from beneath my feet, they've done all in their power to destroy me – I'll not accept it, damn their souls!'

Piers watched him with unblinking eyes. He had a gift of silence and stillness that was oddly owl-like. When his master had kicked a chair and slumped into it, he began again. 'You were foully betrayed in Guyenne, and many believe that to be the case now. Yet still Despenser pours out more lies to justify his own position.'

'He never supported us. Didn't give a ha'penny for all the King's lands over the water. All he wants is money. He'll take it, too, you mark my words. He'll bloody take it. There's no picking so rich that he won't get his hands on it, the bastard!'

'My Lord, you are still young. He is a middle-aged man, while you are in your prime at five-and-twenty. You are an Earl, while he remains a knight. You have years on your side.'

Edmund gave a short laugh. 'You think he will remain a knight? He has already been granted the Temple, and as soon as Despenser the elder dies, my brother the King will endow him with the Earldom of Winchester, whereas I'll be left to moulder. I'm only the King's half-brother – and the youngest of us. Sweet Christ, I'm nothing to them. No, the crafty shite will take all in the end.'

'Not if people can be made to appreciate how badly he let the nation down in the matter of Guyenne,' Piers murmured. 'My Lord, you have been accused of sur- render and accepting a less than adequate truce. We know that was because you received no aid from Despenser. But now there is a need for a lasting peace – and without the King losing all his territories in France. Perhaps if you could be shown to have been instrumental in pre- paring a magnificent arrangement with the French that protected the good King's lands, it would enhance your reputation at the same time as damaging the Despenser's?'

'If you could so arrange matters, I would be even more in your debt,' Kent said. He leaned forward, elbows on his knees. '*Could* you do this?'

Piers was still again. In his eyes Kent thought he saw a little flare of contempt. Surely not. Maybe it was hurt that he could doubt his own spy-master's ability. 'I don't ques- tion your skills, man,' he said briskly. 'Only the numbers of enemies about us. Look at the allies of Despenser . . .'

'There are as many who now profess loyalty to him as used to be loyal to others. A rich man can attract allies, but once let there be a suggestion that he may lose all his money, that his power and influence are on the wane, and see how his friends will flee.'

'Like who?' Kent wondered aloud, for to him it was all

but inconceivable that a man of integrity could desert his master or friend.

'My Lord, you need only look at some of the men of the Church. If you were to be instrumental in winning a victory for peace with France, you would have many of them on your side. Adam Orleton, Bishop of Hereford, is already Sir Hugh's enemy. Then there is Henry Burghersh, Bishop of Lincoln, John of Drokensford, Bishop of Bath and Wells – all these could soon become Despenser's enemies. Even Roger Martival of Salisbury could grow disillusioned with him and turn to your side.'

'None of them have ever been close to him.'

'No, but many have not declared for him. If Lincoln, Bath and Wells and Salisbury were to grow even more opposed to the Despensers, their weight would tilt the balance and others would grow bolder. So many are already disillusioned with the rule of these tyrants, it may take little to persuade them to turn against Despenser. But this time, no exile. The two Despensers must be removed utterly.'

'That would be to the good of the country. But how can we do this?'

'By the judicious use of near-truths, untruths and wholesome lies. Men are always prepared to believe lies, so long as they reinforce their own prejudices,' Piers said with a smile. 'All you need do is lie in the way they wish to hear.'

Queen's Cloister, Thorney Isle

Alicia hurried along the corridor, her skirts held up to keep them away from the mess that had accumulated here. She was on her way from the Queen's rooms to the chapel.

The *Queen's* Chapel. How ironic. The one woman who was not permitted to wander freely, who couldn't write a letter without it being checked, who had seen her children stolen from her, who was incarcerated here without even the solace of her own household – it was named for her. While the woman who had all the real power here, who held in her dainty little fingers the keys to the Queen's chambers . . . she was merely termed a 'lady-in-waiting'.

It was hateful to Alicia, this place. There was nothing here for a young woman like her. Sweet Mother Mary, how could any woman survive amongst such poison? My Lady Eleanor, wife to Sir Hugh le Despenser, was amiable enough, but she had married *him*, and any woman married to such an evil soul was bound to become infected.

Not that their charge was any better. The Queen was a devious and vengeful woman. Alicia was convinced that Isabella would be cruelty personified if she should ever come to power. Which was part of the reason why she was happy to take messages from the Queen occasionally. Perhaps in years to come, her kindness would be remembered.

Alicia allowed a sneer to mar her pretty features. No. She'd be stuck here with the Queen for many long years until they were both old and raddled hags. There would be no peace for them here. Not ever.

At the door to the chapel was a guard. She recognised him at once, of course. Richard Blaket was a good man. He'd been respectful to her as well as to the Queen when she'd been here before. Perhaps if he had been of even moderately good birth, she would have considered him as a mate.

He had the looks. Fairly tall, but not too tall. Bright, dark eyes, almost black, set in a long and humorous face that always seemed to light up when he saw Alicia. It was the sort of look that a girl desperate for a little male attention could hardly miss.

It was the same today. As soon as he saw her, his face softened and his stance altered imperceptibly. 'Maid Alicia.'

'*Lady* Alicia to you,' she responded tartly.

'Oho, yes. My Lady.'

And although she should have been angry at his taunting tone, it lightened her mood a little as she brushed past him and marched into the chapel.

Lydford, Devon

Here, at the edge of Lydford, the town was set atop a little ridge that ran roughly east-west from Dartmoor. Behind the stable was a track, invisible from the house, which led down to a hillside paddock under a line of trees. Simon took this track now, hurrying down until he reached the paddock, where he paused and watched his horses.

For all his amusement in the presence of his wife, he knew that this election had put his job at risk.

For many years he had been a contented Bailiff on the moors, working to maintain the peace between tinminers and landowners, upholding the law among two irascible and sometimes irrational groupings. Yet for all the headaches and strife, that had been easier than his last position. In order to reward him for his devotion and loyalty, the good Abbot Robert had given him a post in Dartmouth, as the Abbot's own representative as Keeper of the Port.

It should have been a marvellous opportunity. Anyone in Simon's position would have managed to enrich themselves quickly, because all mariners were prepared to pay a small subsidy to him to ensure that their cargoes were dealt with expeditiously. And yet Simon could not grow keen on the job. He had been forced to leave his wife and children behind, which was a sore trial, and he found himself growing depressed with the daily grind of checking figures in long lists. He had no *interest* in lists.

And all the while he knew that his patron, the kindly Abbot Robert, was growing weaker. He was wasting away, and Simon was reluctant to add to his troubles by complaining about the job. No, he hoped that soon the Abbot would recover, and then Simon could ask for his old job back. Except Abbot Robert had not improved. One morning Simon had been called to his office to be told that the Abbot was dead, and that his own job was to be passed over to another.

Since then, apart from a short journey to Exeter, he had managed to remain here in Lydford, and he had adapted to the slower, calmer pace of life again. He had learned to accept that his daughter was gone for ever. Where once he had been proud of his little Edith, now it was a source of pride and pain that his occasionally gauche and gawky daughter was grown into a seventeen-year-old woman with all the fire and beauty of his wife. She was a child no longer.

His son had filled the gap. A more boisterous and careless boy could hardly be imagined. When Simon had left to take up the posting in Dartmouth, the child had been some twelve or eighteen months. Now the little monster was almost three, but he had a perpetual smile fixed to his face, and no matter what he got up to, people always looked on him with affection. Even when he got into the neighbour's shed and opened the tap on her cider barrel, leaving it wide as he went out and emptying an entire nine gallons over their floor, the mistress was cold only towards Simon. For Perkin she reserved a special smile and a piece of sweetened bread.

The last months had been very happy. The Puttocks had enjoyed a pleasant Christmas and Simon had been hoping to be left alone with his wife and family, preparing their land for the scattering of crops. It was unreasonable for the Abbey to demand his aid again. Especially since it would be one monk bickering with another.

'Mistress asks you to come up to the house.'

Simon started. He had been so deep in his gloomy ruminations that he hadn't heard his servant Hugh arrive. 'She said so?'

'That's what I said, isn't it?'

Hugh had recently been bereaved, and since then his nature, never better than truculent, had grown more aggressive. Simon understood him well, though, and merely nodded, sighing as he followed Hugh up the path back towards the house.

So which was it? The Abbot who'd been elected, calling on Simon to offer some form of support? Or the one whom Simon despised and felt sure would ruin the

Abbey, John de Courtenay, whose plans would inevitably involve Simon befriending the new Abbot again and then betraying him.

Simon wanted nothing to do with either.

Lesser Hall, Thorney Island

Sir Hugh le Despenser bit at his inner lip as the King stood and stamped his foot. The man's tantrums were as extreme and irrational as any child's. The difference was, that he was the anointed King of the Realm, and anyone who dared to make fun of him could have his head removed. Even Sir Hugh was cautious when Edward was having one of his fits of petulant rage.

'The bastards *demand*, you say?' Edward roared. 'The bastards *demand* that I submit? I suppose they won't be happy until I've passed them the keys to this island and the keys to my treasury as well!'

Today his anger was not abnormal; indeed, since the shameful truce imposed on him by the French, it had grown ever more evident. Despenser remained seated. 'Sire, since the King of France wishes only to reacquire all the lands of Guyenne at as little cost to his pocket as possible, it is scarcely to be wondered at.'

'Do *not* think to lecture me!' Edward bawled. Tall, fair, with the flowing hair of an angel and a manly beard, he was the epitome of a noble English knight. No one was better-looking than King Edward II, and he spent a lot of money ensuring that this remained the case, but his temper was that of a tyrant.

Sir Hugh le Despenser shrugged. 'What do you say, Stratford?'

'As you know, these proposals were thrashed out with the aid of the Pope's envoys, my Lord. If I have failed you, I apologise, but it was the best I felt I could achieve.'

'Summarise them again for me,' the King snapped, sulkily turning his back to them.

'Guyenne is entirely in the French King's hands, my Lord. He says that the province could be returned to you if you do homage to him, and also grant him the Agenais and Ponthieu.'

'So he would snatch all my territories, would he? I suppose he wants Thorney Island too, or is he prepared to leave that for me?'

Stratford rolled his eyes. He had read out the proposals and summarised them three times already. Still, one didn't argue with the King. Taking a deep breath, he began again. 'He has made three proposals. In effect all are connected, and you will have to agree to each being satisfactorily completed before the next takes place. First, he demands that you make over the Agenais and Ponthieu; second, he would return Guyenne – to be held from him, and for that you would have to do him homage; third, do so and he will consider giving you other lands, and will remove his direct control of Guyenne.'

The King threw out his arms theatrically. 'Is this fair? Is it reasonable? He sends an army into my lands – *mine* – and then imposes rules on how I might win them back!'

'There is another matter, my Lord.' John Stratford, Bishop of Winchester, was reluctant to add to Edward's woes, but this was too important not to be raised. At least the King's worst temper appeared to be dissipating, and so the Bishop felt more comfortable about mentioning it now. 'King Charles also complained that you were attempting to form an alliance with his enemies. He mentioned Spain, Aragon, and Hainault.'

'I am a King! I can negotiate with whomsoever I wish!'

Despenser smiled to himself. Any suggestion that someone was encroaching on King Edward's rights always made him jump like someone had jabbed a knife in his arse. Leaning forward, he twisted the dagger a little. 'My Lord, the French King is aware of that, of course. And yet he *is* your liege-lord. You owe him loyalty.'

'Only for Guyenne, damn his soul! That hog's shit has no right to expect me to surrender *my* rights to negotiate! Would he have me submit all my policies to him for approval? That bastard encroached on *my* rights on my territories, and then demanded that I submit to him, and now he intends to make me little more than a puppet king, an arm of French law and nothing more!'

Despenser sat back, the seeds of additional discord already fruiting nicely. He had little care about the provinces which exercised the King so much. He had no need of them. What he was interested in lay here, in the kingdom of England, where he had all but total power. What point was there in him worrying about Guyenne when he was already the wealthiest man in England, saving only the King himself? However, it was true that all power resided in the person of the King. And if King Edward II were ever to be weakened or threatened, Despenser's own position would go the same way. It did not bear considering that he could be left to the mercies of the barons in this country. That had happened to Piers

Gaveston, and he had been captured and slaughtered by them nine years ago. Despenser did not intend to suffer a similar fate.

'My Lord, it is natural that the French King should ask that you go to him to pay homage for lands which are held in fief from him. It is his right to demand this,' Stratford said quietly.

Despenser glanced sidelong at him. Bishop John was a very astute, calm man. He'd been a thorn in the King's side when he took on Winchester, because the King had set his own heart on an ally, Baldock. Bishop John had returned from the Papal Curia, at which he had been *intended* to promote Baldock, with the position in his own purse. Furious, the King had accused him of greed and pushing his own interests, before confiscating all the Bishop's lands. Stratford had been forced to pay twelve thousand pounds to recover his property from the Crown.

However he was a natural diplomat, cautious, shrewd and detached. A dangerous enemy, in fact, and Despenser was unsure about him. What, for example, was the meaning behind this latest suggestion? That the King should go to Paris? How could that benefit Bishop John, he wondered. Not that he was too concerned. He was sure he could persuade King Edward to ignore that sort of suggestion.

He tried a tone of hurt shock. 'You expect your King to go to Paris? You really want him to suffer another humiliation at the hands of the man who confiscated all his French territories last year? When all his enemies are there, living openly and under the protection of the French court?'

'Yes – you expect me to abase myself before that thief?' King Edward raged suddenly. 'Had you heard that traitors are there? You want them to have a chance to assassinate me?'

'My Lord King, I say no such—'

'But you want me to go to Paris, don't you?'

'Perhaps the good Bishop is not aware of the risks involved,' Despenser muttered.

'The risks?'

'Yes!' the King shouted. 'The *risks*, my good Lord Bishop! Don't you know that the realm's greatest traitor, that duplicitous bastard Mortimer, is there at the French court? Eh? And he's not alone, is he? No! There are enough other men in that court who would want to do me damage!'

As he ranted, Hugh le Despenser nodded sagely. It had not been difficult to plant concerns about the King's safety were he to go to France. His obsessional paranoia since the last wars was in fact entirely rational. Edward had killed his own cousin, Earl Thomas of Lancaster, and then embarked on a campaign of reprisals against all those who had attacked him and his authority. That was over two years ago, but rotting limbs of the knights and lords who had been executed were still dangling above the gates to all the major cities in the land, while their heads adorned spikes. Some had managed to slip away without capture, and most of them had gone to the French court, where the King liked to bite his thumb at his English brother-in-law. Now they lived there, more or less openly, at the expense of the French.

'I will not submit to this! I want my host! Send my men-at-arms to France – I will crush this bastard!'

Despenser saw how quickly the Bishop's eye dropped to hide his amusement, and he curbed the smile that threatened his own mouth. To openly deride the King's martial expertise would be dangerous even for him.

'My Lord,' Stratford said quietly, 'you have no host. The French King has right upon his side. You are a vassal for the Guyenne. And do not forget that the Pope wishes for peace, and he begs that you do homage for the lands you hold from King Charles IV.'

'Sir Hugh?'

Despenser made a show of raising his hands and shaking his head. 'My Lord King, I suppose any obfuscation must result in losing Guyenne. My Lord Bishop is quite right to say that homage must be paid.'

'I will *not* go there. Must I accept the demands of this upstart who has stolen my lands from me? No! I would sooner give up my Crown! And I do not have to.' He span on his heel and pointed at the clerk sitting in the corner. 'I will send a delegation to Castile. We will offer my son in marriage to the Castilian woman, this . . . this . . . Sir Hugh, what was her name?'

'Leonor, my Lord,' Despenser said.

'Yes. We will send ambassadors to them there. Demand three thousand men to help protect our provinces from this French King. Then we can . . .'

Despenser saw Stratford fiddling with the parchment in front of him. His unease was all too plain. The King was taking actions that could infuriate the French, who had the most powerful host in all Europe. Despenser shivered, and tried to cover it by lifting his arms over his head and stretching. But there was no concealing the dangers and threats from himself. He had to remain on the alert all the time.

Especially, he thought as he caught another sideways look from the Bishop, from men like this. Stratford knew that the last thing Despenser could afford was to allow the King to leave his sight. If he were to go to France, Sir Hugh le Despenser could not go with him. The French King had already declared that Hugh was an enemy of France and would be executed if he set foot on French soil.

No. He couldn't go to France, and if *he* couldn't, the King mustn't. To be left alone here in England while Edward crossed the Channel would mean an alliance among the barons, and Sir Hugh's neck on a block. There were few in whom he could genuinely place his trust, were the King to leave him to the wolves.

Chief among his enemies was the Queen. She despised him, because when the King lost his infatuation for her, he took all her wealth and property and used it to reward the man he adored. She blamed Hugh for that, he thought with a slow smile. As well she might. It was he, together with the avaricious Bishop of Exeter, Walter, who had hatched the scheme which would reward both by impoverishing her. Only a short while ago she had been one of the wealthiest magnates in the land; now she was reduced to the status of a humble corrodian at the King's court.

All of which had made her Sir Hugh's most implac- able enemy, which was why he had decided she must be removed. To have someone with her resourcefulness, with her injured pride and intense desire for revenge, sitting at court and retaining the title of 'Queen', would be like setting a magnet in a box of iron filings and hoping it would remain clean. Better by far to remove all the filings or – since that was impractical – remove the magnet.

He wondered how Jack atte Hedge was getting on.

Lydford, Devon

Simon scowled at his wife as he entered the hall. She was not alone.

At the table, sitting on Simon's bench and drinking a pot of ale with every sign of delight, was a Lay Brother from Tavistock. Simon thought he recognised the fellow, although he did not know his name, but he had no doubt that whoever had sent him, it would not be for his own benefit.

'Ah, Bailiff, I am glad to see you again,' the man said.

'Yes?'

Meg smiled and left the room with a special grin for her husband. He glowered back.

'Bailiff, I have a message for you.'

'Is it from the Abbot or John de Courtenay?'

The Brother blinked. 'Neither, Bailiff. It came straight from Bishop Walter of Exeter. He wishes for you to join him. In London.'

Chapter Three

The Tabard Inn, Southwark, Surrey

Jack atte Hedge woke before dawn, as was his wont, and did not move in the dark as he listened to the breathing of the others in the room.

This was not the inn where he rested from choice. He had left most of his belongings and his horse over in Chelchede[2], to the south and west of Thorney Island, but he needed to study the place from this, the Surrey side of the river as well. There could be a useful angle which could be seen from here.

The inn was filled with travellers on their way to London, and the snoring and grumbling of the tranters, carters and men of some wealth was loud to his ear. He was used to sleeping apart from others and being so accustomed, he found the noise of this party almost deafening.

In the past he would have woken beneath a tree or

---

[1] 18 January 1325
[2] Chelsea

beside a stream with the sound of birdsong as the thrushes, robins and blackbirds began to warm themselves for the day's work. But that was in the days when he was more hardy. Truth be told, more recently he was grown soft. It had been many years since he had last slept in the open in winter. No one would do so from choice, and he found now that he couldn't face the idea at all. Far better that he should sit in a warmer environment and stop his joints from aching, even if it did mean he must endure the row.

He rolled from the bed, a rough palliasse stuffed with straw, and the man who had shared it with him grunted and swore in his sleep. Dressing quickly, Jack pulled on his belt with his purse, then drew his knife's cord over his head so that the small blade hung at his belly, down inside his shirt. This was his assurance of protection, a small knife that others might not notice. The second dangled from a leather strap, and he pulled that one over his head, feeling it as a comforting weight against his hip. No man with a brain would ever go unarmed, especially here near London. Then he had his purse on another belt, and his horn in case of troubles. With a horn a man might call for help at any time of the day or night. To walk abroad without one was almost a sign of irresponsibility. He took a few moments to stuff his pack, bind it, and then he was off.

The door was opened as he reached the hall, and he went straight out, thrusting his staff through the thongs binding his baggage to carry it more easily. It was a short walk up to the great bridge, less than a half-mile, but he chose to walk along the line of the Thames first, heading upstream as though idly. There was a track which looked as though it was a shepherd's path; it meandered a little too close to the river, but was less muddy than some of the flats about.

It was a very wet part of the country, this. He muttered bitterly when his boot slipped through a thin crust of ice and he felt the first prickling of freezing water at his toes. Looking west from here, he could see some low hovels, but generally this close to the river there was nothing but mudflats and sodden, reeded marshland.

Over at the turn of the river he could see the little vill of Lambeth in the Marsh, a small cluster of houses with a couple of little orchards. He bent his path in that direction, eyeing the far bank as he went. The river here was a good width – almost impossible to cross without a boat or taking the bridge. He had once been a strong swimmer, but looking at the angry ripples on this water, he knew that was no possibility. Since the bridge's building, the river had been effectively slowed, but that only made the currents more hazardous. No, he could not hope to escape by the water unless he stole a boat.

At the vill, a second path led south along the line of the river towards the Archbishop of Canterbury's palace. Another path led about the palace's walls, and he wandered along it idly. Near a gate in the Archbishop's wall there was a landing stage, with five small boats moored. Jack stopped, set his staff on the ground, then thrust his thumbs in his belt and stared out over the water. On the other bank he could see the new chapel on the left, the two-storeyed quarters for the Queen, then the King's own rooms, and his own, newer chapel of St Stephen, before the mass of the Great Hall. The two jetties were clear enough, and so near it looked as though a man might almost reach his hand out and touch them from a boat down there.

But there were problems. A man stood upon the wall behind him. Jack had heard the fellow sniff, hawk and spit a few moments ago, and the whole way over the river would be in plain sight of every guard here in Lambeth and over there at the island. If he were to try anything involving boats, he'd be better served to escape quickly, in any case. Rowing across the flow of the river was no good. It could only slow him, while guards on both banks loaded their bows and sent flight after flight to chase him.

However, perhaps he could use the river to his own advantage? He peered back the way he had come. There, just at the bend, was another little jetty with moorings. It was quieter, with only one boat, for this was by the vill he had passed through earlier, and Lambeth in the Marsh did not justify an enormous flotilla; however, that one little boat could be his saving. Perhaps he could use the landing stage for an escape if necessary? He could leave the island, let the current draw him away, increasing his speed quickly, and then hop off up there. It should be easy enough to escape without too much risk. They'd need boats to reach him, but he could cut the moorings before leaping into the last . . .

No. That would be the act of a much younger man, he grinned wryly to himself. He picked up his pack and shouldered his staff once more, setting off back the way he had come.

He only managed to cover fifty or sixty yards, and was

some ten yards from a thicket, when he suddenly felt a hand grasp his shoulder.

'Wait there, you. I saw you back there, staring down at our boats. What were you thinkin' of, old man?'

Jack found himself pulled around to face a man of maybe two- or three-and-twenty. The fool had a leather cap, and a coif that was stained and marked with sweat. He was a man of no importance, that much was obvious, just a scruffy guard in the pay of the Archbishop, probably.

'Friend, I am just a traveller. I wanted to look at the river, that's all.'

'That's all, eh? I saw you staring out at the river, all right, but you were mainly watching what was happening all about here, weren't you?'

'Why should I want to do that?'

'No honest man would, that is certain,' the man said, standing back a little and eyeing him doubtfully. 'But we've had some things stolen in the last weeks, and my master told me to stop anyone who looked suspicious.'

'Me? Do you think I look suspicious, then?' Jack chuckled. He rolled his eyes. The palace was in full view behind this interfering guard.

'No, master. I suppose not. But you can't blame me for checking, can you?'

'Of course not. But . . .' Jack paused, clutching at his chest, the breath hissing from clenched teeth.

'Master? Christ's ballocks . . . Master? Are you all right?'

'Please, I need to sit under those trees. Their coolness will . . . ah! The pain!'

The guard threw an anxious look over his shoulder. Then, slipping his gauntleted hand under Jack's armpit, he half-carried him to the thicket. There was a log, and he took Jack to it, helping him to sit down on it.

'Thank you.' Jack smiled up at him, and then slammed his right forearm upwards, the hand cupped back. As soon as the palm and ball of his thumb met the fellow's chin, he straightened his arm and simultaneously launched his whole body up with all the power in his legs. There was a snap as the man's teeth crashed together, and then a louder, harsher crack. The body was thrown back, and Jack caught him before he could hit the ground, gently turning him over and feeling the neck to make sure. There was a slight tension there, and he could feel some spasms in the thighs making the torso move, so he set the guard on the ground, put his knee in the small of his back, gripped the head, and pulled sharply backwards and to the side.

There was no one about. He took a rock and eyed the guard speculatively for a few moments, and then brought it down hard on the man's left temple. The rock was tossed to the side of the roadway, and he picked up the guard and set his body down so that the head met the rock. Taking another large stone, he put that near the guard's feet, as though he had tripped and pitched headlong onto the rock, and then he pushed the guard gently until he rolled slowly away from the road and into the drainage ditch at the side of the road.

There was no snow about here yet, but a thick layer of ice crunched and crackled as the body landed on it. There was enough blood on the roadway about the rock to show what he wanted.

And then Jack took up his staff again, and with a quick glance about him, he set off for the bridge once more.

He wanted no one left about either bank of the river who could remember him.

Furnshill Manor, Devon

Sir Baldwin de Furnshill was a tall man in his early fifties, and although he had the aches and pains which were the natural concomitants of his age, he was still proud enough of his past life as a fighter to practise each day with his sword and to ride and hunt as often as possible. He liked to remind his wife, when she remonstrated with him for his over-enthusiastic training, that there was little use to a knight, were he to be unpractised with his most valued weapons.

Not this morning, though. Today he had been asked to join the Bishop Walter Stapledon in his little house at Bishop's Clyst, and the knight knew that he would be well advised to heed the summons.

For some little time past the Bishop had been trying to persuade him to accept an invitation to become a member of government. There were many who would be keen to accept such an advancement, if for no other reason than it gave them an opportunity to visit the realm's first city and see with their own eyes the magnificent court which the King was building about himself. And naturally, most knights would be enthusiastic in case they might be noticed by Edward. There was much that a man might do with the King's patronage.

Baldwin had no interest in any of these matters. Until

the year of this King's coronation[1], he had been a contented warrior for the *Poor Fellow Soldiers of Christ and the Temple of Solomon* – a Knight Templar. But then came the appalling catastrophe. Late in that year, all the French Templars were captured in their preceptories and held. Over the next few years, many were tortured to force them to confess to sins they could not have committed, and several were burned at the stake for resiling.

Since the deaths of his Grand Master and his other comrades, Sir Baldwin had been keen to avoid politics and all other worldly affairs. Instead, he journeyed down here to Devon, where he took up the life of a rural knight, living on his small manor, and avoiding all great affairs of state so far as he possibly could.

Gradually, as he felt the pain and resentment at the injustice done to him and his companions begin to fade, he had befriended Simon Puttock. The result of that was that, with the aid of Bishop Walter II, he had been given the post of Keeper of the King's Peace in Devon. Charged with the responsibility to seek out and capture felons, he had discovered a new interest: to prevent any injustices such as that perpetrated upon the Templars being replicated elsewhere.

And in the last few years he knew that the worst injustices being perpetrated upon a weary and fearful population were those which came from the King himself. There was little an ordinary person might achieve against the tyranny of King Edward II and his atrocious confederate, Hugh le Despenser.

---

[1] 1307

It was that which in the end persuaded Baldwin that he should accept the Bishop's proposal and take up a position with the parliament. He might be able to achieve little in the face of the bullying and dishonesty of so many others in the King's councils, but if he could make even a small impact, that would be some good.

The journey to Bishop's Clyst was not too taxing. He must ride along the line of the river from his home and pass around Exeter. The Bishop's residence was some four or five leagues south and east of the city. Usually it was a fairly easy ride, which would take Baldwin a half-morning to complete, but today, with some ice on the roads, he was less sanguine about the journey.

'You will be careful?'

'My love, I am always careful,' he smiled. His wife Jeanne was exhausted. For once she did not demand to join him on his journey. She had given birth to their son, also named Baldwin, a short while after midnight on Martinmas, and even a month later, she was still too weary to consider a ride to Exeter and back. The child was so demanding, her body had appeared to be sucked almost dry in the first fortnight. Baldwin had been shocked to see how her cheeks began to hollow, how her hair became bedraggled and greasy, and her eyes lost their sparkle.

Now, with God's grace, she was a lot better. Her body had begun to fill out once more, and her eyes had regained their gleaming intelligence, although still with a certain red-rimmed exhaustion about them.

'I shall be home before lunch tomorrow, I pray.'

'Do so, husband. We miss you when you are abroad.'

'Be glad, then, that there is no parliament yet. By the time it is called, I hope you will be able to join me. A journey to London or York would be a fine way to bring the colour back to your cheeks.'

She smiled at him, but shook her head. 'I cannot even dream of such a journey, Baldwin. I am so weary, so weary. The child is strong, though. He thinks nothing of waking two or three times in the middle of the night to suck my pap.'

'He will be strong,' Baldwin assured her, peering down into the cradle where his son lay.

'You should leave, not stand goggle-eyed at the sight of your son.'

'Woman, I am gazing down at my firstborn son and marvelling at his perfection. Which is in truth a proof of the sire's beauty.'

'And nothing to do with the dam's, I suppose?'

'Madam, you merely own my heart,' he swore, his hand on his breast.

'Then stop letting your eyes slide to him, then,' she laughed weakly. 'Go!'

His horse was already waiting, and he was able to make the journey in good time, even with the hazardous roads. In less than a half-day, he was cautiously trotting over the icy wooden drawbridge to the Bishop's well-protected manor. Soon afterwards he was in the Bishop's hall, cupping his hands about a mazer of warmed and heavily spiced cider.

Bishop Walter II was a tall, stooped man in his sixties. His eyesight, never good, must now be supplemented with strong spectacles, which he was forced to hold over his nose with one hand while poring over documents. Still, he was a strong man, and although Baldwin knew he suffered dreadfully from piles, he had few other ailments to show how old he had grown.

'I am glad you were able to come, Sir Baldwin,' he said. For a moment or two he peered at Baldwin through his glass lenses, his eyes enormous and staring, and Baldwin was reminded of a man gazing in terror, until suddenly the Bishop threw the bone spectacles down with a petulant gesture.

'My Lord Bishop? Is there something I can do to help you?'

'Only one thing: I would have you travel with me to see the King. Sir Baldwin, there are matters which are being discussed, and I have been called to give my advice, such as I may. I should like you to join me. There is a need for sound heads. Dear God, yes.'

Chapter Four

Bishop's Palace, Exeter

Simon Puttock rode into the city of Exeter with that tormented feeling of being wrenched from his family again, although this time it was ameliorated by the knowledge that he was at least safe from the politicking of the monks at Tavistock. That was, it was true, some relief.

'How much further is it to London?'

Simon grunted. He had intended to leave this lad behind. Rob had been his servant for a while in Dartmouth, and he had become a form of fixture in Simon's life, no matter what Simon did or said to deter him. When Simon left Dartmouth for (as he hoped) the last time, he had intended to leave Rob as well, but the lad appeared to have developed a highly undesirable devotion to Simon. First he had trailed along with Simon to Tavistock, then to Exeter, which had tested the fellow's commitment significantly, and now he insisted upon

---

[1] 21 January 1325

joining Simon in this, his longest trip overland. All the way to London, in God's name!

'I mean, are we halfway yet?'

'Halfway? All we have done is a matter of a few leagues, boy. We are going to Westminster, which is at least seventy more.'

'Oh.' Rob was quiet a moment, his face scowling with concentration. 'So we'll be a few more days, then?'

Simon groaned. All the way from Dartmouth to Exeter the last time they had travelled together, Rob had kept up a constant demand to know whether they were 'nearly there' yet. Simon foresaw days stretching ahead during which he must suffer the same queries. He could almost feel nostalgic for the old days when he had wandered about the country with his truculent, monosyllabic servant Hugh. But he'd had to leave Hugh at home to protect the place. The country was too unsettled to leave his wife and children there without someone to rally defence.

The palace gate was guarded, which was normal enough, but Simon was a little surprised to see that there were more guards behind the gateway, and all were well-armed. He received some cold, suspicious stares as he let his horse wander slowly inside the court and climbed down, rubbing his arse. The way had not been arduous, but recently his backside was less used to the rigours of saddle-wear.

'Simon! Old friend! It is good to see you!'

Baldwin had his arm in a firm grip almost before Simon had turned, and the Bailiff was struck by his friend's evident joy to see him arrive. 'Didn't you know I was being sent too?' he asked, clapping him on the back.

'I had heard, but I hardly dared to think you would be allowed to join us. Meg is well?'

'Very. I left Hugh to guard her and Edith, although whether or not she'll find that a comfort, God knows. The poor fellow's still not recovered.'

'Hardly likely that he would be. He lost his all in that fire. He is only fortunate that he could return to your service,' Baldwin noted.

Simon nodded. In the last year, a fire had taken Hugh's wife and her child, and although Simon had done all in his power to ease his old servant's mind, there was little any man could do in the face of such a disaster.

'How much have you been told?' Baldwin asked after a few moments.

Simon looked down at Rob and told him to see to the horses, before casting a glance at the palace. 'Little enough. I heard that the Bishop wanted me to join him on this journey, and to be honest I saw only an escape from the in-fighting at Tavistock.'

'You have heard then?'

Simon tilted his head to one side.

Baldwin smiled. 'John de Courtenay has already demanded that the election be set aside and that there be a full hearing into the whole matter of Busse's abbacy. He has alleged that Busse is unsuited for the post, that he used necromancy to win it, that he's already selling off the Abbey's silver, that he's . . . goodness knows what else. I feel sure that you are much better off being away.'

'And what of Jeanne?'

A cloud passed over Baldwin's face. 'She was terribly

sad to hear that we were being asked to go so far. In God's time, I hope we shall return safely, but I am worried for her, Simon. It was a hard birthing. Very hard.'

'The child is all right?'

'Yes. I have called him Baldwin,' the knight admitted self-consciously. 'It was not my own choice, but Jeanne was insistent. I should have liked to call him after my father, or my brother.'

Simon nodded. Baldwin had left England to sail to Acre during the final defence of the city against the heathen hordes, and when he finally returned to his home, both his father and brother were dead. It was a curious thought, that he might have been gone for so long that his family ceased to exist. Simon had no brothers, so he could only guess at the effect such a loss might have upon a man. To change the subject, he shrugged. 'I don't know how much help I am supposed to be to the Bishop.'

'Nor me,' Baldwin agreed. 'But the good Bishop appears determined to have me with him for the benefit of my advice. I suppose I am reluctant to refuse to help him, and yet it is such a bad time.'

In his mind's eye he saw again his wife. She had been determined not to weep before him, both because Jeanne had always been a proud woman, and because she knew it would only leave Baldwin feeling miserable too. She had clung to him when he hugged her before going, and it was only later, on the ride from Fursdon to the ford, that he had felt his shoulder and realised that it was wet from her tears.

'It is one thing for you, a knight and well-travelled

man who has seen much of the world,' Simon muttered, 'but I fail to see what a mere Bailiff from the moors can do to help him discuss matters of great importance.'

'Perhaps he wishes the views of the common man,' Baldwin laughed. 'The most common man he could think of!'

Tuesday before the Feast of St Julian[1]

Great Hall, Thorney Island

The next day was the sort of day that only a frog could like. Cold, grey, miserable, and wet. God, was it wet!

Earl Edmund of Kent detested it. He was happier by far in warmer climes, but he was forced to remain here in England against his wishes, just because any man who left his manors could return to find them filched by that gannet Despenser.

There was a sermon Edmund had once heard preached by the Archbishop, which said that no man should covet his neighbour's property or cattle or wife. But that had never been made clear to Sir Hugh, plainly. Everyone knew what sort of man Despenser was. He controlled access to the King, demanding payment before he would allow anyone to submit a petition, restricting visits to only those whom he knew would not embarrass him. He helped himself to anything he wanted. And now Earl Edmund was sure that he wanted his estates and title too. It wasn't good enough that his father had been made Earl of Winchester and that the

---

[1] 22 January 1325

title would become his on the older Despenser's death. No, Sir Hugh had always been greedy for immediate gratification, and now he wanted his own Earldom.

'The man is intolerable!' he muttered.

'My Lord?'

'*Sweet* Jesus!' Earl Edmund blurted, starting at the sudden interruption to his thoughts.

From behind a large pillar, Piers de Wrotham cast a look up and down the hall before beckoning his master into the darkness, out of reach of torchlight. 'I have news,' he breathed.

'Well?'

Piers was agitated. Even the Earl could see that. His fingernails were bitten almost to the quick, and his eyes were red-rimmed from lack of sleep. 'Master, you are in great danger.'

Earl Edmund felt a tightening in his throat. Ever since the shameful truce he had agreed with the French last year, he had expected to be arrested and held in the Tower, or to suffer a simpler fate, grabbed one night from behind and stabbed in the back while his mouth was covered. 'Who is it?'

'Sir Hugh. He wants you to die,' Piers said earnestly.

'There is little new in that!' Earl Edmund said, unimpressed. 'He never liked the fact that I used to be the King's constant companion. It made me a rival for his affections.'

'There is more. I have heard,' Piers continued, 'that he intends to make it impossible for the King to travel to France. He cannot afford for Edward to leave the country without him, but daren't go to France himself.'

'What could he do to make it impossible for the King to go?'

'He could harm him – wound him sufficiently so that he couldn't travel?'

'Not even *he* would dare do something like that. If his plot became known, the King could well decide to charge him with attempted regicide – and that would mean death.'

Piers shook his head. 'But my Lord, you have to understand, he is desperate. If he is left alone here with the King in France, the barons will undoubtedly slay him. But if he goes with the King, the French have already declared that they will execute him as their own enemy. He must do anything he can to keep the King over here.'

'What could he do?' Edward asked again. 'He must either make King Edward so fearful of travelling that he dare not, or make it appear that our King has committed some crime against the French that would sufficiently annoy their own King ... What could he have attempted?'

'My Lord, because he wishes to ruin you in the eyes of the King, perhaps he could seek to make more of your failings in France last year. Perhaps he seeks to send someone else to make a better truce than the one that exists.'

'Aye.' Better than the one I sealed, Edmund told himself. 'How would that hurt me?'

'If he were to persuade the King that he had learned you were plotting against him, or that you were negotiating with the French to take over the lands which were confiscated from the Crown, you could be arrested.

And of course if you resisted arrest, you could be stabbed in the ensuing struggle. It would make for a simple resolution.'

'The bastard! I shall double my guards immediately!'

'Protect yourself, my Lord.'

'Aye. And take a care yourself, Piers. But find out anything you can about any plots he may have.'

'That I will, my Lord. And you shall be the first to learn everything,' Piers promised.

'What else for now?'

'The same as before, my Lord. I should continue to demonstrate your ability as a politician. You are cleverer than almost any other at court.'

'And what action should I take?'

'You have to prove that you are more worthy of trust than Despenser. Well, you know that he wishes only to keep the King with him here in England. The best outcome for the King would be for a strong negotiator to go to France . . .'

'You think *I* should recommend myself?' the Earl snapped. 'Do you realise I am being blamed for all the ills of the realm since I negotiated the truce last year? It was Despenser's fault, but . . .'

'My Lord, I know all that. However, if you were to propose someone who had diplomatic skills, who knew the French King, who was fluent in his language, even Sir Hugh le Despenser could hardly argue. And it would delay the need for the King to go so soon.'

'How could that upset Sir Hugh? It is all that he could wish too.'

'If you can persuade some of your peers, some

Bishops and others, so that Sir Hugh does not suggest it himself, perhaps it would lead to the Queen being selected on your advice. Then the success of her mission would redound to your credit.'

'You are sure she would be successful?'

Piers looked at him with that unblinking expression the Earl knew so well. 'How could the sister of the French King fail?'

His voice was calm, but there was a faintly accusing tone in it which implied that the Earl should not doubt her ability. 'Very well. So my strength is to advise this before the Despenser?'

'It is merely another proof of your statesmanship compared with his muddle.'

Earl Edmund nodded. It was little enough, but in this context every little would help. He had a long journey to make up the distance he had lost over last year's war.

'Very well, Piers. I shall start on this. You keep on at your sources, though, and see what else I may use to the detriment of the Despenser.'

Piers nodded, sidling deeper into the shadows as Earl Edmund marched off back into the light, his body casting a shadow that lengthened over the floor as he went.

Sighing, Piers turned away. It was sad to betray the Earl, for he rather liked the man. But money was money, and knew no loyalty.

Chapter Five

Hall of the Bishop of Bath and Wells, Straunde
Edmund Woodstock, Earl of Kent, was disgruntled to be made to stand here, kicking his heels until the Bishop deigned to appear. Apart from anything else, he was hungry. He'd come here as soon as he could, before even breakfast, to catch the Bishop first thing after his morning Mass.

He was an Earl, half-brother to the King, an important man, and this petty cleric kept him hanging about like a berner awaiting his lord and master's command to set the hounds loose. He had half a mind to leave this damned palace and make his way homewards to the inn he was renting, when he heard feet on the steps outside.

If only he was home again. Although it was no warmer than here, he liked Gloucester, where he had his main castle and manors. Here in London and the area all about it, he was unsettled. He'd never liked it, not from the first. Give him open lands and his hounds and he'd be happy,

---

[1] 24 January 1325

but here in London he felt cooped like a hen. Especially now he had at least two men with him at all times.

Piers had best be correct. The fellow was too damned uncertain. When they had met the other day, he had looked so petrified. Earl Edmund had hoped that Piers would have produced something rock-solid on which he could plan, but no. Just the same old hints and things of no value, like the news that Despenser hated him and could plot to have him killed. As if he didn't know that already!

Edmund was no fool, but there were times when life was truly confusing. Just now, he knew that all he did must be circumspect and cautious, because otherwise, he could well lose his head. Literally. The messages he had been receiving from Piers left him with no doubts.

The realm needed strong government. The populace were sheep to be herded carefully, and shorn in due season. There were the three classes of man, as all knew: the *bellatores*, the clergy, and the commonfolk. The *bellatores* were the men who had a duty to protect all others; the clergy existed in order to maintain the souls of the rest of society; and beneath both were the commoners, who were there to labour and, by their efforts, feed all others. It was the way of all communities. It was how they functioned.

He had been loyal – no: devoted. All his life, he had fought to support his half-brother, the King. Edward II demanded ever more devotion from his men, even when his household was splintering and his own knights were leaving him to join Thomas of Lancaster, before Edward removed *his* head. When Edward had needed help in allowing the Despensers back into the country after they had been exiled, who did he turn to? Edmund. When he wanted Leeds Castle besieged and Bartholomew Badlesmere captured? Edmund. When he wanted loyal men to take Thomas of Lancaster's chief residence? Edmund. When he wanted his own men to hear Andrew Harclay's trial and judge him? Edmund. He, more than anyone else, had repaid the wealth and honours given to him. God's eyes, he had *earned* his rewards.

All the time he'd felt the sneering, though. Christ Jesus, yes. All the while, while he worked his ballocks off to help the King, he had known that they'd all looked down on him. No matter that he had successfully completed many active battlefield campaigns, they still looked on him as a lesser man. Bloody Despenser, with his airs and graces – when all was said and done, he was nothing more than a knight. Edmund was born the son of a *king*, the son of Edward the Hammer of the Scots. He was a man of honour and breeding.

He heard the mutterings all the more now, of course. Yes, while courtiers reckoned that his star was descending, they all started to show their callous disregard for him. And he knew full well that many of them laughed at him behind his back. He didn't need Piers to tell him that. Christ's bones, it was obvious enough. It wasn't only the Despensers, either. There were some whom he had always looked upon as friends who now were all too content to make his life a misery.

If that were all, he'd not be too worried, but it wasn't. He knew as well as any that among those who laughed at him was his own brother, the King. And his other brother.

Thomas of Brotherton, the older by one year, had never quite enjoyed Edmund's successes. And truth be told, Edmund had always had that feeling that he was the least of all Edward I's sons. He was but six when his father died, and it had left him wondering what sort of a man he had truly been. Perhaps little better than any other. Certainly his brother, Edward II, was scathing enough about him. But then, King Edward I had exiled his son's great friend, Gaveston, and Edward never forgave his father that.

This grudge-bearing trait was one with which Edmund was all too familiar. Ever since he had signed that truce with the French last year, he had found himself marginalised, an embarrassment. And all the others seemed to think that they could manage not only Guyenne, but the whole Kingdom better without him.

'My Lord Kent.'

The suave voice shook him from his reverie. Fitting a grin to his face, Edmund turned and took the proffered hand, kissing the Episcopal ring. 'My Lord Bishop.'

Drokensford was a heavy-set man with a florid complexion. His face was square and lined, as befitted a man who never based himself in any home, but who moved constantly from one manor to another, usually visiting all sixteen of those within his See each year, as well as the other properties dotted about the country. His voice was gruff, and he still sounded like a farmer from that little Hampshire town where he had been born. 'My friend, it is my honour to see you here. Would you like some wine?' He looked across the room at the guards the Earl had brought with him.

'If you please, my Lord Bishop.' He jerked his head at the guards, and they walked out to wait in the screens passage.

'I think that here we may speak as equals,' Drokensford said quietly.

The hall was a large one, but Edmund looked about him carefully. There were hangings on two walls which could have concealed a man. A closed door could all too often hide a listener. He recalled Piers's words, and knew that no one could be trusted.

'My Lord Bishop – John – you will know already that I am not entirely in favour at court.'

'I had noticed your sad absence. I was sorry, for I have always respected your judgement.'

Edmund took the goblet presented to him and sipped, eyeing the Bishop.

Drokensford smiled, then held his arms out as if to indicate that both were a long way from any wall. 'You may speak freely, my Lord Kent.'

'Then I say this: if it were only me, I should be content with my lot. I would give up the governance of the realm to the King and his advisers, and I would retire to my estates. I have no need of political power. I am a simple man, a warrior. The King had need of me, but has so no more. So I should leave. But there are matters which concern me.'

'They are?'

'To speak plainly: Sir Hugh Despenser. When I was in France, he had control of all policy in Guyenne; he did little to help us. The fleet was supposed to sail in August, but did not; he never responded to our demands for men and matériel. No, he sat on his haunches and did nothing, until at the last, we lost all. I was confined in La Réole until I could negotiate a truce, without any help or advice from him.'

'And now we must negotiate if we are to keep even a part of our territories over there,' the Bishop murmured.

'Precisely. And who is advising the King on all this? Despenser. The very same man who has been in control of the affair at all stages. The man who cost us the war last year.'

If the Bishop noted that it was Edmund himself who was in charge of all the forces there at the time of the French invasion and overrunning of the English lands, he kept the observation to himself. 'And you wish to make a point?'

'You know what I'm saying. If Despenser was incapable of protecting the Crown's interests last year, what hope is there that he can do so now? And if he was not incapable, his incompetence begins to look suspicious.'

'You suggest that he was a traitor?'

'Never to his own affairs! I only say what is obvious.'

'I am merely a Bishop, my friend. What would you expect a man of God to do about such affairs?'

Edmund's lip curled a very slight amount. 'Yes – you are a man of God, just as I am brother to the King.'

Drokensford took a long pull from his wine and nodded to himself. 'I am afraid that I have little influence myself. Certainly not enough to interpose myself between the King and his advisers. Especially his . . . his most trusted advisers.'

There was no need for him to emphasise the point further. All knew that Despenser was closer to the King than any other man. Most suspected that the two must be lovers. There were even rumours that Despenser had tried to entice the Queen into his bed, according to Piers, although Edmund found that too unbelievable. The idea that the woman would have allowed him close enough to her to make such an improper suggestion was not credible. She hated him – as well she might.

'And yet all who hold love for our realm must wish to support our territories against our enemies,' said Edmund.

The Bishop eyed him. 'The realm is the King's, and the territories belong to him and the Crown. We are only subjects.'

'But we must still try to protect his lands.'

'And how could we achieve this?'

'There is one way: we must have an ambassador go to the French King. Someone whom he will trust, someone who can speak for our King.'

'I believe I understand your aims now,' Drokensford muttered.

It was not new. In the last day the Earl had visited several Bishops and senior peers of the realm to try to put Piers's suggestion into action, and each of them had listened and then studied him as though wondering whether he had more information he could impart. No one trusted another in this court. The King's household was wrapped in a miasma of fear. Nobody dared to think for himself, and certainly nobody would think of thwarting Sir Hugh le Despenser.

'What else?' he said. 'We must have the Queen go to

France. Who else can achieve anything? If only Earl
Pembroke had not died last year, he could have been sent.
Stratford has achieved much – but he is not capable of
miracles. The only person who can be expected to win
over the French is our Queen.'

'And?'

'You know as well as I do that the Despenser would
not have her sent. He wishes her here. He has never
trusted her, and trusts her less than ever now. I'll wager
you that he fights to prevent her being sent.'

'Come now! He and she appear to be happy in each
other's company.'

'You think so? Then why . . .' He paused.

'Why what? There is nothing more to be said. Sir
Hugh le Despenser is perfectly happy with her, I am sure.
They are amiable before each other, after all.'

'I do know that, my Lord Bishop. In public, I agree,
they seem perfectly content. But there is some news
which I have heard recently. It concerns me, directly. But
I must ask that you keep this to yourself.'

'What would that be?'

'What if I were to tell you that Despenser has already
sworn to kill me? He cannot bear to think that the truth
should ever come out about his malodorous handling of
French relationships. The murderous bastard wants me
out of the way. Anyway, he's always been jealous of my
Earldom. Despenser has always wanted it for himself.'

Drokensford was looking at him with a cynical twist to
his face. The man wanted more. Edmund returned his
stare with resolution. There was little else he could say to
persuade the man. Grasping at the nearest straw, he

blurted, 'You know what sort of man he is: *ruthless*.'

'That is a measure of many a knight,' Drokensford said.

'Not many are in his league. If he dares to harm me, to kill me, who would be next? A Bishop? Would there be any who would be safe?'

The Bishop hesitated, his goblet at his lips. 'You have given me much to consider, my Lord.'

'No one is safe from him.'

'And you think the Queen could make a good fist of negotiations in France?'

'Of course. Ha! She would be grateful too, to be safe from Despenser's clutches.'

'Why do you say that? How could it benefit him, were the Queen to die?'

The Earl had not considered this. His words had only been intended to mean that she would be safer from him were she abroad. Now he grew pensive. 'If she were to die, *he* would be the King's sole companion.'

The Bishop looked across at him. 'You should be more careful with your language, my friend. Such talk could be considered irreverent, even treacherous.'

'My Lord, you have heard the same rumours as me. It is said that the Queen was evicted from his bedchamber some while ago. While the Despenser . . .'

'I do not deal in gossip,' the Bishop snapped harshly.

'Neither do I. Very well. There is another reason for him to wish to see the King's wife dead. She is a great magnate in the land. Her wealth is based in Devon and Cornwall, where she possesses great mining profits and the forestry from the moors. You know how acquisitive the Despenser is. If she were dead, he could perhaps persuade the King to make all that over to him.'

'It would be hard to envisage such bold treachery!'

Earl Edmund blinked. To his mind such ruthlessness was entirely natural from that evil spirit Despenser.

Seeing his frank surprise, the Bishop was forced to look away. He didn't honestly doubt that Sir Hugh would be capable of it either. He could not deny that the Earl's words would make a deal of sense to almost everyone in the land. There was no doubt that if any could consider such a dreadful act, it was Sir Hugh le Despenser. Rumours of his vicious treatment of widows and others who legitimately possessed lands or beasts which he coveted were too numerous to be discounted. He frowned. 'You are sure the Despenser wishes you dead?'

The Earl glowered. 'Yes. He knows I would curb his power.'

'Then, my friend, you must take extreme care in all that you do. He is a most dangerous opponent.'

'I know *that*! In God's name, can't you give me better advice than that?'

Drokensford peered at him, and suddenly his Hampshire peasant's eyes were hard as crystal. 'Yes. If he has determined to harm you, I would pray to God and prepare your soul for death.'

Queen's Chapel, Thorney Island

Seeing the girl walking down the passageway towards him, Richard Blaket felt his heart begin to pound just that little bit harder.

Fair of hair as she was fair of face. In God's name, but

she was his soul's delight. If he could win her heart, he would be glad for ever.

'Master Blaket.'

'My Lady Alicia.' He inclined his head seriously, then grinned as he stood aside.

She looked away, and he felt his heart drop. Still, it was no surprise, not really. They had enjoyed a little banter, but that was common enough in a place like this, where there were so many men and so few women. But perhaps she was offended that he had been too familiar – not in action, but in tone. Even a man's voice could be regarded as an instrument of love-making, so he had heard.

Well, damn her if she did! It wasn't as though he had shown any lack of respect, and for her part she had been saucy enough in front of him, so long as others weren't watching.

And then he saw that behind her was the Queen.

Queen Isabella walked slowly, like a woman on the way to the gallows. Alicia and Mabilla were before her, and Lady Eleanor and Joan followed behind. Many would think that the Queen was merely being accorded the respect due to the most senior woman in the realm, but after listening to Alicia a little, he knew that it wasn't so. It was merely the guard about the prisoner.

It gave him a stab in the heart to see how this magnificent woman was brought so low. She should be up in the Great Hall, entertaining at her husband's side, not locked away in these little corridors to moulder.

He snapped to attention, his chin up, proving his respect by his smart salute, and he was sure that he saw her smile as she passed, acknowledging him with a delicate nod of her head.

Not that he cared a short while later when he felt Alicia's soft, warm hand on his own, touching him as delicately as a bee landing on a rose, he considered, his heart so full he thought it must burst.

Chapter Six

Outside Salisbury

Baldwin looked about him with a faint smile on his face, and Simon noticed and gazed around in his turn. To his eye, the area around Salisbury had something altogether too flat and dismal about it.

'What are you grinning about?' he asked.

Baldwin shrugged. 'I knew this area when I was younger. I came here when the fair was on, about the Feast of the Assumption. That used to be a great fair, Simon. Ten whole days it lasted.'

Simon did not enquire further. He knew that this must have been during Baldwin's life as a Knight Templar, and that was a subject that was unfit for discussion – at least while others could overhear them. 'It is very boring, though.'

'At last you voice your feelings!' Baldwin laughed. 'Your face has grown blacker and blacker with every mile we have travelled since the Blackdown Hills, and that was three days ago.'

---

[1] 25 January 1325

Simon could not argue with that. Leaving his own lands had made him feel odd, like a snail which had left its shell behind. He felt exposed and threatened. All the sounds and noises seemed similar, but strangely different at the same time. The landscape was the most obvious manifestation of just how alien things were, this far from home.

'You find the countryside here curious?' The Bishop had ambled up on his old mare, and was peering about himself with the gently enquiring expression of those with failing sight. 'I rather like it. Does it not give you more of a sense of God's magnificence? With the openness all about me, I always feel more of an affinity for His works. Just look at the sky!'

Simon had to murmur agreement with that. The absence of real hills made the sky appear more vast than usual – although he was sure that it loomed just as large from Higher Willhayes or Cawsand Beacon. Those two hills were so high, to climb to their summits was like ascending to heaven, almost.

'What are they saying?' piped up a voice.

'Rob, whatever they – *we* – are saying is none of your concern. Just try to keep quiet!' the Bailiff hissed to his wayward servant. He had no proof, but he was sure that on the second night out from Exeter, Rob had snared some of the Bishop's guards into a game of hazard. Rob looked only to be some twelve years old, but he had learned his gambling and language from the sailors of Dartmouth. It was thought that he was the bastard son of one. For all that he had a wide-eyed innocent appearance, his speech was as filthy as any whore's from the

Bishop of Winchester's stews, and his ability to palm or move a dice was unequalled by any felon Simon had encountered.

'I was only asking. Is that London, then?'

In the distance they could already see the smudge of a great city. Its fires were belching smoke into the clear wintry sky, and Simon grunted.

It was Baldwin who responded. 'No, lad. That is still many miles away. This city is Salisbury. Soon you shall see the great spire of the Cathedral.'

'Yes. We shall stay overnight with the good canons of Salisbury,' Bishop Walter said. 'I am sure that we shall be made welcome there.'

Baldwin cast a glance in his direction. The Bishop did not sound convinced of their reception, and Baldwin wondered at that, but not for long. A Bishop should be able to expect his brother-Bishops to be courteous and friendly, but he knew as well as any in the Church that such men could be fiercely competitive. They often resented other Bishops, were jealous of their lands and profits.

They had travelled only another mile or two when suddenly through the trees the mighty spire became visible, its structure supported by the poles of larch that comprised the builders' scaffolding. 'Look, Simon. Is it not immense?'

Bishop Walter sniffed. 'If I were not a man of God, I could be jealous of this. My cathedral rebuilding was begun what – fifty years or more ago? And we have only come halfway. Yet this was all constructed in less than that. I cannot hope to see the finish of my cathedral. It began around my birth, and I shall be long dead before it is complete. Yet this marvel has been created in only some forty years or so.'

'The spire is not finished, my Lord Bishop,' Baldwin said.

'No, but even now a man can see what it will be like,' the Bishop said with sadness. 'And I shall never see so much as the roof on my cathedral, I sometimes think. The plans I have for the west front are wonderful – but what chance will I have to see them executed? I shall have to console myself with the reflection that at least others may enjoy what I have worked to achieve.'

He rode on, and his guards, three men-at-arms from his personal retinue, kicked their mounts into a canter to keep up with him.

'What was all that about?' Rob demanded as they hurried after the Bishop.

'He is a man who is suddenly grown aware of his mortality,' Baldwin said wonderingly. 'I have never seen it before in him.'

'He's an old man,' Simon said unsympathetically. 'And right now I expect his piles are playing merry hell with him.'

'You are a rough, untutored fellow,' Baldwin said with a chuckle. 'But you may well be right.'

Hall of the Bishop of Bath and Wells, Straunde, London

It was almost dark when Bishop John of Drokensford heard the horses at his yard, and he sat a moment, his reed still in his hand.

There were many who felt that same anxiety, he knew. The noise of horses could mean many things, but in these sad times, the common fear was that it might be the King's men, or perhaps Despenser's, come to grab someone and take him away. And since the visit of Earl Edmund the other day, he felt more than usually uneasy about the risk of such a visit.

No one was safe. Even those who did not plot to curb the King's powers were at risk, because Edward trusted no one. No one but Despenser, and he was a terror: he was scared of no man. And why should he be? He was rich beyond the dreams of most, with a host of men at his beck and call, with the ear of the King, and the ability to do whatsoever he desired. And this complete power had entirely corrupted him and others.

There were boots on his steps now, and Bishop John leaned back in his chair with a fleeting increase in his heart's pounding. It made him feel light-headed, as though he had partaken of a vast quantity of wine or ale, and then his mind told him to be calm. There were only a few pairs of boots. If Despenser had learned of the message he had sent to the Queen, he would have come with more men than this.

'My Lord Bishop.'

'My Lord Despenser,' he said suavely. 'How can I serve you?'

Sir Hugh le Despenser looked about him with that reptilian coldness Drokensford recognised so well, and pulled off his gloves as three men behind him entered the room, gazing about them suspiciously. 'I would welcome an opportunity to discuss some matters with you.'

'Please take a seat,' the Bishop said drily as Despenser sat. He set his reed aside, glancing down at his notes. His guest was not welcome. 'I suppose you want to protect yourself against me?' he said, indicating the men at the back of the hall.

Despenser gave a half-grunt, half-smile. Turning, he told the men to wait outside. When they were gone, he said directly, 'We are not friends.'

'No.'

'However, the realm needs all magnates to pull together and discuss what is best for the country and the Crown. Just now, unanimity is crucial in the face of the threat from France.'

'Yes. I can agree with that.'

Despenser sat back and considered the Bishop for a while. At last he said, 'The French King demands that King Edward should go to France to pay homage for the lands he holds as vassal to the King.'

'Yes. We all know that.'

'I need hardly say to you how dangerous that could be.'

'You suggest that the French may seek to injure our King?' Drokensford asked with feigned surprise. That was a subject for open conjecture amongst the Bishops, and he was convinced it must be also for the secular barons.

There was no humour in Despenser's face, as there was none in the Bishop's. Both knew how serious affairs were between the English and French.

'They have already taken the majority of the King's lands over there, after creating a pretext. That fool, Kent, lost our King his inheritance.'

'I understood that he received no help from here when he should have been able to count upon it,' Drokensford said mildly.

'There were problems with sending and receiving messages, it is true, but he should have acted on his own initiative.'

'I thought he did.'

'Perhaps. If so, his best was not good enough. His initiative may well have cost us Guyenne.'

'So we are agreed, then,' the Bishop said. 'At all costs this rift between the two Crowns must be healed.'

'Exactly. We cannot afford to see relations damaged further.'

'So we must send more ambassadors.'

Despenser leaned forward. 'Who, though? You know what they have offered. They want us to send them either the King to make his peace with Charles, or to send his son to make homage. But either could be enormously dangerous. We cannot afford to put them into the hands of this French King.'

'He would give safe conduct, surely?'

'What would that be worth? In God's name, Bishop, how much would you trust that Frenchman? He has Roger Mortimer of Wigmore still in his household, so they say. The worst traitor who ever threatened an English King, and the French give him a home!'

'Perhaps you think you should go yourself?'

Despenser looked at him coolly. 'There is no love between me and the French King. If I were to go, I should be slain, and the cause of peace would not be helped.'

'Then who?'

'There is one: the Queen herself.'

Drokensford peered at him. The temptation to gape was almost overwhelming, but he refrained. 'I had thought that you and she did not agree on many matters?'

'To be blunt, I do not like the woman, but she is the sister to the French King, and we must use any lever we may. She could, perhaps, exert some beneficial influence on her brother and save the realm from losing a vast territory.'

'It would surely be a grave humiliation for you?'

'Perhaps, a little. But better that, than a war or the simple loss of so much of our Lord the King's lands. It must be immensely worrying for him to have this matter drag on so.'

'So what do you ask of me?'

'Two things: that you let your friends know that I would seek to let Queen Isabella go to Paris and negotiate with her brother; and that you support me in parliament when it comes to a debate on the matter. Could you do that?'

'I shall have to consider, but . . . yes, I am sure I can support you in this.'

'Good! Good. That is what I hoped to hear.'

He stood, bowed, and strode from the room.

Picking up his reed again, Drokensford sat for a long while, staring at the door with a mild frown on his face. 'So, my Queen, I hope this shall prove satisfactory for you. I wonder what you intend next, eh, my Lord Despenser?' he said aloud, quietly, and then he glanced down at his hand. It was trembling like a drunkard's after missing his morning whet, and as he watched, a gobbet of ink fell from the tip and smudged the parchment beneath.

'Christ save me from that spawn of the devil,' he muttered, and crossed himself.

Salisbury

Roger Martival, Bishop of Salisbury, could have been a brother to Walter Stapledon of Exeter. Both had the same slight stoop, the same slender frames, and the same intensity of intellect. The key difference between them was in age – where Stapledon was some sixty years old, Martival was only some five-and-thirty, in Simon's estimation.

Still, he proved to be a cheerful host, and within a short time of arriving, the whole cavalcade was within the Cathedral's close, the horses being groomed by a small army of ostlers, the guards taken to a small tavern near the main gatehouse together with Rob, while Baldwin, Simon and the Bishop were escorted to the Bishop's palace for a meal with their host.

'Only fish, I fear, my friends, but I hope that your appetites may be tempted by the skill of my cook.'

It was after their meal that the two Bishops chatted for a while, and then Baldwin and Simon were given to understand that there were matters of some delicacy which the two must discuss. Nothing loath, the two friends left them to their deliberations and went to their chamber to sleep.

Later, much later, Simon found himself woken. He lay in the pale light of the sickle moon, wondering what it was that had stirred him. There was no sound of rats about the floor, nor in the ceiling overhead. When he glanced across, he could see Baldwin lying on the bed beside him, chest rising gently with his breath, and that sight itself was almost enough to send him back to sleep. If a warrior who had been forced to live on his wits for much of his adult life had not been jerked awake, whatever the noise was, it was probably natural and of no concern.

Only then did he hear the voices.

'They are doing untold damage to us all!'

'So who would you have in their place?'

Two voices, both raised in anger. The first the Bishop of Salisbury, the second Simon's friend Walter of Exeter. He had no wish to eavesdrop on them both, but when they shouted at each other, it was impossible not to hear every word.

Simon could hear Stapledon's voice, dropped to a murmur now, but insistent. Then there was a moment's quiet, before Roger Martival burst out: 'She has had her children taken from her, do you call that rational? ... I know, but you say she might force her own children to be traitors to their father? Her husband? ... Bishop, do not insult my intelligence! I may be younger than you, but my mind is perfectly able to function. This is not a marital dispute, it is systematic persecution of the lady. She's had her income taken from her, her properties confiscated, her lands – even her household has been dispersed and all the Frenchmen arrested ... Annul the marriage? Could they do that? For *expediency*? In God's name, I deny it! Support this? I should rather support a goat as my chaplain!'

There were more soothing noises then, and the voices

calmed, to the extent that Simon could make out little
more. He frowned over what he had heard, but it made no
sense to him. Ecclesiastical courts occasionally had to
consider difficult cases of marriage breakdowns, when
the only possible solution appeared to be a divorce, he
knew, and he wondered briefly whether they were talking
about a couple in the Bishop of Salisbury's See, but then
he shrugged to himself. It was nothing to do with him.

He rolled over, and would have gone straight to sleep,
had he not caught sight of Baldwin.

The knight was still breathing silently like a man
asleep, but now as Simon looked, he saw that Baldwin's
eyes were wide, and frowning with deep contemplation,
as though he was struck with a new and terrible thought.

Chapter Seven

Saturday, Vigil of the Feast of St Julian[1]

Salisbury Cathedral

The dawn sprang upon them without warning.

Simon had slept fitfully, his aching muscles only allowing a shallow, unrefreshing rest. In the cold pre-dawn light, he rolled from the bed and grabbed for his clothes, shoulders huddled against the chill as he foraged on the floor in the darkness. Tugging on his underclothes, the material of his shirt felt damp against his flesh as he slipped his tunic over his head, pulled on his thick travelling jerkin of leather and set his sword belt about his waist. With his cloak over the top, draped about him, and his gloved hands holding the two edges together, he began to feel a little more normal.

'You awake?' he called to Baldwin, but there was no answer, and when he turned to Baldwin's side of the bed, it was empty and cool to the touch. He had been up some while.

His friend was in the Bishop's hall where they had

---

[1] 26 January 1325

eaten the previous evening. On a large trestle there was a great breakfast laid out, with cold fowls, cuts of beef, and jugs of ale as well as heavy, crusted loaves. Baldwin was seated at the far end with Bishop Roger, and the two looked up as Simon entered. He saw the candle flames glittering in their eyes as they welcomed him, and he smiled in response, but when he took his seat, he was half-convinced that there was a meaningful pause, as though the two had been speaking confidentially on matters of great importance, and his intrusion was unwelcome. Still, the moment passed, and before long they were all discussing the merits of alternative paths onward, before Bishop Walter arrived, and took his own seat next to Martival.

'I trust you slept well, my Lord Bishop?' Martival said.

'Perfectly, I thank you,' Walter Stapledon responded, but he kept his eyes away from the other.

Simon was already on his horse in the greyness before the Bishops were ready to part. They had held a brief Mass for the travellers before beginning the latest stage of their journey, and then Bishop Walter went with Bishop Roger Martival for a few words of private conversation. Baldwin, Simon noticed, was more quiet and reserved than usual, and it gave Simon some pause for thought, but then the Bishop mounted his horse, and the gates to the Close were opened, and they were trotting gently down towards the city gates, waiting for the dawn and the gates' opening. With the help of a canon from the Bishop's retinue, a grumpy porter was persuaded to open them a little early, and then they were on the road to

London, their horses' hooves thudding on the muddy roadway. And when they had gone only a short distance, the sun appeared before them, flooding the entire landscape in golden light.

To Simon it was a surprise. In his experience the sun rose slowly, and the light only gradually washed over the fields and woods. Here, the country was so flat, it seemed to spring up from nowhere. Night became day in an instant.

'You were having a long talk with the Bishop,' he said when he drew nearer to Baldwin.

'You guessed, old friend? Well, I thought it might be as well to be warned about the political situation in London before we arrived.'

'And what did you learn?'

Baldwin sighed. 'There are moves afoot to remove our Queen. That is what we both heard the good Bishops arguing about last night. What I find sad is that it is our own friend who is proposing this action – in order to, as he says, "remove the canker in our King's household".'

'He said that of our Queen?' Simon was appalled. He had always borne great respect for the Bishop. Walter Stapledon had been a heroic figure when he was younger, a man who fought for what he believed to be right at all times, who became Bishop of his Diocese and used his wealth to endow schools and colleges for the benefit of others. He was a great man.

'He said that, I fear, yes. And a great deal more. He said that he desires to see the King's marriage annulled. I believe that is the reason for his journey to London – to seek a way to remove the Queen.'

Sunday, Feast of St Julian[1]

Thorney Island

In the chapel of Queen Isabella's apartments, her Chaplain, Brother Peter of Oxford, was still sweating as he stood, his head bent, before the altar. The fear was with him much of the time now, but rarely so concentrated as today.

He disliked this charge intensely. Never would he have seen himself as a messenger before, and certainly not one who was working against the interests of the King. If anything, he would have tried to support Edward. But when his Bishop, John of Drokensford, asked him to do something, he was not going to refuse. His Bishop held the powers of patronage, and it was important that he keep him contented.

As soon as Peter had knelt with his master to hear his Confession, the Bishop had grasped his wrist and whispered urgently.

'It is vital that you let her know this as soon as you can,' he had said.

'You want me to try to get it to her now?'

'No. You have to wait until there is no suspicion. We have to pray that her enemies will not jump before her next visit to the chapel. Dear God, I only hope that we shall not be too late.'

That was the trouble about being the Queen's own Chaplain, Brother Peter thought: it meant that no one trusted him even slightly. Never had there been a court

---

[1] 27 January 1325

that was so riven by internal politics, or so he reckoned. This place was full of intrigue, and no matter to whom he turned, he knew that, without fail, every word he spoke would be used or at least measured and weighed and recorded, just in case it might, at some point in the future, become useful. And of course there was never an opportunity to see his Queen alone, except at Confession. If he were to ask to see her, it would immediately raise suspicions.

Well, let them weigh and measure. He was no fool, and he was perfectly content to hold his tongue and only speak when he was sure of his words. If any man chose to try a more physical approach, he'd be ready for him, too.

The sun was fading already, he saw. This was an awful time of year. The trees over at the riverbank opposite were all denuded of leaves as though dead. To his eye, the whole countryside looked barren. Skeletal boughs thrust upwards, foul and rotten in their nakedness. Even those plants that retained a few leaves were brown at the edges as though they had been touched with a scorching chill. All was disgusting. It reminded him each year of God's bounty when he looked at this – and he understood the pagan fear that spring might never return. All the peasants felt it, especially as their teeth started to pain them, and the gums to bleed, as the winter scurvy took its toll.

Not here at court, though. Peter sighed. Spring would come, no matter the outcome of all this plotting. Bishop John had been most insistent that he should come here: he wanted someone in the palace who could listen to the

Queen and help her, someone who was above the temptation to take a bribe to see her poisoned. And someone who could maintain certain lines of communication with her.

Such as delivering little notes.

They had a system now. When there was something urgent, he would pass it to her praying hands during Communion, and she'd read it with a face like stone, the little slip of paper sitting in her cupped hands as he passed her the bread, taking it back from her as she sipped the wine and concealing it in his little towel. This time in particular, he was impressed with her resolution. Her face did not change. She could have been a housewife reading a missive from her husband directing her not to forget to feed the chickens, for all the impact that note had apparently had upon her. There was little to show how devastating it was.

Soon after that, she had left him with a gracious nod, swirling from the room with my Lady Eleanor in attendance, the other women about her. Brother Peter noted Mabilla watching the poor lady closely, as if she expected the Queen to run off at any moment. Others, like that little strumpet Alicia, were much more keen on eyeing up Peter himself. She always seemed to have a little curl of her lips for him, and waggled her arse all the way up the passage to the chapel's door in flagrant temptation. Aye, she had somehow picked up that he was no better than he should be. If it wasn't for the fact that the Bishop needed someone with certain ... skills here, Peter knew he would never have been given this job. No, he'd have been left to rot in gaol, where he rightfully belonged.

As he polished the goblet, he eyed his reflection in the shining gilt. His dark eyes stared back at him, serious and contemplative, and filled with self-loathing. Well, at least he had passed on the message. She could do what she wanted with it now.

When she was gone, he had reread the message concealed in his towel. As usual, he was going to eat the little scrap of paper, to deprive unfriendly eyes of the sight of the close, neat writing, but he paused when he saw those words.

My Lady, beware! Sir H plans your murder.

It was dark now. Full dark, with the moon hidden behind a cloud that shimmered every so often with the light it concealed, like a floating ball of silk. This was the kind of night Jack atte Hedge liked. An assassin craved the dark.

He was clad in dark brown hosen and a gipon he had bought in Southwark. It was very tight-fitting, as the modern fashion demanded, and he had dulled its colours by immersing it in the mud of the river for some hours. The stain had made it as dark as the hosen, although not actually black. He disliked black. Many years before, he had noticed that a black dog on a dark night was easy to see – but a brown or grey dog, that was impossible, even from a moderately short distance. So when he took up his new occupation, he decided to make use of that discovery.

He was on the far side of the River Tyburn. It was a strange little river, this. The Abbey monks had only a short while ago had it extensively reworked, apparently, in order to make it more easily navigable, or maybe to make the tidal wheel work the better on their mill. There was no boat or bridge here, but he'd only come here to observe, nothing more.

It was not the first night he had spent out here. For the last five evenings, he had simply sat and watched to see what routines there were in the royal household.

From this position he could look over past the point of the Westminster Abbey wall, straight up to the southern wall of the palace yard. Directly ahead was the Queen's chapel, then her cloister, before the King's own chamber. In low tide, Jack reckoned he could make his way over the mud, through the Tyburn, and onto the thicker mud in the angle between the old palace yard and the Abbey's yard, but if he did, he'd leave clear tracks for others to follow. Better to remain dry, he thought.

The guards at the wall went to their allotted positions, and he watched carefully. This was a special day, the Feast of St Julian, and he was hoping that the guards would be less assiduous than usual, so that he might assess routes of ingress and egress. Not that they were ever that assiduous: from all he had seen, the men were remarkably slapdash about their duties.

At the southern tip, the guard there seemed to give a cursory look up- and downriver, and then he followed the line of the wall to the western point, where he disappeared from view. There was some rattling, and then Jack saw him reappear, now wearing a blanket. He took his metal cap off, set it on the wall between the crenellations, and disappeared once more. Soon there was the sound of a man snoring.

It would be easy to knock him down, Jack thought. Throw him over the wall into the thick mud. He'd probably drown there, and no one would suspect it was foul play. They would simply assume that the fool had fallen asleep and toppled over the wall – if they ever found him. The others knew he slept on duty. They must. Today being a feast day, all would have eaten and drunk more than usual. No doubt half of the guards were snoring already.

He waited until he was certain that the fellow was asleep, and that no more men were tramping over the walkways, and then he slipped quietly along the Tyburn's bank.

Jack had spent the first nights here considering how he might enter the palace yard or wall's walkway – but last night he had thought of another, easier option. If he could just get inside the Abbey's grounds, it must be possible to gain access to the palace area from there. There was only one wall between the two.

Over the Tyburn was one bridge, which led from the Abbey's south gate towards the mill. He walked to it, gazing along its length, and then slipped over it silently. The man at the gate opposite was clearly asleep, because there was no alarm given. Jack reached the gate cursing to himself at the sound of gravel stones crunching underfoot, but when there was no challenge, he began to follow the line of the wall east to the Thames.

At the Abbey's corner, he paused and felt the ground ahead of him. As he had feared, from here to the water it was a thick, silty mess. If he were to step into that, he might sink an inch or a yard; there was no way to tell, and he daren't take the risk. Instead, he began to feel his way about the wall. The mortar between the stones felt solid. Each had been cemented firmly in place, and the quality of the stone-dressing was good. There were no footholes: climbing this would be difficult. Jack swore silently to himself again. Perhaps after all he should find a different place from which to launch his attack.

But then he had a stroke of good fortune. As he stood there, gazing out at the water, disconsolate at wasting his time, he noticed a gleam of light on the ground at his feet. He spun about, thinking a man had spotted him and was holding a candle aloft to observe him, but then he realised that there was another way inside.

Just here, the Abbey had a drain that emptied the yard's waste into the Thames. It was little more than a culvert, here at the point of the wall, and when he leaned down to investigate it more closely, he saw that it was protected with a metal frame, but that the frame had rusted badly. Testing it, he was convinced that he could pull it away with his bare hands. The vertical bars were badly corroded where they were set into the wall above.

He squatted back on his haunches. It was possible to enter now, find his prey, finish the commission and be off. Yet he still had a little time left. Better, perhaps, not to act precipitately.

Rising silently, he crossed the river again, then made his way down to the Thames once more, where he knelt and gazed at the walls. There was the sound of raucous singing from the other side of the wall, and he reckoned that the guards off-duty were making the most of their freedom. As any troops always would.

This was clearly a good time, then. As soon as the main guards had been changed, and when there had been enough time for the new ones to get the first ales inside them, they would give him a little covering noise to hide his steps.

He had his means of entry to the abbey. Soon he would be able to infiltrate the Palace grounds, and do his Lord's bidding.

Chapter Eight

Tuesday before Candlemas[1]

Exchequer's Offices, Thorney Island
Sir Hugh le Despenser woke with that nervousness that had grown so familiar recently. Only a few months before, he had discovered that the devil's own bastard, Roger Mortimer of Wigmore, had plotted to have him assassinated by the use of black magic. Now each morning he anticipated waking to find a stabbing agony in his belly or head to drive him mad, but so far, thanks to God, he had proved immune.

At the time, Despenser had written to the Pope himself to beg for papal protection. The response had been sharp, if couched in diplomatic terms; it advocated that he should look to his soul, beg forgiveness for his sins and make amends. At the time it had made him rail against the arrogance of popes, but gradually the rage had failed. The magician in question had been caught and killed, and now he had other matters to occupy him.

First was the lack of news from Jack atte Hedge, and

---

[1] 29 January 1325

in the middle of the afternoon as he sat enjoying a cup of wine after his meal, Sir Hugh mused over the man.

He was a curious fellow, Jack. Despenser had first come across him when he, Sir Hugh, had been the King's Chamberlain, more than ten years ago. Christ alive, how his life had changed since then! In those days, the King hated Hugh; he was a symbol of the power of the barons who had ousted his lover Piers Gaveston and murdered him. The King resented his appointment, and for many weeks tried to ignore him, as though pretending Despenser wasn't there could make him disappear.

Despenser often had to travel to Winchester, to the old seat of parliament, and in July of the sixth year of the King's reign, he took part in an action against felons and freebooters there.

There had always been outlaws living in the forests of England, and the great forest south of Winchester harboured many. It was forty years or more since the last King, Edward I, had led an expedition to Alton Forest to eradicate the outlaws living there. For a time that had cleared the place of the worst malefactors, but in the intervening years some had returned. A group had robbed merchants at the Alton pass, killing some Hainaulters and stealing from all. Despenser heard, and was keen to join in with the posse sent to capture or kill those responsible.

It was a marvellous forest. The tree trunks were so numerous, they blocked out the view, and the men's passage was silent: the ground was covered in a thick layer of leaves. But when they rode further in, they found the woods less easily passable. Tendrils of wild rose drooped from the trees, tearing at their faces; hawthorn, blackthorn and holly scratched at the men and their mounts. And then, in a hollow, they were ambushed.

Most of the outlaws were themselves trained by the King in how to fight, and they used every aspect of the woods to defend themselves while inflicting casualties on the posse. Arrows hissed through the air, hitting their mark with a hollow, sucking sound. In the midst of the mayhem, Despenser heard the ringing of steel on steel, the shrieks of men, the whinnying of horses. It was a short, fierce encounter, in which several of the posse were wounded. Luckily none of them were especially valuable, but it was still a loss to him. One good groom was killed, which was an inconvenience and a source of annoyance for some little while.

Afterwards, while he and the rest of the men rested, he had seen Jack atte Hedge.

The man was among the captured felons. At first sight, he was not particularly prepossessing; his face was pretty unremarkable, as was his clothing. In fact, there was nothing special about him at all – except for his eyes. They were extraordinary. In them there was a coolness, a steadiness of purpose, that Despenser had never seen before. When he thought about that first little glimpse of Jack, he could still see those cool brown eyes again, even now.

Later, he had come to realise that Jack was more than just some handy warrior or man-at-arms to keep in his entourage. Men like those were ten a penny – fellows like Ellis and William Pilk. The country was full of churls like them, who were capable of killing a man as easily as a rabbit or a hog. They were like good alaunts, hunting dogs which would attack any prey they were launched against, but which were often more trouble than they were worth, fighting amongst themselves or attacking the wrong animal. But Jack wasn't like that. He was more of a hawk. Once he was directed, he would disappear into the air before suddenly launching himself at his prey. Often, his target would not know that he had come, so swift and fierce was his attack. No one could tell when he would appear. Not even Despenser.

Yes, he had seen the difference between that man and the others, and at the trial, Despenser had bribed the judge and some witnesses to have the fellow released into his custody. And then he had made Jack atte Hedge his own. An assassin who could be relied upon.

However, his latest commission was not any common murder. Jack had to do it correctly, or Despenser would see to it that he was punished.

Sir Hugh heard light footsteps approaching outside. He snorted, then placed his elegantly booted foot on the table in front of him. The door opened and he smiled. 'Hello, wife,' he drawled.

Eleanor de Clare, his wife, stood in the doorway a moment, then moved aside and bowed to let in the other woman.

'My Lady,' Despenser said with a courteous duck of his head, but not removing his boot, as the Queen entered.

'I would speak with you, milord,' she said.

Richard Blaket had been a guard for the King for more years than he wanted to remember now. He ached in the chill of the corridor outside the Queen's chambers, grunting to himself, flexing his fingers every so often, pacing up and down as the flags imparted their deathly chill to the flat soles of his feet. The leather was no protection for a man standing still, not at this time of year.

Time was, he'd have been out there in the open with his bow and quiver ready. There was good money to be made in those days, knocking a pigeon from its perch. All a lad needed was an arrow with a blunted tip, and the birds would fall nice and easy, straight to the ground. A fellow had once seen him dulling his arrow, cutting it flat and fitting a thick leather patch to it, and had laughed. He'd said Richard was wasting his time. Richard was content to take his word, and passed him a new arrow.

'But if you kill a bird, you eat it, and if I kill one, I eat mine,' he said. 'Unless you want to pay a forfeit instead.'

Out in the woods near his home at Epping, the fool drew and let loose his arrow. It passed through the bird and stuck in the tree's limb above. The arrow was lost forever. At least the bird fell, but the arrow had passed up from beneath, piercing the guts. The slamming force of a yard of English Ash did not merely puncture the bird's bowels, it burst them, squirting the contents through the entire carcass. The creature was ruined. Richard Blaket took his own arrow and walked on a short distance. At the top of an oak he saw another pigeon. He drew, loosed his arrow, and the heavy, padded tip snapped into the pigeon's throat, breaking its neck and sending it and the arrow toppling to the ground.

The man had to pay Richard a penny not to eat his bird. Richard gave it to a fox that had been raiding his chickens at night, and when the animal was scoffing the bait, he slew it with another arrow he had not modified.

Memories such as that were a delight when a man was standing in such misery. Not so warming, though, as the memories of last night, of Alicia's soft, warm lips against his own, or the feel of her hips under his hands, the sweet roundness of her breasts . . .

This was the trouble. A man was plagued with the most delicious thoughts when he was standing guard in the middle of the night. And yet he had reason to be extra watchful. All knew that the Queen's life was in peril, in God's name, and it was his solemn duty to protect her. He must concentrate on that, not keep harking back to Alicia's gorgeous body in the candlelight, the orange glow making her form so beautifully shadowy before the fire. The feel of her arms about his neck, her breath against his mouth, her throaty chuckles, her gentle fondlings and squirmings under him . . .

There was a rhythmic swishing sound, and his attention was brought instantly to the present, all memories of last night flying from him as he recognised that obscene noise. It was coming from the chapel itself, and he turned to listen, his polearm levelled even as his eyes narrowed.

It was instantly recognisable, of course: the sound of a stone sweeping along a sword's blade. Except there should have been no such sound here.

Gripping his staff firmly, he walked silently towards the sound.

There were some who said that they cared nothing for the woman, but so far as he was concerned, the Queen was his own mistress. It wasn't that he was in love with her – God's teeth, no! His Alicia would have something to say about that! – but he felt some compassion for her. She had been a powerful, wealthy woman for all her life, and now she was brought so low, and yet she suffered all the indignities with stoicism. As her household was broken up and dispersed, she joked with them about when they would all be free to meet again; when the King reduced her income, she laughed that soon he would have her as a pauper living in his hall and would have to save his alms for her. Never did she bemoan her fate before Richard, and that made him warm to her courage. He would do anything for her.

The noise was louder. Standing outside the chapel, he peered around the door which stood ajar, and took a deep breath, preparing himself. Steady, steady, deep breath . . . and shove the door wide! All at once the timbers creaked, hinges complaining, and he was in the chapel's vestry.

'What is it, guard?' Peter of Oxford peered up at him with a bemused expression on his face, the sword on his lap, the hone in his hand. 'Well?'

'Chaplain, I heard a sword being sharpened, and thought it could be someone here to hurt the Queen.'

'Do I look like a God-damned assassin?' Peter said testily. 'Get out – and close the door after you!'

Richard obeyed him, but for a long moment he stood outside, his hand still on the latch. After some while the sweeping rasp of the hone began once more, and he left the door to return to his post.

He would keep an eye on that Chaplain, he told himself.

* * *

Despenser eyed the Queen dispassionately. It was strange. The woman was so beautiful. Elegant, fair-skinned, and with a body that any man would adore to pull to him, and yet she was so cold. The frigid bitch had frozen his advances, all right. Christ, he had wanted her so much, long ago . . . once he'd even contemplated taking her by force. He'd even suggested . . . but that was all in the past now. Since then, her enmity had deepened and strengthened. It was a pity, he thought. Destroying Isabella would be like smashing a perfect ivory carving. So wasteful. But necessary.

'Speak then, my lady.'

'In private, if you please.'

He lifted his eyes to the ceiling, then shrugged at Eleanor. She gave him a close-lipped nod of agreement and went out, quietly closing the door behind her. 'Yes?' he said abruptly.

The Queen walked to a chair and stood behind it as though needing the support. She still had problems with her arms, he knew. They had never properly healed after the fire at Poissy, when she had been badly burned. Sweet God, that was twelve years ago now, he realised with a shock. It was fearful how time hurtled by.

'Milord, I have heard dreadful rumours. Some say that there are men who wish to see me dead.'

'Your Royal Highness, please . . .'

'I believe it. That is why I bend my mind to see who could wish this thing. And I wonder, as I look about me, who could be willing.'

'My Lady, I fear there are many who would be glad to see you . . . It is not a palatable thought, I know, but while your brother rattles his sword and lances across the Channel, many see any French men or women as possible traitors.'

'Their Queen? People dare to suggest I could be faithless to my husband?'

'Some people are terribly gullible.'

'And you? Do you think this?'

'No, of course not,' he lied smoothly.

It was easy, this verbal fencing. Sir Hugh le Despenser had been brought up in the court of the old King, when Edward I's powers were on the wane. To survive in his household in that period, a man had to have acute political instincts. And, under the new King, Despenser had risen to become the richest and most powerful man in the kingdom. Perhaps second to the King – but since he controlled the other man's heart and mind, that was little qualification. A woman was no trouble after such a studenthood.

'Of course,' she continued, 'the idea that an assassin could enter the King's palace with the intention of murdering me is ridiculous, when there are so many guards, eh? Who is responsible for the guards posted about my chambers?'

'Well, I suppose I have nominal responsibility,' he admitted. 'One of my men posts them.'

'Ah yes. The one called Ellis, *non*? He is a very loyal man, I consider.'

'I have none better.'

'Good, because naturally, if any man were to harm me, the King of France, my brother, would never rest until the man who had ordered my death were brought to justice.

He would use all his powers and wealth to hunt the man down.'

'I would expect nothing else, my Lady,' Sir Hugh said. And it was natural enough. Isabella's death would be a grievous insult to the French Royal Family. That was the marvellous second incentive for having her removed. Not only was she a magnet for all the disaffected barons in the country, her death would make it difficult, if not impossible, for King Edward to go to France. News of Despenser's 'close' relationship with the King was bruited abroad. Many would therefore conclude that the King himself might have had a hand in her death. No guarantee of safe conduct would make Edward feel secure in France.

He smiled at her, but her next words caused his smile to disappear.

'I have to say, Sir Hugh, it would be terribly sad if your protection was to fail. My brother is known to hold a grudge. Any man who plotted to harm me would be considered his own mortal and particular enemy. And I fear I may have indicated to him that you and I have not always agreed.'

He liked the sound of that rather less. 'I do not think I understand you.'

'Oh, I think you do, *Sir* Hugh.'

Her face was as cold as marble as she emphasised that word, and he comprehended perfectly. He might be wealthy, he might be powerful, but to her, his lowly birth was reason for contempt. And she had already managed to hint to her brother somehow that, were she to die, it would be down to Sir Hugh. A leaden weight settled in his belly.

'And another matter,' the lady continued, 'one of my maids is very slapdash. I would be glad if she could be replaced.'

'Then you should have mentioned it to my wife.' He felt a rage building. The arrogance of this bitch – to try to threaten *him*!

'I have not felt the need, milord. I leave the affair up to you. I am sure you know which lady I mean.'

'I cannot imagine. The ladies-in-waiting were all carefully picked by my wife.'

'One in particular is not in the same mould as these others. I would be grateful, were you to see that she was replaced by someone a little more . . . ah, *sympathique*?'

He allowed a freezing smile to crack his features. 'My Lady, please do not worry yourself,' he said smoothly, pleased to see her anger and frustration.

'I have a brain. I choose to use it, Sir Hugh!'

'I mean no disrespect, Your Highness. It is only that if a man were to try to harm you, the guards would stop him. And this lady you refer to – we shall have her removed.'

'Please do so. I would not like to have to be forced to take matters into my own hand.'

'I have little experience of such things, Lady. My wife will see to it.'

'Good. And you may see to the guards about me: I would have them increased. Otherwise,' she gave a light laugh, 'some may suggest that *you* could wish me to be removed.'

'My Lady! Why should I want that?'

She turned and looked him very directly in the eye.

'We both know where we stand, I think. I am not so foolish as to believe that I am safe, but I will swear this to you: if you aid me in this, I will shield you from accusations too. My brother, the King of France, would be pleased to learn that you had helped to protect me. As pleased as he would be enraged and vengeful against any man who sought to harm me.'

'But that is all I intend to do, my Lady.'

'Good,' she smiled. 'Then we have an accord. I shall serve you as best I may, and you will keep me safe from any attacks. Yes?'

He nodded and rose as she left, his mind in a turmoil. Was it possible that she was telling the truth – that she had managed to get a message to her brother? Of course it was! He kicked at the chair, sending it flying across the room. There were always people willing to take money to deliver messages, if the price was right. Any number of people could have done so. It was deeply irritating. But perhaps there was something to be salvaged from the mess.

Jack must be told not to continue with this commission. Somehow, Sir Hugh must track him down and let him know that the attempt must be postponed – perhaps indefinitely. How could he call Jack off, though? Well, that was a matter for Ellis.

'Ellis?' he bellowed. 'Get in here! *Now!*'

There was one foolproof way to ensure that the Queen knew he was serious about their agreement. Dangerous, yes, but necessary if he wanted to save his own skin.

'*Shit!* Ellis, find Jack and tell him it's off. He can't attack the Queen.'

'How? He's gone to ground – I've no idea where he is. You know, how he works, Sir Hugh. He could be anywhere right now.'

'Well, find him – any *damned* way you can. Find him and stop him. And in the meantime, double the guards. We can't take the risk you may miss him. *He must not harm the Queen!*'

Chapter Nine

The early hours of Wednesday before Candlemas[1]

Thorney Island

Earl Edmund sat contentedly in his chamber in the Palace of Westminster. Earlier, he had enjoyed a very pleasant evening meal. The face presented to the world by Sir Hugh le Despenser had shown his bitterness and rage, and anything that could have put that bastard in such a foul mood was balm to the Earl's soul.

What the reason for the long face was, Edmund had no idea. Perhaps it was the rumour of yet another attempt on his life, for there had been several in recent months. It was said that the traitor Mortimer had paid a necromancer to try to kill him by magic. Truly, Sir Hugh had very few friends in the world.

Long may it continue, the Earl thought, yawning. There was no one whose death he would have been happier to hear about.

Walking to his bedchamber, a small room near the King's own chamber, he saw a shadow thrown by a torch,

---

[1] 30 January 1325

and stopped. There were dangers in a place like this so late at night: too many dark corridors, places of concealment in alcoves and behind drapery . . . and he was one man who had determined to live as long as possible. His hand reached for his sword even as he saw the pale face peering down the hallway at him.

'Piers! Dear God, what are you doing wandering about the place like this?' he demanded.

'Earl, my Lord, I have terrible news. Terrible!'

Lady Eleanor de Clare walked into the Great Hall with the letters gripped in her hand, and looked to the far end, where her husband, Sir Hugh le Despenser, stood talking with one of the clerks of the Exchequer.

They were a pasty lot, those clerks. She had never had much regard for them, what with their unhealthful complexions and their minds made up of numbers. Nothing seemed to excite them so much as finding a mistake in a colleague's calculations, and none had the faintest idea about honourable pursuits, let alone the finer aspects of courtly love.

Her man was a very different type altogether. Tall, handsome, and with that dangerous look in his eye, he was every inch a knight. Powerful, strong, fair of hair and with a brilliant mind that measured all he saw in a moment. He would assess a man or woman in an instant and always be right. She had seen it.

And now he had seen her. He finished his words with the clerk, and crossed the hall to meet her in a quieter corner, away from the shouting. It was necessary here. Apart from the men calling to each other about the long marble table, the Chancery, there was also the King's Bench and the Court of Common Pleas in this hall, and the din was appalling.

Two men were with him – Sir Hugh always tended to have one or two henchmen with him for protection now – but he waved them away. There was no need of a guard against his own wife.

'My Lady, I hope I see you well?'

She gave the faintest of shrugs. 'You are always considerate, my Lord. Yes, I slept well for the most part. She disturbed my slumbers a little, but not too much.'

'She disturbs all,' he said in a low voice, looking away.

'She will keep up her keening about her children. Since you took them from her, I don't think she's slept a full night.'

'You still have one of the pups in your care with her. Point out to her that he could be taken away as well, and see if that will shut her up.'

Eleanor nodded. He was right, after all. The silly woman should have been grateful. Princess Eleanor and Princess Joan had both gone to be looked after by the Monthermers, but her eight-year-old son John of Eltham was still here.

'Any news for me?' he muttered.

'Two letters,' she replied. 'She is not happy that I look through her correspondence and tried to keep this one secret, but I saw it.'

'What does it say?' he demanded eagerly, reaching for it.

'It is a series of complaints.' Eleanor passed the letter to her husband and spoke quietly as he glanced over the sheet. 'She protests about her lands being taken and losing her income, she complains that all her own servants have been taken from her, and says that you have taken her husband's love from her.'

'That's all?' he chuckled.

'She does describe the King as – what was it? Ah, yes, "a gripple miser".'

'A man who has been parsimonious towards her, but abundantly generous to another, eh? I wonder whom she could mean!'

'She has demanded that her seal be returned to her.'

'You have it still?'

Eleanor took it from within her bodice, where it hung on a cord. 'Always.' It was understandable that the Queen should resent this latest humiliation. Eleanor was not sure how she herself would feel, were she to be kept under the supervision of another, with all her letters read, all her servants removed, her children too, her income drastically reduced, and even her private seal confiscated so that no private or personal correspondence could be sent. For a Queen, the daughter of one King and now effectively the estranged wife of another, it was a proof of how low she had sunk. She was being systematically stripped of all her assets.

'With luck we shall not have to keep her much longer,' Despenser said, smiling at her.

But there was something in his eyes which alerted her to his real feelings. 'My love, is something worrying you?'

'She has been a nuisance at all times, and never more so than now,' he sighed.

'What has she done?'

'Nothing. It is nothing.' His thoughts were far away now, she saw. This foolish Queen was troubling him.

'Is there something I can do to help?' Eleanor asked.

Despenser glanced back at her. 'Dear Eleanor!' he murmured. He would have liked to confide in her, but how could he explain?

Ellis had already been to many of the inns and taverns where they knew Jack had stayed before, but there was no sign of the man. Even now, Ellis was riding over the Surrey side of the river in search of another tavern where they thought Jack might have billeted himself.

The trouble was, Sir Hugh thought moodily, Jack had always insisted that he should be left alone to do his work. When he took a commission, he would fade away, sometimes for days or weeks, and it was impossible to know when or where he would strike. His attacks were inevitably successful, but this time Sir Hugh wanted to *stop* him – and couldn't!

'I'll have to make sure Ellis mounts double the guards – keeps men at the Queen's side at all times. There's nothing else to do, if we don't find the bastard,' he told himself, but even as he thought it, he heard the door open and automatically bowed low, as did all others in the hall.

Eleanor took her cue from him, removing her hand from his forearm and curtseying. Not that there was any need for her or anyone else to bother, as she knew. The King had eyes for only one person in that great chamber.

Eleanor stood a little back as Edward walked straight to her husband, and it was only when she noticed *his* hand at her husband's arm, how he kept it there affectionately and drew Despenser to his side, that she felt that niggle of jealousy once more.

And the squirm of revulsion.

Earl Edmund was at the rear of the room with Piers de Wrotham and Edmund's brother, Thomas of Norfolk. The latter was slightly taller than Edmund, a fact that had never failed to annoy him.

When they were growing up, Edmund had found his older brother's abundant self-confidence and jokes at his expense annoying, but more recently he had grown immune to them. Ever since their joint attack and siege of Leeds Castle, there had been a mutual regard between them. Until, of course, Edmund had been sent to Guyenne to protect the Principality from the invasion of Charles Valois.

Shit, the bastard had walked all over Edmund and his men. Whenever he demanded help from England, from Sir Hugh le Bloody Despenser, the man was too busy stealing lands and property from the legitimate owners to give a stuff. So Edmund could do nothing, just hung about twiddling his thumbs while the King lost his sole remaining territory in France. It was enough to make a man weep.

Not that it reflected badly on the King's favourite, of course. No shit had ever stuck to *his* blanket. No, instead of that it was Edmund who must bear the brunt of the King's reproaches. As soon as he had returned to England, he had realised how the land lay. The King was sulky and uncommunicative – unless Sir Hugh was there, of course. And that jumped-up little prick was all too keen to make fun of the King's brother.

'Look at him now,' Thomas whispered. 'He is all over the man like a cheap tabard!'

Edmund could not help but agree. The King was sickeningly demonstrative. It had been the same with the previous favourite, Piers Gaveston, until the barons could no longer stomach their obvious sodomy and executed Gaveston. Perhaps, with luck, the same would happen to Despenser – except that Sir Hugh had too tight a grip on the Realm's powers, and on the King. He would not allow Edward to put himself into any form of danger. And as for journeying to France . . . well, Despenser would be more likely to suggest that he should fall on his own sword as let the King go there. That was what Charles demanded, though. And Despenser knew that he must do something – find some alternative to the King travelling to Paris. Because as soon as Edward was over the water, Despenser's life would become forfeit.

'He'll never let the King go to France,' Edmund scoffed.

'But he may permit the Queen to go,' Piers said.

Thomas glanced at them. 'Eh? What was that?'

'I have suggested that your brother might benefit from showing himself a better guardian of the realm than the good Sir Despenser.'

'And how do you expect him to do that? The daft sod can't even persuade a wench who's thrown herself at him, to join him in his bed!'

'That is not funny, Thomas.'

'It's true, though, Edmund. Mabilla was teasing your

tarse for days, and as soon as you gave chase, the bitch screamed like a virgin. Virgin, my arse!' Thomas snorted loudly at the joke, turning and walking away.

It was true enough, but that didn't make Edmund any happier to hear the tale repeated, especially not in front of his servant, but before he could respond, Piers was already speaking.

'My Lord, I think that there is one way in which you might defeat Sir Hugh.'

'How, in God's name? There is nothing better suited to my tastes than to see him on the ground and squirming!'

'I think that, were you to espouse the Queen's cause more strenuously, you might injure him. Perhaps you could suggest that, before she were to leave these shores to become Ambassadress to France, she should be re-established in her former position?'

Earl Edmund curled his lip scornfully. 'And how is *that* going to affect the Despenser swine?'

'If the Queen has her lands and rights returned to her, so that if she were to go to France to negotiate with the French King, he could see that our King was treating her honourably, and that her letters to him detailing her suffering were not entirely correct, it may heal the rift between the English and French Crowns. And then a more equitable truce could be arranged. Perhaps the King might even travel to France, and all the glory of the achievement would redound to your honour, my Lord.'

Earl Edmund frowned. 'You are sure of that?'

'Nothing is so uncertain as life in a royal court,' Piers said with a chuckle. 'But let me put it to you like this: if there is one thing the Despenser would not care for, it would be for the Queen to go to France with the King. The King trusts Despenser, not his wife. But she has borne him children, and were she to have his ear for a long journey, Despenser might find his star beginning to wane . . .'

Jack was at the river as soon as the light faded. The sun began to set when he was sitting in the tavern on the road west, and he finished his drink at a leisurely pace. There was no point getting there in daylight, and letting all and sundry see him.

The view was unchanged from the previous night. He squatted down happily enough, eyeing the guards on the walls, and carefully watching at the base of the walls to see whether there could have been a trap laid for him, but saw nothing to alarm him. Next, he walked to the bridge at the southern gate, and squatted again, staring fixedly at a point just above the bridge to catch any stray movements, listening with his mouth open for any strange noises – but there was nothing again.

At last, when he was content that all was well, he committed himself. He crossed the little timber bridge.

The wall to the Abbey reared up overhead, and he glanced up, feeling a curious sense of the height of the place, before carrying on along the base of the wall to the corner. Here he stopped and waited, all senses alert. There were steps along the upper walkway over his head, and he listened carefully as the man spat over the edge. A gobbet of phlegm landed on his shoulder, and Jack looked at it without distaste as it ran down his breast and upper arm.

When the steps moved away, he crouched silently. The steel of the culvert was as rusted as he had thought, but it was still strong enough to make manipulation difficult. He must kneel and wrench at it to make it give enough to leave space for him to crawl inside. Working slowly so as not to attract attention, he was relieved when he heard singing begin, and with that he felt he could work a little faster. Being out here in the open was alarming.

There was a *snick* as a post of steel snapped – and he froze at the sound. However, there were no running footsteps, no bellows for attention. Nothing. He pulled himself nearer and peered at the metal. The bar had a shiny section where the bright metal had broken from its fitting in the wall. He took mud and carefully smeared it over both gleaming edges, drawing in his breath as the sharp metal sliced into his finger. He ignored the stinging pain and continued. One bar was broken. Now he set to work on the next, waiting until that too was broken, and then smearing that with more mud, this time more careful not to cut himself.

When all was done, he painstakingly withdrew the frame a short distance from the wall, and wriggled himself over it and into the drain itself.

The drain, thank God, was not so noisome as it might have been. Recent rains had washed away much of the filth. Fortunately, the majority of the monks' waste would have been captured in the cesspit, ready for spreading over their fields as manure. There were other places he had entered which had been a great deal worse. He wriggled his way along the short tunnel, and peered out into the main yard.

There was a large building on his right, another directly in front of him, and the main Abbey buildings loomed monstrous and black against the sky in the gap between the two.

A step. He slowly withdrew his head into the culvert before he could be seen, and listened intently. There: a man's pacing up overhead. How had he not spotted the guard? Perhaps there was a trap set for him, and there were more men waiting here to catch him as soon as he tried to break in. But the steps moved on, and he began to breathe more easily.

He took hold of his knife and made sure that it would move in its sheath, then he slipped out into the yard, sliding his back along the wall in the shadows. The walkway above him was not high, only about three feet over him, and reaching it should be easy enough. He saw that there were coils of rope and blocks of masonry stashed beneath it, as well as ladders. There had been a disaster of some sort, he reckoned, looking at the ravaged buildings. All to his advantage.

The choice – to continue now, or to wait and reach this far again some other night. Better by far to get the matter over and done with, he decided. He glanced up at the walls again, and then made for the nearest coils of rope.

On the rough palliasse set out for Piers near the King's chamber, not far from Earl Edmund's snoring body, the adviser totted up the money he had been paid so far.

He didn't understand the game Sir Hugh le Despenser was playing, but so far as he was concerned, the main thing was the money, and that was reaching him regularly. For now, Sir Hugh wanted the King to view the Queen as a potential representative for him in France. However, the King had listened to Despenser when he had poured verbal poison into the King's ears about his wife. Queen Isabella was disloyal, treacherous. She could not be trusted.

Earl Edmund had been telling all who would listen that she *was* loyal and would be a worthy ambassadress – and all would remember his words if anything were to go wrong while the Queen was over there in France. Meanwhile, the King was reflecting that his brother the Earl of Kent was a fool if he trusted the woman. Why? Because Sir Hugh was telling him quietly about all the Queen's misdeeds even as Edmund spoke to her credit.

No one else would have been so easily convinced that the Queen should be sent. But not many people were as gullible as poor old Edmund.

Piers rolled over, well pleased with his progress so far. He had worked hard, and was beginning to see the rewards.

There was the sound of cautious steps outside in the corridor, and he sat up a moment, alert, and then yawned and lay down again. It was only someone from the household – a squire seeking the privy, maybe; a page lost after too much ale. Nothing to worry about.

Chapter Ten

Thursday before Candlemas[1]

Thorney Island

Eleanor de Clare stood with her ladies-in-waiting while the Queen entered her chapel and knelt before the altar.

These late-night visits to her chapel were deeply annoying to them all. There was no point to them, yet she insisted on coming in here and prostrating herself before the Cross. Eleanor had nothing against the correct displays of religious fervour; it was to be expected in a Christian. Yet these very loud and tearful visits were wearing, especially when her brat woke before dawn each day, demanding to know in that querulous little voice of his when he was going to see his sisters again. Acting like a baby when he was a big boy of eight. He ought to know his royal birth and behave accordingly. Even his sisters, aged two and four, would be behaving better than him, she thought.

The priest yawned as the Queen continued to speak in Latin.

---

[1] 31 January 1325

'Oh, *damn* her!' Eleanor hissed, but only quietly so that no one else could hear. The woman was so full of her own misery and self-pity, and yet she was all right. She was a Queen. She'd always have her life, be waited on hand and foot.

Earlier, Eleanor had left her in the care of three of her maids, and had gone to the chamber where her husband had been placed. Of course, it was frowned upon for any woman to enter the separate area that was intended for the King's household. As was normal, this household was entirely masculine. The sole feminine elements had always been the Queen and her maids, when she merged her own household with the King's. Usually they would have a separate existence, though, as was natural. And most of her household too would be male, because all the key functions required men. The chaplains, guards, chamberlains and comptrollers. Wives were not allowed to materialise without the permission of the King. Usually that would mean that a wife would have to take a room nearby, and then her man could visit her when he required the payment of the marriage debt.

Tonight, Eleanor wanted to see her man, and since he was one of the most powerful men in the country, she felt secure enough to walk along the corridors and enter the little chamber beside the Lesser Hall, where she knew he ought to be sleeping.

Yet when she entered, he was not there. She went to his bed, and laid her hand upon it, but there was no one inside. Nor was it warm. Perhaps, she thought, he was still discussing matters with the King. There was another possibility, but she had always refused to consider that, and would continue to do so now. It was not the sort of thing she liked to think of, and things which were unpleasant in that way were always better ignored.

The Lesser Hall itself was in darkness, and when she peeped around the old door inside, she saw ranks of servants asleep on their benches. It was possible that her husband was in the Great Hall, and she walked to it, but before she reached it she could see that it too was in darkness. They weren't there.

It was only as she made her way back to the Queen's cloister that she glanced to her left and saw the lights blazing in the Painted Chamber, the King's private rooms. On the wind she heard a low, sniggering chuckle, then a belly-laugh, and she closed her eyes.

Now, standing in the chapel and watching the Queen, she could close her eyes again, this time to pray silently for God's forgiveness. She should never have wished her husband to die for what he was doing. He was in there with the King on business, no doubt. It was wrong for her to assume that they were indulging in those *unnatural* acts again.

The Queen was done. She stood, swaying slightly, giving Eleanor a feeling of grim satisfaction to know that at least the woman was suffering a little of the torment which she inflicted on her entourage. She must be exhausted, for she had to put her hand out for support, and the Chaplain took it, warily eyeing her as though fearing that his touch could hurt her. Then the Queen snatched her hand away swiftly, as though suddenly realising she had touched a man little better than a peasant, turned and left the chapel.

Walking in her wake, Eleanor felt no need to speak, Queen Isabella knew what she was doing – knew that Eleanor was following her. She was in constant attend-ance, just like any chaperone – except in Eleanor's case, the Queen could not send her away. The woman was with her every moment of every day, more gaoler than maid-in-waiting, and both knew it. As was proved by Eleanor reading all the Queen's correspondence, and keeping the Queen's seal. Even now, at this time of late evening, there were two maids before the Queen, another and Eleanor here behind her, and Alicia drawing up the rear. There was no let-up in the women's watchful supervision.

It was all at her husband's command, of course. Sir Hugh said that he and the King were unable to trust the Queen any more. Isabella had shown herself to be unreliable, and the idea that she might pollute the minds of their children was too appalling to consider. So she must be contained, her children protected, while there was this present crisis with her brother in France.

Eleanor knew all this, but it was still hard. She would have preferred to be at her own home, with her own children, and away from this miserable place. With her husband.

There had been rumours, of course. Well, she had heard snide comments about the King from her own husband, back in the days when his infatuation had been with Piers Gaveston, that son of an upstart Gascon man-at-arms. They'd all talked about his friend – his sodomite friend. Hugh himself had been scathing and then, when the barons captured Gaveston and murdered him, his mood was exultant. Hugh had been a loyal friend to Lancaster at that time, and he had been given a role with the King to help control him. Much as Eleanor was monitoring his wife now.

She didn't know when it had all begun to change, when the King had started to exercise an unwholesome influence over her husband. At first it was nothing too overt. It was just that occasionally she would realise that their estates were grown again, with the acquisition of manors and lands which had been owned by the King's enemies. Traitors were being discovered with ever more regularity, and each time their property was forfeit. Someone had to be given it, and all too often it was passed on to her husband.

But it was not only that their wealth was growing. Hugh was frequently being called to advise the King, and had become a well-known political power in his own right; and as his wealth grew, so did his influence with all others in the realm. These days, Sir Hugh le Despenser was all-powerful . . .

There was a sudden stamp of boots, a rattle as a candle was dropped. A door opened, and Eleanor heard a maid draw in her breath. Then there was a flash of silver and a loud scream, a scream that shivered its way down Eleanor's spine, and made her want to turn and fly.

She saw a sudden gout of blood, and heard another scream, which soon turned to a low sob and wail. A maid shoved past her, maddened with terror, a second had already fainted away, and Eleanor saw the other on the floor, writhing in agony, her belly opened with a long slash, while the butcher who had done it stood before them, his long knife slick with blood. The last lady-in-waiting pushed past, but this was Alicia, and she was thrusting forward, putting herself between the man and the Queen.

Lady Eleanor felt sick; she wanted to vomit, but she was a de Clare. Instead, she shrieked at the top of her voice: '*Guards! Guards, help! The Queen is attacked!*'

Friday, Vigil of Candlemas[1]

London

Simon had been looking forward to arriving in London. He had heard so much about this magnificent city, the greatest in the country, and was excited to think he would soon see it.

They had made excellent time, so Baldwin said. Whereas a King's messenger would average a good thirty to thirty-five miles a day, they had managed somewhere in the region of five-and-twenty, even without travelling on Sundays in deference to the Bishop. The weather had been moderate and clement for the time of year.

However, Simon's mood was lowered, even as they approached the city, thanks to the Bishop. Instead of feeling thrilled to see where the King dispensed justice and where the parliaments met most often, the Bishop's foul mood was affecting him and everyone else in their little party.

It had been bad from the moment that they left

[1] 1 February 1325

Salisbury. Bishop Walter had retreated into his shell, snapping at those about him and scowling at the countryside as though expecting an answer to some deep philosophical question, but finding none.

Even at the various halts, it was clear that the Bishop preferred not to discuss whatever it was that was bothering him. He was a powerful man, and his guards and clerks all preferred to avoid him rather than endure his barbed retorts, which meant that Simon and Baldwin were left with him more and more as the others fled. Neither felt that they should leave their mentor entirely alone, so they paced along beside him, mostly enduring his silence, casting occasional glances at each other as they wondered how on earth to bring him out of himself.

It was only as they reached *Cayho*[1] earlier today – some six miles from London itself, he said – that the Bishop appeared to shake off some of his depression. He began to point out places he felt would interest Simon, but nothing could prepare the Bailiff for the magnificence of the sights which were to present themselves.

'And *that* is Thorney Island,' the Bishop said at last as they came through a small thicket and wood and paused on the great road.

Ahead of them, Simon could see a great monastic wall about a large abbey church. Outside the wall was a broad river that had been converted into a canal, and as he watched, a small ship was navigating it. Behind it lay the great sweep of the Thames, with some few buildings on

_____
[1] Kew

the opposite bank, but it was the other buildings behind the Abbey that caught his attention most.

'Is that really a hall?'

'It is the Great Hall,' Stapledon smiled. 'That is where the King meets with all his advisers and listens to their debates. Everything that affects the realm is decided in there.'

Simon heard Baldwin clear his throat in an expression of cynicism but ignored his friend. He would enquire later why Baldwin rejected the Bishop's words. 'What are they?'

'Those are the royal palaces. On the right is the Queen's chapel and her cloister, then the King's chambers and his own cloister is between there and the Great Hall itself.'

Simon nodded, but could not keep his head from shaking in surprise. He had not expected a small city, but in effect that was what he was looking at. The Abbey and palace complex was a small enclosed community, and outside it were roads heading north, west and southwards, and on each of them was a thin straggle of houses and hovels, with their own little patch of garden. The northern road was the most impressive, though. Near the Abbey there were smaller properties, two- or three-roomed dwellings that would be sufficient for merchants passing by. Beyond them were much larger houses – places that would suit a Bishop or very senior courtier. As they marched up towards the north, where the river suddenly bent to the right, the sight there caught his attention, and he whistled.

'That is London?'

'That is London,' the Bishop agreed. 'The greatest city in the country.'

Simon nodded, and his eyes were fixed upon it as they rode on to the seat of government in England.

Thorney Island

In the Great Hall, Hugh le Despenser grabbed the servant by the collar and pulled him towards him.

'What do you mean, you can't find him! I want my man Ellis here now!' He flung the petrified man from him and kicked his arse for good measure as he scuttled away. Turning, he saw a guard. 'Well – do you have any brilliant ideas about any of this?'

'None, my Lord. I was not on duty last night.'

'Have all the guards who were on duty been assembled?'

'Yes.'

'I want them all questioned for this . . . this . . .' Before he could find the right words, he saw the woman at the doorway and motioned impatiently to the guard to leave him. 'Your Highness, you have my deepest condolences for the loss of your maid.'

Sweet Mother of God, he thought. This is all I need.

When Queen Isabella walked in, her face might have been forged from steel, for all the emotion she displayed. Behind her was Eleanor, Despenser's wife, and he threw her a look, but she merely raised her brows and shrugged in expression of her bewilderment.

'Sir Hugh, I would discuss matters with you in private,' the Queen said.

'My Lady, I would be delighted,' he lied. Motioning to the chairs, he graciously invited her to sit.

All he wanted just now was time to consider what had happened. *Jesus!* Jack had never failed before, but this time he'd killed Mabilla instead of the Queen, and Sir Hugh had no idea why. True, the woman was the one whom the Queen wanted removed, and her death was opportune from that point of view, but no one had *told* bloody Jack to kill her. Although it was a damn good job he had got the wrong victim. Sir Hugh was confused, and confusion made him angry. He wanted to talk to Ellis and see what the fool had done. More than that, he wanted to find Jack, grab him warmly by the throat and both congratulate him and shake the truth from him. How could he have missed the bloody Queen?

'Sir Hugh, you and I both know that even in a magnificent hall like this there are places where a man might secrete himself and hear all he wished. No. I should prefer that you walk with me in my cloister for a while.'

'Let me just fetch . . .'

'There is no need for a guard in my cloister,' she interrupted coldly. 'Besides, I am sure that you would be an adequate defence against any assassin, would you not?'

He had no answer to that. Mutely he followed her as she led the way from the hall and out into the Lesser Hall, thence into her cloister. Eleanor started to follow them, but the Queen stopped and stared at her. 'You are not required, my Lady. You will remain here.'

Despenser nodded to Eleanor. There was no need for her to join them.

It was a quiet little corner of the palace, this cloister of the Queen's. He had always imagined that Isabella would have had it decorated in some gaudy colours, for with her French ancestry, she had a love for all fashions. It was not Sir Hugh's way. He had been raised in the court of King Edward I, and there all things martial tended to be exalted, rather than the vanities of the modern court. But much of that was the responsibility of the King, not his wife.

'Sir Hugh, you are investigating the murder last night?'

'Yes. I have men all over the palace to find the culprit, and I am sure that the maid will be avenged.'

'Are you? I am *not* so sure. It would be useful, I think, if there was no great effort to locate the guilty man, *hein*?'

He did not know how to respond to this. Having grown up as the son of a courtier, he understood the dangers of politics better than any other. His man Jack atte Hedge had failed in his original task, but still, he had succeeded in one way. Sir Hugh would like to know *why*, but the result was beneficial. There was a small line of defence *and* attack here which he could use to his own advantage.

'That may not be quite correct, my Lady. Actually, I have already heard that Mabilla had teased a man and flaunted herself at him, but when he tried to respond, she deliberately snubbed him.'

If there was one thing this Queen always adored, it was a salacious rumour. 'Oh? Who?'

'I fear I have been told it was Earl Edmund of Kent,' Sir Hugh said smoothly, lowering his voice. 'You know how downcast he has been since the ridiculous way he was ejected from Guyenne. Well, I think he grew enamoured of her, and pressed his suit too keenly. She was horrified to see how he had misunderstood her flirting, I think, and refused him. There was a guard who witnessed it all.'

'Ah. So perhaps I misunderstood, you mean?' She almost looked as though she was about to laugh. 'Mabilla's removal was *not* your act? In truth, I applaud you, Sir Hugh. You have such skill and wit in the way in which you play with people!'

They parted shortly after that, and it was a curiously contemplative Despenser who entered the small chamber near the Lesser Hall, where he had a parlour. In there he took a seat. Perhaps the Queen was coming round to liking him, after all. There was something renewed in her eyes when she spoke to him – a certain regard, or perhaps respect. She had wanted a sign, and Mabilla's death was the proof of their pact.

Her manner had definitely changed for the better. Perhaps it was his straightforward approach with her. She could see that here was a strong man with whom she could deal, not some feeble-minded dollypoll who relied solely on bribery and violence, as she might once have believed. It was an odd thought, but perhaps he could collaborate with her, after all. She would be a marvellous ally.

His wife entered just as he was reaching this conclusion, and she stood before him, her breast rising and falling with emotion. Although she was silent, he found her presence enough of a distraction to make him look up.

She was furious. It was in her eyes.

'Husband!'

'Eleanor, my love. She didn't want much – I'll let you know later.'

'Husband – was it you?' she burst out.

'Eh?' Despenser was so surprised at her question that he felt unable to answer immediately. 'What do you mean?'

'Did you try to have the Queen murdered? Because if you did, you killed my maid Mabilla!'

'Woman, be quiet,' he hissed. 'That is not the kind of accusation I want to hear in here.'

'And I don't want to have any more of my maids slaughtered before my eyes!'

'Madam, you overstretch the mark.'

'Sir, I will not have any more of my women servants killed.'

His jaw clenched, and then he reached out to her. All his frustration at recent events boiled in his blood. On his feet in a flash, he grabbed her by the throat and spun her around, throwing her against the nearest wall, his fingers tightening.

'*Bitch*, you don't speak to me like that. Ever. And if I hear you talking about me being involved in the death of anyone at all, I shall be seriously unhappy with you. You do not want me to be so angry with you . . . so be still. You have duties. Go to them!'

She dropped, choking, from his grasp, and almost fell on all fours, but he was heedless of her as he strode back towards the Great Hall. He had other things to consider.

'Ellis? *Ellis!*' he roared. 'Where in the name of Satan is he?'

Chapter Eleven

Friday, Vigil of Candlemas[1]

Thorney Island

Richard Blaket was bleary-eyed, weariness battling his fear as he listened to the men talking about the sort of punishment that could be meted out to anyone who held back.

All the guards from last night were down here. The men from the walkways, those from the New Palace Yard, those from the Green Yard, and those from indoors too. First to be grabbed and drawn away was old Archer from the southern wall. The stupid son of a Sheppey goatherd didn't have the brains he was born with. Every night he was wont to put a pack under his head, wrap himself in a blanket, and snooze his duty away. No one minded too much. All the lads on the walkway said that he was a hopeless old sod, and they might as well let him sleep. He'd only get in their way if he was awake.

But last night, even the alarms and screams hadn't stirred him. When the castle's keeper hurried to check all

---

[1] 1 February 1325

the walkways, he found Arch snoring loudly. Kicking him achieved little. The old git was dead to the world.

Well, he was often pissed. The ale barrels down near the kitchens where the guards had their meals were too tempting for an old soak like him. Richard didn't know how he made it up the ladder sometimes. Last Sunday, on the Feast of St Julian, he was so hammered he barely reached the walkway, giggling and lurching from side to side. Richard himself had helped him to his post, and as he walked away he heard Arch singing, then the little clatter as he took off his steel cap and placed it between the battlements before lying down to sleep it off.

He wasn't alone in doing this, but at least the others woke when there was a genuine alarm. Only Arch failed.

The sound of the old fool getting a beating came through the walls perfectly clearly. Arch was being punished for sleeping when a lady was killed and the Queen herself threatened. It was useful for men like Sir Hugh le Despenser to have a focus for their anger, and tonight it was Arch.

Richard himself was one of the few who were in the clear, since he hadn't been on the walkways last night. He had been indoors, and was one of the first at the scene when Lady Eleanor screamed for aid. It was Richard who arrived and stood over the ladies until another party arrived and helped take them back to their chambers.

Because he was safe from accusations of irresponsibility, Richard was treated as a mere servant, and told to fetch Arch out, take him to the gaol.

'Oh, Christ's pains, Arch! What've they done to you?'

It was hard to lift the old man. The blood had made his wrists too slick to grip. He lay sobbing on the ground, his chest bared to the freezing stones, scraped and bruised where their fists had thumped at him, trying to beat a confession from him. The frail old man heard his voice, but both eyes were closed, the lids swollen and purpling already.

'Come on, old friend. Let's get you up, eh?'

Eventually, by putting his hands under Arch's armpits, he managed to drag the fellow to a bucket. There he got Arch to sit while he fetched water to clean the worst of the mess away.

'Why did they do this to me?' the old man wept.

'Eh?'

'I told them all I could,' Arch choked.

He coughed, spat out a gobbet of bloody phlegm and put a hand on his belly. His breath rasped in his throat, and Richard was sure that Arch's ribs were broken. They moved too easily with his breathing. 'Be easy, now,' he counselled.

'But why did they do this to me? Why?' he wheezed.

'Because you always got drunk before you went on duty – and they knew that. No one was going to protect you when they found you still snoring it off. If you'd been awake you could have raised the alarm, but no – you were asleep, so the killer was able to climb inside the palace. If you had been sober . . .'

'But I *was* sober! Last night, I didn't drink a drop! You ask at the kitchens! I didn't have anything last night. I was stone cold sober!'

* * *

The Queen walked about her small enclosure with her hands in a little furred stole, a heavy cloak over her shoulders, feeling the gentle tickle of the squirrel fur at her throat and wrists. As she walked, she hummed a melody from her childhood, 'Orientis Partibus', a pleasant tune that always lifted her spirits.

Despenser wanted her dead. She'd known that for months. Her husband's sudden rejection of her had been a terrible shock, a fearful thing. She had seen how others had earned his enmity and been destroyed, utterly, but she had always thought that she was safe from such treatment. She had loved Edward. And he her. Or so she had thought.

But in the last years his behaviour had grown ever more erratic. One favourite was taken from him and slain, and afterwards her loyalty had brought him back to her. She had never failed him. Those years after Gaveston's death had been lovely. She had possessed him entirely then, and he had even demonstrated his love for her and for their children. But then he had thrown her over for his latest lover.

This second sodomite had taken all his affection. She had tried, she had been as warm and loving to her husband as any woman could be, but his mind was so fixed on the body and person of Despenser that there was nothing left for her or their children. Edward had broken up her household, sent all her friends, companions and servants from her, reduced her to the status of a beggar at his door. It was humiliating!

Milord Despenser was clever, but he had overreached himself.

She had been sure that he was going too far when she had first heard of the threat to her life from Peter, her Chaplain. Bishop Drokensford had many spies, and the news that Despenser might seek her death was shocking. She had not dreamed that he might try such a bold move. Fortunately she had challenged him and his response was clear – he had removed the bitch who had threatened her. But he didn't realise what he had done.

This action was bound to be bruited abroad, and that would only gain her allies. And meanwhile, her letter begging for aid would soon reach her brother the King of France. News of this attack to her lady-in-waiting would add lustre to her tale.

Eleanor was clever. Witty, good company, and kindly. As a gaoler, one who had ultimate power and authority over Isabella, she was quite amiable. But she was also so easy to read. And to confound. When Isabella wanted to write a letter, she did so. Twice. The first she submitted to Eleanor, while the second she secreted about her person. And then she would demonstrate her need for communication with her Chaplain. Perhaps to confess a little sin, or to demand a Mass. And not the first visit to him, not the second, nor even the third would she do anything, but on the fourth or fifth occasion, she would deem it right, when Eleanor was already tired and fractious, just like her darling little Joan.

Joan. Only three years old and these devils had taken her. She was staying with the Monthermers, Eleanor said, but Isabella did not know how much she could trust her. Mother of God, but she missed her children! Her two youngest, Joan and Eleanor, were together, Lady Eleanor said. Of course Isabella had no way of telling whether that was true or not. She missed her boys, too: John and Edward. The girls had been taken from her by Eleanor and Despenser, while Edward had his own household now he was thirteen and an adult. Not old enough to be able to ignore his father, though. The King would not allow him near his own mother.

Only John remained nearby, under the control of Lady Eleanor Despenser, and *she* refused to allow Isabella to see him. It was a means of keeping the Queen under control. 'Behave and I may allow you to see your little son – *mis*behave and you will not.' No. She could not trust my Lady Despenser.

Lady Eleanor could be so like her little daughter Joan in some ways. And in others she could be as unpleasant, scheming and mendacious as the wife of Sir Hugh le Despenser would have to be. Well, Isabella could be even more scheming, even more mendacious. Despenser had taken away her life. She had lost children, authority, friends – all that made up her life but breath itself. Soon he would seek to stop that too. But she would prevent him if she may, which was why she had made him aware that she communicated with her brother. Despenser might doubt it, but he would wonder. And meanwhile she would send her messages by means of her Chaplain. When she received the Body of Christ, she could slip a letter into his hand, and Eleanor was none the wiser.

Like last night. The thought that if the assassin had been successful, she would now be dead, that her letter would have been her last, made her shudder. She would make Despenser *pay* for his actions, she thought, baring her teeth in a feral humour. For every insult, every indignity, every theft. And especially for the proposition. Oh yes. For that, he would suffer the most exquisite agonies she could devise.

The Chaplain looked up as soon as she appeared, and stared behind her to make sure that she was for once alone, before slowly closing an eye in a wink.

Another letter was on its way to her brother.

Baldwin glanced about him with interest, but for him there was far less novelty value. Simon was new to this world, whereas Baldwin had been in London and here to Thorney Island before.

In those days, of course, he had been a man of power and authority, a Knight Templar. On occasion he had been sent here to England to discuss issues with the knights of the London Temple or, more rarely, the English King, Edward I, because it was understood that a knight who spoke the common language of those with whom he was to negotiate would have a greater understanding of the finer points.

That was all a long time ago. Yet he could not but help glancing up along the line of King Street, northwards, to where it met Straunde. Up there, he knew, was the outer wall of the City of London, with the great wall and defences. And just west of it lay the Temple. His heart and soul ached to see it again.

Not today, though. The Bishop was in a hurry to get inside the wall of the Great Hall and begin his discussions. It was no surprise.

Baldwin had been given plenty to think about after his talk with the Bishop of Salisbury.

'I fear I heard you last night,' he had said in the morning at Salisbury, while Simon was still asleep.

Martival looked at him, smiling wryly. 'I dare say most of the servants here heard us arguing the other night.'

'The Queen suffers greatly, so I have heard.'

'It is said by some that she could be a traitor.'

'Only by those who would see her destroyed. Perhaps their actions have made her an enemy to them. But to the King? She has had his children. I refuse to believe that she could be so dishonourable as to be the enemy of their father.'

'There are examples of other women who have been still more . . . unnatural.'

'Bishop, you do not believe that our Queen is capable of such acts any more than I. I heard you, remember.'

Martival had studied him carefully over the rim of his goblet at that. At last he set the drink down. 'You overheard much that you should not have. But very well – no, I do not. This smacks of politicking, and taking advantage of those who are weak or incapable of defending themselves in order to protect others.'

'Is it true, that there are moves to annul the marriage?'

Martival pulled a grimace. 'That is what is said. That the King would seek to have his marriage declared null so that he might seek another wife. Perhaps.'

Baldwin did not rise to that bait. All knew the rumours of the homosexual nature of the King's relationship with Sir Hugh le Despenser. 'That would mean that all their issue . . .'

'Yes. All the Queen's children would become bastards. Our own Edward, the Prince of Wales would be disinherited, no more to be considered than the King's other bastards.'

For all the accusations of homosexuality that had eddied about the King, there was no disputing that he was a virile man. He not only had the four children by Isabella, but all had heard how distraught he had been to hear of the death of Adam, his natural son, while they were on campaign against the Scots some years before.

'They say that he can't father children now. Since the birth of Joan he has grown so infatuated with Despenser that he can't sire another with a woman. It's been some years,' Martival muttered contemplatively.

'There are many couples who cannot breed to command,' Baldwin pointed out.

'We all know that. However, he is the King, and it is his duty.'

'Things have come to such a pass that it is unlikely his Queen would happily accept his advances now, surely?'

'True enough.' The Bishop was quiet for a few minutes, and then he said, 'You are an intelligent man, Sir Baldwin. I get the impression that you are not entirely in accordance with the opinions of Bishop Walter? He would seek to have the marriage annulled. He actually requested my support for such an action.'

'I should consider such an annulment to be a cynical denial of oaths made before God,' Baldwin said heavily.

'You should be aware, then. I would not have you launching yourself into a void without aid. There are other rumours: that Despenser may have tried to force himself upon the Queen,' Martival said.

That stilled Baldwin. All knew how dangerous an enemy Sir Hugh le Despenser could be, and for the Bishop to repeat a story like that, was either astonishingly foolhardy, or meant that it was common knowledge.

'Yes, I know the dangers of repeating such rumours,' said Bishop John, reading the knight's expression correctly, 'but you are going to speak with men such as he, and I would not have you advising the Bishop or others without being fully informed. The Queen has enemies – and chief among them is Despenser. You know what Bishop Adam Orleton called him?' The Bishop cleared his throat. 'Perhaps that is one detail I should not impart. Suffice it to say that the man is viewed with alarm by many of us in the Church, Sir Baldwin.'

'Why are you so assured that I am a safe person in whom you may confide all this? I could be a Despenser ally, or someone seeking preferment.'

'You could – I agree,' Martival shrugged. 'However, I do not think so. Your reputation has reached here. It is said that you detest any form of injustice, that you prefer to see men go free than convict an innocent man. Someone like that is hardly in the same mould as Gilbert Middleton or the other felons from the King's household.'

Baldwin smiled wryly at that. Middleton, a knight from the King's household had been upset when a relation was gaoled for making deprecating comments about Edward and his northern policies. In revenge, Middleton set out on a spree of robbing and killing that culminated in the capture and assault of two papal legates on their way to Scotland to try to agree a new truce between Bruce and King Edward. 'No, I hope I am not made in the same way as him.'

'So do I,' Martival said, and would have continued, but then Simon walked in, and both men turned the conversation to less turbulent matters.

It was interesting, though, Baldwin thought now, that the two Bishops disagreed so radically; maybe that in itself was an indication of the kind of dispute he could expect here at the King's council. Although, of course, he could not be sure of the reason for the Bishop of Salisbury's extraordinary frankness. Perhaps it was largely because members of the Church were growing alarmed at the increasing tyranny of the Despenser family, father and son.

The country needed a counterweight to balance their power. Sadly, at the same time it needed to resolve the dispute with the French King in order to rescue English territories over the water.

All of which should make for an interesting time, Baldwin told himself. He glanced back at the Abbey and the palace area. Both were close enough now that only the grander buildings could be seen above the walls: the enormous belfry in the Abbey's precinct, and the roof and towers of the main abbey church. Beyond was the roofline of the mighty hall behind its own walls.

There was the abbey gatehouse right ahead of them. Baldwin had thought that they would enter here, but instead the Bishop took them about the walls, into Thieving Lane, and up to the gatehouse where King

Street met the Great Hall's wall. Here there were houses built for the merchants who came each year for the Abbey's fair, as well as smaller dwellings for the servants who worked in the Abbey or the palace.

The Bishop's party rode past, entered the King's palace area at the main gate, trotted past an inn, and then all dismounted at the rail near a stable-block.

Baldwin took in the scene. This was New Palace Yard, a wide space, but filled with timber buildings of all sizes, some houses, some kitchens, some storage-sheds. Alehouses lined the walls, and pie and cookshops were mingled among them to cater for those who visited to present their suits at the King's courts or who came to see the clerks of the Exchequer. Stalls had been erected in the middle of the court, and the lawyers and clerks hurrying by were plied with sausages, pies, roasted thrushes, all manner of sweetmeats, and drinks.

Everywhere was bustle. Children played in the freezing mud, dogs snarled and bickered over bones, men gambled at an impromptu cock-fighting pit, while stevedores unloaded cargo from the barges on the dock and carried provisions to the undercrofts. A sergeant cook walked among the cattle, choosing which should die first, while pig and mutton carcasses lay nearby on trestles, a merchant and a carter arguing over their cost. And in among all this, men clad in the King's arms barged past: messengers and purveyors, sergeants-at-arms and kitchen grooms, all hurrying about.

To the south, a wall ran along from the main outer wall down to meet the Great Hall. Beyond that wall were more yards, he guessed, but those would be only for the Royal

Household, not for visitors and the likes of him.

And then he noticed two other things. First, there was the sound of hounds baying nearby, but for once Baldwin took no heed. Of much more interest than hounds or alaunts were the men who stood with polearms ready, each of them studying him and the other members of the party with suspicion.

Chapter Twelve

Thorney Island

On Friday morning, after very little sleep, Sir Hugh le Despenser was sitting in the Exchequer, when he saw from the window the new group arrive. Despite his fatigue, he was already leaving the room before they had dismounted, beckoning a guard. 'You! Come with me.'

This was becoming one of the worst days he could remember. There were those other bad days he had suffered, like the one when he and his father were banished and condemned to exile, or the one when he had been told that he was to lose the Gower. But both times he had prevailed. Other, seemingly more powerful barons had been arrayed against him, but he had beaten them all in the end. This time he would succeed again, he told himself.

'Who are you?' he demanded as he approached the newcomers, his hand on his sword.

Apart from the three men-at-arms who were in the lead, the first man there was a tall fellow in a faded red tunic with an old stained and frayed cloak. He had a hood, but it was thrust back behind his head, and his greying hair and beard were neatly trimmed. He had a scar at the side of his face that spoke of a martial past, but any man reaching his age would have a number of scars. It was a part of life as a knight.

'I am called Sir Baldwin de Furnshill. This is my Lord Bishop, Walter of Exeter.'

'My Lord Bishop, I apologise, I didn't see you there,' Hugh said immediately. The Lord High Treasurer was not a man to insult – not just now.

Stapledon gave him a cool enough greeting, and held out his ring to be kissed, before commanding the others to see to their mounts while he spoke with Sir Hugh. He then set off side-by-side with Despenser to the Great Hall.

'I am concerned that our policy is not being adequately communicated to others,' the Bishop murmured.

Sir Hugh shot him a look. 'That is hardly my province, my Lord Bishop. Our arrangement was, you would convince the Bishops and I would convince the Lords. I have upheld my side of the bargain.'

'I have difficulties with some of them. Martival has rejected our ideas out of hand. We know that Orleton will do anything to thwart you, and now we have others against us too. I am dubious about Bath and Wells.'

'You will have to find a means of convincing them, then. I have enough to do without ordering the obedience of the Church.'

Stapledon nodded. They had reached the Great Hall now and entered, staring up the length of the chamber at the throne with the rock beneath it, the Stone of Scone which the King's father, Edward I, had captured from the Scots. There were two guards in the hall although the place was empty but for them. 'There are more guards than usual.'

'Yes. Someone entered the grounds last night and slew a lady-in-waiting.'

Stapledon frowned. 'What! A man from outside, you mean?'

It was sometimes hard to realise that this fellow had one of the sharpest financial minds in all Christendom. Despenser nodded. 'Yes.'

'An assassin?' Stapledon's eyes narrowed with suspicion. 'Was it you?'

'Why would I murder a lady-in-waiting? It would serve me no benefit, would it?'

The logic of that was inescapable, and the Bishop knew it. 'But why should a man kill a lady-in-waiting? Who was it? Are you sure that the assassin was aiming his knife at her, and didn't simply strike down the wrong woman?'

'Anyone would recognise the Queen, and if he killed the wrong lady, it would have been easy to shove the other women aside and kill the Queen herself.'

Stapledon eyed him doubtfully, but then nodded his head in agreement. 'You're right. There could be no reason to kill a maid. Which one was it?'

'Mabilla Aubyn. You remember her? She was the daughter of Sir Richard.'

Stapledon nodded pensively, but he gazed at Sir Hugh with a frown. It was clear enough what he was thinking.

'Look, my Lord Bishop, she was worth nothing. She has no lands or wealth. I had no reason to seek to harm her.'

'Very well. I take your word for it,' the Bishop said. 'What actions have been taken to seek the assassin?'

'We've searched the whole place, but it seems whoever it was managed to break in, and then escaped as well.'

'How did he get in?'

'We're still trying to find out. The wall has not been breached so far as we can tell. It's possible that they may have got in from the river, but unlikely, I'd have thought. There were no boats seen.'

'Let me know if you come to any conclusions.'

'I will. And in the meantime – those two men with you. One called himself Sir Baldwin de Furnshill. Is he from Devon?'

'Yes. Why?'

'I believe I have heard his name before.'

The news of the attack on the Queen's little party was swiftly spread all over the palace, and nowhere was the news bruited about so speedily as in the New Hall Yard, where all the guests mingled in the taverns and alehouses.

Piers de Wrotham, Earl Edmund's spy, was sitting on an old barrel in a tavern when he himself heard the rumour of an attempt to kill the Queen. Finishing his horn of ale, he set it down with a coin, and made his way towards the Exchequer, slowly absorbing the full horror of his position.

He knew that Sir Hugh le Despenser was behind the murder. It never occurred to him that another could have been responsible. No – Sir Hugh detested the Queen, always had, and he must have been looking for a means of removing her for some little while:

It had seemed odd at the time, when Sir Hugh told Piers to persuade Earl Edmund to extol the virtues of the Queen as negotiator over the stolen territories. At the time, Piers was convinced that the man was playing a different game of his own, because it made no sense for the Queen to visit her brother, King Charles IV of France. Once there, she must be safe from Despenser. But at least she would be out of his hair – and perhaps that was all he was thinking of. If so, then he had gambled badly on this throw: a successful attack upon the Queen was one thing, but a botched effort like this, which only served to kill a maid – that was a disaster. The French King would go mad – immediately demand satisfaction. Only the head of Despenser would suffice.

The woman who had died – Mabilla – was the lady who had given the come-on to Earl Edmund, then rejected him when he got too keen. Yes, and all knew that he had been furious, threatening to rape her when she had done that to him. Perhaps many would see this as a foul act on his part, killing the woman who had spurned him? And all his advice in the last few months would be assessed against this new revelation about him.

His reputation would be destroyed. Aha, Piers thought, and a slow smile spread over his face. Perhaps *that* was what it was all about.

Simon and Baldwin were directed to a small stable set against the northern wall of the court, and there with the three men-at-arms, they unloaded their belongings so that the horses could be properly rested. Rob was left with the horses to groom them – much against his will –

and Simon and Baldwin parted from the others there.

'So that – that's the Great Hall?' Simon asked, awed.

'Well, it's not the smaller one,' Baldwin said drily.

'Is there one?'

'Down the far side of this one. The King uses that more often, I imagine. This one is just too immense for comfort.'

'Especially at this time of year,' Simon agreed. Both had spent enough time in large halls in Exeter and beyond during the winter to know how long it could take for a fire to heat a chamber of any size.

'Come – let us seek some warmed ale,' Baldwin muttered. It was cold, and talking about it only served to remind them just how icy the air was.

They made their way to the inn beside the gatehouse and entered. There was a bar set over two barrels at the far end, and they repaired to this, ordering ales, and then taking their seats on low stools near a little fire that threw out a lot of smoke and not much warmth.

'I wonder when the Bishop will be finished,' Simon said.

'Soon, I dare say. He doesn't enjoy long journeys, and he'll be keen to eat and find a bed.'

'There are a lot of guards here. Do you think that the King always has this number of men about him?'

Baldwin was tempted to say that any tyrant must rely on a large contingent of guards to see to his defence, but forbore. 'This is a large palace, and I suppose he has all the Crown's jewels with him. It's only natural that he should feel the need for protection.'

A grizzled old veteran of many winters in the King's

service had overheard their conversation, and now he leaned forward. To Baldwin's mind his round, flushed features spoke of a better than nodding acquaintance with the ales served here.

'Hadn't you heard?' he asked. 'There was a murder here yesternight. A poor maid was struck down.'

'A lover?' Baldwin asked. It was the usual first question. He always found that in murders, especially the murders of younger folk, the killer almost invariably proved to be someone closely related. A man killed his wife, a lad his girl – sometimes it was the woman killing her spouse. More rarely it was a brother killing a sister because she had brought shame on the family.

'Don't know. The fellow ran off as soon as she was dead.'

'There were witnesses?' Simon asked.

'Four or five of them. It was a lady-in-waiting to the Queen, and the Queen was there with the others when it happened.'

'Did the man show any evil intent towards our Queen?' Baldwin demanded quickly. Coming straight after the news that the King might seek to annul his marriage, it appeared to be the logical conclusion.

'No, not that I heard. He just jumped out and stabbed Mabilla, and then fled the scene.' The fellow clearly had nothing more to tell, other than vague allegations and suppositions.

'What do you think of that then, Simon?' Baldwin asked.

Simon belched, leaned back against the wall and spread his legs luxuriously. 'Me? I think I'm as pleased as a hog in shit that for once, this is nothing to do with us. We can stand back and watch some other poor bastard get on with the work of finding out who was responsible. It's none of our concern. And in the meantime, let's have another ale, eh?'

There was one man who was concerned about the death of the maid though, and he was in the Queen's chapel with Mabilla's corpse.

'Oh, Mabilla! How could you have come to this? Mabilla, my sister, I miss you! I shall avenge you, I swear it, on the Gospels!'

And with that Ellis Brooke, Sir Hugh's most trusted henchman, stood, wiped his face, and made his way from the room.

Despenser left Bishop Stapledon and headed back to the Exchequer through the Green Yard. At least here it was peaceful. This little sanctuary was shielded from the madness and busyness of the main court north of the Great Hall. It might not be as restful as the Queen's cloister, but it was damn near as quiet.

Sir Hugh stopped for a moment. Indecision assailed him, and he stood for quite some little while, simply staring at the Exchequer buildings while a great lassitude washed over him. Never before had he felt so enfeebled. All his life, he had been driven by his passions. He could still remember when he had been a young man, saying to a friend, 'I desire nothing so much as money. One day I will have plenty of it. I will be rich.'

Well, that prophecy had come true. Yet for every new

pound or mark which he accumulated, he grew ever more aware of the risks of his method of acquiring it and the likelihood that he would lose all.

Once he had. When those bastards the Lords Marcher decided to clip his wings, they did so by taking his castles and laying waste all his manors. It was a typical *chevauchée*, a fast ride over all his property, stealing or burning everything. The bastards first wrecked him and then saw him condemned to exile. Well, never again. No mother-swyving churl would ever be able to take away what he had built up, and he didn't give a damn who knew it.

But something was going wrong here for him. Jack should never have attacked Mabilla, and if he did, why should it have stopped him from carrying on and killing the Queen? Although, thank God he hadn't. Jack had been in tougher situations before, and being thwarted by a clutch of women would not normally have prevented him from finishing the job.

Someone else must have killed Mabilla. But who, in God's name? Perhaps the story he had spun before the Queen, of Earl Edmund getting his revenge, had not been so wide of the mark, after all . . .

The thought gave him a new spirit of resolution, and he straightened his back just as a familiar face came the other way.

'Sir Hugh.'

'My Lord Kent. How very pleasant,' Despenser said with a brief baring of his teeth that could have been a smile or a snarl. 'I was just thinking of you.'

Chapter Thirteen

Eleanor de Clare was almost recovered now. She had been forced to drink a great deal of wine last night, just to try to eradicate the sight of all that blood, but it had only served to give her a waspish temper and sore head. Since visiting her husband, that had grown into an ache that encompassed her entire upper body.

Now she sought an answer as to why her husband should have wished to kill poor Mabilla. She had always thought that Sir Hugh was on perfectly amiable terms with her. He wouldn't have permitted Mabilla to be involved with the Queen otherwise, surely? She had been a mild, pleasant enough young woman.

Alicia was with her, placing a cooling cloth on her forehead. 'There, mistress. Be calm.'

'Calm? When I've witnessed Mabilla slaughtered like a hog before me?'

Of course, she knew that Alicia had been there too. Alicia was the one who did not fly or faint. She alone had behaved impeccably, running to block the assassin's path before he could launch himself either at the Queen or at Eleanor. She had acted with a natural courage, and now she was the only one of all who had any ease of mind.

'Oh, get off me, woman!' Eleanor snapped and rose to her feet, a hand to her head.

'Would you like some wine?'

'*No*. I would like to know why poor Mabilla is dead! I would like to know why someone should have taken her away from me! '

'Surely the man wasn't trying to kill her. He struck at the first woman he could barely see in the dark.'

'Then he was a fool! Why should he do that?'

'Madam, he wanted her out of his path so he could attack another, I feel sure of that.'

Eleanor nodded tiredly. That was what she had thought too. 'You think he was after the Queen.' However, she did not add her private fear: that it was her own husband who had commanded someone to try to kill the Queen. His enraged response when she had accused him was proof to her of his guilt. She could still feel his fingers at her throat.

'*Perhaps* the Queen, yes,' Alicia said.

Rubbing gently at her neck, Eleanor almost missed her tone at first – and then, when she realised what Alicia meant, a wave of horror broke over her, her eyes rolled up, and she slipped away into a dead faint.

Earl Edmund of Kent looked quite taken aback to see Sir Hugh le Despenser. He cast a quick look behind him, then one over Despenser's shoulder. 'Lost your little alaunt?' he said insolently. 'I thought Ellis was always at your heel, Sir Hugh.'

'I don't need constant protection,' Despenser said coolly. 'You have heard about the incident last night? The murder of Ellis's sister?'

'You call it an "incident"? A deplorable failure of palace security, I'd have said!'

'Nowhere is entirely safe. Perhaps you would care to have responsibility for the safety of the King?'

Kent hesitated. He could do a better job than this upstart, of course, but there was something in his eyes that said that Despenser was sure he could embarrass him. He was a conniving, devious, lying shite, that man. Instead, Kent decided to attack on safer ground. 'I have heard that the Bishops are all beginning to agree among themselves that the best course of action may be to have the Queen herself go to negotiate with her brother. '

'To set her loose could be an interesting solution,' Despenser said mildly.

'Yes. You would like to have her out of your reach, wouldn't you? You would be content to see her go across the Channel and tell her brother all that has happened here?' Kent said, openly scornful. 'You think that the French King would be happy to learn that you have advised the King to take away her lands and give her only a pittance as an allowance? What is it she is permitted? One pound each day?'

'That is nothing to do with me,' Despenser said smoothly.

'And I suppose the despatch of Robert Baldock and Thomas Dunheved to petition the papal Curia for a divorce, that is not your working either? I fear, my friend, that my sister-in-law believes you may have been responsible. What did she say? Ah, yes, that her husband could never have been so vindictive or cruel to her. Her brother Charles will be fascinated to hear that.'

'What he likes or dislikes is none of my concern.'

'Perhaps. Not yet.'

'You should be more careful of your tone, Earl Edmund,' Despenser said with a hint of steel, but then he added, 'you don't understand. I have already had a talk with Bishop Drokensford and discussed the idea of the Queen being sent as ambassador on behalf of the King. I don't know where people get the idea that I'm against her. I have promoted the idea as vigorously as I dare. I only hope that he and I and others of a similar view can persuade the King that it would be in the best interests of the realm for her to be sent.'

Kent gaped. 'But how could you suggest her, when you . . .' His eyes narrowed. 'You have a scheme, don't you? You think we're all churls with nothing but shite between our ears, but some of us are bright enough to see through your little plots, Sir Hugh.'

He ignored Despenser's easy smile and pressed past him – not so close as to offend, for Despenser was an undoubted expert of sword and lance and it was best not to push your luck – and stalked off towards the Old Palace Yard.

Sir Hugh le Despenser watched him go with his lip curled. The man was contemptible. Even his threats were wasteful of breath. If he wanted, Despenser could have him bent about his little finger in an instant. But he did not wish it yet. No. Better to keep him as a source of confusion for a while longer. That way there would be a point of concentration for any malcontents, and by keeping a watch on him, Despenser and his men would have an accurate register of all those who were his enemies.

It was at that moment that he heard the scream from the Great Hall. Immediately, he looked up at the shingled roof, thinking that there must be a fire within, for the most common fear in a great building like this was that the roof might catch fire. But there was no sign of smoke, no flames, nothing.

And then he saw a man lurch from the Exchequer's door – a clerk, who gripped at the door-frame, staring wildly about him like one who has lost his mind.

'Sweet Christ's cods! Now what?' Sir Hugh swore foully, and marched off to see what was wrong, just as the little cleric bent and spewed all over the cobblestones.

Baldwin and Simon were marching over the gravel to find Rob and their horses just as the cry came, and as soon as they heard it, there was a general rush towards the source, men with polearms running full-pelt, one hand gripping their long weapons, the other grasping their scabbards or horns to stop them clattering against their thighs, while others: merchants, servants and visitors alike, hurried along in their wake.

'Murder! Murder! Murder! Out! Out! Out!'

'It's none of our concern,' Simon said pointedly, grabbing Baldwin's arm. 'The King has Coroners and Keepers for just this sort of eventuality. He doesn't need us.'

'True,' Baldwin said, 'but there is an issue of professional pride involved. I wonder what could have caused such a commotion?'

'Oh – did you miss his shout?' Simon said with heavy sarcasm. 'I believe he may have said that there has been a murder.'

'Oh? Well, it can do no harm to see who has died, can it?'

'I didn't come all this way just to . . .' Simon muttered rebelliously, but followed in his friend's wake.

As they approached the rear of the crowd that encircled the entrance, they heard the beginnings of the rumours.

First was a tranter, shaking his grizzled head. 'Dead, sitting on the King's throne!'

'He was the King's food-taster, and they say he was poisoned,' a tavern slut was gabbling earnestly.

A palace servant sneered, 'Poisoned with steel, most likely. Blood everywhere, *I* heard.'

Baldwin looked at Simon with wry exasperation. 'Very well, I agree. There is nothing sensible to be gleaned here. Probably they are all wrong and it was merely a serving-maid who tripped and stubbed her toe! Let us return to our mounts and wait there for the Bishop to come to us. We should repair to his house and make ready for the first of these consultations we have heard so much about.'

Simon was happy to agree, and the two walked over the yard to Rob, who stood peering at the crowds with bitter disappointment to be missing whatever was happening.

Seeing his mood, Simon tutted and sighed. Then: 'Rob, if you're so curious, work your way up there and see what all the excitement's about, eh?'

The boy was off like a greyhound after a hare.

'He is keen enough on some trails, then,' Baldwin observed, grinning.

'At least he's only interested in simple matters at present,' Simon said. 'Soon it'll be maids, and then I'll be worried.'

'So you should be,' Baldwin sighed. 'That young fellow will be breaking a few hearts before he settles himself.'

'If he ever does,' Simon grunted. 'There's little enough sign of it yet.' He pointed with his chin. 'That was quick.'

Rob was soon back with them, smiling and enthusiastic. 'The Bishop wants you to join him in the Great Hall,' he panted.

'The Bishop does?' Baldwin repeated.

'I suppose they *do* still have Coroners here in the King's household?' Simon asked rhetorically.

The first thing that struck Simon was just how enormous the Great Hall truly was. It towered over them as they marched in, more like a cathedral than a hall.

Rob had taken them by the side way, leading them through a gate into the Green Yard, and thence to the Old Palace Yard. There was a door into the Lesser Hall, and from there they could enter the screens passage. In the middle was the door that led into the hall itself. It was blocked by two guards who stood with polearms crossed, their faces anxious, and the younger man oddly pale and waxen. At a snapped command from inside, the two allowed Simon, Baldwin and Rob to pass.

Simon gaped as he stared up at the gaily painted pictures on the great oak baulks. They were curved in a series of ribs that passed along the length of this massive hall, and Simon found himself studying the rows of columns, hoping that they were strong enough to support the weight of all that timber. It seemed to defy logic. There was an arcade all around, and he was sure that there would be a broad walkway set inside the wall.

The whole was richly coloured, with flowers and faces decorating every surface. Lower, when Simon could bring his gaze down, the walls were designed to prove how magnificent the English King was, and how wealthy. Flags and pennons dangled, moving gently in the draught; where there were no hangings or tapestries, the plaster was painted with brilliant scenes. Each column had shields set about it, their decorations glinting in the meagre light.

When he brought his attention down to the ground again, he was taken with the sight of an immense marble table. 'What's that for?'

Baldwin threw a disinterested glance at it. 'The great courts meet here in King William Rufus's hall,' he said. 'The marble table is for the Chancery, where the king's clerks work. Over there,' he pointed, 'is where the Court of Common Pleas meets, and over there is the King's Bench. This room is usually in uproar when all the judges are here.'

Not today, though. Only small groups of men stood huddled about, a larger congregation at the farther end of the hall, where another group stood huddled over something behind a chair. And then Simon felt a thrill as he realised. Before him was no ordinary chair: *this was the throne of England!*

It stood upon a dais reached by a small series of steps, and Simon eyed it with surprise as well as interest. It was a great deal smaller than he had expected, somehow. He had thought to see a towering seat, more along the lines of the Bishop of Exeter's throne in the Cathedral – an immense, towering construction with rich ornament – but this was nothing more than a well-made, wooden chair with panels in the sides and the back, while beneath it a large rock was set onto a platform. It made him want to go nearer and study it, but already his attention was being drawn to the rear of the chair.

They walked around the fireplace in the middle of the floor, dead just now, the ashes all cleared away, and joined the men standing near the chair, a little way behind it. In the cold, their breath formed long streamers, and there was an unwholesome odour of unwashed bodies.

The Bishop turned as Baldwin and Simon approached. 'My friends, you have some experience of matters such as this. Can you help?'

'What has happened?' Baldwin asked. He pushed his way forward, Simon in his wake, until he reached the wall some distance behind the throne.

Bishop Stapledon was distressed. 'To think that a man could be cut down here, in the King's chief hall!'

'Where is the King's Coroner?' Baldwin asked, eyeing the corpse.

'He is not here at present. I think he must be in London.'

Baldwin grunted. He preferred not to take command when it was another man's responsibility, but if the fellow wasn't around he supposed he could indulge himself. First he gave himself up to a study of the scene.

The man had been laid on his side like a discarded

sack of beans, as shapeless as he was lifeless. He was clothed in dark material, a pair of long brown hosen, a brown tunic and a black hood and gorget. There was no purse about his belt, but he did wear a long knife, and when Baldwin crouched and pulled the blade part way from the scabbard, he saw that it was slick with blood.

Baldwin then turned the man over slightly to look at his face, and almost dropped him. 'Dear God!'

'That was why we called for you, Sir Baldwin,' the Bishop explained faintly. 'Who could have done such a thing to him?'

'Does anyone know who he is?' Baldwin asked. There was no one who would admit to knowing him, so Baldwin let the body slump forward, and then stood considering for a moment or two, his chin cupped in the palm of his hand, his other hand supporting his elbow as he surveyed the fellow. 'I would ask that all those who have no business here, leave the room. And do not discuss this affair with *anyone*! Is that clear? Any man who tells about this body may be arrested. My Lord Bishop, could you have all removed from here other than Simon and me, and the first-finder, of course.'

It took some little while to have all the people ushered out. There were not many, but they were reluctant to leave, and Rob was the most vociferous at protesting that his master might need him. Eventually Baldwin gave into him, on the basis that he might indeed have need of a messenger.

When there was relative silence, Baldwin beckoned to the remaining man, a clerk from the Exchequer. 'You found him?'

'Yes, sir. I had no idea . . .'

Baldwin watched him as he wiped his mouth on his sleeve. He was only young, perhaps in his early twenties, one of those men who would be an asset to a counting-house, but whose pasty complexion and nervous manner spoke of an insecure mind. He had fingernails bitten to the quick, and his eyes were constantly darting hither and thither. 'Your name?'

'Ralph le Palmer. I work in the Exche—'

'Where's that?' Rob asked.

Baldwin snapped, 'Shut up, Rob, or I'll have you thrown out. Ralph, I can see that you're one of the clerks. You are sure you do not know this man?'

Baldwin was walking about the corpse as he asked his questions. Ralph tried to follow him with his eyes, but all the while his horrified gaze was drawn back to the body.

'No, never before, I am—' He swallowed.

'Quite so. Kindly tell us what happened.'

'I had been sent through here to fetch some wine, and I was returning to the Exchequer when I saw that the tapestry there was all lumped, and I wondered what could have happened to it. I thought that the roof might have been leaking, as the material was sodden and misshapen, you see. It has happened before, although the roof is really quite new. All the shingles were replaced only a . . .' He caught sight of Baldwin's face and abandoned any further explanation of the roofing. 'When I touched the tapestry, I felt this man behind it. I lifted the cloth . . .'

'So he was lying *behind* the drapery?'

'He could hardly stand, could he?' Ralph said with an attempt at lightness, but then his eyes returned to the man, and his frivolity melted away. 'Sorry, Sir Knight. I shrieked, and ran from the room. Others started coming in then, and I vomited. I suppose I have raised the hue and cry?'

Baldwin nodded. If a first-finder didn't raise the hue and cry by the manner which was accepted in that part of the country, he would be fined. 'Has anything been taken from him since you first found him?'

'I don't think so,' the fellow said tremulously.

Baldwin attempted a calmer, gentler manner. 'Was there anything you noticed about him in particular?'

'What, other than the way his prick had been hacked off and shoved in his mouth, you mean?' Ralph blurted out, and he had to clap a hand over his own mouth and run from the hall again, almost knocking over Earl Edmund as he entered.

Chapter Fourteen

Earl Edmund of Kent was unused to being thrust from the path of a lowly cleric, and he turned to bawl at the man, but Ralph had already fled.

'What is the matter with *him*?' he demanded. He pushed his way through the crowds, and entered the Great Hall, then stopped dead when he saw the body on the ground. 'What in God's name is this?'

'Who are you?' Baldwin asked coolly, his eyes on the corpse.

'I am Edmund, Earl of Kent. Who are *you* – and what are you doing here?' To Kent's surprise, the fellow was kneeling beside the dead man, behind the throne. And when there was no reply from him, Edmund burst out: 'Will someone tell me what's happened here?'

That earned him a frosty look from the Bishop. 'A man, my Lord Earl, has been murdered.'

Baldwin straightened up and turned. 'I am Sir Baldwin de Furnshill,' he said. 'The good Bishop has asked me to exercise my skills to learn what has happened. My Lord, do you know many people about this court?'

'Quite a few, I suppose. I don't know the servants.' He

walked up to stare at the body before him. 'Don't know him. What is that in . . . good God!'

'Yes. He was killed, and then, I think, *that* was done to him,' Baldwin said. 'Too many people have already been in here, not that there would be much to discover here, I dare guess. Steps on stone are difficult to follow. You see this? There is no sign that he has had his hands bound behind him. If I feel his head . . . no, there is no indication of any swelling there, so I can infer that he was not struck down before this was done to him. What killed him, then?'

His hands were moving over the body as he spoke, and as he ran them over the man's chest, he drew his mouth down into a *moue* of surprise. 'Somehow I anticipated a simple murder from an opponent. Perhaps . . .' He turned the man over and felt his back. 'Ah, here. One . . . no, two . . . three deep wounds. One at least must have pierced his heart, and the others would have struck his lungs. From the look of him, I would expect that the one through the heart killed him, though.'

'Why?' the Earl asked.

'If he was drowned in his own blood, I'd expect to see much more of it about his mouth,' Baldwin answered shortly. He was up from the body already and investigating the area behind the tapestry where the corpse had been secreted. 'There is some blood here, Simon. Not much, though. The moisture appears to be water,' he added, smelling the fabric. He frowned, head set on one side. 'But I can smell wine too.'

The Earl had not noticed the Bailiff and servant, and was startled when he heard Simon respond from behind him.

'You think he wasn't killed here, then?'

'He certainly wasn't killed right here, no. He died somewhere else and was pulled here. Someone cut off his privy member and shoved it into his mouth, and then rolled him away and out of sight.'

'Could this man be the assassin who tried to kill the Queen last night?' the Earl wondered aloud.

'Come now. There is no certainty that anyone tried to do such a thing,' Despenser said smoothly. He had entered from the screens area, and now he stepped slowly and crisply along the flagged floor towards them. 'A man struck down a maid,' he explained to the gathering. 'Unfortunately, the Queen was there, and saw the whole unhappy event, but that doesn't mean that the attempt was on her life. It could as easily have been on my own wife's life. My dearest Eleanor was with the same party, after all.'

He had reached the body and stared down at Jack's bloated face with the repulsive second tongue, and pulled a grimace of disgust. 'Whatever must . . . he have done, to deserve that? It is a repellent act.'

'Yes – why would someone desecrate him like that?' Stapledon asked in hushed tones.

'The normal reason is because of intemperate behaviour,' Baldwin said. Then, seeing the blank confusion on Simon's face: 'Come now, Bailiff, you must have seen such things before? An adulterer discovered in the act, or a sodomite? There are many in the world who seek to punish others for their genuine or perceived misdemeanours.'

'Adultery and sodomy are hardly mere "misdemeanours",' the Bishop protested.

'Perhaps. But the man who could commit an act like this would put more fear in me than either of those,' Baldwin said.

Ellis wiped the tears from his eyes and barged past the guards into the open air. His mood was one of deep, black loneliness. Ever since his childhood, he had been with his sister. Oh, she'd left him when she married, and he didn't see her every day, but that didn't matter. When their parents were gone, when the women he loved left him, he knew that Mabilla was there, somewhere. She was the rock to which he clung when life's waves washed over him.

And now she was gone. Taken from him.

In all his years, he had not wanted anything. He was Sir Hugh's man because they both recognised something they needed in the other. For Sir Hugh, it was simple: loyalty and obedience. He knew that no matter what the task, Ellis would take it on if Sir Hugh asked him. Sir Hugh used him as a last bulwark against the world. When there was a problem in the vast estates he owned, when a man stood in his path, it was always to Ellis he turned.

But Ellis needed his master just as much. Sir Hugh gave him more than a bed and food. Ellis Brooke was an intelligent man, and he did not exist purely for violence. He craved more – the opportunity to see a plan developed and moulded to fit Sir Hugh's needs, and then to be allowed to execute it perfectly. It was not the simple financial reward he sought, it was the personal fulfilment of seeing an intricate design succeed.

There were men on all sides discussing the body found

in the Great Hall, and now he bent his steps that way. He arrived a few moments after the others had left and, ignoring the guards at the door, he marched across the hall, his hand on his sword-hilt, until he reached the body.

'Jack, aye,' he muttered to himself, then angrily dashed the tears from his eyes once more.

The two most important people in his life were his master, Sir Hugh le Despenser, and his sister Mabilla; and now he must avenge one. Walking out into the Green Yard, he stared about him, wiping his nose with his sleeve. With Mabilla gone, he was unsure what to do next, but he was convinced of one thing.

Nothing and no one would stand in his way as he tried to make her killer pay.

They had withdrawn to a smaller chamber, and Baldwin eyed the others as they waited for a servant to bring them ale. He was tempted to send Rob away, but the lad was keeping quiet, and while he behaved himself, he saw little need to evict him. One single interruption, though, and he'd boot him out.

'So no one knew the man?' Simon said reflectively, into the silence.

Baldwin saw Earl Edmund glance quickly at Despenser before shaking his head. '*I* don't consort with assassins.'

Simon frowned. 'Why do you say that?'

'He must be the same man who launched an attack on the Queen. I think we ought to be thinking about who might wish to harm *her*.'

Baldwin saw how he threw another significant look

towards Despenser. Sir Hugh le Despenser was meanwhile watching Baldwin. 'You said your name was Furnshill – and you are the Keeper of the King's Peace in Devon. Have you visited my estates in Iddesleigh recently?'

'I have visited much of Devon,' Baldwin said stolidly. Then, bringing the conversation back to the matter in hand. 'Do you know anything of an attempt upon the life of the Queen?'

'I consider that an offensive suggestion, Sir Baldwin,' Despenser said softly. 'If I had heard of such a treasonous attempt, I should immediately have reported it to the King and the Queen herself. But there is only one man who would seek an assassin to remove someone from power just now. That treacherous hound, the Earl of Wigmore, Roger Mortimer.'

Baldwin nodded. He was glad at least to have deflected the present discussion away from talk of Iddesleigh. There he had thwarted the Despenser plans to evict other landowners, and prevented a minor war from breaking out between Despenser and Hugh de Courtenay. He was pleased with what he had achieved, but to bring it up now could make Sir Hugh le Despenser into a very dangerous enemy. Once Sir Hugh took against a man, his life could be significantly shortened.

'What more can you tell me about the attempt on the Queen's life?' Baldwin said, trying to put that thought from his mind.

'I can provide you with witnesses, should you require them,' Despenser said. 'My wife was there.'

'I shall need to do that. They may be able to provide a clue as to who killed this man.'

'What does that matter?' Despenser asked irritably. 'He was clearly a felon. He murdered a lady-in-waiting, and then was seen and killed. Who cares *who* killed him? He was a murderer himself.'

'Perhaps he was,' Baldwin said, 'but we have no proof of that as yet. He could have been an innocent. The true assassin may have attacked him, dressed him in his own clothes, and then made good his escape in his new outfit.'

'A far-fetched story!' Despenser sneered.

'But in case this man was intending to kill our Queen,' Baldwin went on, ignoring him, 'I shall ensure that no stone is left unturned in finding out whether the right man is dead.'

Despenser narrowed his eyes. 'Surely this must have been the assassin, Sir Knight. Your suggestion is highly unlikely.'

'You are happier to consider that some competent assassin tried to murder the Queen, but failed and was instead himself killed by a retiring manservant? And that the manservant in question has sought anonymity? That is surely more unlikely! His executioner must know that his King would shower money and titles on him for saving the Queen's life?'

Despenser allowed his head to drop. 'Perhaps.'

'You mentioned Mortimer,' Sir Baldwin went on. 'He is a resourceful man. Perhaps he did order this assassin to attack the Queen. But if so, would he have left anything to chance? From all I have heard of him, when one attack fails, he would be likely to have a second ready to try. He was a master of strategy, I think, when he was the King's General.'

A voice behind him answered, 'Yes. He was.'

Baldwin turned, but even as he took in the tall, fair-haired man with the handsome features marred by one drooping eyelid, he was already aware that the rest of the men in the chamber had already bent their knees in submission, and he hurriedly followed suit, relieved to see that Simon had done likewise. Rob stood gaping for a moment, until Baldwin signalled to him with an urgent jerk of his head. Then the servant almost tumbled to the ground, he bent so swiftly.

'My Lord.'

King Edward looked about the room, and when he spoke it was in fluent Norman. 'We are concerned that someone could have made an attempt on a lady-in-waiting to our Queen. It is intolerable that an assassin should feel able to break into our palace and commit such a foul act. If there is the remotest possibility that this could have been an attack from the Mortimer, we must learn it.'

Bishop Stapledon was crouched low. It sounded to Baldwin as though he was speaking directly to the floor as he responded in Norman. 'My Liege, we do not have many who would be capable of learning such secrets.'

'Is there no one used to investigating crimes among you?'

'There is this man, Sir Baldwin de Furnshill,' the Bishop said, and as he spoke Baldwin set his teeth. He did not wish to become the King's own spy and be set to investigate crimes here near London, many leagues from his home. He wanted to interrupt, but he daren't offend his monarch.

'Stand, Sir Baldwin. Let me look at you.'

Baldwin took a deep breath and obeyed. He found himself subjected to a lengthy study, and while the King glanced with some distaste at his scuffed and muddy boots, his sweat-stained and threadbare hosen, and his worn and faded red tunic, he felt himself flush a little.

The King was taller than him, but not by much. Edward II was just over six feet tall, and he had the frame to carry the height, being muscular and powerful. His shoulders were square, with none of the slouching that older knights sometimes displayed. His hair was golden and curling, and hung to his shoulders, while his beard and moustache were neatly trimmed. He was handsome, but there was a kindliness that shone from the crow's feet at his blue eyes, and the broad, high forehead showed that he was no fool. Any man with a head that size, Baldwin felt, must have something inside it.

'You have had success in seeking felons?'

'In my native land, my Lord. In Devon.'

'Then you will exercise your mind here too, and we can say that you have had success in my territories, no matter where they lie,' the King smiled. He glanced at Despenser. 'I desire you to come with me, Sir Hugh. There are matters to discuss.'

'My Lord!' Baldwin said hurriedly. The King glanced back at him, frankly surprised to be delayed. 'My Lord King, if you wish me to investigate, you must allow me to question all whom I deem necessary.'

'Of course,' he said with a nod, and began to walk away.

'My Lord, that includes your wife. May I speak with her?'

The King hesitated. Then he slowly turned and stared hard at Baldwin.

Suddenly Baldwin saw the other side to this man. The blue in his eyes had frozen to ice. 'You may speak to all you wish, Sir Knight, but if my wife chooses to evade you, that is her right. You may not command my Queen.'

Baldwin dropped his eyes and bowed again. 'I have given offence. I apologise, my Liege.'

But the King made no further comment. He gestured to Sir Hugh le Despenser again and swept from the room, leaving Baldwin feeling drained and slightly shivery.

Chapter Fifteen

Sir Hugh le Despenser followed the King along the corridors and up the stairs into Edward's private chamber. From here, in the warm room with the blazing fire, Despenser could see out through the tall, narrow windows over the Thames. Below, vessels of all types and sizes were plying their trade, oars and sails propelling them up- and downriver. In the past he had found the view to be a pleasant, relaxing sight, and he and the King had enjoyed many a evening up here. Not today, though. There was an edge to the King's expression and his voice.

'Sir Hugh, that man. Is he competent? I need no more upsets with my wife.'

'My Lord, I am sure that he is capable, if the good Bishop says so. Bishop Walter is a most wise man.'

'Meaning you accept no responsibility for anything that goes wrong, eh?' Edward muttered petulantly. He walked to the window and put an arm up to the thick stone mullion as he stared out. 'This . . . this attack, and now a man discovered dead. It is a dreadful day. I have never seen such things, not in *my* palace. I do not like it and I *will not* have it!' He span on his heel and stared at Despenser. 'Answer me honestly, Hugh. Was it you? Did *you* instruct an assassin to kill my Isabella?'

'Me? Good God, my Lord, my King!' Despenser took the easier option of falling to his knees rather than trying to play the actor in front of him. Edward II was too good an actor himself not to see the signs of falsity; Despenser had learned that long ago. Now he kept his eyes downcast. 'If I have ever given you cause to doubt my loyalty or integrity, my Lord, take my life now. You know I love you. I would never do anything that could hurt you or harm your marriage. The woman is hard to deal with, I know, but that would be no excuse to have her killed. We need to wait to hear from your envoys to the papal Curia.'

'And then see about sending her to France,' the King reminded him. 'But there she could be even more troublesome.'

'I am sure the lady means you no ill-will or harm, my Liege.'

'Are you?' the King asked rhetorically. 'You do not see how she looks at me sometimes. I swear, I have never meant her any harm, but . . .'

He stopped himself. His old friend knew all the secrets of his mind, and there was little point in voicing oft-repeated fears.

When he had married her, it was in truth because he had been told to. There had been no desire to marry her – he had never met the woman. But there was a vital need for the English Royal Family to strengthen its bonds with the French, so a marriage was contracted. He travelled to France as the contract demanded, and there he wedded his wife – and was surprised to learn that he had acquired a beauty.

She was plump, fair, pale-complexioned, and clearly amiable in spirit. All she could do to please him, she attempted. They were both French-speakers, so they were able to communicate easily, although he could not share all with her. He could not tell her of his love for Piers Gaveston. Not that he needed to. His affection for Piers was all too obvious.

That had led to a troubled early stage in their marriage, but if it was hard for both, they persevered, and he was inordinately glad that this was the case, for when certain barons captured Piers and murdered him, paying two local men, both dregs of the kennel, to run him through with a lance then hack off his head, the only person he felt he could truly trust and go to for consolation was his wife. His royal lady, Isabella.

At that time their marriage flowered into full friendship. He found that possessing a woman with an individual mind could be stimulating. She had a different perception of some matters, and her viewpoint was intriguing. For him, of course, ruling was tedious and dull. He wanted none of it. He wanted to be out, *doing* things, not sitting in a draughty hall dispensing justice or listening to the complaints of the petitioners who came to moan and whine about his barons and what they had done. It was nothing to him. No, better by far to delegate all powers and responsibilities, as he had with Piers. And then he could do what his soul demanded, trying out peasant skills such as hedging, ditching, thatching, or going for long swims to keep himself exercised, and watching plays. He always adored the arts.

But like all the other happy times for him, this could

not last. Isabella took against Sir Hugh from the start. What had *he* ever done to her, to merit her enmity? God's name, but a man had to wonder sometimes at how a woman's mind worked. Here was Hugh, determined to do all in his power to help the King, and yes, of course, he would be rewarded – richly rewarded – for that. But what business was that of hers? None. No, but there she was declaring that a third person had come between her and her husband. Well, Hugh, darling Hugh, was an important part of Edward's life, and she ought to recognise that. She was only his wife, and she had no right to demand more of his time than she had already taken. She had four children, for God's sake. What more could a woman ask?

It was no surprise that Edward was more keen to run to the comforting arms of his lover than stay with his wife.

Clearly it would be no surprise if poor Hugh grew so disenchanted with the treatment she gave him that he turned to drastic methods to remove her. She was the key obstacle to the two men's happiness. Always there, always a morose reminder of a past life, bringing a sour taste to everything. If only she had kept quiet.

Quiet? It was not the way of her family. Her father, King Philip IV, was powerful, autocratic and demanding. All his people were terrified of him, and he was ruthless in pursuit of his own interests. It rather looked as though her brother, Charles IV, was built in the same mould. He saw only opportunities for cheating Edward out of his inheritance. Sweet Christ! They were trying to take Guyenne now. He was damned if he would let them do that!

'Sire? Are you all right?'

He remembered poor Sir Hugh, kneeling on that uncomfortable floor. 'Stand, my friend. Don't tell me about Isabella. I do not want to know what you have done. *Non!*' And he placed a finger on Hugh's mouth before he could enunciate his protests. 'I know you, and I know of what you are capable. Do not deny these things to me. Just love me . . .'

Baldwin felt a shiver run down his spine, and then he puffed out his cheeks and shook his head. He was too old for this kind of behaviour.

'Wait till I tell Meg,' Simon breathed. 'I've seen the King!'

Baldwin gave a pained smile. 'Let us wait until we get safely home before thinking about things like that, eh? Bishop – can you tell me how I can get a message to the Queen? And I want to view the body of the lady who died last night. I must know where she is being kept. Also, the body in the hall – we should leave him there until the Coroner has returned and can view him.'

'The hall is needed for the council,' Stapledon pointed out.

'The law says . . . ah, but I suppose the King is the embodiment of the law. Well, we shall leave the man there until the Coroner returns, if at all possible. When is the council to begin?'

'Tomorrow is Candlemas. If possible the hall should be free for that, and then the council will begin on the Monday after.'

Baldwin caught sight of Rob. Suddenly concerned that

the boy could open his mouth and get himself into trouble, Baldwin asked him to go and make sure that their horses were being well looked after, and then fetch himself some food, and waited until he had gone before speaking. 'Very well. Then we must make sure that the Coroner has a chance to view the body today so that it can be tidied away for the festivities tomorrow. Anything else?'

Kent was frowning. 'If someone has attempted to kill the Queen once, surely he will make another attempt, since he has failed this first time.'

'He is dead,' Stapledon pointed out.

'The alleged assassin is,' Baldwin said. 'The man who paid him is not. It *is* possible he may try again.'

'There are some who have plenty of men at their disposal,' Kent said, with a meaningful look at the door through which the King and Despenser had just left.

Soon afterwards he stood and left the room, and as Baldwin watched him stride off through the doorway, he was struck with a very dangerous thought: at the time he had assumed that the Earl was thinking of Sir Hugh le Despenser when he said that some fellows had plenty of men at their disposal. But now he wondered whether he had understood him aright – was it possible that he thought the King himself could have tried to have his wife murdered?

Queen Isabella sat on a small turf bench in her cloister. At her feet were two ladies-in-waiting, Alicia and Cecily, both seated on small cushions against the chill ground. Queen Isabella had demanded a lighted brazier to keep them all warm, and the red-hot coals gleamed and spat in the basket.

Behind her, she knew Eleanor was resting on a comfortable, low couch.

Poor, pale, downtrodden Eleanor. This afternoon when she had appeared, the Queen had been tempted to ask her to return to her bedchamber. If she had felt even a particle of sympathy for this woman, she would have done so. But Eleanor was her gaoler, Sir Hugh's spy. She was the abductor of Isabella's children. She could no more feel compassion for Eleanor than fly up into the sky.

At least Eleanor was no threat. If anything, the Queen thought that Eleanor would try to protect her from actual physical assault. She wondered if Eleanor knew just what her husband was capable of. Perhaps she did. There was a set of bruises about her neck that looked like a man's hand-mark. One on the right of her throat, just under her jaw, four more on the other side. Isabella had seen men's violence towards women before. She had even experienced it at the hand of her husband. The marks were easily recognisable.

Perhaps that was why, a short distance behind Eleanor, as though she needed any reminder of the terrible attack last night, there was a man with an enormous polearm standing ready to defend her. Such a shame he hadn't been there last night for Mabilla.

There were few places in this palace where Isabella felt she could relax. In the other palaces, her delightful Eltham, or the great castle at Windsor, there were lovely gardens where she could sit and dream. Here she had tried to recreate a little of the splendour of a French garden, with roses climbing and spreading their scent all about, while camomile was sown in among the grasses so that in the summer when she sat, there would be refreshing odours at all times. At this time of year there was little enough to be smelled, but there was still the pleasure of the open air. And yet her pleasure was constricted by the presence of the man behind her and the knowledge that someone had dared to try to execute her.

So they had found the assassin's body. The effrontery! The bare-arsed nerve of the man! To clamber in here and try to slay her! But no less shocking was the mind of the man who had put him up to it. Only one could have dared. Only a man who was convinced that he had all power already and that any misdemeanour on his part would be overlooked by his King. Even the risk of ruining his King's estates in France would not stop a man with the intolerable rapacity of Sir Hugh le Despenser.

She looked down at her hands. They were palm-uppermost in her lap, and if she lifted them but an inch from her thighs, she knew that they would begin to shake uncontrollably again.

It was curious, that. As the attack took place, she was utterly calm, as though she knew that no one could possibly harm her – Isabella, a member of the reigning French Royal Family, wife to the English King, mother of princes and princesses. It was intolerable that someone could even *think* of harming her.

And yet as soon as the man had turned and fled from Alicia's bold defence, she had felt her calmness begin to fail her. It started with her right hand, she noticed. A faint trembling at first, which grew. And initially, she had viewed it with simple enquiring interest. It was a peculiar reaction. There was no apparent reason for her hand to behave in this manner. There were no other indications of alarm or concern, she thought. Except then her left hand began to twitch all on its own, and suddenly she thought that it would be very easy to start sobbing. Only she knew full well that were she to do that, it would be enormously difficult to stop. And that sort of behaviour might suit a lowly washerwoman, but it was out of the question for a woman of French royal birth.

The tears had ceased to threaten; that itself was a blessing. But the trembling had not gone away. She must leave her hands resting at all times just now, in case others saw how fearful she had become. And she would *never* offer that kind of balm to Despenser's soul!

At least his damned assassin was dead.

Palace of the Bishop of Bath and Wells

A single horse approaching was never a problem, and Bishop Drokensford only frowned a little as he listened. It was but a short time before the knock came at his door and the messenger was ushered inside.

'My Lord Bishop,' he said, bowing low.

'You have a message for me?' The Bishop rose from his chair and set his goblet of wine down upon the table.

'Yes, my Lord,' the man said, reaching into his little pouch and pulling out a slim cylinder of parchment.

Taking it, the Bishop saw that the seal was Peter of Oxford's, and he ripped it off, reading the note inside with haste.

'That is well. You may go and seek refreshment. Tell

my steward to give you anything you want until I call for you.'

'My Lord.'

Drokensford scarcely noticed the man bow his way from the room, he was so engrossed. Peter had the gift of brevity, and his succinct message took only a few words. *Assassin dead; Queen's maid dead* left the Bishop without a full understanding. However, there were inferences to be drawn. An assassin had been found and slain, but sadly he had killed a Queen's maid first. Despenser must be feeling enormously fragile, then. Someone might put two and two together and come up with Sir Hugh's name. Almost everyone would think him alone capable of such hubris.

He tapped his reed against his front teeth, considering. The Bishop was not committed to support Sir Hugh any more than he was committed to supporting any other man or woman, but this precipitate attack on the Queen implied to him that Sir Hugh was grown even more arrogant than Drokensford had believed. And it was clear that a man who overstepped the bounds of normal behaviour in so marked a manner could not control his passions. Equally, a man who was not in control of himself would soon fall prey to one of the other men in the court who was seeking power.

Yes. Perhaps now was the time to consider who could take over the management of the realm once Sir Hugh was gone. There might soon be need of a fresh face.

Chapter Sixteen

Tramping boots brought the Queen back to the present. She listened, with her heart fluttering at the thought that it could be men come to destroy her, but then she heard a calm voice speaking, and the confirmation of the guard, and knew that this must be safe.

Nonetheless, Alicia was on her feet before anyone had entered the garden, and Richard Blaket crossed to stand beside her, glowering ferociously, his polearm at the ready, while even Cecily rose to kneel immediately before Isabella. It was in Blaket that she put her faith, though: no one would pass him to harm his Queen.

It was Alicia who offered the challenge. 'You are trespassing on the Queen's private cloister, lordings – what are you doing here?'

'My name is Sir Baldwin de Furnshill, Lady. I am the Keeper of the King's Peace in Devon, and I have been asked to learn all I may about the terrible incidents of last night. This is my friend and companion, Simon Puttock. He is a Bailiff to the Abbot of Tavistock, and experienced in seeking felons. We would like to speak with your Lady to learn all we may about last night's attack.'

Isabella considered a moment. This man's voice was

reassuring, certainly. She had a good ear for a man's voice. Many times she felt certain that her assessment of a man was better than almost everybody else's, because she could hear when there was deceit. 'Let them come forward so that I may see them,' she said, and studied the two for a moment as they bowed. 'Stand up, gentles. I can hardly see your faces when you turn them to the ground, can I? Yes. I like your faces. You may stay.'

'May we speak about the attack, please?' Baldwin said. He spoke in French, and she looked at him appreciatively.

'You have an excellent accent, m'sieur. What would you like to know? A man sprang out at us, he struck at the lady-in-waiting nearest to him, and then fled. Clearly he was appalled himself by his actions.'

'Did you recognise him?'

'Am I in the habit of consorting with assassins? He was masked, in any case.'

'What kind of mask did he wear?' Baldwin asked.

'It was leather,' Cecily interrupted breathlessly. '*Cuir bouilli*, I should think. Shaped in the image of a face with holes for the eyes.'

Baldwin looked at her, a short, plump young woman with a round face and pleasing green eyes. 'How was he clad?'

'He had all dark clothing. Nothing black, but all grey or brown, with a dark green gipon.'

The Queen smiled coolly. 'Are you here to question my maids as well as me?'

'I apologise, my Lady. Did you see his weapon?'

'A long-bladed knife. You know, like those which the

Welsh wear? He had it in his hand before we came along the corridor.'

'I see,' Baldwin frowned thoughtfully.

She was a beautiful woman, this princess of France. Her skin was pale and perfect, her eyes clear blue. She was clad in a pelicon, a fur-trimmed mantle that was quite voluminous, making Baldwin wonder how many tunics he would be able to cut from the one item of clothing. At a rough guess he reckoned six.

Her arm was clearly giving her some pain, for when she moved as she spoke, it made her wince. Baldwin remembered hearing that some years before, maybe ten or so, she had been trapped in a fire when her tent had caught alight, and she had been badly burned. Apparently this was one of those injuries that healed only poorly. However, the aspect of her clothing that struck him more than any other was the almost shameful nature of her bodice – it was cut lower than any he had seen in England before. He was forced to keep his eyes from her décolletage as he spoke to her.

'Could you please take us to the corridor? I should like to see it.'

'Of course. Alicia, you come with us.'

'I shall come too,' Eleanor said quickly, making an effort to rise from her couch.

'There is no need,' the Queen said with disarming civility. 'You were so shocked after last night, you remain here and rest. Cecily, you keep her company. I shall hardly be in danger when Alicia is with me.'

'My Lady, I must insist,' Eleanor began.

Baldwin intervened. 'Madam, I swear I shall bring her

straight back here to you as soon as we have made our investigations. I apologise, but I shall wish to speak to you later as well.'

Isabella smiled sweetly at her gaoler, and strode past the guard to the door that led through to her chambers. She walked along the corridor to the chapel. 'I was in here, and walked back through this corridor to my bedchamber, and it was here where he attacked. Look, you can yet see the poor woman's blood on the flags there.'

Baldwin did not need to touch the washed stones to smell the blood. It had permeated the atmosphere here. Where the Queen indicated, there was a niche in the wall. Just there, a man might hide very efficiently at night when the light in a corridor was invariably dim. The sight affected the Queen, and in the darker light of the corridor she appeared pale.

'My Lady, are you quite well?' Baldwin asked solicitously, and seeing her unease, he sent Alicia to fetch some wine.

'I will be fine in a moment,' she muttered as her maid ran along the passageway.

'I am sorry to have brought you back here, my Lady, but it is important that I see where the attack took place. Now, do you have any idea who could have wished to see you murdered? Is there anybody who has been so angry with you that he might have chosen to order a man to kill you?'

'Tell me, my friend. Do you know anything of your country's politics?' she enquired with mock-seriousness. Then, seeing his agreement, she gave a slow, weary nod in return. 'Then you know who is most likely to wish to harm me. Do not expect me to commit *petit treason* by naming them. You know who they are.'

Baldwin felt as though a knife was in his own belly and being twisted. *Petit treason* was the legal term for any form of treason against a Lord – including that of treachery against a husband. It was enough of a clue.

'Thank you for that, madam. And now . . . just a few more questions. The woman who died – she was . . .?'

'Her name was Mabilla Aubyn. A pleasant enough child, I think, and a bondswoman to Eleanor de Clare.'

'And she was walking with you?'

'Yes. There were five about me. Two before me, and two behind, with Alicia following at the rear. Mabilla was on my right, Cecily on my left, and Joan behind me on my left, Eleanor on my right. As I say, Alicia was behind us all. When the man appeared, we were all struck with fear, I believe. Mabilla was dead in an instant. Ah – I would be wary of trusting to Cecily's memory of the man who attacked us. She fainted away as soon as she saw the man's knife. Only Alicia showed real courage. She thrust herself between the man and me, even when Joan was screaming and flying back towards the chapel in her terror. Only Alicia will be able to tell you what the man looked like. You must ask her. She must have terrified the fellow – he fled before her.'

'And you were all walking in the dark, or was there light?'

'What a question! Mabilla carried one candle, Alicia another. Why?'

'No matter. I just wondered – would a man assume that you would walk before your servants?'

'Not if they know me and this place, no!' She need hardly point out that this palace was to her a prison. Alicia returned with a mazer of strong wine, and Isabella drained it.

'Mabilla had a candle, as did Alicia,' Baldwin noted. 'Tell me, Alicia, did you recognise the man?'

'If any of us knew the man, we would have denounced him for attacking us, of course!'

'Yes. What of Mabilla? Did she scream, turn to run, make any move to show she recognised this man?'

'We were all screaming, m'sieur. It was late at night and a man had appeared before us with a blade in his hand, ready to strike. Of course we were all scared.'

'Naturally,' Baldwin said with a mild smile. 'And now, let me escort you back to your cloister. It is a most pleasant garden you have created there, madam.'

'Thank you. It is a little haven from the storms of political life,' she said and looked down, for she suddenly realised that her hands were perfectly still. There was no more shaking in them at all.

As she walked back to her cloister, she mused on the strange calmness which had come over her, but when they were at the gate to her cloister, the shaking came back.

'*Ce diable!*'

Baldwin heard her hissed words, and followed the line of her sight. At the far end of the Old Palace Yard he saw Bishop Stapledon.

The Queen looked up at Baldwin with glittering

hatred in her eyes, then swept through the gate into the sanctuary of her cloister, Alicia trailing after her.

Eleanor was already on her feet when the Queen stormed in. The two women stopped and stared at each other, Isabella fuming inwardly, and then she picked up her skirts and walked more calmly to her seat again.

Her swift return was enough to make Eleanor easier. Clearly the uncouth knight and his friend had said something to upset her. That was good. She would hardly have given away anything too harmful to Sir Hugh's interests if she disliked and distrusted the men questioning her.

She nodded to Cecily to remain, and walked past the guard out to the Green Yard. 'You said you would return to see me?'

The knight met her look with a dark-eyed intensity that shocked her. Lady Eleanor was no child, but as Sir Baldwin fixed her with that look, she felt uncomfortably like a maiden once more. It was the sort of look that said he knew what she had been doing, what her thoughts were. Only this time, rather than fearing he might learn of an illicit kiss from a groom, she was more concerned about her other secrets. Unconsciously, she drew up the neck of her tunic to conceal the fingermarks of her husband.

'Lady, I am grateful to you for coming to speak with us,' the knight said, and for the next few minutes he questioned her about the attack. Her recollection was no different from Cecily's.

'And then the man fled?'

'Yes.'

'And you have no idea who he was? He was not familiar? Sometimes in a household as vast as this, a man's gait or his way of holding his head can grow known to you.'

'I am sure I did not recognise him in any way,' the lady said with a shake of her head.

'Are you aware of any who may have wished to harm Mabilla?'

She hesitated – it wasn't intentional, and it was only a moment, but she saw his face lower towards her like a dog wondering whether his master was sad. There was the same enquiring, considering frown. 'No. No, of course not,' she said emphatically.

'Did the man make any kind of move as though he was considering attacking another person in your group?'

'Good heaven, no. No, he fled as soon as Mabilla fell.'

Sir Baldwin nodded pensively, and at last his attention was diverted from her. Instead he looked northwards, gazing along the line of buildings. 'What of others? It was dark there. Could one of the other ladies have had an enemy? Perhaps a lover whose affection had turned sour?'

'No. The ladies are all entirely honourable and without any form of . . . of sourness.'

'Lady, you seem a little tired. Would you care to seat yourself?'

His tone was warm and respectful, but she felt a cold certainty that he was watching her every move. He was a shrewd questioner, the more so because he recognised the little guilty signs. He knew she was lying.

'Perhaps the murderer was seeking another, and met us by accident?' she said faintly. 'No one should have known we would be there at that time of night. It was a whim of the Queen's.'

'You would not usually have been there? That is interesting. Where else could the man have been going?'

'To the chapel itself, I suppose. There is nowhere else he could have gone,' she said, and after Sir Baldwin and the Bailiff Simon Puttock had bade her farewell, she watched them leave with a sense of huge relief.

At the same time, she felt a sense of loss. If only she could trust these two. She felt she couldn't trust her own husband just now. Not if he was sending men to kill her maids.

'I didn't understand much of what you were saying to the Queen or that lady,' Simon admitted as they left Eleanor and made their way towards the chapel.

'I rather assumed you wouldn't,' Baldwin said. 'Did you hear what the Queen said when she saw Walter?'

'Hm? No. What was that?'

'It is clear that she detests him,' Baldwin explained briefly. 'It will require a little thought, this. For now though, let us go and seek out the body of this girl. I am more than a little surprised by what we've just been told.'

'I was more surprised by the way the Queen flaunted her breasts.'

'She has an interest in clothing, I suppose.'

'I had an interest in the descriptions of the assassin's clothing.'

'You noticed that too? Cecily's description agreed

with Lady Eleanor's, but neither tied up with the clothes on the man in the hall, did they? I wonder . . . they saw a figure and a face in the middle of the night, by candlelight, while the Queen was naturally under a great strain, thinking this must be an assassin aiming his knife at her.'

Simon glanced at him. 'Baldwin, they're used to candlelight. Lady Eleanor and Cecily were intelligent enough to be assured about the clothing and describe it in some detail. If I had to trust any evidence in this whole mess, I'd trust them.'

'And yet Cecily fainted away, and Eleanor was farthest from the man.'

It took them little time to find a servant in the King's livery who could take them to the body. Mabilla lay in the Queen's chapel, a pretty little room with a high vaulted ceiling. At the rear was a gallery – presumably, Baldwin thought, for the Queen herself. She would pray up there while her household prayed down here below.

'Nice,' Simon commented, looking at the wall paintings. There were scenes from the Gospels on either side, and the great window over the altar was made of panes of coloured glass, lighting the interior with a warm, diffuse light that gleamed on the gold leaf and gilt all about. The space was clear of seats bar one, a small, low chair facing the altar. Before it was a small cushion for her to kneel on in prayer. 'Rather better decorated than Lydford's.'

Baldwin smiled, but said nothing. Before the altar a bier had been placed, and upon that was the body of Mabilla.

She had been laid out by the women of the Queen's household, her wounds cleaned and her clothing changed. Baldwin pulled a face at the sight. 'We cannot undress her in here to see the wounds, can we?'

'Most certainly not!' came an indignant voice.

Chapter Seventeen

The voice came from behind them. Baldwin turned to see a young chaplain, eyeing the two of them with black suspicion.

To Baldwin, he looked much like the Celtic men of Cornwall, with his almost coal-black hair and small, brown eyes. There was a hardness about him, a whip-cord strength, for all that he was short and moderately plump. Baldwin nodded to him, and absently took up Mabilla's right hand, studying it closely with a frown.

'Put her hand down. Stop pawing at her!' The Chaplain entered now and passed Baldwin and Simon, looking down at the woman's body as he did so. 'Rest in peace, daughter.'

There was a kind of naturalness about him in the face of this death that was oddly endearing to Baldwin. The fellow clearly did not look upon Mabilla as a mere corpse ready to be thrown into the ground; he was treating her as a woman still, a person with feelings and a soul, and doing so naturally, without affectation.

'Chaplain, I am sorry if it feels as though we are intruding here,' Sir Baldwin said. 'It was not our intention to be annoying to you, but we have been commanded to come here by the King himself, to learn what we may about this poor child's death.'

'The King himself, hey?' It was plain that this man was not impressed. 'Well – what more do you need to know? The poor chit was slaughtered only yards away from my chapel here, and then her killer – God be praised! – was found by another man, who killed him. It is as simple as that. There is little more to be learned.'

'Could you tell me anything about this lady?'

'Mabilla? Her surname was Aubyn, but I suppose you know that already. Well, as to other things, she was born and bred in a little manor just outside London, a place called Iseldone, I think.'

'Her family?'

The priest looked at him with some exasperation. 'If you need that sort of information, ask Lady Eleanor. Mabilla was one of her ladies.'

'Aren't they all?' Simon murmured. He was standing over Mabilla and peering down at her sadly. She had a pretty enough face and slim body. He could imagine her smiling and laughing, flirting. She had that sort of cheeky look about her.

'Most, yes. The poor Queen has no rights, it would seem,' the Chaplain agreed.

'So all the women are regulated by the Lady Eleanor?'

'Not all. One or two perhaps may be bolder than others.'

'In what way?'

'A household is run almost entirely by men. Yet the Queen has women about her. It is not unnatural for them to form relationships with some of the men about the place.'

'Are you thinking of any in particular?'

'Ach! It is not concealed. Lady Alicia, the same who stood between the killer and the Queen, she has an affection for one of the guards.'

'Which?'

'A man called Richard Blaket. But he is a good, loyal man to the Queen, and I think Alicia has proved her own devotion from her behaviour in the corridor.'

'You have been Queen Isabella's Chaplain for long?' Baldwin asked after a moment.

The man looked at him, and then shook his head. 'What of it? No. I have only come into her service since her previous chaplains were removed. It's a disgrace, the way that they were treated, too. Both of them arrested, and when the Queen offered sureties so that they could be released into her custody, she wasn't even allowed to do that!'

'It is always hard in time of war, Brother um . . .?' Baldwin let the question hang in the air.

'I am Brother Peter. I was asked to come here by my Bishop, Drokensford of Bath and Wells. Naturally I was delighted to help him – and my Lady the Queen herself.'

'Naturally,' Baldwin agreed smoothly. 'Now, should I assume that you yourself have any enemies who may take it into their heads to come here in the dead of night and slay you?'

'I do hope this is merely your sense of humour,' Peter said without amusement.

'I take that as a negative. In that case, is there anyone you can think of who would dare to attempt such a foul attack on Her Majesty?'

Peter rolled his eyes. 'You want me to give you my neck?'

'I am not allied to any Lords. I do not have to tell anyone where I have heard my information. All I ask is that information. If I am to protect her, I need to know who may be thinking to harm her.'

Brother Peter left them and walked to the altar. He stood there with his head bowed, silently considering, and then turned slowly to face them again. 'I will tell you all I may, but if you dare to vouchsafe any of this to enemies of the Queen, I pray that you will have a slow death and that you may spend a thousand thousand years suffering the torments of the devil! Do you agree?'

Baldwin blinked. It was tempting to recoil, for as the priest spoke, he slowly raised his arms as though calling upon God to hear his oath and enforce his punishment. 'I do.'

'Oh. All right then,' Peter said amiably, and beckoned them to join him. He took them through the rear of the chapel, and into a small vestry. There he indicated a stool and chest for them to take their rest, and poured them each a cup of very strong wine.

'One of the perks of the business here is that the King's undercroft is very well stocked with the finest Rhenish and Guyennois wines,' he said, smacking his lips appreciatively – but not as appreciatively as the Bailiff, whose frowning countenance had lightened considerably at the sight of the wine.

'Who could want her harmed?' Baldwin reminded Brother Peter.

'Well, the two most obvious ones are the King and Despenser. But you'll know that, won't you? That supposes that the killer was trying to get to the Queen but was scared off by a single chit of a woman: Alicia. Brave of her, of course, but I'd have thought a hired assassin would not baulk at her. If he was looking to a suitable reward, he'd have got on with the job, even though all five women stood before the Queen.'

Simon had considered this. 'Could the man not have mistakenly thought that he had killed the Queen? It is a dark passageway, and in the excitement, perhaps he thought he had struck her down. After all, I should have expected the Queen would walk at the front of any party. Maybe he did too.'

Baldwin glanced at Brother Peter, who smiled back as though taunting him to display his intellect. 'I think there are two problems with that, Simon,' Baldwin explained. 'The assassin had broken into the Palace, knew where the Queen's chamber was, and even knew that she would pass by that passage at some time that night. So he was very well informed before launching himself on this adventure. If he knew so much, I find it hard to imagine that he would not have learned that she normally walked in the midst of her ladies. Then again, the killer struck Mabilla although she was carrying a candle, so we are told, and could clearly be seen. When you accused me, Peter, of "pawing" at her, I was looking at her hand to see whether there was any evidence of that. There was. On her hand there is a little spattering of wax, such as you receive when you walk along with a guttering candle. So that means that the killer would have seen her. It is inconceivable, I should think, that the man would not know the Queen by sight.'

Brother Peter nodded slowly, a smile on his face now. 'I applaud your logic. It is much the same as my own conclusion. Which was why I was intrigued when I heard that the poor child had been killed.'

'It sounds more and more likely that Mabilla herself was the real target,' Simon mused. 'A curious idea, though. Everyone is convinced that someone is trying to kill the Queen – so why should someone attack the lady-in-waiting?'

'Ah, now that is something for you to learn,' Peter said easily, leaning back against the wall. 'I am only a mere functionary, friend, performing a service for the Queen.'

Baldwin and Simon looked at him. It was Simon who broke the doubtful silence. 'You are very bold for a humble servant, friend.'

'You think so? Perhaps I ought to learn more humility. I thank you for the suggestion.'

'Do you know whether Mabilla had any enemies, then?' Simon tried again.

'Have you had a look about this court yet? It is a hotbed of intrigues and intriguers, full of parasites, rogues, ruffians and the sort of man you would not trust with your purse, let alone your silver. Under the King, these all fight for position, and try to stab each other in the back – and only sometimes do they try it metaphorically!'

'That has no bearing on the death of a lady-in-waiting,' Simon pointed out.

'When there is unrestrained sexual abandon, when man and wife are likely to couple with others, and ignore the order which God in His wisdom imposed upon us for the good and benefit of all mankind, then yes, there is the potential for murder, even of a young woman like Mabilla.'

'Was she free with her favours, then?' Simon asked.

'Mabilla? I don't think so. But that in itself could be dangerous for a woman in a place like this. If she was so courageous as to refuse a man who desired her, who can say what she might suffer?'

'Do you know who could have desired her, then?' Baldwin asked bluntly.

'I believe the Earl of Kent was rather infatuated with her. I do not know, you understand, but I saw the way he looked at her on occasion, and judging by the way she did not look back, I should say there is a possibility that he could have wanted more than she was prepared to give.'

'There have been cases of women who have been captured by those who want them,' Baldwin began.

'But to capture a maid in the King's palace and spirit her away – that would be courageous. The King does not forgive very easily.'

'You paint a picture of a court that is almost out of control,' Baldwin said.

Peter waved his mazer in an encompassing gesture. 'Spend a little time here and see what you think afterwards. For me, it is a view of hell. And that is as a relatively safe outsider. For you? You will both be in danger the whole time.'

* * *

Simon and Baldwin left him in his vestry cordially waving to them, and made their way out of the chapel. Baldwin paused a moment at the woman's body, and then shook his head with a frown and walked out.

'You want to have her unclothed and study her wounds?' Simon asked.

'I considered it, but unless we propose to suggest that the Queen herself and all her ladies-in-waiting have lied about the incident and the murder, which I think could be foolhardy, I think we should take their evidence at face value.'

'I agree,' Simon chuckled with a hint of nervousness. 'I would like to live to see my wife again.'

'So would I. And that means we should do all in our power to learn the truth about these deaths.'

'Do you believe that Mabilla was the target, then?'

'I believe it is more probable than this story of an assassin who was trying to kill the Queen and then got cold feet after striking another lady by mischance. That is, to me, highly unlikely. So, let us note that point and now go and see what we may learn about the man who was found dead.'

They made their way to the Great Hall, but when they reached it the body had been removed. Baldwin had to stop two servants before he learned that the King's Coroner was returned; Simon and he were given directions back out to a stone building in the Old Palace Yard.

Inside, they found a pair of servants with their sleeves rolled up, undressing the corpse. Behind, craning his neck to see by the light of a small candle that burned with a smell of beef fat, was a short, dumpy little man with a beardless chin and gleaming blue eyes set in an almost perfectly circular face. 'What d'you want?' he grunted rudely.

'I am Sir Baldwin de Furnshill, and this is my friend Bailiff Puttock of Tavistock. We have been commanded by the King to investigate these two deaths so far as we may, and to report back to him.'

'You are, eh? Excellent!' In an instant all his snappishness was gone, and the man walked round, holding out his hand. Simon, glancing at it, saw that it was stained with blood, and winced as the man gripped his hand before repeating the exercise with Baldwin.

'You must excuse the mess in here. It's not usually occupied by a corpse, but where else can we store him, eh? No, better to keep him out of the way, that was what I thought. So out here he came. Trouble is, it's damned dark in here, eh? Still, a candle will serve where the sun won't! Did you see him in the hall? Nasty business. Who'd do a thing like that to a man, eh? Cut off his tarse and shove it in his mouth. Barbaric, eh? Oh, by the way, I am Coroner John of Evesham, at your service.'

Baldwin was already at the victim's head, and stood looking down the length of his body. Simon, having a less resilient stomach, had taken up his own station nearer the doorway, where the obscene protrusion from the dead man's mouth was hidden by Sir John's thick little body.

'Was there anything at all about this man that could indicate where he came from, what his usual trade was, or anything of that nature?' Baldwin asked.

'Nothing. All deny ever seeing him before, which is

hardly surprising, but the porters say that they haven't seen him before either, which is odd. If one of them had seen him enter the New Palace Yard, they would surely have said so, and it's not as if there's been too many people for them to notice recently. No, if they say they didn't see him, I believe them.'

'I shall wish to walk about the perimeter of the Palace, then, just to see whether there's an obvious place where he could have gained entry,' Baldwin said. 'Tell me, how easy would it be for a man to learn what the Queen's movements are?'

'The Queen's? Probably very easy. How many hundreds of servants are there here, eh? Any one of them could have been bribed, I dare say. It's all too common.'

'And the Queen has a fairly rigid structure to her day, I suppose.'

'Ah,' Sir John said, smiling and tapping his nose. 'Not all that structured, no. All too often she rises at the oddest hours to go and hear Mass, I've heard. She likes to keep her people on their toes.'

That made Baldwin frown, but before he could continue, the two assistants had pulled off the last of the dead man's garments and Baldwin and John leaned forward with professional enthusiasm.

'Clearly his own tarse, then,' John said with detachment. Simon felt his belly lurch.

'Dead first, I'd think,' Baldwin said.

'Oh, definitely, definitely. He must have had a blow to the heart which killed him, and then the murderer removed his, um, and shoved it into his mouth. It could have indicated disapproval of the assassin's way of life, say, if the killer knew him and resented him for being a sodomite?'

Baldwin shrugged off his words. He had spent too much time living in the East, where men would sometimes form close liaisons with other men. He did not find it as fearful a lifestyle as some.

However, Simon was taken by another thought. 'What if it was an indication of disrespect for someone else, though?'

'Like who, my friend?'

In another man, this patronising tone would have irritated Simon enormously, but he felt himself warming to the Coroner. Sir John seemed affable, but Simon could sense a strong intellect, and felt that he was covering up a sharp mind with his buffoonery. Perhaps it was necessary in a political household such as this. 'I was wondering: if a powerful baron wanted to leave a brutal warning to another, perhaps he could do this?'

'But why?' John said, a smile still on his lips, but a faintly anxious expression in his eyes.

'If he was leaving a message for a baron who was a sodomite, that might be the way he'd do it,' Simon guessed.

Baldwin gave a chuckle. 'I think that's more than a little far-fetched, Simon. No, I feel sure that this is a reflection on the man found dead, and *his* lifestyle. It's surely a little extreme to think that someone could find the right assassin, kill him, and decide to leave a message for the man who could be his paymaster. Now – what else is there?'

And while Simon was left feeling ruffled at the way

the two men had dismissed his suggestion, the Coroner and Keeper bent to study the corpse once more.

'Distinguishing marks – a large scar over his breast here, as though a sword has taken away a flap of skin. He's had that arm damaged, too. Look at it!'

Baldwin nodded. At some time the limb had been badly crushed, the bone broken and reset, as was so often the case, slightly crooked. There was a great deal of scar tissue about it, too. 'He must have suffered every day from that.'

'I wonder how he did it?' Sir John murmured. 'And now, let us roll the fellow over and see if there's anything else to be learned, eh?'

The two men completed their careful investigation and when they were both satisfied that there was nothing more to be gleaned from the man's body, they pulled a sheet over him and wiped their hands on a few rags they found nearby.

Baldwin was first to leave, but when Simon tried to follow him, he found the Coroner in his way: the man had sprung into his path. 'I am very interested in your idea about the dead man, Bailiff. Perhaps we could meet to discuss it further?' he said, to Simon's surprise.

Simon gave a grunt of agreement. The two men had so clearly indicated their lack of interest in his suggestion, yet now the Coroner wished to talk about it. It made no sense.

In the stables, Baldwin and Simon found Rob, sulking at the horses. 'The Bishop said for you to follow on to his house. Told me to wait here for you.' He gave a long-suffering sigh.

Baldwin nodded, glancing at the activity in and around New Palace Yard. As the sun was sliding down in the west, people were starting to make their way homewards. Some were already installed on benches at the taverns, while the hawkers and vendors were packing up their wares and making for the gatehouse.

'Come on, you two,' he said. 'It's time we copied them.'

Chapter Eighteen

It took some little while for them to reach the Bishop's house, and on the journey Simon found himself gaping at all the fine buildings, for it seemed to him that every few yards there was a palace.

'This road is called King Street,' Baldwin said. 'It leads us north for a while, and then we head east on the road called Straunde.'

Rob frowned. 'What does that mean?'

'A "straunde" is a beach, and this is the old line of the Thames, I think,' Baldwin said. 'When I was first here, many years ago, there were still some areas of marsh over there towards the river. It appears all is covered now. They have drained most of the marsh and dumped soil and gravel on top so that they can build on it.'

Rob gazed about him. 'Why bother? Couldn't they go a bit further away and build there?'

Baldwin smiled. 'This is the main road from the kingdom's greatest city to the Palace where the King makes his laws. Courtiers, bishops, innkeepers and pie-sellers all want to be near the seat of power, my friend. It is where the money lies ... and that is all anyone is interested in nowadays,' he added more sadly.

'What is that?' Simon asked. He was pointing at a great open space with low buildings behind it. Before it, stood a magnificent construction. Some five-and-twenty yards tall, it was a spire, with ornately carved sides. In arches on each face were figures, heads bent in mourning.

Baldwin sighed. 'The King's father, Edward the first, put that up, and eleven others, to commemorate his beloved wife, Eleanor of Castile. She was so dear to him, that when she died, he brought her body in procession back here to London. There is a great tomb for her in the Abbey, back there on Thorney Isle.'

'He must have loved her dearly to have that built.'

'Not just that, Simon, it is only one of twelve. She died in Nottinghamshire, and the King had one of these crosses built at each place where the procession stopped each night. And when they returned here, he had her heart buried in the Dominican House in London so that it was near the heart of her son Alfonso. He had died some years before her.'

'A terrible thing for any mother or father,' Simon said quietly. He had lost his own first son.

'Yes. That is a useful marker for us, though,' Baldwin continued, seeing his mood and trying to lighten it. 'Because for us it indicates the end of King Street. Where that cross stands is the royal mews.'

Simon said, 'Ah!' The wide open space behind the cross was where the royal falcons and hawks would be exercised, then, and the buildings beyond were the houses where the birds could 'mew' or moult, as well as housing their falconers. From the sound of baying, he thought that some hounds must also be kept there.

'The King enjoys his hunting, then?' he said, his mind on happier things, just as his old friend had intended.

'He enjoys mostly alternative pursuits, Simon. He likes to go hedging and ditching, or rowing boats or swimming,' Baldwin chuckled. 'Not that that is the worst, sadly. Do you know, he has been known to enjoy acting? There are many scandalised barons who have mentioned that. The thought that a king should enjoy such frivolous pastimes is enough to send some of them into the vapours.'

'Acting, eh? How low can a man sink,' Simon laughed.

'From here, at Charing, the road becomes known as Straunde. It runs from here to the city of London itself, and there it becomes the Fleet Street.'

'Why so many names?' Rob grumbled. 'Can't they make do with one, like other towns?'

'Because this is not like other towns, boy,' Baldwin said, adding with a slightly sarcastic edge to his voice, 'It is too great for one name to suffice. The people here adore display above all else.'

'What do you mean by that?' Simon asked. He was staring at a large building on their right. 'Look at that! It's as big as the Bishop's house at Bishop's Clyst!'

'It's a Bishop's London home,' Baldwin said absently. He gazed at it a moment, brow puckered with the effort of memory. 'Ah yes, I think that is the Bishop of Norwich's place. He is nearest Charing and the cross. Then comes the Bishop of Durham's house, I think. And after that, the Bishop of Carlisle's home. What I meant about display was that here in London, I always had the feeling that people like to make an impression, above

all else. In Exeter or Salisbury or Winchester, or anywhere else, people take pride in beauty for beauty's sake.
They would have a wonderful building because they like
beautiful things. A Bishop might commission a painting
on his walls to make his cathedral more lovely, a
merchant may do the same in his hall – but here, the
aim seems to be sheer ostentation. They want to instil a
sense of inferiority – or fear – in visitors. It is a harsh,
dangerous city. Be cautious when Londoners congregate,
that is my advice to you both.'

Simon could see that he was musing on other things,
but knew better than to press his old friend. And to be
truthful, he was more keen on looking at the huge manor
houses which lined this great road. Ostentatious or not, he
found them fascinating.

'This is it,' Baldwin said shortly.

Simon followed his pointing finger to a range of small
dwellings, mostly little shops and some houses, with an
inn. In the midst of them was a grand arched gateway,
with a small door to one side. Baldwin rode to the gates
and dropped from his horse. This late, for it was almost
dark now, the gates had been closed, and he rapped
sharply on them with his knuckles.

There was a grunt and soft curse, and then Simon
heard footsteps. A panel shot open in the gate and a pair
of scowling eyes peered out. 'Yes? What do you want?'

'The gates opened, old man. We are here to speak with
the Bishop.'

'His inn is just up there. Come back in the morning.'

'We are his guests, Porter. If you wish, we can go as
you say, and you can explain to him why it is that the men

whom he invited to stay with him were turned away at his door.'

The eyes looked Baldwin up and down. 'No one tells me anything!' he grumbled. The panel slid shut, and shortly afterwards they heard the welcome sound of bolts rattling open and the rasp of timbers being drawn back to unbar the gates.

'Please enter, my Lords.'

Simon rode into a space that seemed as large as his village green and sat for a while on his horse, simply drinking in the view.

Ahead of them was the Bishop's residence while in London. It was a great stone hall with a shingled roof, rather like a smaller version of the King's Great Hall. It clearly stood over a large undercroft, because the entrance was up a flight of stairs at the left-hand side, while on the right side was a two-storey block which would hold the Bishop's private rooms and a chapel. Next to that were some stables and working sheds. The middle was one large expanse covered with a thick layer of gravel.

'It's huge,' Simon breathed.

'You forget that the good Bishop is one of the most important men in the country,' Baldwin pointed out.

'But he has the palace in Exeter, and his manor at Bishop's Clyst. I didn't think he'd have a property like this in London too,' Simon said.

'He is a very wealthy man,' Baldwin said quietly.

Admitting it before Simon was hard, but Baldwin too was shocked by the size of this palace. He knew how much the Bishop had been forced to invest in the rebuilding works at Exeter Cathedral, and he had also been patron of schools and colleges. To have bought and built this massive property as well in the last fifteen years showed just how much Bishop Walter Stapledon had prospered. It left Baldwin feeling uneasy: so much wealth was hard to explain. However, Bishop Walter had been Lord High Treasurer twice in the last few years, and it was likely that some of the money used here had had its foundation in the King's Exchequer.

They led their horses over to the stables, and then Baldwin and Simon marched to the hall.

Bishop Stapledon was already seated at his table on the great dais. A proportion of his servants were sitting and eating in the lower part of the hall. As soon as he saw Simon and Baldwin, he beckoned for them to join him. The two men had to wait while a servant scurried for seats and trenchers for them both. Then the laver arrived with a bowl, and both washed their hands and dried them on the proffered towel before setting to with the bowls of meat at the table before them.

'Did you get anywhere, Sir Baldwin?' the Bishop asked when they had taken the edge off their appetites.

'We have learned a little,' Baldwin said, using a piece of bread to soak up gravy, 'but there is more we need to find out. The identity of this strange assassin would be a help to us. However, I have no idea how to find out anything about him. Without a clue as to where he came from, it is hard to imagine that we can get any further.'

'Then perhaps this is the end to your investigation?'

Simon was looking at the Bishop as he said this, and could have sworn he saw a gleam of hope in his old friend's eye. 'Surely not, Bishop!' he exclaimed, shocked. 'How could we give up when the Queen's life may be in danger?' He drank deep from his mazer.

'But if you can learn nothing more . . .'

'We shall,' Baldwin said firmly. 'This was our first afternoon, and already we have discovered much. Tell me, do you know anything about the Chaplain to the Queen?'

'Brother Peter?' The Bishop's tone altered subtly, lost some of its warmth. 'He is a rather disreputable man, from what I have seen and heard. I would not find *him* a particularly reliable witness.'

'Why not?'

'I cannot say,' the Bishop said flatly. 'However, I repeat: I would trust little that he says.'

'I see,' Baldwin said.

'Now. Tomorrow is Candlemas,' their host said briskly. 'There will be no work in Thorney Island, but if you wish, you may join me in visiting the great Cathedral of Saint Paul's for Mass.'

'It would be an honour,' Baldwin said. The Festival for the Purification of the Blessed Virgin Mary was always an important festival in the Christian year. Simon was delighted, keen to see how this great day would be celebrated in one of the country's greatest cathedral churches.

'Good,' the Bishop said, and stared down at the linen on the table before him. There were some breadcrumbs, and he toyed with them, rolling them into a ball and then pushing them forwards and backwards.

All about them the servants were tidying tables, and

men were rising for the second servings of food, when those who had already eaten would serve those who had served them.

'You know,' Walter went on after a short pause, 'it cannot be easy to be a king.'

Baldwin nodded. 'I expect not.' He waited for the other man to explain.

'There are enemies all about. Some are obvious, others less so, but a man who would be King must learn to be distrustful, no matter how much his heart craves the companionship of a friend. Sometimes, rulers pick excellent advisers, and sometimes they don't. But the worst enemies, dear friends, are those whom God has provided – a man's family. No man can pick his family – except perhaps his wife. And for a king, even that choice is taken away.'

'You are thinking of our King?' Simon asked discreetly.

Bishop Stapledon looked at him. 'Yes. I was.'

'You do not trust her,' Baldwin said quietly. 'We have discussed this before.' Vividly into his mind sprang the picture of Isabella as she caught sight of Bishop Stapledon at the far end of the Old Palace Yard when Baldwin was escorting her back to her cloister.

'She could be enormously dangerous to the nation,' their host stated. 'She is not to be trusted.'

'Which is why you advocated action against her?'

The previous year, after the sudden French attack on the English territories in France, Baldwin knew that Walter Stapledon had worked with Despenser to have the Queen's lands taken from her. Now, instead of being one of the country's greatest landowners and magnates in her own right, Isabella was reduced to the status of humble pensioner living from the King's largesse. She had not even been allowed to keep her household. All her servants, her clerks, her maids, even her two chaplains, as Peter had told them, had been removed from their offices. The final atrocious act was the removal of her three youngest children.

'She is the sister of the French King,' Stapledon reminded him. 'We could not run the risk that she might find herself . . . *confused* over her loyalties. Naturally we would like to think that her primary loyalties lie with her husband the King, but it is always possible that she might forget that in preference to those to her brother, Charles the Fourth, King of France. It would be natural enough.'

'I have to object,' Sir Baldwin said bravely. 'I think that the actions taken against her have ensured that her loyalties will have been affected, where before they were not.'

The Bishop waved a hand, then leaned nearer and spoke with more caution, eyeing his servants to ensure that he was not overheard. 'You have not seen how they bicker and argue recently. Until two, maybe three years ago, she was as good and dutiful a wife as any man could hope to possess, but since then she has grown more distant. It is jealousy, I think, which has done this.'

'Sir Hugh le Despenser?'

'You have guessed it. A woman must naturally find it hard to understand the fondness one man might feel for another. Entirely innocent, of course, but still, a man like the King is very affectionate. He craves the companionship of strong, bold men like himself.'

'Sir Hugh has come between the King and his wife?'

'Perhaps she may have *perceived* that to be the case. But women can get the strangest notions sometimes.'

'And often they can be more perceptive than men give them credit for,' Baldwin said quietly.

Chapter Nineteen

The Queen's Chambers, Thorney Island

Lady Eleanor felt better when she had eaten a little supper. She couldn't eat too much, but a slice or two of capon with some wine to wash it down was perfect. It lay happily in her belly, and she settled herself back on her cushions with a sigh.

Alicia was a strange child. She seemed so considerate towards the Queen, almost to the point of fawning on her, even though she knew that their job was to act the gaoler and watch every move the Queen made so as to ensure that no communications escaped from the Palace without their knowing.

And she did have a good brain, it had to be admitted. Others would have automatically assumed, from the way Mabilla died, that the Queen was in danger. But Alicia was the only person other than Eleanor herself to wonder whether another could have been the target.

Of course, Mabilla herself could have been the intended victim. There were plenty of women who flirted outrageously with the men of the King's household, and although Mabilla had seemed quite stable in the past, that was no proof that she actually had remained chaste and sensible when the candles were out. Eleanor only hoped that the killer could be shown to be a jealous lover.

But if it was a jealous lover, who had then executed him in that foul manner? One possibility was that Mabilla had a *second* lover, one who had sought to protect her, or who heard of her death and then chose to avenge it.

Of course, the Queen was only too ready to spread rumours and cause trouble. Hugh had only a short while ago tried to entice Isabella into his bed, so she claimed. He had apparently proposed that she should join him and the King. If she refused, he vowed he would take her on her own at the least. She had told Eleanor all this, although at the time Eleanor had not chosen to believe her. The woman was partly deranged by the removal of her children, and she would have said anything to cause a rift between Eleanor and her Hugh.

Only in this instance of the murder, there was something that had caught at Eleanor's imagination, a kernel of truth that shrieked at her.

Many were already whispering that the King might have conspired with his 'brother' Despenser to remove the Queen because she could be such an embarrassment. If she were to go to France as the Pope had asked, she could cause untold problems for the English King.

Eleanor thought that the motive to remove her could be simpler, though. Isabella found the King's infatuation with Hugh to be frankly, disgusting. And as the daughter of a King of France, and sister to the present French King, she saw no reason to acquiesce to any philandering with Hugh. Perhaps she could have understood and accommodated a female lover, but not a man. If the King sought to kill her, it was to remove the woman who could bruit news of his affair abroad. His sodomy. Were she to do so, Edward II could be excommunicated for heresy.

Eleanor herself had suspected their affair, but she preferred to close her eyes to it. She was no queen. She was a lady, and had some pride, but she was also a realist. A knight had once told her about Sir Hugh's nocturnal visits to the King's bedchamber, and she had laughed at him. 'What of it? He is my husband, and the King his friend enriches us both in return.'

It was true, but tears of shame scalded her cheeks afterwards. She knew that men in the household discussed her husband and the King, and in the same breath, made lewd conjectures about her. Perhaps Eleanor was too frigid, they would say. Perhaps she could not make her old man's tower rise.

When she had first realised that Hugh was being unfaithful, it had never occurred to Eleanor that it might be with another *man*. Then, sadder and wiser, she had swallowed her pride, accepting that such things could happen, but hoping that it would be a passing fad of the King's, and that soon her husband would be free of this foul stain on his soul. But then the affection between them grew, and they became more demonstrative in public, and that was when she faced Hugh with it.

'What of it, woman?' was all he said, looking at her as if she was simple.

She had been lost for words at that. As though it mattered not a jot that he was doing something that was declared a vile sin by the Church. And when he laughed at her, she had burst into tears of humiliation. That was when he had suggested that she might like to join him and the King together in bed – that she could add spice to their love-making – and she had fled at that, hearing his bellows of laughter follow her all down the corridors. Perhaps he *had* made the same suggestion to her mistress, the Queen.

Eleanor had a new and terrifying thought: if the King and Hugh could think of removing Isabella the Queen so that they might more easily indulge their love . . . it was as likely that they could think of removing another – Eleanor herself. Or perhaps Hugh still desired Isabella, and felt that Eleanor was a barrier to his possessing the Queen.

'No!'

It was ridiculous. Why, apart from his irrational outburst the other day, she had never seen her husband look at her with anything other than love or desire in his eyes.

But the thought was there, snagged in her mind. *What if . . . what if he wanted her removed?*

The Temple

Sir Hugh le Despenser knew nothing of his wife's doubts. He sat sprawled in his comfortable great chair in the large solar block of his newest acquisition and looked about him with satisfaction.

'Wine,' he murmured. There was no need to shout. His servants knew better than to miss his commands. Will Pilk looked at him as soon as he spoke and hurried from the room.

Even the King's own servants were not so attentive.

Not to the King, anyway. They tended to obey Despenser, however.

He had returned here late, after a meal with Edward in his private chamber, and although the other man had wanted him to remain, he had gently but firmly rejected his demands. At first the King had been amused, thinking that this was merely some sort of play-acting to taunt and tease, but when he understood that Hugh was serious, he threw a little tantrum. This was developing into a habit now, and it was tedious. If it was anyone other than King Edward, Sir Hugh would have made them appreciate in no uncertain terms, how boorish that behaviour was.

'I must return,' he gave as his excuse. 'My wife is not well after the events of last night.'

'What of *me*, Hugh? *I* may need your protection. The killer could return, couldn't he?'

'I think the man who stabbed a lady-in-waiting is unlikely to try to prove himself as a regicide as well, my Lord.'

'Oh, *do* you? And how do you get to have such detailed knowledge of the man's mind?' the King had snapped.

'My Lord, surely you understand, in the circumstances, I have to ensure first that my wife is comfortable?'

'You try to tell me that you could have misdirected the blow?'

And there it was. In his eyes, in the way that he stood and walked away from Hugh, the way that he averted his eyes from his companion and lover. He was as sure as he could be that Hugh was responsible for the attempt on the ladies. No denial would work here, he had seen immediately, and the two parted on civil, but less than amicable terms.

And the worst of it was, Hugh had absolutely no idea who *had* killed Mabilla, nor who had executed Jack. Jack was an old comrade, when all was said and done, and his loss was hurtful. Sir Hugh did not like to lose his servants. It was the sort of thing that could easily get out of control if people thought that they could kill his men with impunity.

'Where is Ellis?' he asked as soon as the servant returned with his wine.

'I think he is in the main hall,' Pilk said.

'Bring him to me.'

Ellis was soon with him. Pilk had brought another horn for him, and once Ellis was standing before Sir Hugh, Pilk passed him the drink, retreating almost immediately to the door.

'I was looking for you today, Ellis.'

'I was busy,' his henchman said shortly.

Despenser peered into his goblet. His voice was mildly pensive, as though he was ruminating on a new idea. 'I had thought you worked for and served me. Perhaps I misunderstood. When I want my servants, I expect them to be there for me. But you were "busy".' He looked up from his drink and stared at Ellis.

Pilk felt that look in his bowels. No man came here to work for the Despenser without realising that he was entirely ruthless. Pilk could kill – he often had – but always there was a faint feeling of remorse afterwards. It felt as though each death niggled away at him, and someday there must be a reckoning.

Not so with Sir Hugh le Despenser. When he killed a man, there was no compunction at all in his face. Pilk had seen it. He had been there when Madam Baret had been captured by Despenser. The reason was simple: her husband had died and Despenser wanted to acquire all his lands. That meant Madam Baret must give them up, for she was not powerful enough, now her husband was dead, to demand compensation. Not that such a demand could have helped her.

She had been savagely tortured, to the extremity of sanity, and in the end her mind had been broken along with her body. And what had Despenser done? He had found the sight of her ruined figure stumbling away extremely funny – had laughed out loud. All he cared about was his own purse, and nothing and no one else.

'I went to see my sister's body, Sir Hugh.'

'Who?' Despenser appeared genuinely surprised. 'Oh, the wench. I had forgotten she was your sister.'

'Mabilla, yes. She married Sir Ralph Aubyn some years ago.'

'I remember him. Huge man. A good fighter.'

'My sister was murdered by the man who killed Jack.'

Despenser sipped his wine. 'I am concerned. Whoever this killer is, he knew how to offend me. There was a message in the way that they did that to Jack. Cutting off his tarse and shoving it in his face like that was meant for me. It is a challenge, Ellis, and I don't like to be challenged by those whom I do not know.'

'How did he know Jack was going to be there last night? Did you know?' Ellis asked.

'No one knew. You know how Jack worked. He was

always alone. Never trusted anyone else. Not even me, his paymaster.'

'Was there anyone else could have known?'

'No! Hell's teeth, man! I've already said – Jack was always close.'

Ellis glowered at the floor. 'It must have been someone at the palace.'

Despenser was tempted to throw his goblet in the fool's face. 'Is that so?' he spat. 'So, someone at the palace found a suspected assassin and killed him, and then chose not to take a reward for his discovery and for thwarting the attempted regicide.'

'If he knew you were behind Jack, he'd probably prefer to remain anonymous. Most men know what you would do if you found out they had stood in your path or killed one of your servants.'

Especially if they knew I was seeking to assassinate the Queen, Despenser confessed to himself. Aloud he said, 'How could someone have learned about Jack last night?'

'I don't know yet, but if it is your will, I'll find out.'

'It is my will. And when you have done so, come and report to me. Tomorrow I will ensure that this Keeper of the King's Peace does not go anywhere near the Palace. I will have him and his friend come here for the Feast. That will be easy enough to arrange, with the help of the Bishop. Yes, it would be good to know what went wrong for Jack last night. Especially since it would help us to learn whether someone else has uncovered Jack's attempt on the life of Queen Isabella.'

Sir Hugh yawned. 'One last thing, Ellis. Do not let

people know more than you have to. I don't want the
King's officers coming here for me because you've been
talking too freely. Understand?'

'Yes.'

'Good. Now – remind me. At Monkleigh last year
there was some trouble, wasn't there? We were attempting to take over another manor, and someone prevented
us. Sir Geoffrey Servington sent us a full report on the
whole affair, didn't he?'

'Yes.'

'Find it. I have a feeling that the name Furnshill is in
there somewhere, and I'd like to make sure. I suspect that
this Sir Baldwin has been a thorn in my side before – and
you know what I do with thorns? I pull them out and
crush them.'

Chapter Twenty

The Feast of the Purification of the Blessed Virgin Mary[1]

St Clement Danes

The morning Mass was a very special affair, and Baldwin and Simon were up before dawn on the Saturday with the main part of the Bishop's household. To the knight's surprise, Simon's servant Rob appeared quite over-whelmed with the magnificence of the chapel, reverently gawping at the decoration all about.

After prayers in the Bishop's chapel, Walter Stapledon led the way to the great gate at the Straunde, and he and his *familia* strode out into the road.

St Clement Danes was a delightful church just inside the Temple Bar, and Simon immediately felt at home there. It was one of those friendly churches where the congregation greeted strangers warmly. The priest himself was very proud to welcome the Bishop to his little church and urged him and his guests to enjoy their service when he met them at the door on the way inside.

---

[1] 2 February 1325

Simon watched the priest with a mind empty of all except the beauty of the service, and a certain wariness about Rob's behaviour, but as he stood watching, he began to grow aware of Baldwin fidgeting at his side.

The knight seemed to be spending much of the time peering ahead at the altar. It was only after they had finished the candlelit procession that Simon could edge nearer and speak. 'You look upset, Baldwin. Is there something I can help with?'

'No. It is nothing.'

He refused to discuss the matter further, but Simon saw his eyes moving towards Bishop Walter several times during the rest of the service. He seemed no more comfortable when they left the church and walked out into the crisp, wintry air.

'Bishop, if you do not mind, I shall walk on to the Cathedral,' he said. Bishop Walter graciously acquiesced, and Baldwin set off eastwards towards the city, Simon a little way behind him. After a while, he stopped at a great bar set across the road. It was a short distance from the church, and a man had pulled it aside so that it would not hinder traffic, but at night it would lie across the roadway, blocking it.

'That,' he said to Simon as the Bailiff and Rob caught up, 'is Temple Bar.'

'Yes?' Simon gazed at it, seeking inspiration.

Rob said. 'Yeah? It's . . . big.'

'Quite,' Baldwin said, but this time with a twitch of his mouth that told Simon he was amused. 'There are bars like this at every main junction outside the city's gates. The city set them up to stop traffic during the night, and each day they're pulled back so that people can use the roads again. They're only tokens, really. A determined force could easily remove them. But they're useful as symbols of the extremity of the authority of the city itself.'

'Oh. I see.'

'This one is called Temple Bar because it is here. Outside the Temple,' Baldwin said, and he suddenly turned to face the enormous gates that stood a few yards away.

'So?' Rob said.

'Oh!' Now Simon understood Baldwin's distraction.

'Yes. That was the New Temple, Simon – the main preceptory for the whole country. A magnificent building, with orchards, gardens, stables, and the main halls, of course. It was the heart of my Order in this country.'

Simon wanted to rest a hand on his friend's shoulder, but he knew Baldwin would not appreciate it. The knight was too enwrapped in his memories, for Baldwin had once been a Poor Fellow Soldier of Christ and the Temple of Solomon – a Knight Templar.

'I have wished to come here and see the place one last time for many years,' Baldwin whispered. 'And now I am here, I feel that it is a mausoleum only. Dreams lie in there, Simon. Dreams of honour and glory. Dreams of the Holy Land being Christian once more. But no King will honour such a dream.'

'What?' Rob demanded, staring from one to the other.

Simon grunted to himself. 'Lad, I need you to return to the Bishop's palace and keep an eye on our belongings there. Could you do that?'

'Why? It'll be safe enough in there, won't it?'

'Just go and do it,' Baldwin grated. Reluctantly, the lad set off back to Bishop Walter's home in London.

Once he had disappeared from earshot, Simon said softly, 'I am sorry, old friend.'

'No, do not be. This is the Festival of the Blessed Virgin. Come, stop me from continuing with my black mood, Simon. You have a duty today, to keep me happy and cheerful. Prevent me from thinking about my Order. Ach! What of it. Come! Let us find Saint Paul's. It is a wonderful cathedral, Bailiff. Almost as grand as the great one at Canterbury.'

He continued talking as they walked up the road until they reached the bridge over the Fleet River, and there Simon's eyes opened wide to see the huge wall.

It extended northwards in a straight, unimpeded line, with a vast ditch before it. The wall was beautiful, too. There were strings of red tiles that made a pattern of lines going diagonally across it, and it had beautifully maintained castellations, a rebuke to the tatty condition of the walls at Exeter.

But it was not merely the wall that caught his attention. Beyond was the cathedral, standing clear in the grey morning light on its hill.

'Saint Paul's,' Baldwin said.

They entered the great city by the gate, and were soon making their way up Ludgate Hill, Baldwin speaking about the port which supplied so much of the population's needs.

For Simon there was an especial thrill in standing

before the enormous church. Peering at the two towers, the statues and decorations, he was lost in wonder. When Baldwin interrupted him, he was quite startled.

'I think we ought to get a move on, Simon. Here comes Bishop Walter and his retinue.'

'Oh? Oh, yes.' Simon was excited at the prospect of seeing the interior. It was surely not so vast as Exeter, with its massive length of nave, nor as well decorated as the fabulous cathedral of Santiago de Compostela, but for all that, it was a splendid sight.

Except that for the second time that morning, he gradually became aware that Baldwin was very jumpy: his eyes were roving about the people in the street, watching them carefully.

'What is it, Baldwin?' he asked a trifle testily. Only then did he himself grow aware of the terrible tension in the crowds about the Cathedral. There was an almost palpable hatred in the air. As the Bishop's party approached the Cathedral, the babble had dulled, and now the people were glaring at him with sullen faces.

As Simon registered the mood of the people there, a stone was hurled. It flew high over Simon's head, and he heard it smack into the flank of one of the men-at-arms' horses. The mount gave a snort and jerked his head, bouncing up and down. And then there was another missile, this time some ordure from the kennel, and it splattered into the wall of the church not far from the Bishop's head.

Bishop Walter kept calm, and merely clattered on, but there were shouts now on all sides, and curses and imprecations were thrown at him as he passed towards

the hitching posts. A couple of urchins stood there, taking
the reins for all those who were attending the service, and
they gleefully took the Bishop's, gazing about in the hope
of boys everywhere that they might see some excitement.

When he had given away his mount, he stood and
surveyed the crowds. There was more shouting, and
Baldwin distinctly heard someone berating Stapledon
about the 'Eyre'.

The Bishop held up his hand and glared about at the
people in front of him. Baldwin nudged Simon, and
began to walk towards him, pushing through the crowd
with an increasing sense of concern. The guards from his
party were looking from one side to another with
increasing alarm, their hands on their swords. In the
whole space before the Cathedral, the only man who
appeared calm and collected still was the Bishop. He held
up both hands now, in a gesture of mild reproof.

'Wait, my friends,' he called. His answer was a small
hail of pebbles. It was all Baldwin needed. He saw a
young man, probably an apprentice, levering a cobble
from the roadway with a metal bar. Before the lad could
heft the rock, he was aware of a bright blue blade under
his chin.

'Drop it.'

The lad not only dropped it, he took one look at
Baldwin's face and bolted.

But scaring one man was not sufficient to ensure the
Bishop's safety. Baldwin saw that Simon had grabbed a
long staff from someone, and had cracked another man
over the wrist with it. The fellow was standing looking
daggers at Simon while nursing his forearm. Another had

drawn a knife and was eyeing Simon warily, but the Bailiff had seen him, and although he looked relaxed, Baldwin was not for a moment fooled. He knew that Simon was at his most dangerous when he wore that easygoing expression. If the man lunged, he would be unconscious on the ground in a moment.

'This is Candlemas, and you are threatening the peace of this Church,' the Bishop spoke out. 'You have no right to try to draw blood, but if you do so today of all days, the Feast Day of the Purification of the Blessed Virgin, you will be committing a mortal sin. Think of that, all of you! Do you want to be excommunicated? You may escape punishment here on earth, but God watches over all that you do. Do not . . .'

The rest of his words were drowned out in the shouting. Men were shaking their fists at him, and now more missiles were hurled. For the first time, Baldwin saw that the Bishop was worried. His three men-at-arms appeared less than keen to get between him and the mob, and he could plainly see that the door to the Cathedral was some distance away. If he were to run, it was most unlikely that he could make it without being grabbed by someone more fleet of foot, or be felled by a flying rock.

'Christ's ballocks!' he heard Simon say, and the two looked at each other. Then, with a nod, both took a deep breath and plunged into the crowd to try to reach him.

As though by a miracle, the noise and bellowing suddenly ceased. At first Baldwin thought that the sight of a single knight with his sword drawn, or perhaps a Bailiff with a staff, was enough to bring sense to this unruly throng, and he felt a slight uplifting of his heart.

But then he heard the shouted order, the rattle of hooves on cobbles, and the ringing of chains and armour. There was a clatter of steel as men drew their swords, and when he turned, he saw a line of men-at-arms on horseback eyeing the rabble with contempt.

'*Disperse in the name of the King!*'

It was Sir Hugh le Despenser. He trotted forwards a short distance, and Baldwin saw disdain in his eyes – a contempt for the churls who dared to stand before him. Baldwin was convinced that this man would willingly ride down all the people in this street. He cared nothing for any of them.

The people knew him, because their noise was stilled instantly as they froze into fearful submission. Stones were dropped, knives hastily sheathed, and the fellows began to slip away, their faces bitter and surly. One man stood before Despenser with a staff in his hand, but Sir Hugh spurred his great horse onward, and the man was barged aside. He opened his mouth as though to shout defiance, but as he did so, one of Sir Hugh's men drew his sword and casually swung his pommel into the man's skull. He collapsed, blood spurting from a gash over his brow, whimpering with the shock as the horses passed by him.

As people realised that their fun for the day was over, the horde started to thin. After a short while, three women ran to the old man's side, gentling him and no doubt praising him for his courage.

Simon watched them for a moment, relieved that the man was not badly hurt. 'Thank God for that. I thought you and I were about to die trying to protect Walter from that rabble. Sweet Mother Mary, thank God they arrived just then.'

Even Baldwin was prepared to admit: 'I never thought I should be glad to see Sir Hugh le Despenser arrive behind me with a force of men.'

'Really, Sir Baldwin?'

Sir Hugh's voice was nearer than Baldwin had expected. He had left his horse with one of his men, and now was only a couple of feet away, and he eyed Baldwin's sword pointedly.

Baldwin smiled without guile and took it up to sheath it, but Sir Hugh was peering closer, and the knight felt a cold dread that seemed to settle in his bowels. Hurriedly he thrust it home, and put his thumbs into his belt, defiantly meeting Sir Hugh's gaze.

'This was a close affair, Sir Baldwin. You and Master Simon here could have been hurt.'

'We naturally wished to do all we could to protect Bishop Stapledon,' Baldwin said.

The Bishop was already making his way to them. He was pale, and his eyes reflected the anxiety which he must surely feel. 'Ha! The London mob. I have often seen them rise to attack others, but this is the first time I have been on the receiving end of their ire. It is not an experience I should wish to repeat.'

'You'll be safe enough now,' Despenser said. He glanced at Baldwin, then down at the sheathed sword. 'There's no one will dare to harm you here, Bishop.'

'Shall we go inside, then?' Stapledon suggested. For all his apparent calmness, he was plainly nervous, not without good reason.

'Yes. And afterwards, my Lord Bishop, would you honour my little home with your presence at my feast? It will not be a large affair, but I should like to invite a friend. Of course, Sir Baldwin, you must join us too. It would be pleasant to have you and your companion with us.'

'I would be delighted. I am very grateful to you,' the Bishop said, and Baldwin gave a short nod.

'Good. That is settled, then. You will like my home, Sir Baldwin. It used to be the London home of the Knights Templar. Perhaps you know of it?'

Baldwin said nothing. He did not feel safe enough to speak.

Chapter Twenty-One

Ellis had set off early that morning. He had no wish to go and visit a church to watch the Candlemas processions again. Not today. Today, he was bent on revenge.

He walked quickly along the road back towards Westminster. Before he did anything else, he wanted to pray over Mabilla's body again.

The idea that someone had taken his sister away was so inconceivable that he found himself doubting it even as he walked – as though the events of the night before had been nothing but a bad dream. Surely he would soon see her again. She would be there in the palace, smiling and laughing to hear that he'd had such a ridiculous mare. As though anyone could want to hurt Mabilla!

Ellis and she had been born to a squire who lived up in Iseldone, the small vill north of the city beyond the marshes and bogs. Squire Robert had lived a blameless life in the service of King Edward I until he died at the hands of the Scottish on one of the King's forays into that morass of politics. From that moment, Ellis had taken responsibility for the family. He was the oldest son.

Mabilla had married into the Aubyn family soon after their father's death. Then their younger brother Bernard had fallen from his horse and died, and shortly after that, their mother was also dead. When Mabilla and Ellis discussed it, they both felt sure that it was a broken heart that had ended her life, because she had lived for her husband first and Bernard second. Without them, her life was not worth living. And now, only Ellis was left.

He turned off Straunde and into King Street.

Both he and Mabilla had seen what a life of effort and loyalty could bring a man. It had brought their father an early grave. And then there was Bernard – dead at the age of twenty because of a mishandled horse. Ill-luck and Fate – no one was safe from them, however blameless their life.

When Mabilla's husband became vassal to Sir Hugh le Despenser, she formed a close friendship with Eleanor, Sir Hugh's wife. From that it was natural that Mabilla should seek employment for her brother, and soon Ellis was a noted servant. He became Sir Hugh's trusted sergeant, and Sir Hugh grew to depend on him more and more.

The walls of the Palace Yard were ahead now. Most people were in the Abbey for Mass, and the yard was silent as he passed through. He walked from the New Palace Yard into Old Palace Yard, and thence through the buildings until he reached the chapel where Mabilla still lay. Only then, when his face was resting on her breast, did he at last let go and begin to weep.

Despenser trusted him. Sir Hugh knew he could rely on Ellis. If he ordered it, Ellis would break legs, break arms, use screws on thumbs, pierce the flesh under fingernails with splinters, or kill. All would be done as commanded. But that did not make Despenser a friend, and just now Ellis could appreciate that the only friend he had ever truly known was Mabilla. And she was dead.

Simon walked from the Cathedral with a thrilling in his veins.

He often felt this way after a Mass. There was something about the incense, the light, the space, that never failed to excite him. It felt as though God Himself had visited Simon today and touched him. He was elated. The fact that the service had been held in such magnificent surroundings only served to heighten his emotional reaction.

Sir Baldwin, however, remained withdrawn, quieter than usual, as they left the church and began to head back down Ludgate Hill.

'At least while Despenser's men are with us there's no need to worry about the mob,' Simon remarked.

Baldwin did not comment, but cast about him warily like a warrior expecting an ambush.

The two had soon passed through the city wall and were out in the more open ground beyond. Once there, Baldwin said, 'Simon, did you see Despenser's expression as he asked us to go to his house? He was gleeful. Be very careful while we are at the Temple.'

'Why? He seems to have accorded us every compliment and honour.'

'That is true. He has done so to many whom he later destroyed!'

'What could he have against us?'

Baldwin did not want to mention Iddesleigh and

Monkleigh, but he knew that there was one other thing which Simon would appreciate. 'My sword – you remember my engraving?'

'Of course.' He was about to recite the Latin inscription, but Baldwin shook his head.

'No, not the writing. The reverse of the blade.'

'Oh – Good Christ, did he see it?'

'While we were protecting the Bishop, yes. I am sure of it.'

Simon grunted. On one side of the sword Baldwin had had inscribed a quotation, but on the other he had caused a Templar cross to be carved into the metal just below the cross-guard. It was there to remind him at all times of his comrades, the brave men who had endured torture in the defence of their Order. Now, it could lead to dire consequences. Renegade Templars who had not surrendered to the Crown or the Pope were subject to the full rigours of the law. Excommunicated, they could be arrested on sight. Simon was tempted to ask why his friend had considered it necessary to have the blade marked in that way, but he silenced his tongue. Baldwin was his friend, but he was also a proud man. Proud of his past and his companions who had died. It was not Simon's place to question his reasons. If Simon had seen all his friends murdered by the inquisitors and their secular friends, he would probably want to remember them too.

It did take the edge off his pleasure, though, to see that the invitation to the Despenser hall could have been for some other motive than pure neighbourliness.

* * *

Ellis left the chapel and went to look at the walls. He felt sure that the assassin would have made his way to the Palace grounds by some more circuitous route than merely following tradespeople inside. Jack had always been more cautious than that. If it were possible to avoid being seen, he would do so.

The wall guards all knew Sir Hugh and his henchman, so it was no trouble for Ellis to gain access to the upper walkway. Once there, he started with the boats at the dock north of the New Palace Yard. Peering down at the dock, just visible through the murky water, he wondered about Jack coming up here. But the dock was in constant use – the wooden platform was fifty yards long and about twenty wide so that barges and boats could float onto it in high tides, and beach themselves as the tide flowed away again for unloading. Thus there was no time for Jack to appear here and make use of it without plenty of men being about to see him.

Walking on the Thames side of the wall, he was struck with the same thought: if he came up the river in order to scramble over the wall, Jack would be very hard-pressed to do so without being seen. Much easier to come to the palace grounds from the land.

Ellis carefully studied the walls at the north and south, but what could he expect to find? The scratches and stone chips from a grapnel? Jack would not have used such a loud device. The metallic clattering of the hooks would have stirred any guards even if they were asleep. A rope ladder would be more his style, but when he had reached the palace it was late evening, not the middle of the night. In the first part of the evening, Jack would have been seen if he'd come up over the walls. Anyone carrying a ladder that way would have been challenged.

Yet there was one other way to reach the palace . . . from the Abbey's grounds. Sensing that he had guessed aright, Ellis went over to the wall separating the two plots, and as he reached the southernmost point of the palace wall, he saw it.

A rope hung almost negligently from a battlement. Pulling at it, he saw a ladder on the ground below. As he drew up the rope, the ladder was lifted aloft until it reached almost to the battlement. A man could have climbed up the ladder to reach the battlement. Once there, he could have allowed the ladder to topple back silently, using the rope, and then left the rope so that he could pull it back upright for his escape. That way, hopefully no guard would spot that someone had entered the precinct. Not that the guard here was any good anyway. It was old Arch.

Ellis knew the man. Always reeking of sour ale, and Ellis was sure that his guarding was lackadaisical at best. Rumour had it that Arch was asleep more often than awake when he was on duty.

'So that's how you got here, Jack,' he said out loud. 'Now – how were you caught?'

The way to the Temple was along a street between other properties, but soon they were past them and into a wide space. In front of them was the Temple Church itself, and Simon was immediately struck by the look of it. 'Why is that part round?'

'Templar churches were always based on the layout of

the Temple of Solomon in Jerusalem,' Baldwin said. 'The Temple had this same form.'

They were led along the northern wall of the church itself and over towards a large building at the east of it.

'This is where the Templar heretic Prior and his monks used to live,' Despenser said as he dismounted. 'An elegant building, I would say, for those heathens and devil-worshippers.'

He threw his reins towards a boy who scuttled forward to grab them, and then stood at the Bishop's horse to steady it. Bishop Stapledon looked about him with a face that was carefully blank.

Simon knew that he was intensely irritated that the lands and buildings should have been used to further enrich the King's lover. The Temple grounds had been supposed to be given to the Knights of St John, and many were outraged that the King had chosen not to do so. The Bishop clearly felt that if anyone should be rewarded with them, it should be a man from the Church. Simon could guess who he felt would be most deserving. He had begun to understand that Stapledon was not averse to personal enrichment.

'Please, come inside.'

Simon found himself in a sumptuously appointed hall. Along two walls were huge tapestries displaying the Despenser arms mingled with scenes of hunting. Intricately detailed sections showed Sir Hugh chasing a hart, slaying a boar, standing among a pack of hunting dogs – and the last one depicted him sitting with friends and enjoying a meal.

'You like it?' he said. 'I had the full halling from a

tapicer in the city. He was very clever, I think, to get so much life into the picture. Don't you agree?'

'Very good.'

Despenser glanced at him, but he had other things on his mind than a guest's apparent disinterest in his hallings. He called for his steward, and soon tables were set out and laid with a series of linen cloths. Despenser himself took the table at the dais, and courteously invited the others to join him, Bishop Walter at his side, Simon and Baldwin opposite. The rest of the men were ranged about tables in the main hall.

'Yes. This was the Prior's hall, I think. You can hardly imagine the place in those days. I saw it once, you know. There was gold and silver everywhere, and gilt on all the exposed spaces. A marvellous place. Yet when the Order was suppressed, it all just disappeared.'

'Where to?' Simon asked.

'Christ knows. Perhaps the rumours are true, and they loaded it all onto some boats and flung it into the sea. What do you think, Sir Baldwin?'

'Me? I have no idea. I had thought the King took most of their wealth, just as the French King took that which was discovered in the Paris Temple. If you say that much is missing, though, I will believe you.'

'I do not know. Perhaps you are right,' Despenser smiled, but there was no humour in his face. 'So long as none of the illegitimate sons of whores escaped, that is the main thing.'

Baldwin felt his eye upon him, and had to set his jaw to stop from angrily responding. 'You think that all were guilty?'

'Perhaps not. But so long as some were, it matters little.'

'It matters a lot!' Baldwin exclaimed hotly. 'It is better that ten guilty men go free than one innocent man is unjustly convicted.'

'Well, if that is your view,' Despenser shrugged, 'at least you may reflect upon the certainty that God will know His own. The innocent will no doubt be there with Him even now.'

'I am sure that not all were evil,' Bishop Stapledon said, and there was a strength in his tone which Baldwin had not expected. 'There were very many with whom I had dealings who were entirely honourable. Like most of the other knights Templar.'

'The Pope convicted them of unimaginable crimes,' Sir Hugh reminded him.

'Oh yes, and then when the Order was destroyed, the same good Pope allowed all those Templars who wished it, the opportunity to go to another religious brotherhood. Some joined the Benedictines, some the other Orders. They were men of honour and integrity.'

'Then why were they arrested?'

'That was much the fault of the French King.'

'Ah, of course,' Sir Hugh sneered. 'It's often down to him.'

Food arrived, and the party set to with gusto.

Sir Hugh le Despenser was the first to finish his thick stew, and he took a hunk of bread to soak up the juices as the mess bowls were taken away with their valuable contents to be given as charity at his door. As he chewed, he watched the servants clearing away the dishes, and then said to the Bishop: 'Did you notice during the candlelit procession that I spilled some wax on my hand? Never a good omen, that.'

Simon was not credulous, but he did have some superstitions. 'Where I was born they used to say that if you spilled wax, someone you knew might die.'

'Really?' Despenser said shortly. Too late, he told himself. Jack was already dead. 'How interesting. I hope it won't be my wife. She is with the Queen again today.'

'That was a dreadful event yesterday,' the Bishop said quietly.

Despenser looked at him. 'Dreadful' hardly covered it. He could still remember that body on the floor behind the throne. Jack, the man on whom he had come to depend so much, because he was the most expert killer, had himself been killed. But by whom? And how? Anyone who could lull Jack and slay him was an enemy to be feared.

He managed, 'I agree. One finds it difficult to express one's horror at such a foul murder.'

'The maid, yes,' Stapledon agreed.

'It is hard to understand how any man could wish to hurt the Queen,' Baldwin said.

His words had an instant impact. 'You think that?' Despenser said. Beside him, Bishop Walter winced.

'Surely any man who has taken an oath to obey the King has simultaneously taken an oath to protect his wife?' Baldwin said.

Despenser was studying him closely. 'Perhaps some do not think that she merits such blind devotion?'

'I am surprised to hear you say that, Sir Hugh.'

'Her brother makes it difficult for a patriot to support

her. Just as the Bishop pointed out, the French cannot always be trusted. They covet our lands and kingdom.'

'You say that is an excuse for not honouring our Queen?'

'I say that we who have responsibility for the security of the realm have many difficult decisions to make,' Despenser said. 'It is like the matter of the Templars – perhaps some, as the good Bishop suggested, may have been innocent. But for the protection of Christianity as a whole, it was essential that they were all arrested, was it not?'

'I could not say,' Baldwin said. He shifted in his seat. This felt too much like denying his comrades, but if he were to become known as an escaped Templar, it would not serve to aid them. It would only ensure that he was arrested, and likely executed, for no purpose. Then a small flame of defiance flared. 'I could only say this: that as Keeper of the King's Peace I have witnessed enough injustices at the hands of the incompetent, the dull-witted and the corrupt. I should not be in the least surprised to learn that some of those who prosecuted the Templars were no better than those I have seen in the last years in Devon.'

'Really? Ah, but of course, you are the same good knight who has been involved in so many interesting cases in Devon, are you not? You were in Iddesleigh last year, I believe, and Dartmouth, too. I seem to remember hearing of you.'

Baldwin looked at him very directly. 'You wish to complain about my impartiality?'

Despenser was expressionless. 'No, I merely wanted

to ensure that you were the man I was thinking of. It is always refreshing to meet someone whose reputation precedes them.'

Baldwin nodded. He was perfectly aware that this was a warning, but he did not know what he was being warned from. It would warrant consideration. 'Will your wife attend upon the Queen again tomorrow?'

'Of course. She is with Her Majesty every day.'

'Good. I should like to speak to her as well.'

'Why?'

'Just to confirm her impression of the figure she saw kill Mabilla.'

'What is there to find out? He was there in the hall.'

'Did we find a *cuir bouilli* mask to cover his face? No. A green gipon? No again. Cecily was very certain in her description, but it does not tally with the man we found there. I would like to speak to your wife to see what she recalls.'

'I see. Any others?'

'Certainly. I shall also be speaking with Alicia when I have an opportunity.'

'Interesting, that superstition about candles, don't you think?' Despenser said, still eyeing Baldwin. 'Do you think someone here at this table will shortly die, Sir Knight?'

There was a lightness to his tone, as though he was making fun of the superstition, but when Baldwin looked up at him again, he saw only death in the man's eyes.

Chapter Twenty-Two

Now he knew how Jack had got into the Palace, Ellis set his mind to considering how Jack's killer could have found him.

Jack was no easy target. He'd not have spoken of his commission to anyone else. He was far too aware of the dangers of betrayal, especially with a job like this one.

He had made it from here, the south-western point of the wall, into the passageway that led from the upper gallery in the Queen's chapel to her solar. But how on earth had he got there?

Ach, he was wasting his time! He shouldn't be here running about trying to put himself in the mind of a man who was dead. It would do little to help him find the murderer of his sister . . . and yet the fact of being busy lent him some comfort, was helping him to concentrate. Very well, then. *Concentrate.*

Ellis turned away from the Abbey and stared hard back towards the Old Palace Yard. The new cloister and Queen's chamber and chapel were ahead of him. He glanced to left and right. The walls here were completely open from the guards at the other walls. There were some parts where the farther guards would have been hard pushed to see too much, and of course their attention should have been directed outwards, away from the palace itself, to keep an eye open for any possible intruders approaching from outside. Someone already on the walkway would have been at an advantage anyway, because many of the guards would see a figure at the other side of the wall and assume it was one of them. In the darkness it would be natural enough.

Still, if he had to bet, Jack wouldn't want to walk too far on the walkway. No, he'd try to get down to the ground as quickly as possible. There were stairs over to the left, and a . . .

Ellis looked ahead of him. Just in front of him was a small stone building used for storing provisions, and Ellis grinned to himself coldly. That made sense. He had already found a ladder and rope. It would hardly be surprising if he'd found another length of rope. With that a man might let himself down from here, to a place just behind that stone building, so conveniently positioned to conceal someone climbing down the wall.

He strode along the walkway, down the staircase, and over to the rear of the building. There was a small heap of rubbish there. From the look of it, it was clearly a convenient repository for waste from the kitchens. He found a long stick, and thrust it in about the edges, but found nothing. Then he reasoned that Jack would hardly leave a rope in a damp muck heap. Looking about, he could see no sign of one hidden anywhere else, though – until he looked at the roof of the storage room. Eaves overhung the walls by a significant amount, he noticed. Reaching up beneath the shingles, he found that there was a slight shelf at the bottom, and as he ran his fingers along this, he collected a splinter, and then his fingers met a piece of rough hemp. Excellent!

From here, Jack would have had just the one route to the Queen's quarters – across the yard and in by the garden door. Ellis set off in that direction, reaching the door in a few paces. There was a guard waiting there, who watched Ellis as he approached.

'Who are you?' Ellis asked.

'Richard Blaket.'

'Is the Queen in her cloister? I want to see inside – just for a minute. The murderer who killed Mabilla came in this way, I think,' Ellis explained. 'Sir Hugh le Despenser wants to find out how, on behalf of the King, to make sure it doesn't happen again.'

Blaket opened the door for him, and Ellis entered, but once inside, he paused and looked back at him. 'That door, is it locked at night?'

'Usually, yes.'

There was an anxious look to him that told Ellis all. Clearly it hadn't been, the night Mabilla died. Was that because someone had been making it as easy as possible for Jack to come here? Could he have had an accomplice inside the palace?

Suddenly Ellis reckoned he was making some headway.

Baldwin and Simon left the Temple a short while before dusk. To Baldwin, his departure felt like a rout. Despenser had threatened him, that much was quite plain, but Baldwin was unclear what he was being threatened about.

'Do you think it was something to do with Iddesleigh? The damage done to his manor at Monkleigh was bound to have been reported, and then there was the fight down at Dartmouth,' he said.

'You have never been allied with him.'

'I have never allied myself with any political grouping other than the King,' Baldwin said fiercely. 'I demand the right to live in peace with my King. Nothing more.'

The Bishop had collected his horse and he and his men trotted up to join the two. 'Sir Baldwin, I trust you enjoyed your meal? Sir Hugh is an excellent host, is he not?'

'Oh, yes. Most courteous,' Baldwin replied, thinking that it was true, so long as you ignored those brutal, black, unforgiving eyes with the promise of death in them.

'If you do not object, I shall continue to my hall,' the Bishop said wearily. 'I shall see you there. After this morning, I think it would be for the best.'

'Of course, my Lord Bishop,' Baldwin agreed, and the Bishop and his men were soon riding off towards the royal mews at Charing.

'He is a man with a lot on his mind,' Simon said musingly as the others rode away.

A thin rain had begun to fall, and Simon and Baldwin both pulled their hoods up over their heads as they walked. Baldwin was wearing a cloak, but Simon only wore his gipon with a hood incorporating a gorget.

'Simon, have you seen any displays like that in Exeter?'

'What, like the mob outside St Paul's? No, never.

Nobody would dare to insult Bishop Stapledon down there. He's known to be an honourable, decent man back at home. I think it was just the Londoners. You often hear about them attacking the rich and important. They seem to think it's their job to pull people down a peg or two. I doubt it was more than that.'

'I am not so sure. I heard someone mention the "Eyre". I wonder whether the good Bishop has sat on an Eyre, or whether he enforced some decision against the interests of the people of London?'

Simon shook his head. He knew little of any matter outside his own county.

Baldwin sighed. Out here now, he remembered how he had denied his companions within the Temple; he had run at the first moment when asked for his views on his comrades. It felt shameful. He felt defiled.

Soon they were back at the Bishop's house, and they found him sitting up and waiting for them in the main hall. A fire had been lighted in the middle of the floor, and the smoke rose up to the rafters before leaching out between the shingles. It gave the room a warm, homely atmosphere, which was only enhanced when the Bishop's servant brought out a large jug of wine and three cups.

Simon took the proffered cup, his eyes fixed upon the Bishop, and was aware of a vague sensation that something was not quite right. He sniffed his cup, but the wine was good, it wasn't that. The Bishop was watching him closely, and Simon could have sworn that there was a gleam in his eye. It was only when he heard a snigger that he looked again at the servant.

'Rob! What in . . .' He quickly swallowed the heretical

curse, 'What are you doing in the Bishop's uniform?'

'It was my idea, Simon. I thought that his old clothing needed cleaning,' Bishop Walter explained. It was true – after their journey, Rob's clothes were both smelly and threadbare. 'I have many servants here, and the idea of fitting this young fellow out in old clothing seemed not unpleasing. I trust you do not mind?'

'Of course not,' Simon said, eyeing his servant from the corner of his eye. Rob did look much improved. If Simon didn't know better, he'd think that Rob had been washed, too.

'Sir Baldwin, Simon, I offer you a toast to the King: may he confound his enemies!'

The two men drank, then Simon pre-empted Baldwin's question. 'Bishop, what was the matter this morning? The crowd wanted to rip your head off, if I'm any judge.'

Stapledon grunted and peered at Simon over the top of his cup. 'You are right, of course. Well, it's perfectly simple, I'm afraid. Londoners don't like me at all. It's because they don't see the state of the nation's finances, only what I have to do as Lord High Treasurer.' He drew in an irritable breath.

'A King cannot finance a war on his own. The cost of paying troops and buying their arms, armour, mounts . . . in the past, it was easy: a man offered his service to the King, and if the King accepted him, he would provide spending money, food, drink and clothing, and the man would serve the King all his life with honour and fidelity. Now? These days, every man is a mercenary. They come and go depending upon where the money is, and they don't expect to make any oath, other than, "For as long as

Your Lordship pays me".' He grunted and shook his head. 'Well, when I was first Lord High Treasurer, in the fourteenth year of the King's reign, the King asked to hold a Grand Eyre in the city. He wanted the money. That was what he said, but in truth I think he wanted to punish the city for trying to support Lancaster in the disputes earlier that year.

'The Eyre was held along the same lines as those of King Edward, the King's father. So all who possessed a franchise of any form must come to open court in the Tower and declare it and prove their ownership with any documents. If they could not prove their right to hold it, the franchise was lost. Men who had the rights found that they were taken away. And all blamed me for it. It was not fair, but then so much in life is not fair!'

'That crowd was determined,' Baldwin mused. 'Should you not travel with more men to defend you when you enter the city?'

'Oh, they were just a small mob. They had no intention of harming me seriously. I was just a convenient target this morning. If someone else had been there, they would have attacked him.' He gloomily drank off the last of his cup and refilled it. 'What of you, though, Sir Baldwin?'

'Me?'

'Yes, you. I am not in my dotage yet. I saw the way that Sir Hugh stared at you. I tell you plainly, Sir Baldwin, that look worried me.'

Baldwin was about to deny understanding, but then he remembered that feeling from when he had been walking back here, that he had been forced to retreat and not stand up for his companions. In response, he drew his sword and offered it to the Bishop. 'Look at the blade.'

'The Latin?'

'No – the reverse.'

The Bishop peered, tracing the lines with his forefinger. He stiffened, and then nodded very gently. 'A cross?'

Baldwin was surprised, wondering whether the Bishop's eyes were poorer than he had realised. 'It is a specific *type* of cross,' he said.

The man gazed at him very hard for a moment, and then passed the sword back. 'As I said, it is a cross. The symbol of all that is great about our Lord Jesus Christ, and an honourable mark for a knight to wear on his sword. No, the main thing is, you must watch yourself with Sir Hugh. He is a constant ally to the King – but he can yet be prey to strange fancies, and when he grows upset with a man, sometimes he can be quite unforgiving.'

'My Lord Bishop,' Baldwin began, taking back the weapon and thinking that the Bishop had not realised the cross was a sign of the Temple . . . but even as he thought this, the other man turned to him again and met his look with a raised brow.

Suddenly his defence of the Temple in Despenser's presence was explained. This was another man of the Church who had no truck with the fanciful allegations against the Order. He was one of those who recognised that the persecution was nothing more than that: a vicious assault on an innocent brotherhood for motives of profit.

Baldwin sheathed his sword, and bowed his head in

gratitude. 'Let me offer you another toast, my Lord Bishop. To you: your health and long life.'

Ellis reached the Temple late that evening, and strode straight out to the hall where he knew his master would be waiting.

'Good. You're back. What did you learn, then?'

It took Ellis some little while to describe all that he had seen at the Palace that day. When he was finished, Despenser sat back, mulling over the news. 'So – we are no further forward with the facts, then. We have learned much about how Jack got *in* there, but nothing about his killer or why he would want to kill your sister.'

Ellis watched him coldly. He knew his master well enough. Despenser would consider the facts carefully, weighing them, and then reach a conclusion. Although there was something different about him today. Sir Hugh was distracted. There was something else on his mind, obviously. Ellis wasn't blind or stupid. He knew that there were arguments about the Queen's visit to the French, that men had been trying to control Sir Hugh's authority over the King . . . there were plenty of matters to take up the knight's time.

It was all one to Ellis. He was his master's henchman, and no one else would ever have his loyalty. While Sir Hugh lived, Ellis would be his man, and he would die to save his life. Ellis had no time for others. He had made his choice many years ago when he had first come to understand that his master would protect him, and in that time Ellis had never wavered in his loyalty.

'It comes to this, Ellis. We know that someone must

have let an ally of the Queen understand that her life was in danger. And whoever that was, he knew that your sister was helping us to monitor her. Other men would have assumed that the only person spying on her was my wife. Who knew about Mabilla?'

Ellis felt as though his stomach had fallen to his feet; there was a curious rushing noise in his ears. 'Pilk was there that night when you told Jack . . .'

'No, Ellis. He wasn't. Jack threw him out of the room and Pilk went down the stairs. There's no way he could have learned anything about the plan. And it wasn't Jack, because he was always too careful. I know how much you adored your sister, Ellis, so it cannot have been you. And I hope you'll believe me when I say it wasn't me either. No. So – only one other man knew the plan and could have affected our plot.'

Ellis knew who Despenser meant. They had met him in the cloister yard on the day that they briefed Jack. Just before they saw him.

'Yes,' Despenser breathed. 'It must have been him. Piers de Wrotham.'

Ellis frowned. 'But you didn't tell him about Mabilla. How would he learn about her?'

Despenser gave a shamefaced grunt. 'I am afraid I may have mentioned her to him the next day, while you were out. I let it slip to him.'

Chapter Twenty-Three

Sunday, the Morrow of Candlemas[1]

Bishop of Exeter's house, Straunde

Baldwin was already gone from his bed when Simon awoke. It was still dark, and freezing cold. Walking to the window, he peered out, only to find that the inside of the greenish glass was smeared with ice. Shivering, he hurriedly dressed and strode out to the hall.

'Ah, Simon, it is good to see you awake,' Baldwin said as he walked into the room.

Baldwin was standing at the hearth in the middle of the floor, holding his hands to the flames. Although he was the most abstemious man Simon had ever known, regularly drinking fruit juices through the summer when he could, today he had a quart of good ale warming in a jug by the fire, and Simon eyed it jealously before striding to the barrel in the buttery to fetch one for himself.

'You slept well?' Baldwin asked as Simon warmed his knife in the flames and then stirred his ale with it.

---

[1] 3 February 1325

'I think I was asleep as soon as my head hit the pillow. The Bishop has magnificent beds. It is impossible not to sleep well on them.'

Baldwin pulled a grimace. 'Old friend, you could sleep on a bed of rock.'

'I have grown used to a degree of discomfort,' Simon agreed happily as the warmth began to seep slowly back into his fingers. 'It is what a man has to do when he lives on the moors. I had to stay out in all weathers while I was a Bailiff. It makes one appreciate a comfortable bed all the more.'

A servant heard their voices and peeped around the hall's doorway. Baldwin asked for some food and he disappeared, only to return with a platter filled with bread and cold meats. Baldwin and Simon gratefully sat on a bench at the table and broke their fast. It was early for the rest of the household, but as they were not sure what they would be doing this day, the two men were keen to take advantage of meals when they might.

'The Bishop is celebrating Mass in his chapel with his confessor,' Baldwin told Simon, cutting himself a slice of cold chicken. 'I said that we might go to the church here later. Is that all right with you?'

'Yes.' It did not matter to Simon where they celebrated the Mass so long as there was time for them to do so at some point.

In the event, it was late in the morning before they made it to St Clement Dane's Church. They had to look to their horses first, and Baldwin noticed that their packhorse had a degree of lameness. He wouldn't leave the animal until he had seen the Bishop's hostlers and asked them to put a good poultice on it to draw out any bad humours.

Later, when they had returned and eaten a late meal, the two decided to walk about the Bishop's gardens.

It was still cold as they left the house and walked along gravel pathways towards the river. The way had been landscaped. There was a pretty garden of raised beds with vegetables for the kitchen, followed by bushes of soft fruits for the summer, and then an orchard and nuttery. This last was a very recent planting, and the nut trees were a long way from bearing fruit. However, they gave what would in a few years become a shaded walk down to the private jetty where a boat remained tied up.

Baldwin turned and looked back up towards the house. 'Look at that.'

'It is a lovely place,' Simon said. 'I can see now why the Bishop stays up here so often.'

'It is not from choice, Simon. He is forced to stay in London, and I would think much of the time it is against his will. Did you not notice how pale he was last night? That event at the Cathedral terrified him. The mob there could have torn him limb from limb, and he knows it.'

'From what he was saying, it is all because of a misunderstanding,' Simon said.

'That would be little comfort if the misunderstanding led to his death, would it?'

Simon shrugged and grinned. 'It will hardly come to that. Bishop Walter is a friend of the King.'

'Simon, Earls and great Lords have been killed in recent years. Do you think that the London mob would hesitate to kill a Bishop if they thought he had been a tyrant to them? I tell you this: Walter should be careful, and he knows it. He is anxious.'

'If you are right, then he's already being careful, I expect.'

Baldwin looked at him, then nodded towards the river. 'How many guards do you see there?'

'None, but his men are all at the house, of course.'

'What of a wall, then? What is there to deter a man from launching an attack up here from the Thames?'

Simon had to concede that. 'But I am sure that Bishop Walter would be assured of his own safety.'

'I hope so, Simon, because if the Queen herself is in danger, no one is safe. And if an assassin managed to get so close to her . . .'

He was silenced by a call from the house. Glancing that way, both saw a man on the path clad in the blue of a King's messenger, Rob standing at his side and waving at them enthusiastically.

King's Cloister, Thorney Island

'My Liege,' Baldwin said, dropping to his knee. Simon copied him, stifling a curse as he felt a stone that seemed to pierce his knee through his hosen.

'My good knight,' the King said in his French-accented English. 'I asked you to investigate matters for me, I think? But I have heard nothing in return from you. I expected to have news earlier than this.'

'Your Royal Highness, we are continuing to seek to learn all we can.'

'You have no news for me?'

Baldwin was reluctant to apportion blame yet,

especially since the main suspect in his mind was Despenser. He stared down at the gravelled pathway, then sighed. 'This is all I have learned, my King,' he said, and explained how he now felt that it was likely the Queen herself was *not* the intended target. 'Perhaps this was more mundane than we first thought. A man fell in love, he desired Mabilla, but she would not, or could not reciprocate his feelings. So he decided that she must die.'

'The dead man, you mean?'

'I think that he was a hired killer. An assassin. Everything about him seems to show that he was not supposed to be in there. He was not a part of your household, not known by the servants or others. He was a stranger. What would a stranger be doing in your palace at night, Sire, if he was not up to nefarious business?'

The King was silent a moment or two. 'But this is incomprehensible! Why would a man have set himself against an innocent lady like Mabilla . . . I know that my wife has enemies, and it would be understandable if someone had attempted to harm *her*, but Mabilla? She was nothing.' He was bewildered by the thought.

'Why do you think someone could have tried to harm the Queen?'

But King Edward's mind was rushing ahead. The Despenser had been reluctant to explain anything about the attack on the Queen. No, that was not true. The King himself had told him not to explain anything because he was anxious lest he learn something he did not want to know. If he was to discover that Hugh had indeed tried to kill his wife, that would have been an appalling situation. For then Edward would have had a responsibility to protect the Lady Isabella. To do otherwise would have been the grossest treason to her. Unthinkable.

And yet . . .

Hugh was perfectly capable of such cold reasoning. King Edward had seen that in him before. He was a most competent rationalist. When he wanted something and there was an obstacle, he simply sought the most effective means of bypassing it. Sometimes it meant capturing people and torturing them; occasionally he merely had them executed.

The King did not doubt Hugh's personal devotion to him. Their feeling for each other went deep, like the love of those whose souls were united. It was inconceivable that Hugh would do anything directly to harm Edward. But if he *had* sought to hurt the Queen, King Edward needed to know.

King Edward was no ruthless tyrant. He wanted a happy kingdom, for all within it to be content. But he was the King, and that meant he had responsibilities. One was to ensure that if a man thought he could remove the Queen, he should be warned away. He should have been more masterful the other day when he first tried to tax Hugh with the crime and then changed his mind.

'What else do you propose to do?' he asked the knight rather absently.

Baldwin sighed deeply. 'My Liege, there is little more a man like me can do. I have no authority here. Surely it would be best for Your Majesty's own Coroner, John of Evesham, to investigate this matter?'

'A Coroner? What use would that be? I need someone who is used to hunting killers, not a glorified clerk whose only interest is to record details of wounds and weapons so that a bill can be set against someone at a later date. No, you are better placed to seek the truth here, Sir Baldwin.'

'You have other Keepers of your Peace in London, though,' Baldwin continued to prevaricate. 'Surely they must have better information than I? Would you not be better advised to ask one of them to look into this and—'

'Mon *Sieur* Baldwin, I am *commanding* you to continue to investigate this matter and find who is responsible for committing this terrible murder of my lady-in-waiting to the Queen!'

'But there is another possibility, My King. Have you considered that the lady could have been murdered by the dead man found behind your throne? Perhaps he killed her and then was killed in his turn. The man who punished the assassin was responsible for bringing justice on his head.' There was a new idea there, one which made Baldwin frown again. The body was discovered *right behind* the throne. Suddenly he wanted to be away from this King and talking to Simon.

'My friend, if someone was to kill an enemy of my Queen, he would also be killing an enemy of mine. There is no difference between us. An enemy of one is an enemy of both. Were he to do that, do you think he would not have come to me for a reward?'

Baldwin nodded slowly. 'That is possible, but . . .'

'No, it is more than possible! Sieur Baldwin, you do not understand life in a royal court, I fear. I do. I know the men here, and their motives. They would not hesitate to inform me of anything whatever which redounded to their credit. Oh yes! If one of them had killed this foul assassin, they would have been knocking on the door to my private chamber no matter what the time.' He permitted himself a cynical smile.

Baldwin could see the logic of this, but he dared not raise the possibility which had just occurred to him.

'So, Sieur,' King Edward continued, 'the lady was undoubtedly murdered by this other man. He learned that he had a competitor, and killed him too. That is my conviction. Someone had desired to kill the Lady Mabilla, and succeeded, but then met with this second man and had to kill him too.'

Baldwin smiled and nodded. 'Of course, Sire.' He was in a hurry to leave this chamber and escape out into the fresh air where he could think again.

'So please continue,' the King concluded, 'and as soon as you learn something that might explain this whole sorry affair, let me understand your thinking.'

The royal audience was at an end.

Out in the Old Palace Yard, Baldwin grabbed Simon's arm and drew him away to a shed that had been built against the western wall.

'Baldwin, are you all right?'

'The body, Simon! The body of the man,' Sir Baldwin said urgently. 'Where was it found?'

'Right behind the throne, of course.'

'And what sort of symbolism could have been meant by that?'

The Bailiff winced. 'Ah. The power?'

'Yes.' Baldwin closed his eyes and leaned back against the stones of the wall. 'I do not understand how I could have failed to see that! The body was set out behind the throne, his prickle cut off and shoved into his mouth. It was obviously a warning to his paymaster, to a man who is a sodomite, but who is also the power behind the throne. *Despenser.*'

'So what do you want to do now?' Simon said quietly.

'What do I want? I want to escape this madhouse, fly back homewards and never return,' Baldwin said bitterly. 'What am I doing here? I am a good Keeper back in Crediton. I can read the laws and help keep them in Exeter. I can show my skills as a questioner and usually I can bear down upon people to find the truth. And that is all I ever seek, Simon. Just the truth. It is the only thing that matters in the end.'

'So what is the truth here?'

'Here? The truth is, I think, that the dead man was hired to come here to kill someone. Someone else learned of his plans, met him here and murdered him instead. When he was dead, his body was defiled in that abominable manner, and then the man responsible sought poor Mabilla, killing her.'

'You still think that the Queen was not the target?'

'If that was what our assassin intended, he would have been able to finish his task. There were only two women opposing him: Alicia and the Queen herself. How could they have protected themselves against one ruthless man with a dagger?'

'Perhaps he wasn't that strong?'

Baldwin looked at him. 'The fellow had got to the

palace where he was not permitted. That demonstrates at the least a level of determination that many would like to be able to copy. No, I believe he would have entered here and . . .'

He was suddenly still. Simon looked at him warily. 'You have had another thought, haven't you?'

'Well, it's just that if he didn't come from hereabouts, he must have used a horse, which will be tethered somewhere close. However, a man on horseback at night is a rare sight, and always suspicious. More likely this fellow was bright enough to walk here. But he couldn't come here on foot from too far away, could he? No, he would want an inn or tavern as his base. Perhaps he rented a room?'

Simon latched on to what he was saying. 'Think, Baldwin! If a man came here and succeeded in killing, say, the Queen, the first thing to happen would be that the King's men would smother the neighbourhood. If he had taken a room in a house nearby, the owner would know if he rose in the middle of the night and trotted off. No household is so quiet that a man could go abroad without someone being aware, and as soon as the men-at-arms arrived, mine host would become thoroughly talkative. If this fellow was staying nearby, he was either sleeping rough . . . no, it is too cold – unless he made his own camp, but about here that would be too obvious. So, not a camp . . . I would guess he stayed in a small inn or tavern. A place large enough for him to be anonymous, not a small house where his coming and going would be too obvious.'

'Yes – you are absolutely right. He would have to be

staying in a place where his movements would be easily concealed – possibly somewhere that was already so busy, that he could justifiably demand space in a barn or hayloft,' Baldwin said thoughtfully.

'Because then he could slip away in the darkness and no one would see him,' Simon agreed.

Baldwin set off across the yard.

'Hey – where are you going?' Simon called out.

'We need some men to search all the little inns and taverns hereabouts. If I understand my orders, I have been instructed to find out all I may about this man. I shall do so, then. I will command the King's Sergeant to send riders to seek this place.'

Chapter Twenty-Four

Ellis had been at the palace from an early hour, and at midday he was in the main hall again, leaning against one of the pillars and staring at the throne. There had to be some reason why Jack had been killed and left here to be found. What that reason might be, he had no idea. All he was certain of was that if Jack had been there when the Queen passed by, he would have killed her. Of course, if another woman was in his way, like Mabilla, he might have been forced to hurt her, perhaps even kill her, in order to achieve his end. But none of those women would have been able to stop him.

Which meant that the man who attacked Mabilla *was not* Jack; thus her murderer was still abroad.

He was about to go and study Jack's body again, just to see if anything else occurred to him, when he heard shouts and the rattle of horses' hooves in the New Palace Yard. No man who was handy with a weapon could ignore the sound of cavalry. He hurried out to watch, and saw thirty or forty men on horseback streaming from the gate. Another twenty or so marched out with pikes on their shoulders.

'Where are they going?' he asked a cleric nearby.

'They've been ordered to look for the place where the assassin may have been staying.'

'Who ordered them to do so?'

'Those two.'

Ellis took in the sight of Baldwin and Simon over at the far side of the yard. He was not surprised. However, when he saw the pair of them make their way to the Exchequer, he was intrigued. They must surely be going back to the hall as well, just as he had. There was a connecting door from the Exchequer to the dais behind the throne.

On a whim, he decided to listen to them, and he hurried off into the Green Yard before entering the Great Hall at the screens. Peering within, he could see the two men crouched behind the throne, and he slipped inside silently, walking up along the line of pillars, out of their sight, until he was only a matter of yards from them and could hear their conversation.

The Bailiff was saying, 'Look at it. There is not enough.'

'Let us take a look behind the tapestry. No – nothing there either. But the fact remains that the man was stabbed, had his tarse cut off and shoved into his mouth. Any of those wounds will have caused a deal of bleeding, but there is nothing in here.'

'It's hardly surprising, of course,' Simon Puttock said sensibly. 'This hall is constantly being used as a corridor between one or another chamber. No one in his right mind would come here and do something like *that* to a man's body in full view of anyone who might walk in.'

'Well, the lack of blood bears out your thoughts,

Simon. So, the next question has to be: where on earth is all the blood? Where was he killed?'

'If the killer was a man from here, from the palace itself, he could know any number of little nooks and crannies.'

'And yet . . .'

'Yes?'

'If the man knew his victim was an assassin, we can suppose that the assassin was killed on his way to the killing or on the way back. If it was on the way back, we know that he did *not* intend to hurt the Queen, but was merely attempting to worry her, or had another motive and was always planning to kill the girl who died. The Queen in that case becomes merely an innocent witness.'

'So where was he killed?'

'Well, Simon, there are two entrances to this hall. We came in through one, the Exchequer. The only other one is the main entrance at that end there. The man was not too heavy, but I'd guess that even he would have been an uncomfortable weight to drag or carry too far. I would bet that he was near here when he died.'

'In the hall here?'

'That would be one possibility, but I have looked about the place a little, and have seen no sign of blood. No, I think we should look outside in the screens passage, the service chambers and the lower rooms near the King's rooms.'

Ellis listened as they marched along the hall, gradually sidling about the pillar as they grew level and passed by him. Then he walked down the outer aisle, careful to move quietly and keep from the view of the entrance. Soon he heard them again.

'Nothing here. If there were, we'd have seen it when we were in here the other day.'

'Very well, Simon. Come, we must check in the buttery and pantry.'

There was a pause, and then a call full of dejection. 'Nothing here, either, Baldwin.'

'Nor here, Simon. This is madness. Logic says that the man must have been killed nearby. To carry a dead weight in the middle of the night with no candle or other aid would be extremely difficult.'

'Baldwin . . .'

'What, Simon?'

'What of that door there?'

'It leads to the King's chapel, I believe.'

'Is it locked?'

There was a pause for a few moments. 'It is open, Simon. Come on.'

Ellis sneaked to the opening and listened carefully. He knew the door in question. It led into the ground-floor level of the King's chapel. It was always locked usually, to ensure the King's privacy, and his steward would only unlock it for Masses during which the King's household would join him in prayers. It oughtn't to be open.

As he peeped around the doorway, he heard them again.

'Look here, Baldwin.'

Ellis leaned forward to see what Simon was speaking of, but as he did so, he felt a boot hit his ankle, and his leg was swept away, in an instant he was on the ground. He snarled as he rolled over to spring up, only to find himself gazing along the length of Sir Baldwin's sword into the knight's dark eyes.

'I would like to speak with you, friend.'

William Pilk was with his master as Sir Hugh le Despenser left the Temple and set off along the road towards the Great Hall at Thorney Island. Not solely William, naturally. The Despenser was so convinced of his importance that he always tried to travel with a large entourage of men.

A good thing too, if the events of yesterday were anything to go by. The Bishop could have been dead with all those men throwing rocks at him. It would only take one to knock him down and the mob would have been on him. Pilk had seen it often enough before. When someone in power could be shown to be vulnerable, the crowds would enjoy ripping them limb from limb.

'Pilk. Here.'

'My Lord?'

'When we get there, go and see how Ellis is doing. I want someone to keep an eye on him.'

'Eh?' Pilk stared at him.

Despenser favoured him with a look. 'I don't entirely distrust him, Pilk. But if I am to have a replacement for my steward and henchman soon, I'd best make sure that the man whom I trust is the one who watches him, eh?'

William Pilk felt his breast swell with pride. The idea that his master could think of installing him in Ellis's place had never occurred to him. It was a proof, as if he needed it, of how much trust his master was putting in him now.

'I'll do it.'

'Good. If there's something urgent, come to tell me. I'll be in the King's private chamber, I expect.'

Pilk settled back, trying to look forbidding and strong, as he should now he had the Despenser's full trust. A man like him was powerful. There were few others who could hope to emulate him. This was the sort of thing he'd dreamed of when he was younger, that he'd get to be the senior man in a great household like Sir Hugh's. And now it was coming true – Sir Hugh was giving him responsibility.

His master didn't trust Ellis any more than he should – that was obvious from the way he had asked Pilk to watch the man. No surprise there. Anyone with a brain could see he was unreliable, whereas Pilk had never failed. He was clever, he knew that. With a little luck and by using his brain, he would make his fortune.

With such cheering thoughts, he scarcely noticed their way. Long before he expected it, he could see the enormous belfry tower of the Abbey up ahead, and then they were off King Street and were riding in under the great gatehouse.

All here knew Sir Hugh, of course. The porters ducked their heads as he passed, whether he noticed or not. If they had not, he *would* have noticed, and as soon as he saw a dereliction of respect for a knight like himself, he would have them arrested instantly. He could make use of his authority as a household knight and member of the King's inner council to ensure that any servant's life could grow uncomfortable or downright painful. And any man who tried to complain would have the King to contend with, which would usually mean an even greater punishment, because Edward was ruthless towards any who caused trouble for his friends. Since the capture and murder of Gaveston, no one had been in any doubt that Edward would visit unequalled retribution upon them.

Pilk was still feeling that sense of warmth as he dropped from his mount and threw the reins to a waiting groom. The fellow caught them, frowning slightly at the arrogance of the action, but Pilk knew he was safe. Even grooms knew their places here, and the man's eyes flashed to Despenser briefly before he took the horse away to the stables.

As Sir Hugh dismounted and made his way towards the Green Yard, tugging off his gauntlets as he went, Pilk walked to the Exchequer to see where Ellis could have gone. There was no sign of anyone there, though. The door was locked. So Pilk walked out to the Green Yard, and from there, he went in by the screens door to the Great Hall.

There he immediately saw his master standing before the knight Sir Baldwin.

'I demand to know the meaning of this!' Sir Hugh was bellowing.

Sir Baldwin was calm, but his eyes did not blink, which Pilk immediately thought made him look dangerous, as did the sword which was in his hand. Behind him on the floor lay Ellis, while another sword lay resting on his breast, the grinning Bailiff holding the hilt.

'I was asking this man why he was following me and eavesdropping on my conversations with the Bailiff here.'

'And you had to knock him down to do that, I suppose?'

'Yes. I didn't want him to try to attack me,' Baldwin said. He still hadn't blinked, Pilk noticed. The man stood very still, his sword's point towards the ground, across his front, so that whenever he needed to, he could flick it straight up at his opponent.

'Let him up at once!'

'Certainly, but it will be your responsibility if he tries anything foolish,' Baldwin said. He stepped back swiftly, and nodded to his companion, who withdrew his own sword.

Ellis looked up at the two men, and as soon as he was sure that he was safe, he rolled over and pushed himself upwards. His sword was in his scabbard still, and for an instant he thought about drawing it. Sir Hugh was silent, and Pilk wondered whether this was a part of the Despenser's plan, to see Sir Baldwin provoke Ellis into an indiscreet attack. It would be sure to be helpful either way – whether Ellis killed Sir Baldwin or the other way about. Best, of course, would be for both to kill each other.

But Ellis was not angry enough to miss the danger in the Devon knight's eyes. There were plenty of knights who bought their knighthoods with money that they had accumulated through their mercantile ventures. As soon as a man reached a certain value of income, he was expected and required to become a knight. It was how the nation kept its stock of warriors. Not this man. Although the sword looked almost new, without the scratches and nicks that spoke of past battles, that proved nothing. Plenty of men had nice, new, shiny swords because they had over-used their old ones. If he had to guess, he'd say this man was in possession of two or three swords that had seen good service.

'I'll ask you again: what were you doing following us?'

'I was just walking along the hall, and when I reached this door, you knocked me down for no reason,' Ellis growled.

'There. Clearly this has been a misunderstanding,' Sir Hugh said with a smile. 'I suggest you put up your swords, lordings. We aren't in the West Country now. It must be good for you to come to civilisation once in a while. Oh . . . Sir Baldwin. How is Iddesleigh? Have you been to see my manor at Monkleigh recently? It is not in very good shape since you were there last. Still, your little manor at Fùrnshill is all right, is it not? A nice place, so I am told. And I believe that you have a lovely wife and child there.'

Baldwin's face did not alter. Pilk could have sworn it was graven in stone, he was so still. And then he smiled gently, and carefully pushed his sworn into the scabbard. 'My Lord, I have a wonderful family. They are so precious to me that if any man were to try to *touch* them, I would see to his immediate destruction.'

'You think to threaten me, man?' Sir Hugh said. Pilk reckoned there was no anger in his voice, only a kind of mingled wonder and amusement. 'And what would you do if I, for example, burned your house to the ground with your family inside it, eh? And Sir Baldwin, I *could* do just that, if I chose. So don't make me choose. Let me remain contented and at peace, so that you and I do not fall out. I am a good master to my vassals and friends, you know. There is no need for you or your companion there to look for strife. Consider it. We could be friends.'

'Why do you seek to offer me this, Sir Hugh?' Baldwin said. 'What use could my friendship have for you? What value, what utility, would I have for a great magnate, the King's own friend?'

'Nothing. I make the offer freely,' Sir Hugh said, his hands outspread, palms up in sign of openness.

'No,' Baldwin said consideringly. 'You wish to have something concealed about these murders. Perhaps it could be convenient for you to have me silenced.'

'I think that things would be rather more advantageous for you, if you were to listen. It will mean you have a strong ally. Of course, if you prefer, I could be an enemy.'

Pilk smiled at that. The last few words had been spoken in that gruff voice which he and the others in the household recognised only too clearly. When he spoke like that, Sir Hugh le Despenser meant that he'd break someone's leg if they didn't do exactly as he wished.

Baldwin's eyes narrowed. 'So clearly it is something you are very worried about. I think that will make our investigation more interesting.'

'It will,' Sir Hugh said. He smiled. 'Indeed, it will.'

Coroner John was unhappy. This new Keeper, Sir Baldwin, was a companion of Bishop Walter of Exeter, and that meant he was a close ally of Despenser, so his words could scarcely be trusted on any level. A friend of Despenser was an enemy of justice, in Sir John's simple belief.

Yet the man had been instructed to find out what had happened to Mabilla, and who had killed the assassin. That should have been a weight off John's mind, but in many ways it left him feeling that the entire investigation was to be whitewashed. Nothing of any importance would be discovered by men like that Sir Baldwin. The Bishop and Despenser had carved up the realm between them, and they were not the sort of men who would threaten their own positions. If there was skulduggery afoot, it was more than likely due to those two, so their own placemen would uncover nothing.

John didn't like that. Which was why he was now descending into the filth of the main gaol to visit the guard from the southern wall, Arch.

It cost him a whole shilling to bribe the gaoler to open the ancient door so that he could enter the foul chamber.

'Leave me, please leave me!'

Sir John had seen enough torture victims in his time to be unshaken, but from a professional viewpoint, he was disgusted. To have so destroyed this man was unnecessary and pointless. He had been broken in spirit, and from the look of his arms, in parts of his body too. Anything he had said at the extremity of his pain was irrelevant. Everyone knew that, who had ever questioned a man in this condition.

'I will leave you, but I want to ask you some questions first,' he said.

'I know nothing more – nothing! Please, I can tell you nothing!'

'The night – you know the night I mean. You were drunk.'

'No! No! I had nothing!'

'You fell asleep at your post.'

'No! I was awake.'

'You kept no watch. The assassin crept past you.'

'He must have been there already.'

'You saw him?'

'No. I only saw the Queen's guard on his rounds. No one else.'

John smiled. 'And he knocked you down?'

'No! No, he was keeping lookout. There was nervousness in the palace.'

'You were asleep as soon as you arrived, I suppose? Everyone says you were lax in your work.'

'No! I was awake until late. It was after the moon when I got hit.'

'The moon?' The Coroner was puzzled by that. 'What of it? What do you mean?'

'It had a halo. I haven't seen such a one before. A halo all about it – the man must have come after that.'

And that, John told himself later, was the most perplexing aspect of it all. The man repeated those words several times – about the moon and its halo. And yet that had no bearing on anything, surely.

Simon followed Baldwin into the open. A fine rain had begun to fall, but Simon wanted to get as far away from the hall as possible. He stood in the rain with his eyes wide open, staring up at the heavens.

'Sweet Christ, Baldwin! Did you have to antagonise him like that?'

'Simon, he was testing us. Trust me. While we have

the King's favour and he wants us to carry on with this investigation, we are safe from Despenser.'

'What, even down a darkened alleyway? Or near the river? It's easy for a man like him to pay some felon to loop a rope about our necks, tie us to a rock and just throw us into the Thames. It's easier still for him to pay a man to slip a dagger between our ribs. Sweet Christ! He threatened Jeanne, man, didn't he? He more or less warned you off, or he'd burn the manor to the ground.'

'And what would you have had me do, Simon?' Baldwin asked with torment in his voice. 'Would you prefer me to have bobbed my head and act obedient, like any number of those fools who work for him? I cannot do that, old friend. I am a knight, when all is said and done.'

'But Baldwin . . .'

The knight turned to face him. He stood so close, Simon could see the fine lines at the corners of his eyes, the way that his beard curled back from the point of his chin to face towards his ears, the small tracery of thin veins that crept across his nose. And last of all, Simon saw the great misery in his eyes. The all-encompassing anxiety.

'Simon, do you think I do not know what danger Jeanne and my children are in? Despenser is the most powerful baron in the country. He has the King's ear. They could easily destroy me and mine in a moment. But what else could I do? Back down and agree to find nothing? What would the King say, were I to tell him that? Or I could tell Despenser that I would actively do nothing, in which case he would own me and be able to tell the King that I had lied to him. I could do nothing other than what I did, unless I wanted to be owned, body and soul, by Despenser in the future.'

'Our families, Baldwin,' Simon whispered.

'I know. But what would you have me tell him? That I'd support any lie, that I'd agree to have another man declared guilty, when perhaps he was innocent? That is the sort of sport in which Despenser revels. He would toy with us, find a man who had nothing to do with the killings, and have him hanged just for pure devilment. He is a man without compassion, Simon. All he knows is the abuse of power and how to force others to his will.'

'So what can we do?'

Baldwin sighed and looked away. 'My fear, my great fear, is that *he* was directly responsible. He is the sort of man who would have a multitude of assassins at his beck and call. He can give them money, and he can protect them. If one was found out and arrested, Despenser could use bribery or coercion to have him released. Who else would know where to find a man like that dead one? And then, as you said before, the symbol of the tarse shoved in his mouth – that to me looks like a warning. To the man who is the power behind the throne.'

'But you told me . . .'

'Simon, old friend, you were talking in front of the Coroner. He is a stranger. He could be an ally of Despenser, for all we know. It was dangerous to speak frankly in his company.'

Simon privately thought it was a great deal less dangerous than talking back to Despenser as he had just done.

'I am sorry,' the knight said quietly. 'I wish to God that

we had never come here. I knew it would be dangerous.'

'You never wanted to come.'

'No, but the Bishop persuaded me. I thought, looking at him, listening to him, that it was not possible *not* to come. The way that the Queen was being treated was too deplorable. I felt I ought to make an effort – that was why I agreed to come to London. It is not a parliament with the representatives of all estates, it is to be a council. But that itself means that each voice will have more authority. I thought I could make a difference, Simon. And the only difference I am likely to make is to alienate my family from the King. Sweet *Jesus*!' He clenched his fist. 'I was a fool, and now I've upset the King's best friend.'

There was no need for words. All knew how the Despenser was likely to treat an enemy. Simon cleared his throat. 'Well, we're still alive for now. Surely the best thing for us to do would be to find the blood, if we can. I don't know – perhaps if we discover the answer to the killings, we may also find some arrows we can fire back at Sir Hugh le Despenser and protect ourselves?'

'Perhaps,' Baldwin said. He stared at the ground.

The rain was steadily worsening. Already little puddles were forming on the thinner gravel, and Simon could feel a rivulet trickling down between his shoulders. He rubbed a hand through his hair and pulled his hood over his head. 'Come, old friend. Standing here will serve no useful purpose.'

'Where could he have died, though?'

'Baldwin, I do not know. Christ's pains, perhaps we were right about the chapel? It would explain why Sir

Hugh and his man were so interested when we arrived there.'

'True.'

It would have been good if he was right. Sadly, the two had only chosen that position because they had seen the shadow of the man listening to them and following them. The dim light from the windows had at least served that useful purpose. And when Simon saw the door, he had thought to draw out the spy. It had worked, but there was no indication that a body had lain there, nor that a man had been dragged from the place.

They found a small shed which had an open door, and sheltered inside. 'It would be ironic if that *was* where the man was killed,' Baldwin said musingly.

'Perhaps it will grow more obvious as we discover more about the killing.'

'How can we learn anything about the murders? We cannot even be sure about the intended victim yet. I can guess – but I cannot *know* for certain. Perhaps he was an inexperienced assassin, who killed one woman and was afraid to find another woman challenging him.'

'We have learned about other murders often enough when there was less information,' Simon pointed out in an attempt to cheer him.

'But without the risks to ourselves,' Baldwin said gloomily. 'Whether we succeed or fail, I do not know which is the greater danger.' He slumped against the wall, staring out at the rain.

Simon had never seen him like this before. His friend had always been strong, purposeful, focused. To see him in this dejected condition was alarming – especially now, when both of them had been warned by Sir Hugh. His concern, not only for his friend, but for the position they found themselves in, lent acid to his tone.

'Then ignore them!' Simon snapped. 'Baldwin, we're in this now. There's no point complaining. All we can do is our best, and the devil with Despenser. We have a duty to learn the truth and report it to the King. That is our duty – so let us do it!'

Baldwin looked at him and gave a half-grin. 'You should have been a general, Simon. You have the gift of motivation.' He stirred himself and stood again, and suddenly the light was back in his eyes.

'That's better. I feel like a hound who had lost the scent in a river, who mournfully sat down, unsure where to go next and how to find it again – only to be guided by his berner to greater efforts. You are my expert berner, Simon. I should change your name to that. Right! We have had no joy in seeking the place of the man's death. We had assumed that it must be near to the place where the body was discovered. Ah! But we think that the same person killed the assassin and then went on to murder the lady-in-waiting. That would mean that the killer had to go from the hall, or wherever the assassin died, to the corridor where the Queen's party was assaulted. Yes! Come, Simon, let us try this new theory.'

Chapter Twenty-Five

Great Hall, Thorney Island

The Coroner made his way to the kitchen, where he learned that the sergeant-cooks could remember nothing about seeing Arch in there on the night of the murder.

'Yeah, he's usually here before dark, long before he has to get up to his post, but I think he was knackered after the day before, and he didn't come down as usual. Not that I remember, anyhow.'

John left the kitchen with a vague feeling that something was beginning to come together into a coherent story. On a whim, he went up to Arch's post and gazed about him. These walls were solid stone, and stood yards high. When he peered over the top, he shook his head. Anyone throwing a grapnel up here would be heard. If Arch was truly sober, he must have been alerted by the ringing of steel. A man might muffle it with a cloak about the metal, but that held its own dangers, for the metal could miss its mark.

No. He must have been drunk.

Returning across the Old Palace Yard, he saw a guard standing at the gate and recognised him as Blaket.

'Do you recall anything special about the moon on the night the Queen's maid died?'

Blaket looked at him blankly. 'The moon?'

'Yes. Did it have a halo?'

'Oh, yes. It was still and cool, and when the clouds cleared late into the evening, there was a great halo about it. That was late, though. About the middle watch.'

'Was it really?' Coroner John said to himself. He gazed about him, leaving the guard at his post.

If Arch was awake enough to see the moon that late, then the man couldn't have been drunk, as had been alleged. He had been knocked down, if his story was to be believed. The assassin must have done that. And then he made his way down to the corridor to kill Mabilla, leaving Arch lying unconscious up on the wall.

Arch was not guilty of dereliction of his duty. He had been tortured for no purpose. But that was of secondary interest just now. John had to see whether he knew any more.

Pilk found himself alone. Sir Hugh had entered the King's private chamber, and Ellis remained outside the door together with one of the King's own men, both guarding their masters. It left little for Pilk to do, so he wandered aimlessly along the corridor, then went down the staircase to the ground floor. He was about to leave by the Great Hall's screens passage, when he heard the voices approaching.

There was nowhere to hide. He could have retraced his steps, but before he could try that, the Bailiff and the knight turned the corner and stood facing him.

'You are with Despenser, then?' Baldwin said, eyeing Despenser's arms on Pilk's breast.

'Yes. I am one of his trusted men.'

'I am sure of it. You look a trustworthy fellow. Tell me, did you know the dead assassin well?'

Pilk curled his lip. 'No. I hardly knew him at all.'

'But you *did* know him?'

'Jack? Many of us did.'

'And by "us" you mean?'

Pilk was aware of a sharpness in the knight's voice. It made him wary. 'Just people. Nothing more.'

'You weren't thinking of any group in particular?'

'No.'

'Your name is?'

'I don't have to give it you.'

'No, you don't. However, if I were to go to your master and tell him how grateful I was for all your help, and the fact you told me that all his household knew the dead assassin . . . do you think he would be happy? You see, Sir Hugh had already told me he knew nothing about the man. I doubt he will be glad to know you've shown him to be a liar.'

Pilk said immediately, 'Jack was known by some of us, that's all. Sir Hugh probably never met him.'

'Don't lie to me, fellow! I have been lied to by experts, and you are not one of them. *What is your name*, I asked.'

'Pilk. William Pilk.'

'Well, now, William Pilk. What did you know of this assassin?'

'Nothing. He was just one of those men you see about occasionally.'

'And when did you last see him?'

'I don't know!'

'Days ago? Weeks? Months?'

'Weeks, I suppose.'

'Where?'

'In the . . .'

'In the Temple,' Baldwin completed for him. 'And who was there with him?'

'You ask Sir Hugh. Leave me alone.'

'Good, Pilk. So it was Sir Hugh, then. And who was Jack supposed to kill?'

'I don't know.'

'The Queen?'

'No! If I knew anything like that, I'd not have— I'm no traitor, and I won't have anyone say I am!'

'Then I must ask you again: who was Jack told to kill?'

'I don't *know*! I wasn't there.'

'Where were you?'

Pilk looked at him resentfully. 'I was with Jack when he first got there, but they sent me off. Didn't want me listening, I expect.'

'A shame. Still, perhaps you could still be of use.'

'Oh, no.'

'Where were you on the night that the assassin Jack and the woman Mabilla were killed?'

'Me? I was at the Temple. We all were.'

'Your entire household?'

'Yes, probably.'

'Who was not there – *probably*?'

Pilk looked at the knight, bitterly angry. 'Are you like

this all the time? I don't know. The man, Jack – they say he tried to kill Mabilla and died early in the morning. I'd have been asleep, and so would all sensible folk. I don't know more than that.'

'You know the palace, though, don't you?'

'What palace?'

Baldwin allowed a gentle silkiness to infect his voice. '*This* palace, Pilk. This one in which we stand right now. Do you know the thoroughfares here?'

'I know a few corridors, if that's what you mean.'

'It is precisely what I mean. Can you show us the quickest way from the Great Hall to the Queen's solar?'

Pilk looked at him and then shrugged. If that was the way to get rid of them . . . 'Yeah. If you want.'

With his assistance Baldwin and Simon soon reached the Queen's cloister. They were led along a passageway with windows that looked out over the river, then up some stairs and down others with enough turns to make even Simon confused.

'It is easier in the countryside where you can keep an eye on the sun,' he grumbled.

Pilk said nothing, but his contempt for rural peasants who could not make sense of a simple set of corridors was evident in the look he gave Simon. At the door to the Queen's chambers, he left them with a scowling pair of guards.

'We are looking into the murder of the Queen's lady-in-waiting, on the orders of the King,' Baldwin said, but the guard shook his head.

'I've been told no one's to go through here today. If I

could, I'd let you pass, Sir Baldwin. I want to know who was responsible for killing Mabilla as much as the next man, but I can't break my orders.'

'Could you do the next best thing then, and pass a message through to the ladies inside? We wish to speak with Lady Eleanor and Madam Alicia.'

'I can try. If you'll wait here,' the guard offered, and when Baldwin and Simon agreed to wait, he opened the gate and passed inside.

He was gone some little while, and then the gate opened, and a petite blonde woman came through it.

She was young, with a round face and thinnish lips that could have looked hard, if it were not for her laughing eyes. They were slanted, and the clear blue of cornflowers in the summer. When she looked at Simon, he was convinced that she was a flirt. She had that kind of slightly over-wide eye, an appraising look to her, that spoke of a maid keen on the natural pleasures.

'I am Alicia. You wanted to speak to my mistress, Lady Eleanor? I am afraid that my Lady received a message this morning advising her against aiding you, gentles. Perhaps it was thought that your interrogation might unsettle her delicate spirits?'

'Perhaps it was,' Baldwin agreed. He smiled. 'I assume you would not suffer in a similar manner, then?'

'Oh, Sir Knight, I do not think that there is anything a man could do would alarm me overmuch.'

'I believe you, if all I have heard is true.'

'You mean the attack when Mabilla died? Yes. That was a dreadful experience.'

'Can you describe the man?'

'No. I am afraid I didn't take much in – I was so shocked and fearful. All of us were.'

Simon frowned. 'But we heard that you were fine. You stood up to the man boldly enough.'

'Ah, but I am only a woman, sir. He was a fearsome man, masked and armed. The picture of masculinity and malice. I could not recall anything about him.'

'You are sure of this?'

She looked up at him with wide, less-than-innocent eyes. 'But of course, Sir Baldwin. Why, would you like to put me to the test?'

There was a lazy eroticism in the way she spoke, tilting her head and moving ever so slightly, the skirts of her tunic swaying suggestively. And as he coloured, she laughed with genuine delight, walking back through the gate, nodding to the guard, and glancing once over her shoulder at them, before she disappeared.

'You shouldn't trust all she says.'

Simon and Baldwin turned to see Joan. She was the lady-in-waiting to the Queen who had fled at the sight of the man, Baldwin recalled. 'Mistress?'

Unlike Alicia, who appeared fully recovered, Joan had clearly not got over her shock yet. Baldwin supposed that it was natural enough in the circumstances. Sadly, it made almost anything she could tell them largely irrelevant. Baldwin had often found that eyewitnesses were unreliable, but the worst were those like this woman, who had been so terrified that, after a mere glimpse of the scene of horror, she had run away.

'Alicia says things to spice up her life,' Joan explained. 'She likes to flirt, Sir Baldwin.'

'What would you not trust about her evidence?'

'She said she did not remember the man? I think she did.'

'Do *you* remember what he looked like?' Simon asked.

'Of course, sir. He was a little under your height, Sir Baldwin.' She stepped towards the knight and studied his face. 'And younger. Much younger. Less of a paunch, I would say, and very light on his feet, like a dancing man.'

'I thank you for your observations,' Baldwin said, smiling a little. 'Why do you think he was younger than me?'

'You mean because of his little mask? Ah, even in the candlelight there were very few wrinkles or worry-lines about his mouth. And his hair had no hints of grey,' she added, reaching up to gesture at his own greying temples. 'And the way he moved, it was plain to me that he was a fit, young man – although he wasn't a knight.'

'Oh? How do you know that?'

'His neck was not so thick and muscled. A knight who is trained to the joust will always have a neck that is built to hold the weight of a tilting helm, will he not? And this man's shoulders, too, were not so bulky. He was altogether a smaller-framed man than you, Sir Knight.' She glanced back towards the gate to the garden.

'His clothing?'

'He had all grey and brown, except for his gipon. That was different, because although it was not emerald, it was a good, fresh green.'

Sir Baldwin gruffly cleared his throat. 'Joan, we are

keen to learn all we can about the man who entered the palace and was killed. Do you know of anyone who could help us?'

'There is one, I think,' she said. 'Arch, the guard up at the wall, was found the next morning, snoring.'

'Yes?'

'It's said that he's often up there in the morning, usually snoring because he drinks so much.'

'What of him?'

Joan shrugged and pulled her mouth into a little moue. 'I am often sent to fetch wine and ales for my Lady and the other ladies-in-waiting. When I spoke to the steward in the buttery next morning, he said that Arch hadn't been near the ale that night. He reckoned he must have gone somewhere else. But I wonder whether Arch could have been telling the truth, and had been on the wall as he should have been.'

'He was a heavy sleeper? He snored?'

'A man may snore and sleep heavily without ale, Sir Baldwin,' she said, but there was no cheekiness now. 'If he is knocked down, he will also snore.'

'Who would have done that?'

'An assassin entering the palace clandestinely would want no one to give the alarm, would he?'

Ellis was exercising his brain, an activity to which it had grown unaccustomed, and he was finding his conclusions more confusing than enlightening.

If what he had heard from the discussions between his master and Sir Baldwin were correct, someone had been trying to kill his sister and not the Queen after all. But who could have wanted Mabilla dead? She was a sweet girl, no one's enemy.

Except the Queen's, he thought with a start.

And then there was Jack's death.

The only people who'd known about Jack were him, his master, and Jack himself – and Ellis knew full well that Jack would never have told anyone about his mission. Equally, he knew that he himself had said nothing, and so perhaps the confession from Sir Hugh that *he* might have given away the plan to Piers was not so wide of the mark.

Piers was a spy. His trade was lying and passing on news to others. Perhaps he had sold Sir Hugh's plot to someone else. Earl Edmund was his master when he wasn't with Sir Hugh, so had he mixed his loyalties and found solace in the fact that for once he was acting in some form of good faith by aiding the Earl? The only alternative to that was that the Queen herself had plotted to remove Mabilla.

And surely that was unthinkable.

Simon and Baldwin soon found their way to the gaol. It was down a dank corridor far beneath the King's chambers, close to the river itself, and as the gaoler opened the door to the cell, Simon was very aware of the great river just a short distance beyond the walls. There was a perpetual trickling, tinkling sound, and it was impossible for him to ignore it. He had never much liked being underground. The thought of the weight of stone and timber overhead was always unpleasant to him, and never more so than here.

There was a scattering of straw on the ground, but not enough. A bucket held some water, brackish and foul from what he could see, and there was a stench of urine and excrement about the place.

Not that the occupant appeared to care. He lay crouched in the far corner, his eyes on them like those of a whipped hound, his arms wrapped about him against the cold.

'Dear God,' Baldwin murmured. 'Are you Arch?'

At first Arch didn't seem to understand. Simon saw him shake his head and pull his arms tighter, ducking his chin to his breast as though that would hide him from his tormenters.

They had been busy on him. Blood marked him, and mucus and slobber had drawn trails in the filth on his face. His hair was awry, but there was more blood among it, and Simon thought that clumps had been wrenched out. And then he saw the missing fingernails and felt sick.

'Leave me, masters, please leave me. I know nothing.'

His whine was pathetic. Although his eyes looked towards them, it was plain to Simon that he did not see them. Instead, he saw his tormentors returning to inflict more pain.

Baldwin crouched near him, sniffing at the bucket. Suddenly angry, he stood and would have kicked it over, but for the fact that it would have added to the chilly misery of the cell. Instead he gritted his teeth. 'Arch, I want to know what happened on the night that the maid was killed.'

'I've told you all . . .' Arch was huddled away from them, rocking gently.

'Not me, my friend. Just tell me: did you see anyone up there on the wall that night?'

'I was just looking out over the river, and I heard a rat. That was all. But I didn't have a drink, not that night. I was sober. It was just a rat.'

'Arch, look at me. What sort of noise?'

'It was a rat eating at wood. I heard the crunching. You hear them down here. They're all over the place.'

'Are you sure you didn't drink anything? You were still sleeping the next morning.'

'I was just so tired. And my head hurt.'

'You had a hangover?'

'No. My head hurt.'

Baldwin shrugged and glanced up at Simon helplessly.

But Simon was convinced. 'This headache – is your head sore?'

'Ach!' Arch rolled into a ball, his hands gently covering his head. 'No more, please, no more . . .'

Patting him gently on the shoulder, Baldwin signalled to Simon that they should go, and leave this poor fellow in peace.

Chapter Twenty-Six

'Was that any help?' Baldwin wondered. 'I should have liked to take a look at his head, but the poor fellow was terrified.'

Simon was more sanguine. 'If Alicia's right, and he didn't get any drink from anyone, then why would he have a headache? I think Joan was right. I knew a miner once. He was struck on the head by a felon, and he was found out on the moors because he was snoring so heavily. Sometimes a man who's been knocked out will snore like that. I don't think it was a rat that Arch heard: I reckon it was someone creeping along the walkway behind him, and who then knocked him down.'

'The assassin? Unless it was the other killer, the one who killed the assassin,' Baldwin mused. 'Who on earth was that, though?'

As he spoke, he was leading the way to the stairs that gave onto the walkway about the inside of the palace walls. After speaking to another guard, Simon and he learned exactly where Arch would have been standing on duty. There was another man there already.

Baldwin explained who they were and asked for the man's name. He was wary, but gave his name as Will

Fletcher, and was helpful enough when he realised that they were only interested in the morning when Arch was found.

'He was often drunk up here, I know, but I never heard of him still sleeping the next dawn.'

Simon listened as Will said a little about Arch, how he was always scrounging ale and wine, and was looked down upon for his laziness. 'But he's no traitor, I'd wager. He's honest enough in his own way, but he's too old for this job; at his age he needs a warm fireside rather than a chilly, wet wall like this.'

Simon was peering over the walls at the wetlands beneath. From the look of it, the mud there would be waist-deep. No one could clamber across that without making a row about it and broadcasting his presence to all the guards on the walls. When he looked eastwards, there was only the Thames itself. Even a quiet boat would alert guards. No, Simon was convinced the man hadn't come from the south wall or the east. Which meant that either he had climbed over the north wall, or the western one. Since there was no point approaching from the north and having to pass all the other guards on their rounds, surely he had come from a nearer post.

Satisfied that his logic was solid, Simon walked to the nearer part of the western wall and peered over into the Abbey's grounds. 'What's happened here?'

'That? They had a fire there thirty-odd years ago. They're still trying to clear the ruins and rebuild them.'

Simon could see the ladders and ropes, and, like Ellis before him, knew that this was how the assassin had entered the precinct. He said so.

'I agree. It is likely,' Baldwin said. 'The abbey grounds would be easier to enter than the palace walls by the river. There must be several places to enter the abbey quite easily.'

'And not even clandestinely,' Simon noted. 'A man could have entered the place pretending to be a workman, hidden himself until nightfall, and then climbed up here.' He drew away from the wall, peered back into the Palace yard. 'So we can be sure that the man came up here, struck down the guard Arch, and then sneaked into the Queen's cloister, before perhaps losing his way in his panic following Mabilla's death, and heading to the Great Hall by accident,' Simon theorised.

'Unless he had been paid not to harm the Queen – whom he didn't approach – but instead to kill another. Eleanor? Cecily? Joan, or Alicia? Or was he *meant* to kill Mabilla?'

Simon shrugged. 'Who could have wanted Mabilla dead?'

'Earl Edmund is the obvious man.'

'And he is not fond of Despenser.'

'No. Neither is enamoured of the other,' Baldwin agreed. 'Perhaps that has some bearing on the murder.'

Earl Edmund of Kent had been drinking, and seeing the rain falling so steadily outside, he chose to remain indoors with his two henchmen.

Usually he did not bother with guards, especially when he was in the palace grounds, but today he felt jumpy. Sir Hugh le Despenser was a dangerous man at the best of times, but never more so than when he felt himself in a

corner – as he must do now. The discovery of the assassin
had come as a shock to him, Edmund was sure, and the
fact that he lied about knowing him meant little: the
Despenser was almost incapable of telling the truth,
Edmund knew that. Who else would have considered
hiring an assassin to come and murder the Queen? There
was no one apart from him who could have been so
brazen in their actions.

Mad. Bloody mad. As soon as the Queen died, her
brother in France would demand the heads of those
responsible, and all knew exactly how much Sir Hugh
hated and feared her. He would be the number one suspect.

At that moment, Sir Baldwin and Simon appeared.
Seeing the Earl, Simon pointed him out to Sir Baldwin,
and the pair crossed the yard towards him.

'My Lord, would you object to answering some
questions?' the knight asked. 'As you know, your brother
the King has asked us to investigate the murder of the
woman Mabilla.'

Simon was eyeing the Earl as Baldwin introduced
them, and try as he might, he could not shake the
description which Alicia had given them from his mind.
She had said young, which was fair enough, but she'd
also described a less muscled neck, and shoulders that
could not have graced a knight. This man was living
proof of his skills with lance and sword. His shoulders
were broad as befitted one who trained with weapons
every day of his life; his neck was strong enough to hold
a man sitting on his head. Still, he could have hired a man
to kill the woman, he supposed.

'If you must,' the Earl said with a bad grace.

'We have heard that you knew the woman Mabilla.'

'Have you?'

'Is it true that she rejected your advances?'

Earl Edmund coloured with anger. 'What is that to you? Oh, I forgot, my dear *brother* told you to investigate this little affair, so naturally you had to come here to me. Well, yes, the brazen little bint did waggle her arse near me once too often, and I succumbed. It was after Christmas, and she was obviously demanding some attention. Christ, you know what some of the bitches can be like. She was on heat, and I was ready. So I chased her out of the hall and into the yard here. It was clear what she wanted, and I was happy enough to supply it. I mean, last year . . .'

What could he say? That last year hadn't been his best ever? By the Gospels, that was an understatement. He had been sent out to Guyenne with the King's host to protect the lands, and then when the French arrived, his military career was shredded. They had the son of the devil himself, Count Valois, there, and that experienced old bastard had trounced Edmund at every turn. There was nothing to do but retreat, and finally Edmund had been surrounded at La Reole. By late September, Charles Valois had conquered all, and Edmund was forced into a humiliating truce.

When he finally returned to England, he had hoped for some sympathy, but no. There was nothing, only contempt for his actions and failings. No one wanted to listen to him or to hear his side of the story. All they cared about, as the King himself had said, was the loss of their lands. Well, so did *he*!

Mabilla was the only one who ever gave him the time of day during those miserable lonely weeks. She obviously had the hots for him, and he thought she was lovely, although he waited for a signal. And when she seemed to give him the come-on, he rallied, set his lance to the rest and charged.

'She was a lovely wench, I'll give her that.' The Earl sighed heavily. It was dreadful to think she was dead.

'But she rejected you?'

'Look, I'm a man, and I've had many maids – most willing, some not – and I know when one of them wants to play hide the sausage! She was keen – she made that obvious. And then, when I followed her out from the hall, and tried to grapple with her in the Green Yard, she swore at me, screamed and accused me of rape, God help me!'

Simon said, 'You'd been drinking?'

'Oh, you can look at me like that if you want, Bailiff, but you hark to me! That wench knew how to wriggle her arse as she passed by, how to bend just low enough to give me a view of her bubbies, and she would sit so close to me I could hardly put my hand down without resting it on her thighs. That went on for weeks. And then, the first time I gave chase, I got the brush-off and accusations of rape. It was ballocks! Pure ballocks. She'd been drawing me on, and as soon as she had my blood up, she lost interest. She's damned lucky I didn't rip her clothes off there and then and give her a good bulling!'

'Why didn't you? She deserved it, for being a tease,' Simon said sarcastically. It was the excuse he had often heard in his own court.

'I'm no rapist,' Edmund said hotly. 'And in any case, if

I was found to have done something like that, I'd have had my arse in gaol instantly. My name is no protection – not after last year.' He said bitterly, 'Even the King would have been happy to see me, his own brother, out of the way.'

'Interesting,' Baldwin said as they walked away. 'What do you make of that?'

'The Chaplain told us he thought that there was a gleam in Edmund's eye towards Mabilla. But surely if he had killed her, he would have denied any flirtation between them. Why should he admit it, and tell us the story straight out like that?' Simon shrugged. 'It didn't seem the act of an ashamed or guilty man.'

'I agree. Which means that the rest of his tale could also be true. In which case, what was the girl doing, teasing and tormenting a man like him until he felt he had no choice but to bed her? Clearly she did not want that, so why tempt him?'

'What motive could she have had?' Simon agreed.

'I do not know. But it is something I intend to try to understand,' Baldwin said.

They were almost at the gate to the Green Yard now, but then they heard Baldwin's name being bellowed, and turned to see a messenger running towards them at full tilt.

Earl Edmund was still at his table when he heard the shouting and saw a rider approaching through the rain. He rode in at full tilt, yanking the reins about as he cleared the gatehouse, so that his beast thrust both forelegs out stiffly; the man was out of the saddle almost before the horse registered that he had stopped.

'What's his hurry?' Earl Edmund wondered aloud.

The man pelted in towards the palace, but before long he was running out again. He grabbed the reins, pulling the horse to a mounting block near the gatehouse, he sprang up into the saddle again, and then sat waiting for someone else.

Men were running about, and two more horses were quickly brought out and saddled. Then Baldwin and Simon hurried over, and in a moment the two and their guide had spurred their mounts and hastened off through the gate, heading west.

Edmund finished up his drink, belched, and wiped his mouth. If they were going, it left much of the palace empty. That was good. It gave him a little time to do a few things himself.

The news that Jack atte Hedge's lodging had been found gave Baldwin a whole new view on their position. As though this mere snippet of information could protect him and his family, he grabbed at this chance.

Chelchede was the name of the small vill to which the messenger took them. It was one of those places which Baldwin always disliked; built in the loop of the Thames, the area was prone to flooding. It was very damp now, in the middle of the winter, and puddles and mud predominated. The trees which survived were stunted and unhealthful, because of the sodden soil. At least the people looked fit and well. Their diet must include a large quantity of the wild fish that swam in the river, Baldwin guessed.

'Where is it?' he asked, and the messenger led the way to a quiet little inn at the far side of the village.

Walking into the single broad chamber, Baldwin was struck by the thought that only very few men could have come here from outside the village itself, and that must be why it had been selected by the assassin. For him it was ideal – secluded, and only a short walk from Thorney Island.

'Who are you?'

The innkeeper was a portly man called Henry atte Swan, the tavern's name. He stood at least five feet eight inches tall, and was clad in a tatty linen shirt, a thick jacket of fustian that looked as if it had been made for someone a lot thinner, and a heavy leather apron. He had been brewing when the messenger arrived, apparently.

'I don't want to be in here while my wort's heating. I have to get out there and see to it.'

'Then you should be attentive and help me quickly so that you can hurry back to it,' Baldwin said easily.

'I don't see how I can help much.'

'You can begin by telling us about the man who stayed here.'

'I told him all about the fellow,' the innkeeper said, jerking a thumb at the messenger at Baldwin's side.

'Good. Then you can tell me as well, now you have refreshed your memory,' Baldwin said, a hint of steel entering his voice.

'Ach, Mother of Christ, I don't . . .' Then the publican caught sight of Baldwin's expression and shrugged. There was a barrel near the wall. He walked to it, poured a couple of jugs full and placed them in front of Baldwin and Simon, then fetched another for himself.

He had a ruddy face with watery eyes, and he looked like a dangerous witness to Simon. The Bailiff was all too used to men who would seek money by entering a court and telling fantastical tales of other men. Many believed that all judges wanted to convict men, that any case should be treated neatly: for every crime there should be an equal and corresponding number of felons discovered and gaoled.

If this had been his old courthouse at Lydford, Simon would have looked at this man and instantly doubted him. He looked too much like someone who depended upon the ale he brewed for his opinions. One who was incapable of thought without a large jug in his fist.

However, to be fair, although Henry atte Swan may have enjoyed the results of his brewing, there was nothing in his manner or his delivery to suggest that he was anything other than reliable. There was no hesitation, no 'humming and hahing' to indicate invention.

'His name was Jack atte Hedge,' he began. 'I've known him for many years. Used to come here to stop fifteen year ago when he was a sailor. Back then, he was in trouble all the while. I had to knock him down once for upsetting a villager. If I hadn't, he'd have been killed by the locals here. A wild boy, Jack was.'

'What was a sailor doing here?' Baldwin asked.

'Sometimes he'd get into a fight or something, and the master would throw him from the vessel. He had several jobs up and down the river, working with the barges. After some years, he was said to have killed a man and ran away. I heard he went to become an outlaw – I think that was where he met Sir Hugh. That's what I heard, anyway. He was not the sort of man to talk about such things.'

'What else did you hear?'

The innkeeper gave Baldwin a long, considering look, then glanced up at the other faces around him. 'Yeah, well, anyone else here will tell you: I heard he joined ships that preyed on others. Lived out of a port on the South Coast and turned pirate. When Sir Hugh le Despenser took to the seas as well, Jack got hired.'

'As a perfectly ordinary seaman, I do not doubt,' Baldwin said mildly. He looked up at the messenger. He did not know whether this man was in Despenser's pay, but he was sure that, were news of this story to get back to Despenser, it would be dangerous for him, especially after that curious outburst with Ellis earlier. 'You may wait outside.'

The man left eagerly – which almost persuaded Baldwin that he was wrong to suspect the fellow – but then he concentrated on the innkeeper again. '*Was* he just an ordinary seaman?' he said in a lower voice.

'I don't know. You would have to ask the men down there who knew him. All I do know is, he got a reputation. He certainly knew Despenser. When Sir Hugh was up here in one of his palaces, Jack would come here sometimes. Always had a polite word for me and the missus.'

'Where did he live?'

'Now? Don't know. Somewhere back up the river, I think, because he always came here from the west and went home again that way.'

'Did he have a mount or walk here?'

'He used to walk, but this time he rode, and on a magnificent beast, too. Lovely animal.'

'So he has come into some money?'

'Well, I don't think he's a horse-thief, if that's what you're asking.'

'Quite. So when did he come here?'

'This last time? It was around the Feast of St Hilary. Hmm. That was the Sunday – I think he got here early on the Monday after, so the morrow.'

'You sound very sure of that,' Simon said.

'Yes, I am. I have a good memory for days.'

There was no guile. Not even offence that Simon had suggested he was lying. Simon nodded, content for the moment.

'So,' Baldwin continued, 'he was here then. What did he do?'

'That same night he joined a little boat and went for a ride on the river. I know that – I saw him. Then most days he stayed in and kept quiet.'

'He stayed here in the tavern with you?'

'No. He wanted to sleep out in the hayloft above the stables. Said he always preferred peace and quiet. Plus he was worried that someone might steal his horse.'

'Did that not strike you as strange?'

'No. Why should it? More strange was that he used to come here at all. Unless it was for the value of my company. I never pretended to understand that.'

'When was he last here?'

'About the Feast of Michaelmas last year. Then he was here about the Feast of Honorius, too.' He gave them three other dates in the previous year.

'This time he has been here two weeks – no, more,' Baldwin said. 'Was he usually here so long?'

The innkeeper shook his head slowly. 'No. But this was unlike other occasions in many ways. Normally, he was never here for more than a couple of evenings, and when he was, he'd stay here and be social. Not this time.'

'What do you mean?'

'Generally he was here almost all the while during the day and off out at night. He even stayed away for a few nights.'

'You reported this?'

'No. He was no felon out robbing, or I'd have heard. What should I have reported?'

'That a man was known to wander at night. After curfew, that is illegal.'

'I saw no harm in it.'

'Then you are a fool.'

'I don't deny that, Sir Knight. I am only a lowly tavernkeeper, after all,' Henry said sarcastically.

'The night before last. Did you see him then?'

'That was when he disappeared for good. From what your man said, it'll be the very last time, eh?'

'You heard what happened to him?'

'Of course I have. Everyone hereabouts is talking about how a stranger climbed into the King's hall and was killed there, and then your man comes here and asks me about Jack. What would *you* think?'

'What would he have wanted to do there?'

'Look – I don't know what he was up to, but whoever did that, they picked the wrong man. Jack didn't deserve that sort of treatment. He was a good fellow. He always paid for his rooms and things, always happy to buy an ale for another man. He was a pleasant character.'

'Really? We have heard it said that he was an assassin, a man who took money to murder others.'

'I've heard of worse. Ha! I've *had* worse in here!'

Baldwin was too astonished to respond. He tried not to gape, but he could not help his expression showing his shock.

'Oh, come now!' the innkeeper said with a hint of anger. 'You know men who have killed. So do I.'

'Was he a nervous, fretful man?'

'Jack? Good God, no! He was calm, considerate. The sort of man any would want as a companion for an evening.'

'But he was a murderer.'

'You probably have killed men yourself. Are you any different from him?'

Chapter Twenty-Seven

Baldwin's anger made his voice high with outrage. 'He took money to kill people – and you ask me whether I am different? I would not take money for murder. I would not commit murder. You say I would?'

'No, not murder, but I'll bet you've killed in the heat of the battle, eh? And you wouldn't accept pay for going to war, perhaps, but you'd take a new robe each year from your Lord and all his food and expenses . . .' He eyed Baldwin's shabby tunic, and Simon cringed, fearing some smart comment about obviously not accepting the free clothing . . . but thankfully Henry said nothing about that, merely continuing, 'Well, Jack looked on himself in the same light, I dare say. He didn't think of himself as a mercenary or a murderer. Not that we ever discussed such things, of course.'

'You had best show us where he slept,' Baldwin said, still smarting over such a gross insult to his chivalry. It was a matter of honour to him that money meant nothing. It could not possess him because he had no interest in it.

Henry led the way through the cross passage to the yard beyond. From here Baldwin found he could look over the river to the grassy and bramble-smothered banks at the other side. The yard itself was muddy, with pools and puddles where the water had collected from the rain, which had, mercifully, stopped for a while. Perpendicular to the inn itself was a stable-block, with space for three horses. Not a profitable tavern, then, Simon found himself thinking.

Baldwin walked inside and remained there for a few moments. When he came out, he whistled and jerked his head towards the open door. 'If he was able to buy *that*, he had recently come into a lot of money,' he said.

Simon walked in, and admired the beast over the half-door. 'Did you say he had never ridden here before?' he called out.

'Never,' the innkeeper said. 'Always walked.'

'Clearly he could ride, when he needed, eh?' Baldwin said. 'That is a fellow that would put fear into the hearts of many.'

Simon nodded. It stood with its head above Simon's, a large monster with gleaming coat and rolling eyes.

'You will need someone to exercise the horse,' Baldwin said.

'I have a groom enters here often enough.'

'I hope he's brave,' Simon said seriously. 'That thing would eat my servant for its breakfast!' He grinned at the thought of Rob's expression, were he to ask him to mount this stallion.

'Where is this hayloft, then?' Baldwin asked.

Henry gestured, then said he was off to check on the wort. They knew where to find him if they wanted him.

Simon was about to leave when he noticed a mark in white – bleached hair. He reached out to pat the horse, and was rewarded with a nip on his shoulder. He pulled his hand away swiftly, rubbing at his shoulder, and peered in carefully. The mark on the horse's shoulder was a brand – not one he recognised so far from his home, of course, but a brand nonetheless.

He walked out, and saw Baldwin disappearing into a chamber above the stables, his legs still resting on a sturdy ladder of larch poles with flat rungs nailed between them. 'Anything up there, Baldwin?'

'If you think you can search faster than me, you are welcome to try,' Baldwin retorted in a muffled voice. 'It is dark in here.'

His eyes acclimatised swiftly enough to the light that filtered in from beneath the thatched eaves. It was a chamber the length of the stable, and was still half-filled from the previous harvest, the area here nearest the door being clear, loose boards. The thick dust was cloying, and he began to feel it in his nostrils as he moved about. All he could smell was horses and hay, and he wondered how easily the man Jack would have slept in here. At least it wouldn't have been too cold, with the heat rising from the horses, and the warm hay.

At the far side, a small pile of it had been collected into a mattress and a heavy fustian blanket laid over the top. Baldwin could imagine the fellow lying down here and resting, a blade ever ready in case of attack, ears straining, his eyes wary. What sort of a life would it be, he wondered, accepting money to go and kill men or women you have never known? Was Jack atte Hedge extraordinarily callous, simply devoid of any feeling whatever for others? From all that the innkeeper had said, he was a pleasant enough fellow, or had seemed so.

He thrust about under the blanket, but there was nothing there. The hay itself was piled into a great heap, and he was reluctant to sift through the whole lot. Instead he took his sword and began to prod in amongst it. Probing here and there, he felt the blade strike the wooden boards six or seven times before it met something more soft and giving. Parting the hay carefully, a little squeamishly, he reached in. Once he had thrust into his own hayloft and found something inside. When he sought it, he had almost been bitten by the enormous rat he had unwittingly stabbed.

There was no rat this time, only a large soft package. He pulled it out, undid the knots, and opened it.

'You all right up there, Baldwin?'

'I'm fine. Wait a moment,' he shouted towards the ladder.

Inside was a linen shirt and a pair of rough sailor's hosen – both slit from the sword's blade – a belt of good thick leather, a small lead badge from Canterbury to show he had been there on pilgrimage, and a purse of coins. Inside the purse there was also an indenture, a half of a contract written up with a lord, defining the responsibilities of both parties for the contract. As was usual, the contract had been ripped in half roughly so that when the two parts were joined it would be easy to see that they both comprised the one contract by the way that the tears matched. Baldwin stared at this for a short while, then thrust all together again into the pack and retied it. He searched about the hay again, but if there was anything else there, he couldn't find it. Walking to the ladder, he tossed the package down to Simon before making his way down once more.

'That horse has a brandmark on it,' Simon said, jerking his head towards the stalls.

'Innkeeper, do you know whose brand it is?' Baldwin shouted into the yard.

'You ask that messenger brought you here. See if *he* recognises it,' the man shouted back, busy with his fire and apparatus.

Baldwin glanced at Simon, frankly surprised, then called the messenger in. The fellow was only in with the black horse for a very short while before rejoining them.

'We are foreigners up here. Do you recognise it?' Baldwin asked.

'You are serious, Sir Baldwin? It is the mark of my Lord Despenser.'

Bishop of Exeter's House, Straunde

The two men rode back in a contemplative manner, neither wanting to say anything of the fears which both now harboured. Not until they were in the Bishop's house, in the small room where they slept, did they broach the subject again.

'I feel I need a pint of strong wine,' Simon said, staring at the indenture. Across the top in large letters was the name of Sir Hugh le Despenser, beside some date which was indecipherable, apart from the year. It was dated in the eighth year of the King's reign, so had been drawn up somewhere between July 1314 and June 1315. 'It's clear enough, isn't it? The man was Despenser's own, had been in his pay for ten years or so, and he was trying to kill the Queen.'

'Yes – and Sir Hugh gave him that horse down in the stable, either to bring him here to discuss the murder, or as a gift in advance payment.

'Simon, when news of this gets out, as it will, we will inevitably be viewed by the Despenser as being implacably opposed to him.'

'What should we do?'

'We should report this to the King at the first opportunity. However, I do not expect you to do so with me, Simon. Indeed, I would prefer you didn't.'

'What?'

'Old friend, I have to report this. I was the one charged with finding out what I could about the murders and the assassin himself – *me*. It was also me who had the argument with Despenser, not you. He wouldn't worry about you, only me. I am a knight, whereas you . . .'

Simon gave a half-grin. 'Yes. Whereas me?'

'You are an irrelevance, to his mind. I am sorry, but I know the arrogance of knights, Simon. In his mind you have no value, and therefore you are no threat. Whereas I am a knight. I am no powerful, wealthy man like so many of his enemies, but I have some position in Devon. I am a knight of the shire, I am a member of the next parliament, and I have been asked to come here to help advise the King. All that makes me a potential threat to him, and he will not allow me to grow to become a worse one.'

'How much risk are we thinking of?'

'Me to him? Little. He is the King's favourite.'

'What of him to *you*? You think he may kill you?'

Baldwin's face hardened, but only with recognition of his own danger. 'If he was to feel that I could be a danger to him, yes. He would kill me with as little compunction as a pit owner wringing the neck of a fighting cock.'

'What of Jeanne?'

'Perhaps you could take a message for her from me. If it comes to it, I would like you to tell her that . . .'

'She knows all that already,' Simon said, uncomfortable with this sudden turn of events. 'Baldwin, there must be a way around this.'

'If there is, I wish I could see it. From tomorrow morning, I must try to tell the King the truth about his favourite adviser and friend: that Sir Hugh has been plotting to have the Queen killed.'

'But . . . should you do that?' Simon wondered, eyes narrowed.

'What other course do I have?'

'To find the man who killed the assassin and Mabilla, of course.'

'I must find them too, Simon, but I cannot allow the man who seeks the Queen's death to continue to walk abroad safely, can I?'

New Palace Yard, Thorney Island

William Pilk was in the yard as the dribs and drabs of men returned from their searches. Him, he was still angry at the way those two churls had dared to question him. They'd made him feel a fool; moreover, they'd got more from him than he should have given, as he was uncomfortably aware. He kicked a stone disconsolately, wondering how long it would be before they accosted his master and told *him* what he, William Pilk, had told them about Jack.

He knew how his master would respond, and he quailed at the thought.

Sighing heavily, Pilk watched dully as another man rode back into the yard, just as Ellis appeared at the gateway from New Palace Yard out to the Green Yard. Ellis stood peering about deliberately as always, ensuring that the way was clear, before standing aside for Sir Hugh to stride out. There was nothing abnormal about any of this. Sir Hugh always sent Ellis on ahead, and William scarcely gave it all a second glance. Just now, what he was more interested in was how his master would respond to the idea that he had . . .

The flash of metal came from the right of the little alehouse, the one which was patronised by the palace guards. That was odd, Pilk thought, despite himself. There shouldn't be anyone there. The area was used as a general midden, nothing else. All kinds of garbage and trash went out there, along with slops from the old barrels, the solid stuff sinking down and gradually filling the pit dug there for that purpose, the liquids all leaving by the little channel that led through the wall to the spur of the River Tyburn.

The midden was the sort of place any normal person would avoid if they had any sense. So who could have gone there?

In that moment he made the connection, and time stopped for him, before he bellowed, ''*Ware! Archer!*'' and threw himself across the yard towards the midden.

All appeared to happen so slowly. He couldn't understand afterwards, how those few seconds had seemed to last his lifetime. Every moment was firmly imprinted upon his brain as though seared there with a brand.

'Ellis! Archer!' he shouted again. And now he saw him – a thin, ferrety fellow with a green gipon and brown hood. He had a small crossbow – and as William hurtled forwards, he saw the bow shudder and the foul bolt fly off. Horrified, William was about to throw himself to the ground, when he realised the thing had already buzzed past his ear like an angry wasp. He imagined it slamming into his body, the point like a bodkin sheathing itself in his breast, the steel tip penetrating bone and shivering it into pieces with the massive shock of the metal and the hardwood shaft. He had seen men hit by bolts, and the wounds were always hideous. Terrifying.

He was at the midden now, and the man was hurrying away to the right, behind the stables. William kept on slogging forward. His heart was thudding painfully, his head light, his ears hissing and his thighs complaining. It felt as though his whole body must explode with the effort.

Then he saw the man again. He was climbing hand-over-hand, up a rope towards the wall's walkway.

'Stop that bastard! He tried to murder my Lord!' he gasped.

A guard turned, saw William, then spotted the murderer. He gaped, but only for a moment. Then he was rushing at full speed towards the rope. The killer saw him, made two ineffective lunges upwards to reach the safety of the walkway before the guard, and recognised defeat.

Instead, he let himself fall from the rope, hitting the ground hard and rolling. In an instant he was up again, but he was winded. His weapon was beside him on the ground, but he knew there was no time to reload. Instead, he drew his sword, a wicked, dark-bladed weapon.

William had no time to think. He was closing with the fellow, and as he drew his own sword, an ancient, rusty-bladed one with more nicks in it than a saw, he heard a loud crack and his quarry suddenly fell to his knees. There was a noise like a hatchet striking a log, and he saw the man's eye erupt with blood as an arrow-point came through it. He toppled over.

Staring all around, William saw the four archers on the walkway, one with another arrow nocked and ready. Two were gibbering and capering at the destruction their arrows had inflicted.

William Pilk walked forward slowly, and studied the man. The last arrow had penetrated his skull from behind, the arrow protruding a bloody twelve inches or more from the ruined mess of his eye. Another, the first, had taken him in the thighbone just above the knee and shattered his leg. It was no wonder he had crashed to the ground like that. The other two had both hit him full in the chest, one of them sinking so far into him that not even the fletchings were visible. All the clothyard had gone through him at that range, and was sticking out behind him. The man shivered, and then his right foot twitched with a curious rhythm. It was still doing that when William realised that Ellis had joined him.

'Know who he is?' Ellis asked.

'My God, no! I've never seen him before. Did you see

him go down? It was like someone had taken his legs away. Look! He is still moving.'

'Calm down, Will. He's not the last dead man you'll see,' Ellis growled, his eyes up on the walkways. 'Someone's going to pay for letting him in with a crossbow. How'd he get in?'

'I just saw the flash over there, and I thought, Why's someone there in the midden? That was all. And then I knew, see, I *knew* – so I ran, and—'

'Yes. You did well, Pilk,' Ellis said with finality.

A messenger was running to them, and he hailed Ellis.

'Not now, man!' Ellis snarled at him.

'But, master, I—'

'Are you deaf or just thick?' Ellis said, and suddenly pirouetted. He took the messenger's gipon in one hand and hauled the man, squeaking, towards him; Ellis then booted him in the backside and he fell to the ground. 'Now shut up!' And he was already making his way back to his master.

'Shit! He's the stupid one, the bastard!'

The man's evident distress forced Pilk from his self-absorption. He reached down to help him up.

'That man obviously wants to see his master dead,' the messenger said viciously, dusting his uniform down.

'Why's that then?'

'Because I know something that would be to his benefit.'

'What?'

'Why should I tell *you*?'

William had not had a good day so far. He was still feeling a little shaky after his sprint and then witnessing the death of the assassin. 'How about because if you don't, I'll break your legs. Or I'll tell Ellis you held something back from us. He wouldn't break your legs, though. He'd . . .'

'Christ's bones, all right. You've made your point, mate! Tell your master this, then: the knight who's looking into the death of Lady Mabilla and that other man, he's found out where the assassin came from. He's found the man's name and his horse, and the horse has the Despenser's brand on it. Understand? The knight knows the assassin was one of your master's men.'

William nodded. He looked back at the body. The foot had stopped its little dance now, and there was only a tiny movement of a finger, which was unnervingly like a beckoning gesture. It made William feel sick, but then even that stopped. There was another shudder that ran through the man's frame, and then it seemed to almost sink in upon itself. It was odd, like a pig's bladder when someone had taken all the air out of it and it slowly collapsed. The man seemed to just – well, *end*.

Sir Hugh was calling. Still in a slight daze, William Pilk realised he was being summoned, and he tried to go to his master, but his feet wouldn't obey. He looked down at them, and it was only with a physical command to his legs that he was able to stumble forward.

'Pilk, you did well. You saved my life.'

'I only did what I . . .' He didn't know how to continue.

'You did it well. I am proud of you. There will be a reward for you when you return to the Temple this evening.'

Even Pilk could see that Sir Hugh was shocked.

Usually so urbane and suave, just now he was frigid, like a man holding his breath to stop the shakes taking him over. His attention was not even vaguely directed towards the walls or the possibility of another threat, though. His eyes were fixed on Ellis, Pilk and his other men.

'Does anyone know who he was?'

'No, my Lord,' said Ellis. 'I don't recognise him. Some discontent, I'd guess. Some bastard prickle from the household of Lancaster, or maybe another paid man from Mortimer. Christ knows how many there are would like to see you hurt.'

'Find out where he bloody came from,' Despenser spat. 'I don't pay you for "guesses", Ellis! I pay you for results. Just now Pilk saved my life and you did nothing. I am unimpressed with that.'

'Master, I —'

'Go and see if anyone else here knows the man. Get that lazy prick the Coroner out here and see what *he* can achieve. What is he paid for? Where is he? Sweet Jesus!'

His rage was understandable. Pilk knew that his master, the Despenser, was suffering from the shock. Had it not been for Pilk's warning, the bolt would have passed through his throat and he would be dead. It was only Pilk's shout and his quick appreciation of the danger he was in that had saved Sir Hugh's life. That and Ellis. Ellis had thrown himself in front of his master even as the bolt flew towards them.

That nasty missile had found its mark in the gate-post to the Green Yard, and Sir Hugh went to it now, touching the hardwood shaft and goose-quill fletchings. 'Have that taken out and saved for me,' he ordered the guard standing and gawping at it. 'I will keep it as a reminder.'

It was only now that Pilk suddenly recalled what the messenger had said. 'My Lord Despenser! May I speak?'

As he repeated what the messenger had told him, relief flooded his entire body. There was now no need for Sir Hugh to learn that Pilk had told Sir Baldwin about Jack. The innkeeper had done so. Yes – Pilk was safe!

But others were not, not if the expression in Sir Hugh le Despenser's eyes was anything to go by. William Pilk was inordinately glad to have been the sole bearer of good news today.

'That *fucking* tavernkeeper?' Sir Hugh cursed. '*Right!* I'll have to show my appreciation for all his help, damn his bowels!'

Chapter Twenty-Eight

Bishop of Exeter's Hall, Straunde

Simon and Baldwin were late into the Bishop's hall for the main meal of the day. This was usually eaten late in the afternoon, but today being Sunday and the day after the celebration of Candlemas, there was less food and no meats available for the Bishop's guests. Neither Simon nor Baldwin felt remotely hungry in any case.

Baldwin was looking so pale and fretful, most unlike his normal self. Simon had only ever seen him like this once before, when he had been about to ride into a tournament to the death. It had been a similar situation to this: knowing that the likelihood of his surviving was remote, and also knowing that his death would have repercussions for others. On this occasion, those at threat were his own family, and Baldwin had been like a man half-asleep since the full danger of his position was brought home to him.

The Bishop was already seated. 'My friends, please join me and try this delicious dish. It is a little pie which my cook has created to tempt my appetite ... Sir Baldwin, are you quite well? You look as though you are feeling indisposed.'

'I thank you, I have had a shock today,' Baldwin said.

'Please – tell me, that I may try to help you.'

'It is not a pleasant tale, my Lord Bishop,' the knight said sadly, and related all that they had learned.

The Bishop listened, his eyes almost staring. 'But this is ridiculous! My friend Sir Hugh would never plot to have the Queen killed!' he whispered.

'My Lord Bishop, I really would be happier to think that this was conjecture or simple error, but it is not. We saw the horse, we heard from the innkeeper that the guest was this man Jack atte Hedge, and when we left, I asked him to come tomorrow and view the body. He agreed, after some persuasion. I am sure that he will be able to confirm that the body is that of Jack atte Hedge, and then all follows logically: we have the contract, we have the horse, and we have the dates when the man was there. It is plain that Sir Hugh paid this assassin to come and kill Queen Isabella, and that the attempt failed only because someone killed the assassin first.'

'When the King ordered you to seek the killer, did he ask you to learn exactly who had sent him?'

'He asked me to find out who was responsible for the deaths of Mabilla and Jack.'

'Perhaps . . . I do not mean to make the waters muddier for you, but I do have some experience in political matters, Sir Baldwin. Sometimes the art is to avoid the unwholesome repetition of details which can serve no useful purpose. In your case, I think you are worldly enough to be aware of the risks you take in letting the King know that his favoured companion has planned a peculiarly evil act. Better, perhaps, if that aspect could be avoided, simply not mentioned. Would it really serve any useful purpose? All it could do would be to expose you and your family to danger. Let us not be foolish – Sir Hugh has a dreadful temper, and he has many men at his command. If you embarrass him, it can do you no good, but it will probably not even greatly affect him, because he can deny it all, and the King will probably believe him.'

'The King ordered me to perform a task for him, and you are asking me to be dishonourable?'

'To be dishonourable, you would have to lie. You would apportion blame where it did not truly lie, you would put another man in danger instead of yourself. Those would all be deeply dishonourable acts. To *not* put yourself and your family in danger, that is logical and sensible. To avoid hurting a man who is so much more powerful than you – that is nothing more than commonsense.'

'Perhaps.'

'The indenture you speak of: do you have it safe?'

Baldwin hesitated, then tapped his breast.

'You carry it with you?' the Bishop demanded, appalled. 'And what if you are attacked on the road? There are footpads all about the palace, Sir Baldwin. If not that, it could fall from you and become illegible in a pool of mud, or, or . . . please, let me have it. I can store it safely.'

Baldwin and Simon exchanged a look. Simon was happy to allow the Bishop to hold it for them. He had known Bishop Walter for many years. His friend was more reluctant, he saw, but that was perhaps because Baldwin knew how dangerous the scrap of parchment might be. Still, there was force in the Bishop's arguments, and after a moment, Baldwin passed it to him.

'I will lock this away in my chest tonight.'

The Bishop continued with his attempts to persuade Baldwin not to tell the King, and as the evening wore on, the knight gradually began to wear a more composed look about him. By the time the Bishop yawned and said he was off to bed, Baldwin was apparently back to his usual affable humour.

In their bedroom, as they undressed by candlelight, Simon looked over at his friend. 'Well?'

'Hmm?'

'Did he convince you with all his arguments?'

Baldwin crossed his arms and drew his linen shirt over his head. He stood silently, naked, the shirt still dangling in front of him, sleeves held at his wrists. 'His arguments? I tell you now, Simon. All the while he spoke, all I could see was the look on the Queen's face when she saw him the other day as we escorted her back to her cloister, and I had to wonder what it really was that lay at the back of his mind. I did not like the conclusion I reached.'

'What was that?'

'You remember I told you that the Bishop wished to see the King's marriage annulled? A man with no scruples might seek a swifter resolution. I am sure that Sir Hugh is ruthless enough for that. I now begin to wonder whether Bishop Walter could himself be an accomplice.'

New Palace Yard

Coroner John squatted near the inn and peered down the length of the yard towards the gate to the Green Yard. Try

as he might, he could make little sense of this. He had
been told how the Despenser had walked this way, ready
to leave the yard and go home, when this second assassin
tried to kill him.

Pensively, the Coroner walked along the dirt and mud
to the gatepost where the squared hole showed the place
at which the bolt had struck.

This was all growing just a little too dangerous. It was
bad enough that he had been given the job of Coroner to
the court, without assassins springing up and trying to kill
all and sundry. There were too many demented fools with
sharpened lumps of steel dangling at their hips already, in
Sir John's opinion. He would be happier in a world where
only those who needed such weapons were given access
to them – men such as coroners.

Not rural knights like this fellow from Furnshill. They
were . . . *unreliable*. Coroner John wanted only one thing
– to clear up this mess and ensure that the King and his
Queen were safe. That was all that mattered to him.
Because no one, no one at all, was above the law. Not the
Coroner, not Sir Hugh le Despenser. But this Furnshill
man wasn't so interested in seeking the truth, Sir John
was sure of that.

There were several reasons for his conviction. The fact
that the man had arrived in Bishop Stapledon's retinue was
against him, for the Bishop was known as one of the most
self-serving and avaricious of all the King's advisers – after
Sir Hugh himself. Second, Sir Baldwin had obstructed him
when he tried to speak to his friend Simon Puttock about
his thoughts as they looked over the assassin's body.
Interesting, that. The man had the right idea, too: that one

baron could have been making a comment about another. That in itself was interesting enough, but Coroner John had immediately seen that the court's politics were likely involved. It was hardly a great intellectual leap: there were enough petty disputes at all times, and many involved men who would stop at nothing in pursuit of their own advancement. Men like Despenser.

Until this latest attack, the coroner had assumed Despenser to have been involved in the two killings. Mabilla's death was incomprehensible, as was the assassin's, but John was sure he would learn that they were both to be laid at Despenser's feet. It was the natural assumption to make whenever Sir Hugh was involved.

But here was another attack, and this time it was against the Despenser. Was it possible that this was the third in a series, that the three murderous assaults were all connected? That was something to make a man take note. However, more interesting was the fact that it might mean that Sir Hugh himself was innocent just this once. And someone else was leaving a message for him: *Next time we could do this to you*, perhaps. Or: *Next time, do not hire a killer to do your own dirty work.* If he had to gamble, that would be the construction Coroner John would place upon it.

But what an intriguing thought – that Sir Hugh might not have intended that assassin to die; that he was not, just this once, guilty of a murder . . . but could instead be a potential victim.

An intriguing, and a wonderful thought!

Swan Tavern, Chelchede

Henry was tired out after brewing the latest batch of ales. He lay back in his soft palliasse with his arm about his naked wife, pulling her close. At this time of year, the only way to keep warm was the oldest, and he nuzzled at the nape of her neck until she responded and allowed him to turn her on her back.

His lips had found her breast when the noise of hooves came from outside.

'What the devil . . .?' he muttered.

This late at night there was never usually any sound from outside, other than the occasional owl screeching into the blackness or the murmuring of dozing cattle in their byres. Even the dogs were asleep. His wife had stiffened at the first sound, too, and now she sat up. 'Who is it, Henry?'

'Don't fret, woman. No one you need worry about.'

But as he spoke, he rose and pulled on hosen and a shirt against the freezing cold. He slipped his knife's thong over his shoulder, the easier to grab it at need, and walked over to the shutters. Pulling one aside, he peered out.

There was a sizeable force of men down there, some gripping torches in their fists, and as he watched, two men came from his stable with Jack's great horse. 'Oh, Christ's knackers!'

'Henry? What is it?'

'Despenser's men.'

That was enough to still her. All knew what that evil bastard was capable of. At least the knight today had said he wouldn't tell Despenser, and Henry had believed him.

Until now.

A voice from outside shouted up at him. 'Keeper, open your door. We want ale, and lots of it.'

'You've got your horse back, masters,' Henry said. 'I'll be happy to sell you ale any time, but just now we're abed.'

'Bring your wife too. We don't mind.'

Henry grimaced to himself. He was ready to bet that they wouldn't. 'She's happier to stay up here and sleep.'

'Just you, then, master keeper. Come down here and let us talk to you. We understand you had a knight here today. We want to know what you told him.'

The man doing the talking was a short, pugnacious-looking fellow, and Henry looked at him a while, debating with himself what the safest course would be. But against a force like this, there was little he could do. He grunted to his wife to slide the timber bar over the bedchamber door when he had left, closed the door behind him, and made his way reluctantly down the stairs.

'Ah, good man,' William Pilk said when the door opened. 'What, your lady not here to serve us?'

'She will remain in her bed, master,' Henry said firmly.

'Nice for her,' Pilk said, smiling without humour. Then he snapped his fingers, and two men grabbed Henry's arms. Pilk stepped forward and jerked the knife from about his neck. 'I think some of my men would like to keep her warm up there, though. She'll enjoy that, won't she, eh?'

Chapter Twenty-Nine

Feast of St Gilbert of Sempringham[1]

Great Hall, Thorney Island

This was not his first meeting in the Great Hall for affairs of great importance to the realm, of course, but this time Sir Hugh le Despenser did not feel the usual lifting of his spirits as he walked in and gazed about him. Instead he was aware of a shrinking sensation, as though expecting at any moment to feel the thud of a bolt strike his spine.

Ever since Jack's failure and death, all had gone wrong for him. It was one thing to lose an assassin, but to have the target remain to threaten him was highly disagreeable. And dangerous, because he was always open to potential counter-attacks: anyone could get close enough to him to slay him.

But not a jot of nervousness could be shown in here, among all his peers. They would try to capitalise on any sign of weakness immediately.

There were already some thirty or forty barons and prelates gathered there. He nodded without expression at

---

[1] Monday, 4 February 1325

some few. To smile or acknowledge them any more than that might make them think that they ranked higher in his estimation than they did, and he had no need of them or their patronage. No, he was the *giver* of patronage here.

Look at that man over there – Earl Thomas of Norfolk. He had acquired several manors in recent months, and it had nothing to do with him being the King's brother. It was because Sir Hugh had seen that keeping the man on side would be more beneficial than not. Occasionally it was best to have a man inside the tent and pissing out, than outside pissing in. Although sometimes it was best just to remove that man altogether. Still, Norfolk had his uses. Unlike his younger brother, the cretinous Kent. He was there, too, standing with that suspicious look in his eyes. Ach, the arrogant prickle made him sick. He was so blown up with his own importance and the affectation of rage at Despenser. Perhaps some time he'd have to get rid of the little prat. A dagger between the ribs could be a wonderful silencer. Sir Hugh had detested him ever since King Edward had given him his earldom. Despenser had expected that for himself, but still, in retrospect it was no great loss. He had much of Wales now, as well as the other little gifts which the King had showered on him.

Yes. He had been fortunate. He had always intended to be rich, and that was the end to which he had bent his mind, but he'd never expected to be able to win such a fabulous position so quickly. It seemed as though Edward only understood how to keep his lovers by giving away his own inheritance to them. Some would say it was simple generosity, but Despenser knew better. It was weakness.

The King was scared that someone could try to remove his Despenser as they had taken his Piers, his lovely Pierrot. Sweet Jesus! And now Edward had been told that, last night, someone had tried to do so.

Sir Hugh smiled grimly to himself, recalling the sight of Pilk rushing forwards, bellowing something incomprehensible, while that useless tub of lard Ellis stood gaping . . . and then the thrumming through the air as the bolt flashed past, so close it almost felt that the fletchings must cut his temple, and Ellis knocked him to the ground. Christ's bones, it had left him entirely confused: he scarce knew whether to be furious or shit himself, the bolt had come so near!

At one long side of the hall a series of tables had been set out with cups and horns. Next to these were racks of ale and wine. Sir Hugh beckoned a servant, who nodded, drawing off a pint and hurrying to bring it to Sir Hugh. The strong red wine made his belly warm and he felt a voluptuous shudder run down his back and into his buttocks.

He had thought that no one would dare to stand in his path – not since they'd seen how traitors and those who'd fallen out of favour with the King were likely to be treated. Since Boroughbridge, the King had launched a series of relatiatory attacks against all those responsible, and the ferocity of his revenge had been a lesson to all those who'd ever considered thwarting him.

Hugh le Despenser had been secure in the patronage of the King, unassailable, feared by all. The fact that someone had dared to attack him left him furious – and feeling strangely impotent. His problem was, if people thought others would dare assassinate him . . . more might take up the challenge.

Which made him still more angry to think of that innkeeper. The man should have come to him, told *him* about the horse, not gone shooting his mouth off to those other men.

And the knight Baldwin would have to be persuaded to mind his own business. His investigations into the death of the bitch killed in front of the Queen and Jack's murder were exercising him a little bit too much. He was starting to poke his nose into affairs that were none of his concern.

Perhaps the fate of the innkeeper would be a lesson to him.

Simon entered the hall with a feeling of awe.

He had grown up knowing rich and powerful men – his father had been steward to the Baron de Courtenay at Okehampton and Tiverton, and it was not as though Simon could be daunted by the sight of a man wearing a coat-of-arms, but as he stood in the entrance to the screens passage, he felt the weight of the authority in that enormous chamber oppressing him. It was as though the wealth and power of the entire realm had accumulated in that one spot. Lords and Earls, Bishops and Archbishops stood in their finery, and Simon was aware only of the shabbiness of his jack and hosen, his stained gipon and worn boots. In this company, he felt as out of place as a nun in a brothel.

'Can we go home now?' he whispered to Baldwin.

'If only that were possible,' the knight responded. He

walked in, glancing back at Simon and beckoning him with a tilt of his head.

Simon took a breath and nodded, walking in. The Bishop was already there, talking to some other churchmen, and Simon bowed as he saw one of them looking his way.

It was then that he saw Despenser. The knight was standing in a small group; to Simon's eye it was a curiously fawning little assembly. All were clearly trying to win the approbation of the man who scarcely listened to any of them.

Despenser said something, and the men about him turned as one to stare at Simon and Baldwin, and then guffawed with sycophantic laughter. Each, though, was laughing with one eye on Simon, the target of their mirth, while the other eye was on Sir Hugh. In those circles, Simon thought, no one would feel safe. Their backs were always waiting for a metaphorical – or literal – dagger.

Baldwin snapped his fingers at a servant and soon he and Simon had large cups of wine. Baldwin sipped cautiously – he knew that in the past, the King had provided strong wines, and this was no exception. At his side, Simon was similarly careful. He had no desire to make a fool of himself here with the magnates of the realm watching him.

Yet he soon realised that no one was terribly interested in Baldwin and himself. All eyes were on the Despenser, who stood in all his finery, and yet whose face was mottled, like a man who had not slept well. Simon would have said that his features reflected the dissipation of his soul and the repellent arrogance that led him to believe that he could capture, torture, or even murder with impunity.

'Have you seen his expression?' Baldwin grunted. 'Either he is sorely tormented with constipation, or he has something to fear.'

His voice was not quiet enough. A man behind them overheard his words. 'Sir Knight, you are quite right. Have you not heard about the attack on him last night? As he was leaving the Green Yard, an assassin tried to shoot him with a bolt. The assault failed – just. It was a close thing, though.'

'Ah. And who was the assassin?'

'No one recognised him. He wore no arms.'

'Has he said . . .'

'He was struck dumb by three or four arrows. They had to shoot him to keep him from harming others,' the man shrugged.

Baldwin nodded. No one would be very likely to live after being hit by three clothyard arrows.

'So that would explain his temper today,' Simon whispered.

'Yes. And whoever had the guards silence his attacker ensured that the fellow would never speak about who had hired him to try to kill Despenser,' Baldwin noted.

There was an excited chattering from the door, and then the room was hushed. A herald entered, slammed his staff on the floor three times and bellowed, 'My Lords, the King!'

Chapter Thirty

Baldwin nudged Simon as he bowed low, going down on his knee. Simon was unused to court etiquette, and the last thing Baldwin wanted was for his friend to be arrested for a failure of simple manners before the King.

It was many years since Baldwin himself had needed to worry about such things. The last time he had seen the King had been in that small chamber with only a few men about. This was different. A failure of protocol here could result in a painful chastisement, and Baldwin had no desire either to suffer that nor to see Simon do so. He had to remind himself, though, of the rules of such encounters: never look the King in the eye, keep the head bent, always face him: even when leaving the King a man should walk backwards, head bowed, until out of The Presence.

He should have warned Simon, he reflected with irritation.

The King was walking at a stately pace along the hall. He nodded occasionally to those whom he wished to acknowledge: his brothers, a Bishop here or there, and the Despenser.

Sir Hugh was the only man who bowed but did not

kneel, Baldwin saw. For some reason that struck him as the most appallingly conceited action of the man. Sir Hugh was clearly so settled in his power that even in public he felt no need to show his respect to the King or the Crown. Instead he walked over to the King and led him to the throne.

There was a ripple that passed through the crowd as the King took his seat, resting his hands on the throne's arms. At last he lifted a hand, palm uppermost. The men in the hall stood straight once more, and the council was begun.

'My Lords.'

Baldwin was slightly shocked, for it was not King Edward who was talking, but Despenser, standing beside the throne and reading the King's words from a parchment.

'There are matters pertaining to the Crown and the security of the realm which require that you advise me. I am your leader, and have supreme responsibility for the protection of our realm and Crown, doing all necessary to save them with your help, advice and guidance and all your strength. I have never acted without your counsel, and think that I have shown that I have always listened to your advice. I have asked you all here today to discuss matters affecting the realm, and I ask that you all individually speak at your peril to let me know your minds.'

Baldwin felt his own mind wandering. There was a great deal more in a similar vein, telling the assembled men that King Edward wanted their views, point by point, both from the laity and the clergy, and that they should be put in writing too, so that no man could deny his advice later. There would be no covering-up or evasions.

'My Lords, the King of France has demanded that I go to him to swear allegiance for the provinces which I hold in France as Duke. I wish to hear your thoughts and deliberations.'

One after another, different Lords spoke, and all was quite civil until at last a man near Baldwin cleared his throat and cast a look on all sides.

'My Lord King, my Lords – we are in this position because the French King illegally and unreasonably began to undermine our King. We all know what's been going on. Any petitioner who comes to listen to our King's justice and doesn't like it can then go to the French King to demand his aid – and King Charles always sides with them against our own courts. And he used that as a pretext to make demands of us. He took our lands by devious and unreasonable means, my Lords, and he will take more. He will take over all our King's possessions if he can, and none of us will be able to keep our lands. Make no mistake, that is what he intends, my Lords: to remove all our estates, and then, perhaps, to expand over here and take our country as well. At present our King is expected to go to France every few years to swear allegiance to their King for the lands he holds in fief. But if we leave him an opportunity, if he has an excuse, he will eventually be here, sitting there in that throne, demanding allegiance for *all* our lands.'

At this a Bishop began to shake his head emphatically. 'That is nonsense, and my Lord of Norfolk knows it! The French King has justified claims upon those who attacked and murdered his officials. He has every right to ask that our King should go to France to give homage. He has done so to other members of the French Royal Family in recent years. Why should this one be any different?'

Bishop Stapledon had joined Baldwin and Simon, and now he whispered softly, 'That is Bishop Orleton. He is most unhappy about the recent disputes and wishes for peace.'

'What of that man?' Simon asked, nodding towards the first to have spoken.

'He is the King's brother, Earl Thomas of Norfolk. He is distressed to think of the damage being done to our lands in France, for if the King should die, they would come to him,' the Bishop said drily.

Another man had started to speak, and as he subsided, so another took over, and thus the debate rolled about the Great Hall, while the sun moved slowly across the sky and the shadows from the great windows roved across the faces of those present.

The Bishop who had spoken already, Orleton, spoke again, scowling about the room. 'My Lords, the King has already given homage to this King's brothers, and to his father. What is so different now? If our King were to go to France, surely Charles of Valois could at last see how he means the French Crown no ill-will, and their friendship could swiftly be renewed.'

Earl Thomas lifted his eyes to the heavens. 'You mean that, my Lord Bishop? You think that this French King would be satisfied with our Liege's apology and humble homage? He has Aquitaine already. We have lost Normandy, we have had Guyenne overrun – all on a pretext that will not hold water – while he gives sanctuary and friendship to our most hated enemy, Lord Mortimer. You really think it makes sense for our King to go there under those circumstances?'

'I think it would be better for our King to be proved honourable!'

'*Honourable!*' the Earl sneered. 'I suppose you would think any defeat for our King, for our Crown, for our *honour*, to be preferable to fighting for them.'

'I would see blood preserved and not shed needlessly,' Orleton said, his own voice rising.

'And I say, a pox on that!' This was Earl Edmund. He had been standing at the side of the chamber out of Baldwin's view, but now he crossed the hall to stand before the King. 'The French have invaded our lands and say that they are forfeit because our King has not paid homage. Charles laid siege to Saint Sardos and then to Montpezat, because he said there was no one in Guyenne for him to treat with. He is false, I say, and we should not allow our King to be sent into a land where he may be in danger.'

It was Sir Hugh le Despenser himself who finally opened the new line of discussion. 'My Lords, there is one possible alternative to our King's dilemma.'

His intervention caused a certain surprise. The men all about turned to him.

'My Lords, we know that here in the King's household there is one who could be sent as an ambassador to the French King. Perhaps we should consider this as an alternative.'

'You mean to send the Queen?' Earl Thomas was

disbelieving. 'How would that help us?'

'Queen Isabella is a skilful negotiator. She could perhaps find a way to her brother's heart and appease him without costing us further hardship. If she were to go to France, I am convinced that the French King would permit the return of the King's territories in France. And that has to be our aim.'

Baldwin frowned with some surprise. He would have expected Sir Hugh to be less favourably disposed to such an idea. But when he looked at Bishop Stapledon, all he saw was dismay – and he realised that this had come as a complete shock to him too.

It was a relief when a halt was called to the proceedings. Throughout the morning, arguments had flowed forwards and back, the protagonists bellowing at each other, then cooler voices taking up the gauntlet and putting forth new, calmer points of view until one of the hotheads again raised the temperature of the debates.

Simon was surprised at the rowdiness. 'Baldwin,' he whispered as the two stood back and let the Lords and Bishops leave the room, 'in my court at Lydford there are often blazing rows between different parties, but when that happens, I separate them myself, or have other men do it. It's too dangerous to have tempers fray when everyone carries a knife or a sword – matters can so quickly escalate. Yet at no stage did the King even speak to stop the arguments from developing into a battle.'

'He was listening and concentrating on the issue at hand, I suppose,' Baldwin said.

'Perhaps it is the upbringing of the men involved.

Lords are simply better behaved than peasants.'

Baldwin looked at him long and hard. 'You really believe that?'

'Ah, Sir Baldwin.'

'Sir Hugh,' Baldwin said, without bothering to fix a smile to his face. 'I understand congratulations are deserved. Your attack last night – I trust you were not greatly discommoded?'

'Not so much as the pile of cow dung who had the temerity to try to kill me.' Once again, the memory of that hideous hissing as the bolt scorched past him and Ellis came to him, and Sir Hugh had to swallow the curse at all those whom he paid and who failed in their duties.

Baldwin smiled wolfishly. 'And how can I serve you today?'

'Not you I, no. I can perhaps serve *you*. I heard of a dreadful attack last night – on an inn not far from here. The innkeeper was a known horse-thief, and do you know, one of my black stallions was there in his stables. A fortunate thing that one of my men happened by after the attack. He could report it *and* rescue my horse. But I understand you had some interest in the man. I am sorry if this is evil news for you.'

Baldwin was so overwhelmed with fury, he scarcely trusted his voice. 'How did he die?' he demanded at last through clenched teeth.

'The keeper? Badly, I expect. They told me that he had been . . . roughly treated before he died. A place so far from any town, it's hardly surprising.'

'Those responsible will suffer for this!'

'Perhaps. And then again, maybe those who try to

make life difficult for those who seek only the good of the kingdom will themselves find life short and painful. Beware dark alleys, Sir Baldwin.' Despenser retreated a pace or two, then span on his heel and stalked off towards the entrance.

'He threatens me,' Baldwin said with a cold ferocity.

'Let him. There is no point taking on the most powerful man in the kingdom,' Simon said. He had a hand on his friend's elbow to restrain him. 'Baldwin, please. Do not think of assaulting him.'

'And have him think me a coward?' Baldwin hissed.

'Better let him think that than know you're dead.'

A messenger appeared in the doorway and stood gazing about him at the hall. Seeing Simon and Baldwin, he made for them.

'Sir Baldwin, I have been sent to ask you to join the King. He would know what you have learned about these unfortunate deaths.'

'Wait for me here, Simon. I shall be as swift as I may be,' Baldwin said coldly.

'Baldwin! Be careful, old friend!' Simon called after him.

Coroner John was already exhausted when he reached the Great Hall, and the sight of all the people thronging the New Palace Yard made him pull a face and mutter a short curse about all the 'horses' arses' milling about and slowing the King's officers about their duties.

He left his mount with a groom, and then made his way into the hall. Almost immediately, he saw Simon, and grinned broadly. 'Aha, Bailiff! I have been wondering when I would see you again. I would like to talk a little more about your theories about the dead man and what the significance is of the way he was treated.'

'I am waiting for my friend, I fear.' Simon was disinclined to talk. 'Perhaps another time would be better?'

The Coroner drew down the corners of his mouth. 'Perhaps so. I too have business to attend to. Have you seen the good Sir Hugh le Despenser?'

'He was here a short while ago,' Simon said, on his guard. 'Why do you seek him?'

'I have just returned from a rather hideous murder. An inn was fired, the keeper and his wife left inside. But they were not killed by the fire itself, Bailiff. I fear both were first stabbed,' he said. 'One of those pleasant affairs where the lady was entertained by her murderers first, and her man made to watch, I fancy. Their bodies were hardly scorched. It was clear enough what had happened to them.'

Simon shook his head. 'Henry and his wife? God's balls!'

'I had heard that a knight and a man clad in clothing much like yours visited the fellow only last night,' the Coroner continued. There was an edge to his tone now, and he looked at Simon with his head set slightly to one side.

'Yes, we were there,' Simon said, but no more. He had no desire to give any more information than was necessary. This man gave the impression that he was a cheerful, amiable soul, but Simon was painfully certain that he was in fact very shrewd, and that he might well be an ally of Sir Hugh.

'Why did you go there?'

Simon smiled, but there was no humour in it. 'We were seeking information about the dead man here, of course.'

'Aha! And you learned something then, I can see it in your eyes.'

'Yes – and my friend is telling the King even now, I expect.'

The Coroner smiled. 'Could you tell me, too?'

'I think it is best that the King should be informed first.'

'Bailiff, do you not trust me?' the Coroner asked, a trace of hurt in his voice which was supremely irrelevant to Simon. 'I have the impression that you prefer not to discuss any aspects of these deaths with me.'

'Oh, Coroner, no. That is not true!' Simon protested mildly.

'Then answer me a few little questions, please. Was there any suggestion that the dead man from the Great Hall had stayed at that inn, for example?'

'I think so,' Simon agreed.

'Was there anything still there which could have assisted us in investigating his death? Oh, come now, Bailiff, surely there can be no difficulty in telling me that much!'

Simon hesitated, but in all fairness he could see no reason to conceal that matter. 'Very well. Yes, there was proof that he had stayed there.'

'And what was that proof?'

Simon was relieved to see Baldwin return. 'Our friend here wants to learn more about what we discovered last night.'

'Really? Did you tell him that it is not safe to be seen with us? We are become leprous, Coroner,' Baldwin said heavily. 'Do not approach us unless you wish to become afflicted in the same manner.'

Coroner John looked from one to the other with a perplexed expression on his face. 'I do not understand you. All I wish is to discover the truth behind the death of this man, and you are both officers of the law. You ought to want to help me, but you're obstructing me instead. Why is that?'

'We have too many other matters to discuss. If you would excuse us, Sir John,' Baldwin said firmly, and took Simon's arm to lead him from the room.

Chapter Thirty-One

'Baldwin, what is the matter?'

'You would hardly believe it, Simon,' Baldwin said, his teeth gritted. 'The King denies that there is anything to be discussed. He agrees that we have found where the man was staying, but apart from that says we have nothing. He said that the assassin, Jack, was a known felon, so whoever killed him was doing the King a service, especially as the man was obviously here to kill the Queen – and possibly Mabilla too. In God's name! Have you ever heard such nonsense?'

'What of Sir Hugh's horse?'

'Oh, he knew all about that! Sir Hugh had already told him that a known horse-thief had taken one of his mounts and it was found last night as people were trying to put out the flames at the inn where the man was staying. The King actually made it sound as though he was unimpressed with us, Simon, because Sir Hugh had learned of this place within a little while of us ourselves, and he more or less accused me of being dilatory and lazy. Me! Dear heaven, what can I do to escape this iniquitous den of malevolent, mendacious, manipulative, meanminded . . .'

'Don't forget "mercenary",' Simon prompted.

'Go fall from a horse,' Baldwin growled. 'Look about you, Simon. The King wished to be deluded about the true nature of his chief adviser and friend; here, all try to gallop to a better position compared with others by telling the King and his companion what they want to hear. There may be a short interval while a man seeks to do something for the common good, but that is over in the blink of an eye, because if it suits neither the King's dreams nor his adviser's ambitions, it will be forgotten. There is nothing that so embitters a man as to see his good intentions discarded by another for the simple reason that he can see personal advantage by so doing. Dear God in heaven! What must a man do?'

Simon was frowning. 'Has the King heard about the attempt on Despenser's life?'

Baldwin nodded. 'Yes. He knows all about that – his guards kept him informed. He is furious about it. I think that was why he did not make his own speech today. Partly because his voice could have betrayed his rage, and partly because he wanted to demonstrate that his favourite still has his full trust and support.'

Simon looked about him at the walls. 'It didn't occur to me before, but there are more men about here today.'

'The King is treating it as a serious attempt. So is Despenser. The bolt flew very close, so I have heard. The King asked me to forget all about the attack on the Queen, and instead to seek the men who decided to pay an assassin to kill his friend.'

'What did you say?'

'I said I thought the Queen was more deserving of my

protection. Despenser can go hang! He has his own men to guard him, and he is responsible for breaking apart the Queen's household and imprisoning or sending abroad all her own guards. Why should I seek to help him compared to her?'

'You said all that?' Simon felt a leaden-like weight in his belly. In that case, the die was cast. If Baldwin had summarily rejected the King's request for help, they would both have lost any patronage which might have been flowing their way.

'No. Only the first, that the Queen was in more need of my help, and that as her husband he would naturally want me to bend all my efforts to her protection,' Baldwin said. He turned away from Simon and put a hand to his temple. 'In God's name, I swear I wish I had never come here to this cursed isle! There is no good can come of it, not for you nor I. All we can do is hope to survive and not be consumed in this political morass.'

'What's a morass?'

'A bog.'

'Ah,' Simon smiled brightly. 'Yes. It is that.'

He was inclined to fear for a while, but then he remembered the sight of the dead Mabilla, and was disgusted that any man could want to divert attention from her murder to an attempt on the life of Despenser. 'Sir Hugh is a repellent character. The more I see of him, the more easily I can understand someone trying to kill the bastard.'

'He is worse than you can imagine,' Baldwin said.

'What of the King, though? Would he punish you for refusing to seek the attacker of Despenser?'

Baldwin shook his head. 'He was very upset that someone could have attempted to hurt his . . . his friend.'

He drew Simon away to a shadowy corner to speak his mind. 'Look, Simon, if he were to punish me for simply seeking the person who tried to kill his wife, it would put him in bad odour with everyone else, even those in his own court. He cannot do that. What he can, and may do, is find some other pretext for harming or hurting me. At least at present you are secure. There is no one who can link you to my refusal. You have to keep yourself out of the way so far as is possible.'

'I am not going to leave you to hunt this man on your own. I have my own pride, Sir Baldwin. I am keen to bring Mabilla's murderer to justice if I may.'

'I know, old friend.' Baldwin gripped his shoulder. 'We merely have to keep our heads on our shoulders long enough to make sure that we can.'

Simon set his mind back to those earlier murders. 'Do we agree that the man Jack was here to see the Queen killed?'

'Of course he was! But someone was defending her.'

'Then the best course for us would be to meet her again and warn her that another could be sent to achieve where he failed.'

Baldwin looked at him. 'You are right, but I do not take on that task with any great enthusiasm, Simon. If the Queen has a brain, she will be fully aware that her life is in danger. In her heart she must be praying to be sent to France to negotiate with her brother.'

'Surely the danger to herself will only spur her on to *demand* that she be sent?'

'Yes,' Baldwin grunted, and then his brow furrowed. 'What?'

'I was thinking that if Despenser wished to be rid of her, the easiest option now would be to ensure that she was sent off to France, urgently. Having an assassin found making an attempt on her life would be no bad way to achieve it. If she could tell the King of France that her life was being threatened, he would send messengers demanding safe passage for her in an instant.'

'Despenser is a devious, political man,' Simon said.

Baldwin shook his head. 'But . . . although I would be happy to believe anything evil of him, and it is easy to imagine that he is ruthless enough to have a loyal servant destroyed to fulfil a desire, surely he would not have a man cut off his tarse and shove it in his mouth in sign of his sodomy with the King.'

'Yes. It makes no sense,' Simon agreed. 'I'd more easily believe the Queen had arranged it herself.'

'At least the foul symbolism would be more believable,' Baldwin nodded.

Sir Hugh le Despenser was still feeling that creeping sensation at his back as he walked past the Great Hall on his way to the King's rooms. Ellis was not with him, and he felt uneasy.

He was startled when a burly figure appeared before him.

His sudden panic was reflected in his speedy grabbing at his sword-hilt, and his hasty attempt to draw steel, but before he could do so, he suddenly recognised the man. 'Oh, Coroner. I am glad you have deigned to visit me at last!'

'I am a man with many calls on my time – rather like you. We both appear to be busy just now, do we not?'

'I am always busy in the service of the King. You should be too. You heard about the man who tried to murder me last night? A crossbowman out there in the New Palace Yard.'

'Yes, I heard a little about it. However, I was more interested in the matter I was shown this morning. There was a little inn over at Chelchede – the Swan. Did you know it? A nice little place, it was. It was taken by some men last night and fired.'

'Yes, I heard about it. A thief there had stolen a horse of mine. My men found it as they tried to put out the fires. I hope you will have held an inquest on the dead and issued the usual fines. But more serious is an attempted assassination against the King's own adviser. What are you to do about that?'

'About the attempt on your life? What should I do?'

'You are the Coroner! Do your job!'

'My "job", as you term it, is to record all cases of sudden death, to note the methods by which death occurred, and to hold those records until a man can be put on the county before the jury. I am no investigating angel.'

'Then who is?'

'If you want a man to seek out a killer, you should ask the good Keeper of the King's Peace to do so. He has a good deal of investigative experience, and I am sure you know him well enough to engage his aid.'

'What are you talking about!' Despenser spat. 'I hardly know the man!'

Sir John smiled cynically. 'Of course not. You are mere acquaintances. No matter – I need to speak to you about the death at the inn. Your men were seen there.'

'I told you. A known horse-thief had taken one of my horses. My men went to retrieve it.'

'I have been told that they were seen tormenting the innkeeper and then firing the place.'

'You'll find no witnesses to give any evidence to that. They were mistaken, clearly. No man of mine would do that. Now, if you don't mind, I have business to attend to.'

'I see.'

'However, Coroner, if you want to be useful to the King, you should seek to find out who could have sent that crossbowman. He might have been intending to harm the King, you realise?'

Sir John bowed, keeping his eyes on the man all the while, and as Sir Hugh stalked away, he wondered aloud: 'So, was he lying again, or was he telling the truth this time, and you are not really a companion of his, Sir Baldwin?'

William Pilk was satisfied with the efforts of the last day or two. He had successfully carried out my Lord Despenser's command about razing the inn to the ground, and now he was assured of an improved position at the next opportunity. What with money and promotion, he felt much was all right with the world.

Ellis was at the alehouse by the gatehouse as William walked past, and he shouted to William, 'Hey! Where's Sir Hugh?'

'You talking to me?' William returned disdainfully.

Ellis was unused to being challenged. 'Yes, you *pilcock*. Where is he?'

'He has been having talks with the King. I think he's still there now.'

'Has he asked for me?'

'No. He has enough men about him already.'

Ellis peered at him disbelievingly. This timid little arse was being cheeky. 'Hey, are you pissed or what?' he asked.

William looked at the alehouse and then down meaningfully at the pot in Ellis's hand. 'No. Are *you*?'

'Why – you little *shit*!'

Ellis hurled his pot at William, and as the latter lifted a hand to shield himself, Ellis was up on his feet and hurtling straight at him, fists already bunched.

William had no time to wipe the ale from his eyes before the first punch hit him. It knocked him backwards, and he fell over a loose cobble. Looking up, Ellis was nearly on him, and Pilk rolled quickly away at the last moment. Ellis blundered by, trying to change direction, but too late. As he went, William Pilk reached out and caught his ankle. He gave a twist and Ellis uttered a shriek.

William rose to his feet, wiping his face. Ellis too, more cautious this time, going gently on his right leg where the pain was shooting up from a badly twisted ankle.

At William's side was a stall where a fishmonger had a display of fish from the sea and the Thames. He picked up a whole eel, and as Ellis came on again, he flicked it like a whip. The head struck Ellis in the eye, and he had to turn his face away even as William vaulted towards him and wrapped the thing about Ellis's throat, pulling as hard as he could.

Foolish! It was slippery in his fist. Ellis jerked and strained, and reached over his head to grab at William's nose. William felt as though it was going to be wrenched from his face, and let go the fish to save it. Immediately an elbow slammed back towards him. It just missed his belly, but his flank felt like a donkey had kicked him.

It put Ellis off-balance, though. William gathered both fists together and swung them at his opponent's face. They pounded into his temple by the already swelling eye, and Ellis fell back, shocked. William went in closer, and clubbed his nose. There was a crunch of gristle, and he was enjoying the sight of all that blood spraying around when he felt a sudden explosion in his abdomen.

He curled up, bent double, eyes wide as his lungs screamed for air, air he couldn't possibly take in. While he gasped, Ellis stood, shaking blood from his face. His fist bounced wildly from the back of William's skull. It was a glancing blow, but enough to topple him to the ground. And then Ellis began to kick. He had two good boots into the kidneys and then clipped William's head once, before a slamming blow struck his own head and he paused. While he reflected, the cudgel crashed into his head again, and he fell to his knees.

'I think you ought to stay there a moment and reflect,' Coroner John said happily. He swung the cudgel on the little thong that encircled his wrist, but seeing that there was little likelihood of the squirming, choking and weeping William returning to the fray any more than the dazed Ellis, he took the thong from his wrist and tossed it gently back towards the innkeeper.

'Don't think they'll be any more bother,' he said. 'You two, I suggest you buy each other an ale and make up your differences before my Lord Despenser sees you. He won't be too happy to see his two best boys beating each other up like this, will he?'

He saw that Ellis was staring at him now with a fury that was only matched by William Pilk's as he gazed at Ellis, but the Coroner was unconcerned. Their master was a threat to him, certainly, but these two were hardly the kind to give him sleepless nights. They would only attack him were their master to consider him a threat, and sadly the Coroner knew he was nothing of the sort. Who would dare to be a threat to Sir Hugh le Despenser?

Sir Baldwin and his friend were a curious pair. It was plain enough that neither of them trusted him. It was a little hurtful, but understandable in this madhouse of intrigue. Even after Sir Hugh's words, John didn't trust Simon and Baldwin yet, either.

Chapter Thirty-Two

Coroner John was soon in the little chamber where before, he had studied the body of the first assassin with Sir Baldwin. Today, standing there alone, he winced at the sight of the arrow through the second man's eye. To facilitate moving the corpse, someone had snapped the arrow off about six inches from his ruined eyeball, and the red stick protruded like an obscene stem.

'Who are you?' he muttered. It was wrong for him to be here. All was wrong, though. There should have been an inquest on the man in the yard when he was found there, with witnesses enrolled on the Coroner's records. If truth be told, the yard should have been closed, and all those in there at the time should have been held. But who was going to force the King to adhere to every aspect of his own laws? No one, was the short answer to that question.

He started undressing the body, seeing what he could learn. The clothing was simple enough. It was a thick woollen material, closely stitched. There was nothing to learn from that. When he pulled the man's belt off, though, he was impressed by the quality of the dagger. It was expensive workmanship.

'What are you doing with this?' he asked. He continued taking things from the body, but it was only as he got to the man's underclothes that he found the little leather purse dangling from his neck, inside his shirt. It contained more than a pound in coin.

'Little enough here to justify dying, my friend,' he said sadly as he pocketed a shilling. 'Compensation for bribing Arch's gaoler,' he explained to the corpse.

Baldwin found his way barred twice en route to the Queen. Guards who had stood aside the last time he and Simon came through here were either deliberately obstructive of him because they had decided they didn't trust anyone, or they were being difficult because someone had told them to stop Sir Baldwin from getting to the Queen. Not to protect her, but to stop Baldwin from talking to her.

As it was, it took a long time before Simon and he could persuade the last of the guards to permit them to see her – and when they had passed the man, they found their way barred once more at the entrance to the chapel.

'She's at prayer just now.'

'Good. Then we can wait outside the chapel for her,' Baldwin said reasonably.

'You should seek refreshment, Sir Baldwin. The King will return within the hour to continue his debate.'

'Since when has a lowly guard been privy to such information?'

'Since the King's chief guard hurried past only a few moments before you arrived,' the man said, deadpan.

Baldwin grinned. 'Good fellow. I know your face.

Weren't you somewhere else, last time we spoke?'

'I am Richard Blaket, Sir Baldwin. Last time you saw me I was in the garden with Her Majesty.'

'Of course. Well, good Master Richard, I still wish to visit the Queen. I have news for her.'

'I have been told to keep all from her. It is for her safety.'

Baldwin's temper was already frayed, and now he felt his face flush. 'You suggest that I am a threat to Her Majesty?'

That earned him a direct look. 'No, I don't think so. I should recognise an assassin.'

'Good. I do have information which may be of use to her, to help the Queen protect herself.'

'I think she already knows how to do that,' the man said lightly, as though he knew something they did not.

'What do you make of that?' Simon asked as they marched away.

'He is a fool,' Baldwin snapped. 'Damn his soul! Who does he think he is, to prevent me, a knight, from seeing the Queen?'

'A man who takes his duty seriously,' Simon said. 'Come, Baldwin, how would you feel if he had let anyone in to see her after the other evening? If a guard is to do his job well, he must assume that any man approaching is a potential enemy. Why should he consider you any less of a risk than another?'

'I am a knight!'

Simon was very tempted to remind him that so was Sir Hugh, but forbore. 'What now? Is there anything else we can achieve here?' Simon wondered aloud as they strode along the corridors.

'I would learn who was the killer of the assassin and the girl, and who told that man to seek them. There must be a reason why Mabilla was killed. Who could have done that?'

'And don't forget the innkeeper,' Simon said.

Baldwin shook his head, then stopped suddenly. 'Simon, we can do *nothing* in all probability. You understand? That man was certainly killed at the command of Sir Hugh – probably because he learned what we found there. Henry and his wife are dead because of our investigation.'

'It is not our fault we sought where Jack had lived, and found his inn.'

'But it is possible that the assassin was commanded to kill the Queen by Despenser, and that Mabilla died because of him too. Whichever way you look at it, Despenser is in the middle, like a spider at the centre of a web.'

'And yet someone else killed the Despenser's assassin, and may have killed Mabilla too.'

'But why did the assassin's killer not claim his reward?'

Simon was suddenly stilled. 'Christ's bones! Because the man who killed Jack knew full well that he'd be killed too if his deed was discovered.'

'How so?'

'Anyone finding a stranger would raise the alarm. The assassin was killed out of hand, with no alarm.'

'Because he wanted peace to kill Mabilla?'

'Perhaps. But a guard, or some other legitimate person who killed an assassin bent on killing the Queen, would expect a reward. He could say that Jack killed Mabilla *first*, and then he killed Jack in his turn.'

'True. So?'

'So the man knew that admitting to killing Jack would put him in danger. He knew the Despenser was behind Jack, that was why he cut off Jack's prick and shoved it in his mouth. So he daren't confess. Despenser would be furious about that, as well as losing his best killer. He'd be sure to execute anyone who admitted it.'

'We shall need to discuss this further,' Baldwin said.

There were footsteps, and he held up his hand when Simon opened his mouth to speak. The approaching man turned out to be Despenser; he looked quickly from one to the other, not with fear, but with that vigilance that told he was aware that he might be in danger. Still, he was no coward.

'Ho, Sir Baldwin. Are you here to ambush me? So you incline your head, eh? No more than should be necessary to a knight – we are equals theoretically, after all.'

'Sir Hugh, you have no henchmen with you after what happened yesterday?'

'Inside the palace here I feel safe enough,' he lied.

'Even after that man Jack atte Hedge got in? I am surprised.' Baldwin glanced behind him at the way he had come. 'You have been seeing the Queen? I had thought she was in her chapel. But perhaps you were joining her in her chapel for prayers?'

'You sound bitter.'

'I was waiting to see her, but the guard refused me access.'

'A good thing too. I do not want her being interrupted by any petitioners. She had a terrible shock when the maid was killed.'

'Did you know her?'

'Mabilla? Yes, of course. She was the sister of my man, Ellis. I have known her many years, especially since recently she has been a member of my wife's household.'

He had begun to walk towards the Great Hall again, and the others kept in step with him.

Baldwin said, 'But that is interesting. Did you find her friendly?'

'You suggest I may have shoved my hand up her skirts? Sir Baldwin, were I to do that, my wife would be most displeased. It is not the sort of behaviour which is expected of a knight. Well, not here or in London.'

'Meaning that you would expect such rough treatment from a horny-handed rural fellow like me?' Baldwin smiled. Simon could see that this smile never even tried to approach his eyes.

'Oh, Sir Baldwin, please. There is no need to be like that. I meant no insult, my friend.'

'Oh, no. I am sure you would only offer an insult when it was necessary and you felt justified.'

'Quite. I am glad we understand each other.'

'I think we do, Sir Hugh.'

'I am glad to have had my stallion returned, anyway.'

'Ah yes. And I was glad too. We collected some of the man's belongings before the fire.'

'Clothing? Was he your size?' Despenser wondered with an insolence that scalded, glancing at Baldwin's shabby tunic.

'I am not like you, Sir Hugh. I didn't look for items to snatch from a dead man. He left some interesting reading, though.'

'Reading?'

'Do you indenture all your servants?'

Sir Hugh was still now, his eyes unmoving. 'Often. Yes.'

'I suppose you have to buy loyalty. However, to ensure that we are both perfectly acquainted, let me just say that I intend to move all obstacles in my search for the true culprit of the other night. I will find him.'

'The *culprit*? How quaint. I thought that the dead man was the "culprit".'

'Perhaps,' Baldwin said coldly. 'And perhaps the culprit still lives. As does the man who ordered the attempt on your life yesterday.'

'Do you know anything about that?'

On hearing the eagerness in his voice, Baldwin gave a very slow smile. 'Oh, no more than you yourself, I expect.'

As they left Sir Hugh and walked away, Baldwin was struck by the feeling that Sir Hugh's reaction to his words was not quite right. Surely he should have been distressed to be left in the dark, or furious that the archer was unknown and his paymaster anonymous, but when he glanced back over his shoulder, all he saw in Sir Hugh's face was a cold and unfeeling calculation.

* * *

It was a little less than an hour later that Queen Isabella saw Sir Hugh.

She nodded to the priest at the end of her Mass, and made her way back through the little door under the careful eye of Madam Eleanor. The woman was insufferable. She would not leave the Queen alone for even a moment. It wasn't enough that she had seen to the removal of Isabella's royal seal and her beloved children, now she must steal all Isabella's spare moments too.

Despenser was waiting in the corridor with a face like thunder. He beckoned his wife and spoke to her with the deliberate precision of extreme rage, then span on his heel and strode away, his tunic snapping crisply with the speed of his march.

'Lady Eleanor? Your husband looks most angry.'

'No. He is fine. It is your husband who has lost his wife,' Eleanor said tartly.

This wife of Despenser, Isabella thought, could once have been her friend and companion, but when her husband Sir Hugh first made his most improper suggestions, and Isabella told her of them, Eleanor was not surprised. She seemed to have expected something of the kind.

It was nothing new, true enough. Isabella knew that her brothers had enjoyed the favours of women while they were princes. It was natural. They were men, and a prince or King had rights. A man like Despenser, who was setting himself up as a prince in all but name, clearly felt he deserved the same dispensation. Somehow he had persuaded dear, weak Eleanor that he should be permitted similar latitude. And he would, of course, have asked his close friend the King before making his suggestion.

At the time she had thought it was one of his jokes in bad taste. Asking her to join him in the King's bed . . . then suggesting that the King could be there too . . .

Beds were for couples, she'd responded icily, and he had laughed, as though her view was deliciously quaint. And soon thereafter her husband had begun to view her with a degree of suspicion, as though she had betrayed him in some way. It had been a coolness in those days, little more. But then Sir Hugh had tried to force her to swear to support him no matter what, pinning her against a wall with his hand about her throat, as though he could scare her – *her*! The daughter and sister of a King, not son of a brain-addled knight of poor birth like him. But afterwards, when she refused and spat out her rejection of him and his evil ways, Despenser had grown cold, and she had wondered whether he would actually dare to throttle her right there in the hallway, as though she was just some servant girl, a wench from the stews or a cheap alehouse.

The grim suspicion had never left her husband's face after that, as though Despenser had told him that she had refused to declare her devotion to him, her husband.

Despenser would be happy to see her destroyed. He had told her as much, but by then their enmity was so deep-rooted there was no surprise in the revelation. And she knew about her other enemies. Dear heaven, there were so many! Most of them hating her purely because she was French. Not for any rational purpose, but just because of the accident of her birth. They were determined to see her removed if they could. Perhaps

Despenser had stirred up hatred against her, spread lies to malign her reputation at court? Some would have needed little supposed evidence of her misdeeds, of course. There were many who would look on her as an enemy because they coveted her lands, her manors, her riches. Walter Stapledon. She knew she was hateful to him, and she knew why: he wanted the tinmining. It was worth a vast sum each year, and with Isabella's control of the better mines, Stapledon's jealousy knew no bounds. She'd seen it in his eyes.

He had attacked her with every means at his disposal. First, there was the removal of her servants, her chaplains, her physicians. Then her estates were sequestrated, her children taken from her, and now, the final indignity, even her seal was snatched and given to her gaoler, Eleanor, Despenser's wife.

Alone, without money, her family taken from her, all the trappings of her wealth removed, she had been able to spend much time considering her situation. It was not pleasant. She had been a royal princess in the House of Capet, and she was used to being treated in a manner suitable to her rank. Not now, though. She was reduced to penury, to the status of a humble petitioner by that gripple miser, her husband. And most recently, she knew, Despenser and Stapledon had attempted to have her marriage annulled by the Pope. Oh yes, she knew of all these little schemes of theirs. Just as she had known that Mabilla was intended to be Despenser's especial spy. Mabilla was the one who searched through her clothing and writing tools to see how on earth she had managed to get so many messages to her brother.

But they would not succeed in blocking her channels of communication any more than they would succeed in having her marriage declared void and her children declared bastards.

Poor Sir Hugh, he had looked so anxious this morning, she thought with a smile. Usually all he exuded was a vicious cruelty when he visited her. Not today. Today, for once, the fear was all on his part, no one else's.

It was *delicious*.

Chapter Thirty-Three

At about the same time, Simon and Baldwin were returning to the Great Hall again, after taking Blaket's advice and seeking a small meal to settle their bellies. There they met Bishop Stapledon almost as soon as they entered.

'Baldwin, you look as though you have had a shock. Is it true that the King asked to see you?'

'I fear so, my Lord.' He studied the Bishop. To his eye, Walter looked even more careworn and weary than he himself felt.

'Why "fear"?'

'The King asked me to stop enquiring about the attempted murder on his wife, and instead commanded me to look into the attempt on Sir Hugh last night. I left him in no doubt as to where I thought my responsibilities should lie.'

'Did he see you alone?'

The Bishop was peering at him in that short-sighted manner which was so familiar to Baldwin. If they were in his parlour, Walter would by now have reached for his enormous spectacles, and even now would be holding them at the join over his nose, staring at Baldwin with eyes magnified to giant proportions.

It was a curious question, Baldwin thought, but he shrugged and nodded. 'There was only a door-guard in the room with us. No one else.'

'He was angry, you would say?'

'Absolutely. He was quivering with rage at the thought that someone could be so bold as to attack his favourite in his own palace yard. I think the audacity of the attack was what affected him so dramatically.'

'Perhaps,' the Bishop said musingly.

Baldwin cocked his head and raised an eyebrow. 'You know more of this than you are telling. Why do you question my view?'

'You are an astute reader of a man's mind, Sir Baldwin,' the Bishop acknowledged. Then his face grew more serious even as he dropped his voice. Simon had to lean forward to hear him. 'Let me put it like this: if a man were to attack your wife in *your* yard, how would you respond?'

'I would be enraged . . . I see.'

'But he cares little!' Simon protested.

Baldwin shook his head. 'His affection is given to another, Simon. He is most angry because of the attempt on the life of his beloved.'

Simon's mouth fell open in comprehension. Of course: Despenser was the King's especial lover, if all he had heard and seen was correct.

'That could explain it,' the Bishop said.

Shortly afterwards, another Bishop, a man whom Baldwin heard described as Bath and Wells, arrived and engaged Stapledon in conversation. Suddenly his mind was taken back to the Chaplain in the Queen's chapel. He

said he had been installed by Drokensford, the Bishop of
Bath and Wells, and Baldwin studied the latter with
interest.

He was a tall, handsome man, with curling grey hair
that almost sprayed out from beneath his mitre. Grey it
may have been, but it was thick and gleaming. There was
no weakness in his face, either. Baldwin saw astute eyes
set in a face that gave nothing away, but clearly the man
missed little. Even as Baldwin studied him, Drokensford
looked across at him and murmured a question to
Stapledon. Soon afterwards the Bishops were before
Baldwin and Simon, and the two had to kiss another
Episcopal ring.

'I believe you are the knight who was looking into the
attempt on the Queen's life?'

'That is right, my Lord Bishop,' Baldwin agreed. He
was surprised that this great Lord would have any interest
in the affair. It appeared to have all the hallmarks of a
rather grubby attempt, not the sort of thing that should
have appealed to a man in Drokensford's position. He
was intrigued to learn what his interest was.

'I have heard from my Lord Walter that you are not to
look into the man who last night made an attempt upon
the King's especial adviser.'

'I take the view that the person of the King's consort is
of more moment than a man who, though he is important,
is nonetheless merely a knight,' Baldwin said firmly.

Drokensford smiled at the certainty in his voice. 'Your
judgement shows great honour, Sir Baldwin. However, I
simply wonder whether there are aspects which may have
evaded you?'

'I am scarcely omniscient!'

'Perhaps. I merely wonder whether it could be advantageous to seek the attempted assassin of Sir Hugh, since I should have thought that two assassins in one palace in a week is enough of a coincidence for anyone.'

'I do not think I follow you, my Lord Bishop.'

'Come – I think you follow me perfectly well! We have passed many years without a single assassin appearing. Then within a week we have two. Surely both should merit investigation, in case this unseemly rash of murderers might have a logical explanation behind them.'

'Of course,' Baldwin nodded.

'I merely leave the thought with you, Sir Baldwin. If you look into one assassin, why not look into both?'

'And if I seek neither?'

His words took both the Bishops by surprise. Stapledon thrust his chin at Baldwin and scowled with the attempt to see his face, while Drokensford's mouth fell open for a moment before he realised how unedifying his expression must appear. 'What do you mean?'

'Both assassins are dead. The second, it is true, died in his attempt on the life of Sir Hugh. The first, though, was killed without any comment. No one claimed responsibility. That is curious, is it not? If a guard had come across him in the palace in the middle of the night, recognised him as an intruder and killed him, would he not be in front of the King's steward the very next morning, demanding a reward for his selfless devotion to his duty? And he would have raised the roof that night with elation, for having done a job so well. Have you ever known a guard do the right thing and then *conceal* it?

Have you known any servant hide his behaviour when it only redounds to the benefit of his reputation? Good heaven, Bishop, the more I think about this matter, the more certain I am that the man who killed the assassin was desperate to hide his part in the matter. And he killed the assassin to protect someone – perhaps even to protect his true prey.'

'The assassin killed that lady, Sir Baldwin.'

'No – *someone* did. And I have to wonder why. It is stretching credulity too far to consider that Mabilla was being sought out by one assassin, a second was seeking another victim, and the two met in the palace with disastrous consequences for the one found dead.'

'I agree. That scarcely holds water.'

'Yet there was an assassin. And he was killed. So somebody in the Palace wished to stop his murderous attempt. I think it is fair to consider that the man who killed Mabilla was almost certainly the same man as he who killed Jack, the assassin.'

'You have his name?' Drokensford was shocked. 'I had thought he was a complete stranger to all in the Palace.'

'Oh no. He was commissioned by someone here to go and make his daring assault.'

'Then who could have ordered that?'

Baldwin felt Stapledon's eye on him warningly. 'Somebody who wished for the Queen to be killed,' he replied. 'You may have more idea of that than me.'

The Bishop eyed him doubtfully. 'I have a feeling that the sooner the poor lady, our Queen, is away from here and back at her home in France, the safer she must be.'

'I cannot argue with that, my Lord Bishop.'

'Are you quite sure that this dead killer was not the man who killed Mabilla?'

'Quite sure. The man who killed Mabilla was witnessed. He was someone who was dressed quite differently from Jack atte Hedge, and interestingly, Mabilla's killer wore a mask. I feel sure that Jack felt no need of such a device. He would kill any who saw him; as an assassin he could kill without compunction, after all. While the fellow who killed him, and incidentally Mabilla as well, had his face hidden so that the ladies in our Queen's party would not recognise him.'

'What reason would this second man have for hurting her, then?' Stapledon demanded.

Baldwin was saved answering that by the blaring of trumpets. The King was returned.

The rest of the afternoon passed as had the morning. Men stood and made their feelings known, while the matter of whether the Queen should be permitted to cross the water and negotiate with her brother exercised all the minds there in the chamber.

'This is pointless,' Simon muttered to Baldwin. 'Surely they're all aware that something must be done, and if they want to send anyone, isn't the sister to the French King the best possible ambassador?'

'Only for those who are convinced that she will act as a free and fair agent on behalf of the King,' Baldwin muttered back.

'Who could doubt that?'

But once more Baldwin was saved from responding to

a difficult question by the King, who nudged Sir Hugh in the ribs and pointed to Baldwin.

Sir Hugh nodded and motioned towards him. 'Sir Baldwin. The King would hear your opinion.'

To Simon's eye the whole room became still as people craned their necks to stare at him and his friend. Colouring quickly, he felt more conspicuous than his friend under their steady contemplation. He wished that the ground would just open up so he could wriggle away through the mud and filth which was where, he reckoned, all these grand men assumed he must live.

Baldwin was in no way affected in like manner. He bowed to the King. 'My Liege, I think that there is no possible alternative to your using your greatest asset in these negotiations. You must either go yourself, or send an ambassador, but if you are to send someone, you should use the one to whom the French King is mostly likely to listen. It is clear who this must be.'

'You would send the Queen?'

'Certainly.'

'And what if she were to prove more devoted to her brother than to her husband?'

Baldwin did not flinch. 'I am sure that my King would not have given her reason to commit petty treason, any more than I would think her capable of such a betrayal.'

'You may find yourself nailed to a door by those words, Sir Baldwin.'

'Perhaps. But I think it better to behave towards others as a Christian should, and hope in that way that others will also treat me honourably, Sir Hugh,' he said firmly, and there was a sudden laugh at the rear of the room, quickly stifled.

The King sat in his chair, unspeaking, but pale as he stared at Baldwin. For his part, Baldwin obeyed etiquette and did not meet his gaze, but instead kept his eyes firmly welded to Sir Hugh. And then the moment of tension passed as Sir Hugh moved over to speak to another man behind Baldwin.

Drokensford sniffed and glanced at Baldwin. 'I have to say, Sir Knight, there are not many in here would have tested their balls against that man. You are a bold fellow, sir.'

'No. Just one who senses he has little to lose. Backing down before him in a room full of my peers and superiors would not help me.'

'True enough.' Drokensford turned away, but as he did so, he rested a hand on Baldwin's shoulder. He spoke very quietly. 'You should know that there are many rumours that the woman Mabilla was a spy for Sir Hugh. He didn't even trust his wife on her own. He had Mabilla watching *his own wife* as well as the Queen.'

The debate in the Great Hall moved on, forwards and back. There were many Bishops who demanded that the King do all in his power to prevent war again. He should go to France to prevent the loss of his French assets. Others were vehemently opposed to such a course, pointing out that their King would be entering a den of thieves and criminals, set upon the destruction of the English throne.

A scowling, black-haired Lord from the North spoke;

Baldwin later learned that he was called Leicester, the brother of Lancaster, although he had not been allowed to inherit the title of 'Earl' after his brother's execution by his cousin, the King.

He agreed with those who counselled against Edward going to France.

'It is a ridiculous suggestion! You want the King to throw himself upon the mercy of a household of traitors, felons and murderers? The French court is little better than the house of a mercenary knight. In God's name, if you send our Lord there, you may be sending him to his doom, and I for one oppose it with all my strength.'

It was at this point that Earl Edmund pushed himself forward. He had been talking with a slender, short fellow in a corner, Baldwin had noticed, and now he held up a hand and spoke loudly and clearly. 'My Liege, my Lords, there is surely an easier option. Rather than disputing whether the King should himself go or not, why should we not seek the easier option? Another who could pay homage in his place?'

'Whom do you suggest? You want to visit the French King again?' someone jeered from the rear of the room, and Edmund's face worked a moment.

'Since you ask, Stratford, no. I do not propose to return there to be insulted by the man who broke my army while I waited for reinforcements which did not come. No, I suggest that if my Lord the King cannot go to Paris, as indeed he cannot, why do we not perhaps send his wife to negotiate the arrival of another.'

'We've already agreed to send the Queen to discuss

your peace treaty,' Despenser said with an unkind chuckle.

'Yes. And would it not make sense for her to negotiate the arrival of the man who holds the Duchy of Guyenne?'

'The King will not go!' Despenser spat.

It was interesting, Baldwin thought, that the man was growing so agitated about this. Clearly he was determined that Edward, his protector, should not leave the country. He must appreciate his own danger, were he to let the King away from his side. And no number of safe passages would convince him that it would be safe for him in France, whether with the King or not. Some years before, he had been forced into exile from the King's side, and he had turned pirate, robbing several French ships. Ever since, he had been a wanted man by powerful French mercantile interests.

'No,' Edmund agreed. He turned to glare at Despenser. 'If you would listen to your betters, you might gain some understanding of my proposal, *sir*! I say, my Lord King, that you allow your good lady Queen to travel to France so that she may negotiate the arrival of her son – your son – whom you shall elevate as Duke of Guyenne. In that capacity, he can give homage to the French King. The French will not harm him, for he is King Charles's own nephew and has no dispute with him. The Queen will herself aid and protect her son – *your* son. And when it is time, they can travel homewards together. What more elegant and simple solution to our problems could there be?'

Chapter Thirty-Four

It was an enormous relief when the King stood, a short while later. All those in the chamber bowed, facing him, and waited while the King's footsteps passed through their midst and out to the main doors at the rear of the hall. Then, and only then, did the room begin to empty. Suddenly there was a lessening of tension, the occasional chuckle or muttered joke to relieve the mood.

Baldwin was still musing over Bishop Drokensford's final words about the Despenser having his own wife watched, as Simon and he made their way through the screens passage and out into the light of the Green Yard.

'Ach, standing in that place made my head ache,' Simon groused. 'Sweet Jesus, but the smell of other men in there was overwhelming.'

'Did you hear what the Bishop of Bath and Wells said to me?' Baldwin asked.

'No. Why?'

Baldwin quickly told him what the Bishop had said about Mabilla being a spy for Sir Hugh.

'You recall what the Earl told us about her?' Simon asked.

'Of course. That she drew him on, and when he showed her some interest, she fled.'

'But if she was a spy for Despenser, that could all have been an act intended to entice him. But she wasn't expecting him to be quite so enthusiastic in his response.'

'Perhaps. But that would still mean that the Earl could have had a wish to kill her, as could many of the women in the Queen's entourage.'

'And the Queen, Baldwin. Don't forget her.'

'How could I? But of all the people who wanted her dead, most would have had to hire proxies. The women would have known, surely, if it was one of their group who attacked Mabilla. That would be too obvious.'

'Yes,' Simon said. The two men were walking further from the crowds now, voices low. 'So whoever it was who stabbed her, it must have been another paid assassin, or perhaps a man who was known to a woman who serves in the Queen's household.'

'Either that or the Earl himself paid someone. But if he did, would he have been quite so honest about his feelings towards her?'

'Is he intelligent enough to see that?' Simon wondered. 'He was not the brightest man we have met here. Although, to be fair, he seemed to astonish everyone in there, myself included, with his idea about sending the Prince to France.'

'Perhaps he hides his intelligence until he needs to show it.' Baldwin was quiet a moment. 'However, what I find most astonishing is that Earl Edmund appears to be one man who is moderately secure from accusations of trying to kill Mabilla. Despenser probably paid Jack to kill the Queen, but it is clear enough that the man who killed Mabilla was paid by someone else, and I should guess it was someone who had learned about Despenser's attempt on the Queen, and was determined to thwart it. The idea that it could have been someone who was asked to kill Mabilla, and his attack happened coincidentally on the same night as a second assassin was making an attempt on the Queen's life . . . well, that seems to me to be quite ludicrous.'

'So, we are looking for someone who sought to kill Mabilla for her faithlessness? Or, since she was a spy, someone who sought to punish her for that?'

'There is one person who may be able to help us,' Baldwin said ruminatively. 'Perhaps we should speak again to Lady Eleanor.'

'What more could she tell us?'

'Perhaps only a very little, but I would say this: if she found out that she was being watched by her untrusting husband, she may have grown deeply insulted and angry. Who can say but that she might not have decided to pay a man to remove her husband's spy?'

'And hired her own man?'

'Someone did,' Baldwin said with a shortness that was unlike him, as though he knew that the story sounded implausible, but it was the best he could concoct at the time. 'Let us at least see whether we can meet the Lady or not.'

Earl Edmund left the hall with a warm conviction that he had done himself some good in the eyes of most of the Lords and Bishops in the room. Perhaps it was not what his brother, the King, had wanted to hear, but it was the sensible option. What else would simultaneously take the sting from the French demand that the King should go and pay homage while ensuring the King's safety from the murderous bastards over there who wanted to destroy him? While men like Roger Mortimer were living freely at the expense of the French King in the latter's court, it was impossible for King Edward to set foot on French soil.

Piers de Wrotham, Edmund's adviser and spy, had done a wonderful job. Edmund grinned. His proposal today had clearly irked Despenser. The poor fellow! He was only a knight, when all was said and done, and if he ran the risk of crossing verbal swords with men of significantly better position, he shouldn't be surprised when he came off worst.

Standing in the Green Yard, Edmund felt the February sun on his face and sighed happily. He'd already drunk a good measure of wine in the Great Hall, but he was still thirsty. A small ale might help clear his head.

The gate to the New Palace Yard was crowded, and it took him a few moments to make his way through. He began to march towards the alehouse at the northern wall, and it was then that in the shadow of one of the buildings, he caught sight of Despenser talking to a man with the unmistakable dark looks he knew so well. Piers.

His thirst quite gone, Edmund turned and began to make his way to the gate back out of this yard, his mind racing.

Piers was *his* man. He'd given Edmund so much good advice in the last few weeks, all genuine and clear, and all aimed at ruining Despenser – so what was he doing, having a cosy little meeting with Sir Hugh now? Piers had told him that Despenser was his own most hated enemy, so to be with him now was surely proof of a terrible deceit! If Piers was so friendly with Despenser that he could stand in a dark shadow and make conversation . . . what topics would they be discussing?

Edmund had a nasty suspicion what one of them would be: how to make a certain Earl look even more foolish than he already did.

'You *shit*!' he snarled, and slammed his fist into his gloved left hand. He'd have his revenge on the bastards, both of them.

Simon and Baldwin found themselves confronted by an apologetic-looking Blaket once more.

'Sir Baldwin, you know I can't let you in.'

'But we don't want to talk to the Queen, man, we only wish to speak with Lady Eleanor for a little while.'

'I still cannot let you in. I have my orders.'

They were forced to turn away again, Baldwin muttering imprecations against idiot guards who couldn't recognise the difference between a cut-throat and a friendly knight.

'This is farcical,' he said with disgust. 'All we need is a few moments with Lady Eleanor, to see whether she can aid us at all, whether she knew of Mabilla's position or not – and yet even in that we are to be blocked.'

'Perhaps not,' Simon said with a nod behind Baldwin.

There in the main yard was Peter of Oxford, Chaplain to the Queen, strolling along happily, taking great bites from a loaf of bread which he had broken in two, one half in each hand.

'Aha, Sir Baldwin! It is a delight to see you again. And your good friend, Bailiff Puttock. To what do I owe this pleasure, I wonder. Perhaps you want to come and investigate another poor corpse in my chapel, eh?'

'Is the poor woman buried?'

'Well, she's not in my chapel any more. I think that her mortal remains are to be taken to her parents' home in the wilds of Middlesex, somewhere called Iseldone, far to the north of our fair city and this thorny little isle.'

'We were not here to see her again,' Baldwin admitted. 'Rather, we are keen to speak to Lady Eleanor – but the guard on the gate to the cloister there is particularly scrupulous in his duties. He has been ordered not to let us pass, and will not suffer us to even pass a message to her.'

'Why do you want to speak with her?'

'Why do you think? We are seeking the murderer of Mabilla, and to do so, we must question all those who might know something about her death.'

'You think that the Lady may be able to tell you something?' the Chaplain asked with a smile. 'I have to warn you that generally, she is less than communicative when it may be something that reflects badly on her husband.'

'This has little to do with him, I think,' Baldwin said. 'It is more likely to have a bearing on her.'

'I don't think I understand you.'

'Did you know that the dead woman was herself spying on the Queen *and* on Eleanor?'

The Chaplain's smile faded. 'What! Who could have asked her to do that?'

'You tell me,' Baldwin said sourly. 'Not only that, Mabilla was used by someone to spy upon others as well. In particular, she was used to tease the Earl of Kent and try to learn what was going on in his mind.'

'Ah – which would be why I had heard that he and she were not happy together in each other's company,' the Chaplain nodded. 'I begin to understand.'

'So you see why I would wish to speak with the lady herself? I want to learn what she can tell me about the woman Mabilla.'

'I can understand that, yes. But if you are sure, why not simply tell the King about the matter? He would soon be able to extract any information he needed.'

Baldwin winced. That was one suggestion he could never agree to. He had heard too many stories of the tortures to which his comrades in the Templars were subjected, to ever permit something remotely similar to be inflicted upon another man or woman. The sight of Arch rolling in his own blood and vomit had shown the futility of torture to extract a confession. 'I would prefer not to see that.'

'Well, if you want to do everything the hard way, I'll see what I can do for you,' the Chaplain said. 'But it will take a little time. Wait in the Green Yard. I'll speak to my Lady Eleanor, and either I'll be there to see you, or I'll have someone else come to speak with you.'

Piers de Wrotham watched the Despenser walk away in the direction of the stables, and smiled slyly to himself.

There were times when he wondered whether he was being a fool, and many, many others when all he could think was that the world was filled with idiots, apart from himself.

Here he was, a simple fellow, who was being paid, fed and clothed by my Lord the Earl of Kent, while at the same time Sir Hugh was paying him handsomely to pass on certain snippets of information, or to persuade his master to behave in such and such a way. In the past, it was a matter of manipulating the Earl to act in such a manner as would ruin his military reputation. Now it was a matter of feeding him certain convictions about his future behaviour. If he spoke out in favour of having the Queen sent to France, Earl Edmund would be thwarting Sir Hugh, *in theory* – except that Piers knew as well as Sir Hugh that to have Isabella removed from the court, potentially allowing her to defect to her brother, the King of France, would leave the King depending still more upon the advice of Sir Hugh. At least, that was what Piers reckoned the Despenser wanted. It made sense.

He crossed the yard towards a large wooden hall where there was a little bar set up. An enterprising woman from King Street had brewed too much ale, and she was there now, selling quarts of a good brew. Piers took one and settled to drinking.

Life today looked good.

Except when he looked up after a short while, he saw his other master, the Earl of Kent, at the gateway to the Green Yard, and caught sight of the expression on his face.

It was enough to sour his ale.

* * *

Sir Hugh left Piers with no easing of the frustration he had felt all day. Ellis was nowhere to be seen just now, nor was Pilk. Useless arses, the pair of them! Since he'd had that chat with Sir Baldwin, he'd been struck with a sense of urgency.

He'd managed to speak to Bishop Stapledon, and the good Bishop had promised his help. Oh yes, he'd promised. But that wasn't really good enough. Stapledon should have come and told Sir Hugh as soon as the indenture had been given to him. It had been a shock, to hear about it from Sir Baldwin. Sir Hugh would have expected a 'friend' to let him know as soon as it turned up. Still, the fact that it had been given to the Bishop for safe-keeping was good. It was under lock and key now.

Still no sign of Ellis. The Despenser ground his teeth. Here he was, unsure when another blow might fall, and his man had disappeared! It was quite intolerable! He and Pilk had better make themselves more useful, or they would learn that neither was indispensable. There were plenty of men who'd be happy to remove them to take their places at Despenser's side. And just now Sir Hugh would be happy to receive their replacements.

Chapter Thirty-Five

The Chaplain was as good as his word, and soon he returned, holding a skin of wine and three wooden cups. 'I thought you looked like men who would appreciate a little drink.'

'We thank you, most sincerely,' Simon said. He jealously watched the wine being poured and all but drained his cup in one draught. 'I often find that investigations can be thirsty work,' he said hopefully, and was reassured to see his cup refilled.

Baldwin glanced at him. There was one question which still troubled him about this Chaplain. 'Tell me, when I mentioned your name to the Bishop of Exeter, he was not fulsome in your praise.'

Peter was still for a moment, and then he gave a short shrug. 'He does not like me. I was a failure for a while. Until Drokensford rescued me.'

'How so?'

Peter grunted. 'I have no need of secrets from you. I was a priest in a hellish little hole in Kent, far from any civilisation. There I fell in love with a woman. The wife of my patron, and we ran away together. We hoped . . . well, we intended to escape Kent and

England and find a new life in France.'

'You were captured, though.'

Peter could see that moment again. Waking beside his lovely Margaret to see Sir Walter above him, sword in hand. Peter had escaped only by a whisker, but she was killed by that blow, and Peter had taken the sword and thrust it again and again into Sir Walter's breast. They found him there at noon, still cradling her dead body. And then he was sent to the Bishop's gaol until Bishop Drokensford found another little job for him.

'My Lord Bishop thought that I would be the perfect man to help our Queen. I dislike seeing women caged,' he said after a moment. And the Bishop kept a close eye on him to make sure he didn't seduce Isabella, too, he thought. Seeing a flash of colour, he looked up. 'Ah, here she is,' Peter said.

Turning, Simon and Baldwin saw the Lady Eleanor crossing the yard. She looked pale. But having witnessed the murder of her servant, it was scarcely surprising that she was wan, Simon thought.

'My Lady, I am grateful indeed that you could spare us a little of your time,' Baldwin said.

She nodded, but to Simon she seemed barely aware of the courtesy. To him, she appeared so enwrapped in her own thoughts that the real world could scarcely intrude. 'Peter told me that you might have information that could help me?' she said.

'I fear there can be little comfort for you,' Baldwin admitted. 'But you would hardly expect that in this court, would you?'

She said nothing, but a slight fluttering gesture of her

hand, like the beating of a butterfly's wings, appeared to confirm his guess.

'I shall not attempt to conceal anything from you, my Lady. I feel it is best to tell you what we have heard, so that you are forewarned.'

'Please do.'

Baldwin glanced at Peter, who began. 'Very well, my Lady. Mabilla, we have heard, was the brother of Ellis, your husband's henchman. She was also, we have recently been told, an especial spy for your husband.'

'No. No, that can't be right!' Eleanor said with a shake of her head. 'He wouldn't need another in the Queen's household. He knew I was always there.'

'Lady, I fear it is true.' Baldwin's tone was calm, but relentless. 'She not only spied on the Queen, but . . . on *others*, too.'

As the Lady Eleanor grasped his meaning, her complexion became quite waxen, the colour of a church candle, and Simon moved closer to her, fearing that she might faint.

'I do not wish to upset you,' Baldwin said, but now his voice had changed. Instead of the confident retailing of the story, he began to sound quite wretched as he took in her appearance.

'Continue, I pray,' she said.

As Peter passed her a filled cup of wine, Baldwin obeyed, clearing his throat.

'We know that she was used to spy on Earl Edmund of Kent, for example. When he came back from Guyenne, he was desolate after the shameful truce he had agreed with Charles Valois. Mabilla's apparent kindness to him persuaded him that she was interested in him, and he tried to force her to lie with him. However, she had no intention of sleeping with him and gaining a reputation for unchastity purely for your husband's benefit, so she rejected him. It confused him greatly, I think. To this day, I believe he doesn't understand why she refused him.'

'So Earl Edmund killed her?'

Baldwin shook his head. 'No. Why should he do that? If he had been that upset, he might have stabbed at her when he thought she was insulting him, but not weeks later. No, I do not think so.'

'No,' she said bitterly. 'You think it must be my husband, don't you?'

Baldwin was silent. At moments like this, when someone was considering betraying all that they had held dear for many years, it was best to let them speak at their own speed. But when she spoke, her frankness shocked him. He was unused to such glacial anger, even from women whose men had foully mistreated them.

'I am sure it was him,' she spat. 'He always wanted other things, other women. And men. I was never good enough, you see. I was adequate at first, because I brought him valuable property in Wales, but now he's built up his own estates he scarcely needs me.'

'You cannot think he intended to kill you?' Simon said.

'What would *you* think, master?' she demanded. 'He sends an assassin to kill me, and he killed Mabilla by mistake.'

'Lady,' Baldwin said, 'I think you are wrong. If he had wanted you to die, he would have ensured that his man killed you.'

'But Alicia pushed herself before me. She protected me – and the Queen, of course.'

'One woman? No, if the assassin wished to kill you, he would have pushed all the ladies-in-waiting from his path. Just as, if he had intended to kill the Queen, he could have done so. No, I think that he was there to kill one person and one person only: Mabilla.'

'You do not know my husband.'

'I think I know him well enough, Lady. What advantage would your death bring him? Money? Power? Land? No, nothing.'

'What would he gain from Mabilla's death?'

Baldwin had to shrug in defeat at that. 'It is very difficult to think of anyone who could have had a motive to kill her. The man whom you saw that night – I do not suppose you recognised him?'

'No. His mask was enough to strike terror into my heart, and when I saw the knife, I lost all will. I just stared at it. Pathetic, but I could do nothing else!'

'The man did not have a candle, though,' Simon said.

'I . . . no, he cannot have. If he had, I should have seen the light as we walked along the corridor.'

'Was there the scent of a snuffed candle?' Simon pressed her.

'No, nothing.'

'So he must have known his way about the palace in the dark, surely?'

Baldwin and Peter were both frowning at him. It was Baldwin who nodded slowly, and murmured, 'A very good point, Simon.'

'He must have been someone who knew the passage-ways as well as knowing where the Queen would be,' Simon said.

'Did she walk along that corridor at the same time every night?' Baldwin asked.

'The same time?' Eleanor gave a sharp little laugh without humour. 'She would have us up at all hours of the evening. She has needed the consolation of her priest every night since . . . well, since her children were taken from her.'

'We have heard about that,' Baldwin said, and his tone was colder.

Simon was still thinking about the corridor where Mabilla had died. 'That means it could have been anyone in the Palace guard.'

'Or someone who bribed a guard to learn where she might be,' Peter offered helpfully.

'True,' Baldwin agreed.

Eleanor put in, 'It could have been one of my hus-band's men, too. I told him all about the Queen's noc-turnal wanderings. Any of his men could have overheard. No doubt Mabilla could have done, too.'

'What of the assassin himself – the man found murdered, this Jack atte Hedge?' Baldwin said. 'Did you know him?'

'The name is known to me.'

'There is no need to be wary,' Simon said bluntly. 'We found one of your husband's horses at the inn where Jack was living. The innkeeper told us it was the horse which Jack rode in on.'

She let her head fall a little. 'Yes, I think Jack atte Hedge was a man whom my husband knew. They would meet occasionally. Only occasionally, though. Not often.'

'How often would your husband have had need of a murderer?' Baldwin asked pointedly. 'This man Jack – do you know whether he was used to kill many people?'

'That is not the sort of topic my husband would discuss with me,' Eleanor told him. She trembled. It was hard to lose the conviction that her husband had been attempting to kill her when the figure jumped out at Mabilla that night. Alicia's words had brought all that home to her.

'I believe that this Jack was hired to come here to kill the Queen,' Baldwin said. 'I think that someone knew he was coming, and was determined to stop him. To do that, he stabbed and murdered the man, hiding him. And then he decided to kill Mabilla too. But my difficulty comes from this: if your husband chose to hire an assassin such as this Jack atte Hedge, I do not think he would be foolish enough to tell many people. He would surely try to prevent anybody from learning about it. And so whoever killed Jack must either have been enormously lucky, and guessed that the man might enter the palace to attempt to murder the Queen . . . or it was someone very close indeed to your husband who sought to frustrate his plan.'

'Someone close?' she repeated.

'Only a man *very* close to Sir Hugh would be able to

learn his mind, I should say. I only know him slightly, but that much is clear enough.'

'Yes,' she said, but her voice was little more than a whisper.

'There is one aspect that confuses me, though. The man clearly knew that the Queen would pass by that corridor. Would your husband know that?'

'He knows that the Queen regularly passes by there, yes,' she said quietly. 'I have told him.'

Yes, since you are her gaoler and spy, Baldwin thought. Still . . . 'But the man was not there as you walked *to* the chapel? Only when you returned? Or could he have been there, but so well concealed . . .'

'No. He was not there as we walked to the chapel – we should have seen him.'

'Strange,' Baldwin said. 'That would almost seem to imply that the killer was warned of the right time to be there. He was told beforehand, or heard people's steps – or perhaps he knew that the Queen walked there most nights and was simply lucky that one evening. But that would mean that Jack atte Hedge and Mabilla's deaths were simple coincidences that night, and I do not believe in such things.'

'One of my husband's men,' she said again, and then she looked scared.

'You can think of someone?' Simon pressed her.

'There are only two men who could have known and attempted to do something like that: William Pilk and Ellis. But it could not be Ellis. He was Mabilla's brother. He loved her, and would never have laid a finger on her.'

Simon and Baldwin exchanged a look. Baldwin's face

was carefully devoid of all emotion, but Simon could not dissemble so effectively. On his was a savage delight.

'William Pilk.'

As they learned his name, William Pilk had other concerns. He was wearing a bruise that was growing nicely under his right eye. His shin was sore, his kidneys felt as though he'd been kicked by a donkey, and his ballocks were swelling – they felt like they'd grown to twice their normal size. He couldn't remember half of the wounds being inflicted, and he only prayed that Ellis felt as bad as him.

There was a deep-seated sense of resentment as he limped, careful to protect the more tender aspects of his anatomy, from the gate towards the Green Yard. The place was filled as usual, because whenever there was a council meeting or parliament here, all the traders turned up from miles around. They wanted to make as much money as they could while the realm's magnates were all collected here on this muddy little island by the Tyburn.

There were some he recognised, and some who were less familiar, but one face in particular stood out as soon as he saw the man. It was the black-haired fellow who had been in deep discussion with his master Sir Hugh on the night that Jack atte Hedge first appeared at the Temple. Here he was again, sitting on a bench, supping a cup of ale. William was intrigued. If the man was here, he must be someone of more importance than Pilk had realised at the time.

Retaining power in the Despenser's household was

often a question of being more astute than others, more aware of what was happening, and then keeping any information you gleaned from that to yourself. Well, Ellis had plainly succeeded in that, because William knew bugger all about the man.

Without thinking, he bent his legs towards the fellow. He would buy him another ale, he decided, and learn all he could; but even as he limped towards the fellow, the latter rose and began to make his way from the court. As Pilk watched him, disappointed, he saw the dark-haired man glance back towards him. But not directly *at* him. No, he was staring at someone nearby . . .

Finishing his drink, Piers de Wrotham rose and set off towards the main gate. He had no more business here today, so far as he knew. He had ostensibly advised his master, Earl Edmund, and then been well rewarded for it by his other, secret master, Sir Hugh. Now, since catching sight of the Earl, he had a strong desire to leave here. Urgently. There was something in the look on Edmund's face that spoke of danger. Had he seen Piers with Sir Hugh? That would account for it. Perhaps he should make a run for it now. It would be easy enough – he could either just disappear and make his way homewards to Kent, or perhaps return to Despenser and offer his services on a more permanent footing? Sir Hugh was definitely the man to keep friendly with.

The great gates were wide, and he reached them with a sigh of relief. Premature, as it happened, as with an inward groan, he saw the Earl, standing near where he had been before and casting about as though seeking someone. The moment he spied Piers at the gate, he strode up to meet him.

'I am glad to see you. I need to talk to you,' he said shortly.

'Of course, my Lord.'

'Outside, then. Not in here. Too many ears flapping.'

Piers nodded sagely, and the two made their way out and up King Street, the Earl all the while gazing about him as though the whole area was new to him.

'How much?' he demanded.

'My Lord?'

'How much did he pay you?'

'Who, my Lord? I don't —'

'I saw you with Sir Hugh just now at the side of the tavern.'

'You must have *thought* you saw me.'

Edmund turned, grasped his tunic in his fist, thrusting him up against a wall. 'You really thought that you could pull the wool over my eyes and gull me while taking Despenser's money, didn't you? That offends me, old friend. It really offends me.'

'Why should I do that, my Lord?' Piers gasped.

'Money, of course. It is what makes all transactions happen now, isn't it? Everybody wants money – nothing else matters. Except I have some men who are more loyal than that. I don't need to buy them. They are my honoured vassals. I trust them with my life, you know.'

Piers opened his mouth, but only a squeak came out. Suddenly he was petrified with fear, for in the Earl's eyes he saw nothing. Not hatred, not anger, just . . . *nothing*! It was as though he was already dead: an irrelevance.

The Earl let him go, and Piers almost fell to the ground. He wanted to leap up and flee, but his legs would not move. All he could do was stare up in horror, and then it was too late. There were steps behind him, and he saw the Earl nod once.

'You know what to do with him.'

'My Lord!'

'You are filth.'

'Let me tell you! I can help you.'

'And then sell me again?'

'Sir Hugh le Despenser, he was behind it all. Mabilla was his spy in the Queen's chamber, and Sir Hugh wanted Mabilla dead so that the Queen wouldn't tell the King Sir Hugh was plotting *her* murder. Mabilla was the trade. The Queen would live but the spy in her household would go. That was the arrangement!'

'You think I care?'

'But my Lord, you can sell this! It's information people want! You could —'

But Earl Edmund wanted to hear no more. He did not hesitate or glance over his shoulder as the two men bundled Piers into an alleyway, hurrying him along until they came to a darker doorway.

Chapter Thirty-Six

Simon and Baldwin found William in the yard still. Peter of Oxford had come with them, and he pointed out the Despenser's man at a table nursing a large horn of ale. He was staring at the gate with a frown of consternation on his battered face.

It was strange, the way that the Earl had hurried after the black-haired man like that. The Earl had looked really pissed off when he got here and Piers was gone, but then he caught sight of his man in the gateway, and strode after him. It looked as though the two knew each other.

'Are you William Pilk?'

He glanced up to see the tall Bailiff, and then he recognised the knight behind him. 'What d'you want?' he asked, although he was sure enough. Seeing Peter behind Simon, he leaned forward truculently. 'And what are *you* grinning about?'

Simon introduced himself, studying the figure in front of him. He looked as though he had just been in a fight, and had probably come off worst. Pilk was the sort of guard who would do well because of his native cunning, but Simon was sure that he was not terribly bright.

'Well? What do you want?' Pilk repeated to Baldwin, without showing a shred of respect.

'First, just to ask you some questions.'

'I don't think I want to answer any.' Pilk stood. 'I have things to do.'

'So do we,' Baldwin said and thrust hard in the middle of Pilk's chest, forcing him to sit down on the bench again with a gasp of pain as his sore arse hit the wood. 'If you wish to leave, please do. However, when I report to the King later, I shall tell him you didn't want to help investigate the murders. You were *too busy*. I am sure the King will understand.'

Pilk sneered despite the pain he was in. These prickles didn't understand the first thing about the palace. 'You do that,' he said insolently. 'I am on my Lord Despenser's business.'

'And we are on the King's,' Baldwin said. As Pilk stood up again, Baldwin grunted with irritation and pushed him down a second time. This time his hand connected with a large bruise over his abdomen, and in a reflex action, Pilk slapped at his hand. Suddenly there was a bright blue blade at his throat.

'I asked you politely, and now I am *telling* you to sit down,' Baldwin stated through gritted teeth.

'What do you want?' Pilk demanded, scowling as he sat again.

Baldwin sheathed his sword as Simon beckoned a serving maid. She looked a little reluctant to go to them, for she had seen the sword flash, but when Simon grinned broadly and held up a coin for her to see, her fear dissipated.

When she was gone to fetch their drinks, Baldwin hooked his thumbs in his belt.

'I think you could be in serious trouble.'

'I have nothing to fear.'

'Your master cannot protect you from everything, Pilk.'

William looked up at them and curled his lip. 'He can from anything *you* threaten.'

'Not I, Pilk. The King.'

He shrugged. Edward was hardly a threat. 'If you say so.'

'Let me tell you what I think happened,' Baldwin said. 'You were with your master, and he decided he had to stop Jack from killing the Queen. But he didn't know how to do so. What should he do? Ride the streets shouting Jack's name? No. All he could do was try to intercept Jack in the palace, even though no one knew from which direction, or when, Jack would come. Is that a good guess so far?'

'I have work to attend to. If all you're going to do is ask daft questions . . .'

Baldwin was unimpressed. He continued: 'So Sir Hugh le Despenser asked you to come here and do it all for him. You came here to the palace, and you stood and waited. You know the place well enough, don't you? So seeing where the Queen would be was no trouble. Except, would Jack have known where the Queen would be?'

He was struck with a sudden doubt. *Would* Jack have known about the Queen's night-time wanderings? Had she already begun to walk about the place at the time

when Jack was briefed and commissioned? No matter –
he must continue now he had begun.

'So you entered the palace, you went to the corridor
where the Queen would pass you, and you stood there
waiting. When Jack arrived, you spoke to him. You knew
him, after all, so you were able to calm his doubts. But
then, when he turned his back on you, you stabbed him.'

'I don't know what you're on about,' Will said, and
spat on to the cobbles. His eye was closing now, and he
felt like shit. 'It's nothing to do with me. I was back at Sir
Hugh's place – the Temple. I can get plenty of people to
tell you that.'

'Oh, I'm sure you can,' Baldwin said. There must be
dozens of Sir Hugh's servants who would be keen to
demonstrate their loyalty by giving Pilk an alibi. And
Baldwin would believe none of them. 'So who was it who
stabbed the man in the back, I wonder?'

'Maybe you should talk to Ellis,' Pilk suggested, and
sniggered to himself. 'He may know something. He has
investigated how the assassin got in. Perhaps he knows
more than he's let on.'

'This is Mabilla's brother?' Simon confirmed.

'You know him?'

'If he's the henchman who looks like a mastiff with his
brain removed,' Simon put in, 'then, yes.'

'Perhaps he found this man wandering about and
killed him,' Pilk said. 'There are enough died around here
just recently. If it wasn't for me, Sir Hugh himself would
be dead.'

Despite himself, Baldwin was intrigued. He had
learned nothing of the attack on Despenser from his own

choice, but his interest was piqued. 'You were there?'

'No. *Here*,' he said with emphasis. 'My master was coming out from the gate to the Green Yard, and I was up there, just a ways ahead of him when I saw the flash of the bolt up there.'

Baldwin looked away. 'I can't see where you mean from here – the man was behind the stables?'

'No! He was beside the alehouse, beyond the midden there.'

'And you saw him cocking his weapon?' Simon asked, peering up by the alehouse.

'He must have done that earlier. It was ready.'

Baldwin nodded. 'So you saw him aiming his bow?'

'I suppose so. I was in front, so he probably moved to aim around me.'

Simon frowned. Baldwin had plenty of experience with horses and lances, but the Bailiff's knowledge of bows and shooting was more extensive.

Noticing his friend's expression, Sir Baldwin set his head to one side enquiringly. 'What is it, Simon?'

'Just that if this fellow here was out in front, there'd be no need for the archer to aim around him. He would already be out of the point of aim. Look at the ground there. The gate from the Green Yard is out near the Abbey's wall, and the main gate is a little in front. A man aiming from the alehouse would only have to lean out a short way to cover the whole area. Certainly this fellow wouldn't impede his aim.'

'Then why'd he do it, then?' Pilk demanded truculently. 'I definitely saw him lean out to aim around me.'

'So Despenser was near the wall?' Baldwin asked.

'No. He was off to the left as I looked back at him. Away from the wall. It was Ellis who was nearest the wall.'

Simon shook his head. 'That makes no sense. Perhaps there was a cart or something in front of you? Or at least in front of Sir Hugh?'

'Aw, I don't care. This is so much ballocks! You have no right to keep me here, do you? I think I ought to report you to my master for wasting my time.' He stood this time, grimacing from the pain all over his body, and barged between Simon and Baldwin.

'Baldwin, I don't like that man,' Simon said.

'Nor do I. I rather think that this matter of the bowman attacking his master has upset him, although I have no idea why.'

Simon drew a triangle in the ground. 'It makes little sense for the bowman to have had to lean out to attack Despenser, not if he was out in the open and this idiot was heading straight for the gate.'

'He probably made a mistake. Still, do you think that Pilk could have killed Jack.'

'Yes, he could have. But if so, *where* did he do it? Wherever Jack died, there must have been plenty of blood. We've still not found it yet.'

Baldwin sighed and spoke quietly. 'Simon, we have looked fairly carefully about the palace, haven't we? There are only two areas which we haven't considered.'

'You aren't serious, are you?' Simon breathed. 'The two royal chambers?'

'Yes. It must have been either in the King's or the

Queen's chambers. There is nowhere else.'

'And how can we check them?' Simon asked.

'I think we need someone who can get us into the palace again,' Baldwin said, and turned to look over Simon's shoulder.

Simon followed his gaze, and gradually a smile spread over his face.

'Yes? What are you two smiling at?' Peter asked, suddenly nervous.

Ellis was tired, and the back of his head, where Coroner John's cudgel had whacked it, hurt like buggery. He was in torment. The loss of his sister was one thing, but the lack of any evidence to show who was responsible was worse. He was her brother, it was his duty to find the guilty man and make him pay, but instead he had almost seen his master killed by a bolt, and had had his own position weakened by that donkey's arse Pilk.

Mabilla – how he missed her. Who on earth could have killed her? It could have been Jack, he supposed, but he didn't think Jack would have stopped there. If he'd been told to kill the Queen, he'd have gone right on and done it. So it wasn't Jack, unless he had suddenly decided he didn't like the idea of killing anyone else. Not very likely.

He couldn't stay at the palace. It was growing late, and his head was hurting too much to think clearly. His body ached where that fucker Pilk had hit him. He'd return the favour when he had an opportunity. Later. For now, his bed was appealing. Sir Hugh had told him he would be staying here tonight, and there were enough bloody guards set around the place to protect his master. He needed to get his head down for a little. There was a palliasse in the gatehouse where he could rest.

With that decision made, he walked over the court towards the gatehouse, but while doing so, he saw Earl Edmund walking back in.

There was something about the masterful manner of his gait that stopped Ellis in his tracks. Usually the fellow was so pathetic, he could be entirely discounted, but today he was like a man renewed. His head was set high and proud, his back was straight, and he covered the ground like a warrior in a hurry. It was enough to set a warning bell tolling in Ellis's bruised and battered head. He wasn't aware of anything that could have made the Earl develop a spine all of a sudden.

As Edmund walked through a couple of waiting men, he pushed them from his path like a dog scattering cattle. The warning bell clamoured again.

And then the Earl looked over and saw him. 'So, you're still here, loyal to your master to the end, eh?' he sneered. 'Miss Mabilla, do you?'

Ellis set his jaw. How dare this man insult his sister! She was hardly cold yet, and this pathetic churl thought he could . . .

'You don't realise, do you?' Edmund went on, and gave a bark of laughter. 'You don't see what's in front of you, man. Your sister was *exchanged*, Ellis. A fair deal. She dies, and the Queen won't tell her husband that your master dared to try to have her killed. That was the deal, because your sister was a spy in the Queen's camp. You heard about her leading me on and then dropping me? That was all part of the same game. The Despenser set her on me, and when I responded she grew afraid. But don't worry. You continue to serve your master as only you know how, my friend. You do that. Don't worry about avenging your sister. What does *she* matter?'

Ellis was turned to stone, unable to move. Meanwhile, having said his piece, the Earl had walked on through the gate into the Green Yard and was gone.

'*No.*' It wasn't possible. The man was tormenting him because he hated Despenser and all his men. It was a lie – an evil lie. There could be nothing in it.

'Ellis?' It was a young messenger in the King's livery. 'Your master wants you to go to the Bishop of Exeter's house and fetch something for him. He said to give this to the Bishop's steward.'

The lad thrust a note into his hand and disappeared.

Ellis stood staring down at the slip, still without moving for a moment or two, and then he turned and made his way to the gatehouse. All he knew was obedience to his master. Without that, there was nothing. Time enough later to learn whether the Earl had been telling the truth.

Earl Edmund did not care about the impact of his words. All he knew was an overwhelming rage that he had been so duped by that worm Piers, and his master the Despenser.

'Shit!' he muttered. All the advice given to him by Piers was the result of devious plotting by Despenser, was created solely for his benefit. The Earl's closest man, the adviser he depended upon most of all was in fact an agent of his enemy, so the line he had taken recently to promote the Queen's journey to France – that must also have been what Despenser wanted. It wasn't going to hurt him at all, if Piers had promoted it.

Hell's teeth! He needed someone to help him. Standing here in the middle of the yard, he stared about him, and all he saw was hostility. Not a friendly face among the multitude.

At least there was no risk of an imminent attempt on him here. After the crossbowman's near-assassination of Sir Hugh le Despenser, his men had been all over the palace, and even now the Earl could see four of them on the walkway at the north wall and six more at the wall nearer the Thames. The guards were taking no risks, and anyone who so much as showed a bow in the yard would be pierced by a dozen arrows before he could nock his first one.

Earl Edmund did study a few of the men from beneath his brows, but it seemed that Despenser had not ordered his death yet. There was no apparent interest in him, and he didn't feel endangered as he saw armed men gazing down into the crowds. No, it was just good to see that there were men who were keen to stop any more nonsense. Three deaths in only – what? – four days? First Mabilla and the murderer, and then the second assassin with the crossbow last evening. It was becoming almost embarrassing, that the King's palace should have so many men expiring.

And now there was a fourth dead man, of course. Mustn't forget him, Edmund told himself.

No, that dog's turd. Piers was the most deserving of the lot of them.

Chapter Thirty-Seven

There was a time, Pilk reckoned, when life had been easier. When he was a lad, for example. Those days, he'd never worried too much about anything, except where his next ale was coming from. Now his head was throbbing, and he was unpleasantly certain that Ellis was going to want to cut out his bowels and strangle him with them. It was the sort of thing he'd enjoy.

Slowly, he walked through the crowds beginning to pack up their wares and leave for their lodgings or homes. When he spotted Ellis among them, he quickly turned – God, he couldn't take any more punishment today – but the man didn't see him, was hurrying through the gates, as if he couldn't get away from the palace fast enough.

Everyone was running about today, William reflected. Not him, though. He just wasn't up to it. The bastard Ellis could go and swyve a mule. If he tried anything with William again, he wouldn't hesitate – not this time. No, he'd grab a knife and gut the bastard. As long as it wasn't today.

It had been a dreadful day. Not only because of the fight with Ellis, but also because of the questioning: those two appearing and accusing him of killing the girl and perhaps Jack too. Christ, that had been unsettling. Even now, his bowels felt as if a rock was stuck in them, a heavy ball that wouldn't move, no matter what. That was how fear always affected him.

With any luck, Pilk thought wearily, he'd be able to see the back of Ellis for good soon. That'd make his day.

'I really should not be doing this.'

'No, Chaplain. You oughtn't,' Simon said with happy agreement. He poked his head around a doorway and beckoned the other two.

They had entered the palace from a doorway beneath the Lesser Chamber, which had led them to a small corridor going southwards through a small range of storage chambers. The other side of them, Peter explained, was the King's cloister, and that itself met with the Queen's. This passage would end there, and there was a small gate to allow them inside. A guard would be stationed there, of course, but Peter had learned that the guards were not aware of all the entrances. For example, he knew of a stair that led to the second floor just before the Queen's cloister.

'If we go up there, we can easily get into the upper corridors, and thence to the place where Mabilla died.'

'That is good,' Baldwin said. 'Even better would be to get inside the connecting passage from the King's to the Queen's chambers. What I wish to do is look to see whether there is any evidence of murder having happened in the King's chamber or near it.'

'Why? I don't understand.'

'Because someone,' Simon said, 'killed this man Jack

atte Hedge. Whoever it was, killed him somewhere else, and then carried him through to the Great Hall. There wasn't enough blood where he was found for him to have died there.'

'So you say he died somewhere else and was carried there? Why?'

'That, as they say, is the interesting question,' Baldwin said. 'If he was found in the King's chamber, perhaps that would have made for embarrassment.'

'Especially with his tarse in his mouth,' Simon grunted.

'That is the reason why I feel that the King's chamber is not so likely,' Baldwin said. 'Whoever killed him left that mark upon him as a symbol of contempt for Despenser, I am sure.'

'So you don't want to go there?'

'The Queen's chamber first would perhaps be more sensible,' Baldwin said.

'Apart from the fact that if the man *was* killed in her chamber, or near her, the killer would have had to carry his corpse all the way along the corridors to the Great Hall where he was found,' Simon pointed out. 'How could someone do that and hope to escape without being detected?'

'Maybe he bribed the guards,' Peter offered. 'Or he was simply an enormously bold, courageous fellow.'

'Perhaps,' Baldwin agreed. They had reached a staircase. 'This is it?'

'Let me go first and make sure all is safe,' Peter said. He walked up the stairs and opened a heavy little door at the top. 'It's fine.'

Baldwin and Simon followed him and stood at the top.

Baldwin thrust his head through the gap and found himself in a narrow passageway that led off towards the river and met up with an upper storey in the old palace building. Soon he was up and standing beside Peter, Simon clambering after them.

'It is usually safe here. That is why it's sometimes popular.'

Simon tilted his head. 'With whom?'

'Lovers. They use this route when they want secrecy. I've seen some few.'

'Such as?'

He looked at Simon with a smile. 'I mentioned Alicia and the guard before. They have been along here, when Alicia should have remained in the Queen's quarters and Richard Blaket should have been in the guardroom. But lovers cannot be kept apart, eh?'

This new corridor ended in a small chamber, in the next wall of which was another small door. Peter again went ahead and peered through. He jerked his head at them, and they walked along the flagged way after him. Periodically, on their right, were a series of tall, narrow windows which gave out over the Queen's cloister. At this time of the evening no one was there. They would be eating, Baldwin thought, from the odours that rose to his nostrils.

Peter led them to a door set into the wall at the end. Here he looked at them seriously, then drew a key from a chain about his neck, and put it in the lock. The door opened easily and silently, and Simon and Baldwin found themselves in the chapel once more, this time in the upper storey.

'Here you are.'

'The Queen will be eating? I suppose that means we cannot enter her chamber,' Baldwin mused.

'No, she's dining with the King in the old palace just now.'

'Why?'

'They are putting on a show of matrimonial normality,' Peter said cynically. 'There are too many who would like to portray them as loathing each other, so they sometimes put on a little display to frustrate all of them.'

'Then let us see her chamber.'

Peter chewed at his lip. 'What will you do if there is blood in there?' he asked without moving. 'You mean to accuse the Queen of murder?'

'No. There is no doubt that the man who died was an assassin. We have had him confirmed in his profession,' Baldwin said. 'My interest is to learn about Mabilla and who actually killed her.'

Peter led the way slowly out through the rear of the chapel and along another corridor. 'But if you find blood in her chamber . . .' he said again, still anxious.

'It will simply mean that someone killed the assassin in order to protect her.'

'Ah. Good point. That man should be rewarded,' the Chaplain smiled. He threw open a door. 'Here it is.'

They were in a long chamber that looked out over the Thames. The walls were decorated with a pattern of tiles, the floor comprised good broad elm boards, and there were decorative tapestries and hangings to stop the draughts. Baldwin glanced about him once, and was then off along the chamber, his eyes to the ground, walking from side to side like a questing hound.

'Is he always like this?' Peter asked.

Simon, who was finding it hard to drag his eyes from the hangings, from the gilded carvings at the ceiling, from the fabulous tableware and the gleaming plates and bowls of silver, could only nod.

'Stop! In the name of the King!'

Peter winced and threw a look at Simon.

'Oh! Hello, Master Blaket,' Simon said, and attempted a sickly smile as the long pike's spear-point came to a halt at his breastbone.

Sir Hugh le Despenser watched as the two men were pushed in, the Chaplain apologising profusely behind them, all of them bowing low as they came into the King's presence.

King Edward could have been unaware of their arrival. He was sitting at his comfortable seat and eating, making no comment, but Sir Hugh knew that studied disinterest of old: it was a certain indication of his extreme anger.

Studying them himself, Sir Hugh saw that the Chaplain had every appearance of fear. Good. So he should! He'd been found leading these two in among the corridors to the Queen's quarters when they'd been told to leave the place alone. If nothing else, he'd lose his comfortable little posting here. No matter that he had 'benefit of clergy,' his crime was one that would undoubtedly lead to a punishment. That was a sly little game for clerics who were guilty of fondling some matron's titties, but it wouldn't serve for a man considered a traitor to the King. And leading strangers into the Queen's accommodation was surely a treacherous act.

These two rural officers! Look at them! One a country-knight with barely enough money to keep himself in equipment and horses, while the other was a mere peasant. Pathetic! Yet they had challenged his authority and now they sought to embarrass the King himself. Good God – what a pair of *cretins*!

The Bailiff was worried. It was there in his quickening breath, the narrowed eyes, the slight flushing at his cheeks. As he walked in, he had looked calm, perhaps a little anxious, but not more than that. Now, though, he stood with his eyes downcast, a man who knew his peril and daren't meet the eyes of his judges in case he saw death in them. He'd be fun to break! If the bastard didn't confess to his crime in five minutes of first meeting Ellis and his tools of torture, Sir Hugh would be happy to eat his cap!

It was then that he saw Sir Baldwin's gaze on him. The man had the nerve to meet his eye! Sweet Christ, he'd have the man's ballocks off for that! And there was no fear in his face. If anything, he was like a man who had already lost all he cared about and now was prepared to stand up for what he believed.

The King finished his meal in a leisurely manner, and beckoned a laver, who hurried forward with a bowl and towel as the Chaplain behind the King read a short Grace giving thanks for God's bounty.

Dabbing at his lips, the King did not so much as cast a look in their general direction. 'You were in my lady wife's parlour. You had been told not to go there, but you did so.'

Sir Hugh stared from one to the other. He saw the

Bailiff glance at his friend, but Sir Baldwin made no sign; he merely stood utterly still, his brows lowered as he listened.

'I had asked you to investigate the murderous attack upon my good friend Sir Hugh here, but you chose to slight me and suggest that I should be more careful of my wife's life. And then you broke into her chambers.'

'You asked me to investigate the murder of Mabilla and the death of the assassin in the Great Hall. I am doing that to the best of my ability, my Liege.'

'You seek to correct me? You presume to tell me I am wrong again?' King Edward snapped.

All in the room stiffened. Despenser could *feel* it: the sudden gathering for the explosion of violence that would surely ignite in the King's breast. He'd seen it so often since the Battle of Boroughbridge. The King had made it his mission to seek out all those who'd decided to challenge his holy authority, his God-given right to rule in his own name, in the manner which he chose. They had been hunted down, every one, and destroyed. Broken, ravaged, they were hanged until almost dead, and then their pricks and ballocks were cut from them and burned before their eyes to show that their line was cursed. While they choked and struggled, gagging, the noose about their necks, the executioner would hack open their breasts and rip out their still-beating hearts and throw them onto the fire. Only then were they beheaded, their corpses butchered so that their limbs could be displayed on the city walls as a deterrent to others.

'I intend to seek the man who could have sought to murder your Queen, my Lord,' Sir Baldwin said flatly.

'This is the task you gave me, and I will serve you as best I may.'

'I told you I wanted the man who intended my friend here to be killed. *That* was the man I wanted you to find for me.'

'And I said that your friend here had enough men of his own. The Queen suffers from the loss of her household. Who is to protect her?'

'She has my protection!' the King snapped.

Baldwin set his head slightly to one side and said nothing, but his manner was clear.

Sir Hugh intervened with acid in his tone. 'You mean to accuse your King of deceit? You say that he seeks to harm his wife?'

Sir Baldwin looked at him. 'No man could dream of such a thing! I merely state the obvious, my Lord. You have your household to protect you. The King's household exists to serve him. Yet the Queen, who is the lady whose life must be in peril, has had all her guards dispersed, her friends and knights removed. She is little better than a petitioner at the court where she is supposed to rule. If a man were to make an attempt on her life again, it would be easy enough.'

'My men guard her!' Sir Hugh spat.

'I am sure Her Ladyship would be comforted to know that,' Sir Baldwin said expressionlessly.

'You doubt his integrity?' the King demanded. 'Sir Hugh is my fondest companion. I trust him entirely.'

'I am glad to hear it, Your Majesty.'

'You disbelieve me?'

'Your Majesty, no man could doubt your honour.'

'That scarcely answers my question.'

Sir Baldwin said nothing, but his dark eyes changed subtly. Sir Hugh saw it: there was a sudden chill in them. All warmth left them, and all that remained was like the black ice that formed on the paved ways in winter. Even Sir Hugh was affected by them, and felt compelled to look over at the guards and make sure that they were all ready in case of an attack.

'You are a bold fellow, Sir Baldwin.'

'There are times when a man must choose integrity compared with living a lie, Your Majesty. I feel sure I would be uncomfortable behaving any other way.'

'Yes. Perhaps you would,' the King muttered. He subsided into his chair, and now his anger appeared to have left him. He studied the two men before him with a quizzical expression in his eyes. 'What were you doing there? You sought to search her rooms. That doesn't sound as though you were seeking to protect her – quite the opposite. Are you guilty of treason against your Queen, Sir Knight?'

There was a teasing note in his voice which Sir Hugh did not like to hear. 'Your Majesty—' he began.

'Let him answer, Hugh. Does he look like a burglar to you? No. Nor the good Bailiff, I'll be bound. Come, Sir Baldwin. Answer: do you mean her some harm?'

'Your Majesty,' Baldwin said, 'I would never dream of harming her or you. I am a loyal servant of the Crown.' He inclined his head. 'If you have any doubts about me, you must immediately take away my writ to serve you as your Keeper of the King's Peace in Devon.'

'Come now!' the King said a little testily. 'If I was that

worried, you wouldn't still be standing here before me, Sir Baldwin. Plainly I do not distrust you altogether. No, I am inclined to believe you. But what were you doing in her rooms?'

'I sought blood.'

'Blood?' The King's eyes widened. 'What?'

'The assassin died somewhere. One of only a few places where I had not yet searched for his place of death was in the Queen's chamber.'

'And did you find it?'

'I fear, Your Majesty, I was interrupted before I could complete my search. But I do not think I shall find anything there. There was nothing to indicate that there had been a fight. Surely wherever this man Jack atte Hedge was murdered, he will have left traces of his death.'

'Perhaps. So you will not be feloniously persuading some mischievous Chaplain to grant you access to her rooms again?'

Baldwin allowed himself a small smile. 'I rather think that my experiences tonight with your most efficient guards would put me off the idea of further enquiries.'

'Good. Oh, rise, rise, all of you!'

They did so with relief. Simon always suffered from a bad back, and after bending for so long he was uncomfortably certain that he would soon be suffering again.

'What will you do now?' the King asked.

'I think I am close to a decision on the matter of the murder.'

'But have done nothing about the attempt on my good friend Sir Hugh's life?'

Baldwin smiled. 'I have discovered an interest in that too, my Liege.'

'You have!' the King exclaimed. 'What tempted you to start to think of this?'

'Naturally your desire to see me look into it, Your Majesty. That, and a chance comment from a man earlier. It has made me look at the matter afresh.'

'Ah. Very good. You may leave us, then, and continue your search for the truth.'

Baldwin nudged Simon, and the three men backed away, bowing low. They managed to reach the door without stumbling, and once outside the room they looked at each other, Simon blowing out his cheeks as he sighed with relief. 'Baldwin, Brother Peter, I thought I was going to have to compose a letter to Meg to say, "Farewell"!'

'Come, Simon. Don't exaggerate! There was little enough to fear in there.'

'Little? When we were hauled in front of the King?' Peter squeaked.

'It was to be expected.' Baldwin sighed. 'Only it does mean that further investigation will be difficult. How can we learn where the assassin died if we cannot look in the King's and Queen's own chambers?'

Simon shot him a look. The guards were still close, but as he and Baldwin walked away from the last door, Chaplain Peter behind them, he leaned to the knight.

'You mean you didn't see?'

Baldwin was puzzled. 'See what? I was looking at the King.'

'On the floor beside the table, near Despenser's foot. A large stain on the flags and carpet.'

'Was it blood?'

'I'd bet on it. *That* was where he died.'

'Good. In that case we have almost all the chain of events in our hands, Simon,' Baldwin said, and rubbed his hands together with glee.

Chapter Thirty-Eight

Ellis was almost back at the palace when the man stopped him.

The fellow was young, and quite slim for a man-at-arms, but from the heraldry on his breast, he was a servant of Earl Edmund. He wasn't the sort of man to upset, but Ellis didn't care.

'What?' he demanded ungraciously.

'A present. For your master from mine,' the man said. 'Do not open it yourself, though, it is for Sir Hugh le Despenser and him alone'

Ellis took the leather package and hefted it. It was quite heavy, for all that it was about the size and shape of a pig's bladder. He jerked his head to have the man move out of his path, then strode onwards.

The gate was busy, as ever. There were always traders entering, politicians idling their way past, guards sitting and gossiping with pots of ale or wine, and the sound of thousands of men and women talking as loudly as possible, selling wares, shouting for attention, demanding people stop and consider their goods.

Not for him today, though. He had been sent to the Bishop's house with an urgent mission, and now he had a gift for his master too. He shouldered his way through the crowds and out to the Green Yard gate. 'For Sir Hugh le Despenser,' he said, holding up the package, and was soon through.

He had been told to bring his message to the King's chambers, so he made his way there now, easily getting past the different guards. All knew him. All worked for him. All were paid by him.

The last pair were at the King's doors. Ellis motioned for them to stand aside, then rapped smartly on the timbers. Hearing the King's command to enter, he opened the door and walked in.

'Ah, Ellis,' Despenser said. 'You have it for me?'

'Yes. I went there as you asked, and his servant gave it to me.'

'Good. Where is it?' He took the small scrap from Ellis and glanced at it with relief. Then he saw the leather parcel slung from Ellis's shoulder. It was a simple bag, with a thong that passed about the mouth, and this had been tied firmly. 'What's that?'

'It's a gift from Earl Edmund.'

'Really?' Despenser said. He was intrigued. The Earl was more likely to send an assassin, like the one who had tried to kill him on Sunday.

The King was surprised too. 'I didn't think my brother would usually consider sending you a present, Sir Hugh.'

'Nor did I, my Liege,' Sir Hugh said, but added with a smile, 'yet he and I have discussed many matters recently, and we find ourselves often in agreement.' He set the package down on a table and fumbled with the bindings.

It felt like a pot of wine or something. It was quite a weight.

The leather bag opened, and he pulled the drawstrings wide, reaching in and then giving a short gasp and pulling his hand away again, his eyes wide with revulsion. 'What the—'

'Sir Hugh?' the King cried, leaping to his feet.

Ellis's more practical response was to draw his knife and step to his master's side. 'Sir Hugh, what is it?'

Sir Hugh tipped the bag over. Piers's head rolled out a short distance, the eyes half-lidded, the neck obscenely shortened.

'I don't understand you,' Simon said as Sir Baldwin stood in the yard with hands on hips, and looked up and down with excitement.

'Simon, it is easy. I wouldn't trust that son of a leprous whore any more than I'd trust a snake. Not true: I'd trust a snake more than him.'

'You mean Despenser?'

Baldwin threw him an exasperated look. 'Come along, Simon. This was your fault, after all.'

'Mine?' the Bailiff protested, but Baldwin was already striding up towards the alehouse's midden.

'He must have hung about here in order to be hidden,' he said, pointing up at the wall walk. From almost all angles, Simon could see, they were concealed from view here. And nobody would have bothered to keep much of an eye upon this noisome place.

'But look,' Baldwin said, gesturing back towards the Green Yard gate. 'See? If that fool Pilk was out in front, he would be unlikely to block the archer's view of Despenser.'

'So?'

'So, as you pointed out, there was no need for this man to lean out to fire at Despenser. All he need do was stand here and fire along the building.'

'Unless there was someone else in the way.'

'Pilk said not, and we can trust his words, for he actually *saw* the bowman. If there had been an obstruction, Pilk would not have seen the man.' Baldwin leaned against the wall with satisfaction. 'No, I think that explains much. This fellow wasn't aiming at Despenser.'

'What? Who, then?'

'There was one man he'd have to lean out to hit, and hit safely without hurting another – and yet leave it looking as though he'd been trying to kill Sir Hugh.'

Simon swore quietly and slammed a fist against his thigh. 'But why would Sir Hugh conspire to kill his own servant?'

'If Despenser had paid to have Mabilla killed . . . how would her brother react?' Baldwin asked.

Simon nodded. 'A good point.'

'A very good point,' Baldwin said with a brief flash of his teeth. 'And the best of it is, if we can persuade Ellis of the truth of our words, he might just agree to tell us about his master's business. This could be the last little thread of the story that ties the whole tapestry together.'

Despenser pointed at the head and barked at Ellis, 'Take that thing away! Throw it away!'

Ellis was staring at it still, open-mouthed. 'Why'd he

send that to you? It was the Earl's servant himself gave it me, master. I am sorry.'

'Get the damned thing off my table!' the King screamed. 'Who was it? Dear God in heaven, whatever was my brother thinking of when he—' He stopped. Never a fool, Edward knew a revenge slaying when he saw one. 'Who was he?' he repeated.

'A man I knew, named Piers de Wrotham,' Sir Hugh said cautiously. 'No one of significance.'

'He isn't now, anyway,' the King said drily. The shock was wearing off, and both men could eye the head with interest as Ellis picked it up and shoved it back in the bag.

'I'll take it back to Earl Edmund.'

'Do that. And tell him that I am grateful for his gift, and that I intend to reciprocate in due course,' Sir Hugh said, his anger already rising at the thought that the King's youngest brother could have dared to taunt him in this way. No matter. He would have his revenge.

Ellis walked from the chamber with the repugnant package in his hand, hoping against hope that he might meet with one of the Earl's men, and be able to dump it on him.

'Master Ellis, I must speak with you!'

He saw Sir Baldwin and his friend, but didn't slow his pace, snarling, 'I've urgent business. Leave me alone.'

'Pilk told us that you were investigating the assassin. Did you learn how he got in?'

'Speak to the fool Arch who was on the wall. He was the weak link. The man knocked him down, I think, and climbed in that way.'

'Where did he go then?'

'Down to the Queen's rooms, I suppose. Now leave me alone! This is business between my master and the Earl of Kent. I will not be delayed.'

'But *we* need to talk to you about your sister,' Simon shouted after him, but he was beyond listening.

Ellis was seething. He wanted to kill someone. For the offence given to his master – and for the murder of his sister.

Sir Hugh excused himself. 'My Liege, I fear that my man could get into a fight again if he meets with one of the Earl's men. Would you allow me to leave you and ensure that there is no bloodshed?'

'Why was my brother willing to decapitate a man and send the head to you?' the King demanded.

'It is a question you must put to your brother,' Sir Hugh said firmly, and he bowed.

'It is a question I have posed to *you*, Sir Hugh,' the King said sharply.

'My Lord, if I leave this a moment longer, there will be more blood shed for no purpose!'

'Oh, go if you must, then,' the King responded petulantly. 'But be quick! I will have an explanation from you, and from him too. I am not in the habit of receiving heads at my table, Sir Hugh. I do not like the thought that others may consider you are receiving such leniency from my hand.'

But Sir Hugh didn't wait to hear any more. He bowed his way from the room, and when he had passed through the doorway, he turned and hurried away to the yard. But rather than follow Ellis, he took the path that led him down to the Great Hall and out by the Exchequer. It was that which saved him from bumping into Sir Baldwin and Simon, who were hastening along in the wake of Ellis.

Despenser saw Ellis in the yard as soon as he reached the New Palace Yard, and immediately began to cast about for Pilk. Ah, there he was, over at the main gate, sitting on a bench. As soon as he saw Pilk, Despenser waved to him. The slow-witted idiot seemed not to recognise him at first, but then lumbered to his feet and made his way towards Despenser.

Ellis, meanwhile, was moving at a faster pace. A pair of the Earl's men were standing at a brazier of charcoal, hands held out to it. Ellis recognised the young man who gave him this 'gift', and did not break his stride as he approached them, but instead gathered the bag to his breast, elbows out, and both hands behind it, thumbs under to support it, before flinging it like a stuffed bladder in a football match. It span twice through the air before slamming into the shoulder of one of the men.

He fell, cursing loudly, and his companion had his sword out in a moment. Ellis ignored it, drawing his own and snarling incoherently as he held it aloft and advanced.

And in the midst of the fight, Despenser saw his opportunity. 'Pilk, in God's name, stop Ellis. He's gone mad! Look at him!'

Pilk needed no second urging. He drew his own sword and hurried after Ellis, who meanwhile had kicked the Earl's man in the head where he lay, and was now attacking the second.

He cared nothing for the scratch he had already

experienced on his left arm, but instead attacked relentlessly, his blade always before him so that no further stab might win through. There was no sense to the fight, it was the culmination of the horror of his sister's death, and then the increasing frustration he felt at not finding her killer. He wanted to lash out until all those who had hurt his sister were dead. And these gilded little popinjays were representatives of the man whom Mabilla had accused of trying to feel up her skirts. The *good* Earl had tried to rape her, and then sent his man to have Ellis carry that head to his master. Well, Ellis would have *his* head in return. Tears filled his eyes at the thought of Mabilla's body lying cold in her grave, and the anguish of loss gave his damaged arm more vigour. He slashed and stabbed faster and faster.

'Stop that! *Stop*, Ellis!'

He didn't register who it was. His blood was up, and any man who approached him was there to try to kill him. So as soon as Pilk was near enough, he span quickly, his sword flashing red, and whipped it past Pilk's throat. There was a gout of blood, and he sprang forward to plant his fist in Pilk's face even as Pilk staggered. Then he was back on his other opponent.

But the Earl's man had not been idle. As soon as Ellis turned to attack Pilk, he reached forward, so low that his hand went to the ground to support him, and his sword thrust up from just above the buttocks. It was not a deep stab, and Ellis hardly seemed to notice it, but when he returned to the attack, he was slower, more ponderous. He could feel it, even though he was unaware that his liver and a kidney were both ruptured. But as he continued, a growing pain in his back told him something was amiss. He tried to return to the assault, but found his eyes growing heavier and heavier, his feet leaden, and suddenly he pitched forward to his knees. He remained there for a moment, blinking, baffled and too tired even to maintain his anger.

But not for long. His opponent would take no risks. His sword whirled once and Ellis's head was catapulted through the air to join the one still in the bag over by the brazier.

Baldwin and Simon had heard the screams and shouts, and turned to rush back to the yard, but they were too late to stop the fight. They only reached the ground as Ellis sank to his knees, the back of his jerkin and hosen a reddened mess of blood, and just in time to see the Earl's man bring his blade around and sweep the injured man's head from his shoulders.

'A sore loss,' Despenser said, coming to join them. But there was no sadness in his tone. No, as he gazed at the two bodies, at Pilk's still shivering from the throes as the last of his blood leached into the gravel about him, and at Ellis's, where it had fallen forwards to lie on the ground only a matter of yards away, all he knew was satisfaction at a job well done.

'I hope you are pleased, Sir Hugh?' Baldwin spat.

'Me? I have lost two good men here, Sir Baldwin. Naturally I am distressed,' Sir Hugh replied. But he smiled.

Baldwin clenched his fist; Simon saw and gripped his wrist. 'Baldwin!' he muttered in the knight's ear. 'Think of Jeanne, and Richalda and little Baldwin. Do not throw away your life and their future in anger!'

'You are right,' Baldwin said, taking a deep breath. 'We have evidence enough already to see you ruined, Sir Hugh.'

'I had nothing to do with all this, Sir Baldwin. These men started a brawl without my egging them on. They are simply the victim of their own violent natures. And now I shall have to find more men.'

'Yes. And explain all that happened on the night Jack was killed.'

'I don't know what you mean.'

'I think you do. You commanded Jack to kill the Queen, but then you changed your mind. For whatever reason, you decided to stop Jack. But how to do that? The only way was to kill *him*.'

'You call me a murderer?'

'I call you much worse than that.'

'Be careful how you speak to me!'

Baldwin was about to say more, when Despenser shook his head.

'Sir Baldwin! You think you have some marvellous evidence against me? You do not. I knew nothing about this Jack atte Hedge. Nothing. And you cannot prove otherwise.'

'I *shall* prove it!'

Despenser shrugged and grimaced without humour, then walked slowly away, from the scene of slaughter, content that with Ellis dead, he was safe.

Chapter Thirty-Nine

Bishop Walter was happy to accede to Sir Baldwin's request, and met with Simon and Baldwin in the smaller of the royal chambers, the Lesser Hall. They were only there a short while before Coroner John opened the door and peered inside. The night was falling, and it was growing dark. Simon was glad to see that the Coroner had brought a candle, and servants entered with him, quickly lighting candles in a pair of floor-standing holders. Soon the room was illuminated with a cheerful orange glow.

The Coroner ushered the servants out, and then said, 'My Lord Bishop? I was told to come here.'

'You have seen the two dead men out there?' Baldwin asked the Bishop.

'I am afraid so. Two of Despenser's men and one other, of whom we have only the head. I am shocked by these deaths. What could have led to such a violent assault?'

'Three dead. Three more dead,' Baldwin said heavily. 'And all for so little reason.'

The Coroner stirred in his corner. 'I should not overly tax your sympathy on their behalf, Sir Baldwin. I am sure that one of those men was involved in the murder of the innkeeper over at Chelchede on Sunday.'

'That is a terrible thing to say of the dead!' the Bishop said, startled.

'Perhaps. Yet I believe you said that you have evidence I could use?'

'Yes, indeed, Sir John,' Baldwin said. 'We have much. For the first, we know that the assassin who was found in the palace here was in fact in the pay of Sir Hugh le Despenser. He was named Jack atte Hedge, and was a known killer.'

'You have proof?'

'Yes. He climbed the wall at the south-western point where the wall meets the Abbey grounds, knocking out the guard on duty there, before making his way into the palace.'

'Where he died,' John noted with satisfaction.

'After killing Mabilla,' Simon growled.

'And then there was the supposed attack upon Despenser himself. The bowman who tried that had a perfect shot at Despenser, from what we have heard. Despenser was walking away from the wall, one man well ahead of him out in the front, and the other nearer the wall. Yet the bowman leaned right out to fire.'

'Yes. I thought the same when I studied the ground,' John agreed.

'What do you infer from that?' the Bishop asked.

'That he was not aiming for Sir Hugh. He was aiming at another,' Baldwin said.

'How much, I wonder, would a man be paid for killing the Despenser?' Coroner John wondered aloud.

'At least twenty, maybe five-and-twenty pounds. Maybe even more, if he was being paid by someone who had a serious grudge against the man,' Baldwin said. 'There are some who would no doubt pay any price to see him removed.'

The Bishop said, a little stiffly, 'I hardly think that this sort of speculation is helpful.'

Coroner John nodded – although he was remembering the coins he had found in the dead bowman's wallet. The sum had amounted to less than a pound. Hardly the King's ransom that Sir Hugh's enemies would have paid for *his* head.

But as he calculated, the door behind them all was kicked shut. 'Who else would they have been aiming at, then, Sir Baldwin?'

Simon felt his hackles rise at the sound of that voice. Sir Hugh le Despenser had been standing at the door for some little while – how long Simon didn't know – but it was plainly long enough for him to get a feel for what was being said.

'Well? You have been making accusations against me with joyful abandonment. Am I the only person to miss the full depth of your ingenuity?'

Simon instinctively felt for the hilt of his sword as the man swaggered over to stand by the candles. He stood facing his accuser.

Baldwin nodded. 'Very well, then. I know that you had your man Jack atte Hedge enter the grounds. I think that he knocked a guard, Arch, on the head and all but addled his brains. I believe that you had commanded him or another man to kill the maid Mabilla.'

'My. Wasn't I busy!' Despenser observed coldly. He held a hand to the flame nearest him as though seeking the warmth.

'However, after the death of Mabilla, you knew full well that your man might come to recognise your part in her murder. You did not wish him as an enemy within your household, so reluctantly you decided that the dead girl's brother Ellis too must die.'

'"*Reluctantly*" eh? You do me that honour, at least.'

'A man like you will only reluctantly lose a competent and reliable servant like him,' Baldwin said with confidence. 'But the last days must have been disastrous for you. You lost Jack atte Hedge, then Ellis and William Pilk. At the same time you have lost your best spy on your wife and the Queen.'

'You step too close to the brink, Sir Baldwin!' Despenser hissed.

'Yes,' Baldwin smiled grimly. 'I, who interpret the facts, may imperil my life, while you, who are responsible for all these deaths, may threaten me with impunity! But I am not finished, for you also comprehended your danger and sought to alleviate it somewhat. And how? By having a bowman execute your man Ellis. Except he missed his target, didn't he? He was to have killed Ellis, and then you would have had him slain immediately. But no matter. When William Pilk saw him and called attention to him, Ellis ran to save you! What irony! He ran to save the man who had paid another to kill him. And then your guards on the walls slew the bowman, as you had anticipated. What, did you tell him that he would be able to escape safely because you had warned the guards to let him loose?'

'This is all most fascinating,' Despenser murmured. 'Pray, what else am I guilty of? Perhaps I also caused the famine? Did I slay the officer in St Sardos and precipitate the war with France?'

'Do not be flippant!' Baldwin said. 'You, who have been responsible for so many deaths, should at least show a little compassion and humility! Do you have nothing more to say?'

'I have plenty to say. I say this is nonsense! I say that the tale is built upon your remorseless enmity to me and my people. You, Sir Baldwin, have tried to thwart my people all over the country. I know of you from old. And now you have created this fiction!'

As he spoke, he had removed himself to the other side of the great candle-holder, and Simon thought that he was moving in order to defend himself from attack. But then he took a small parchment strip from his scrip and held it to the flames. For a moment Simon wondered what he was doing, and then he gasped. 'Baldwin, the indenture!'

'This?' Despenser smiled wide-eyed at Baldwin. 'Did you want this? Ah, but it was a nothing.'

It had flamed like an oil-soaked cloth, flaring in a moment, and he dropped it quickly. But there was no point attempting to rescue it. As it landed on the ground it was clear enough that it would be ash before Simon or Baldwin could reach it. A few words might have been legible, but only a few.

'Did you want it? Oh, I am sorry. It was only a scrap of mine,' Despenser said, and now there was a harsher edge to his voice, 'So, Sir Baldwin. What proof exactly do you have of my crimes? You allege that I had this man Jack working for me – I deny it; you say I had him killed – again, I deny it; you say I had Mabilla killed – that is nonsense; you suggest that I attempted to have my man Ellis killed – and all this without the slightest hint of proof. I am tempted to demand justice from the King for such disgraceful accusations. But no, I can afford to be lenient. You have much to learn about this little isle, Sir Baldwin. It will be a pleasure to witness your education. Do not mind if I leave you now. I do not think that there is any point in continuing this discussion.'

'I shall carry on to find who . . .'

'Yes, yes, yes,' Despenser said with an elaborate yawn. 'I am sure that you will, Sir Baldwin. Be careful, though. Such a task could prove to be a heavy *cross* to bear, eh?' and he glanced at the sword sheathed at Baldwin's hip. 'Do we really wish to rake over old ashes?'

'Well!' Coroner John said when Sir Hugh was safely out of earshot. 'I think, my Lords, that he has you by the short hairs. There's little enough to be said, I think.'

'I am sorry,' Baldwin said. 'I appear to have wasted your time.'

'Yes. Well.' Coroner John paused, shot a look at the Bishop, then held out his hand to Baldwin. 'Friend. For all the good it will do, I would say that the Despenser was right. You have much to learn about this place. The Palace appears to be built on solid foundations, but in reality its bedrock is politics, and that means lies and deceit. Don't worry yourself unduly, eh? Ach, what do I know? I'll take my leave, lordings. My Lord Bishop.'

The Coroner nodded to Simon and Baldwin, made a cursory bow in the direction of the Bishop, and walked from the room.

He had misjudged the two men. They were no more dishonest than he himself. Perhaps less so.

After he left the room there was silence for a while.

'Baldwin, I am sorry,' Bishop Stapledon said. 'Truly. I did not expect to—'

'My Lord, you knew that piece of paper was the vital link between him and the assassin, yet you kept it back and gave it to him?'

'I did.'

'You had sworn to keep it safe for us,' Simon pointed out, aghast. 'Why did you give it to *him*?'

'Do you think it will be best for our Kingdom to be thrown into disarray just now?' Bishop Stapledon demanded. 'Look about you, gentles. Look at the King's council. Did you see much by way of rational, logical debate? Was there much unanimity? Was there agreement? No! There was a bear-pit of dispute, and then Sir Hugh Despenser was able to close it down and bring matters to a reasonable conclusion. What would that scrap of paper have achieved?'

'It could have brought a murderer to justice,' Baldwin said with ponderous emphasis.

'Do you think that one, or two, or three, or even four murders would justify removing the last baron capable of maintaining the realm? Sir Hugh is unique. He has the King's ear. With his arguments, we may be able to renegotiate a truce with France. You think we can afford to lose such a man, just now when the whole of the King's French territories are under threat? You would not destroy Sir Hugh, but you could bring him under such scrutiny that his ability to command men would be restricted, and then where would we be?'

'My Lord, you justify his murders?' Simon asked quietly.

'No. I do not condone murder. But there are times when commanding a kingdom, when a man must look to the necessities of the ruler, not the ruled.'

'I will have no part of it!' Baldwin spat. He turned on his heel.

'Sir Baldwin,' the Bishop called. 'I do not expect you to understand me in this matter. But do not condemn too swiftly. Your anger may be misdirected.'

'*Misdirected*,' Baldwin fumed 'My arse!'

Simon glanced up and down the corridor. 'Old friend, I think it would be best were we to leave this place as soon as we may.'

'I agree. There is nothing for us here. All here are shallow and dishonourable. My God – I despair of this. That the Bishop himself could suggest that I might condemn too swiftly! Dear God in heaven, what must a man like Despenser *do* to be found deserving of punishment? He is safe from accusations of murder, so how may a man find justice?'

'I don't know. It was an odd thing, though.'

'What?'

'The way the Bishop said that – about not condemning too swiftly. Did you hear his words? That "when

commanding a kingdom, a man must look to the
necessities of the ruler" – could he think that the *King*
was responsible?'

Baldwin looked at him and there was some wildness in
his eyes. 'You think that the Bishop considers Despenser a
gentle, kindly fellow? Simon, we have merely seen a
glimpse today of the Bishop's own heart. He would prefer
stable government to honesty! A man must not rock the
balance of power in the state in case it topples. I suppose
that was what he meant. But for my part, I would see
Despenser accused, gaoled and hanged if there was even a
remote scrap of evidence.'

'But there cannot be,' Simon said. 'You cannot find a
man who would have seen Despenser walking the
passages during the night, because you know that the
killer was the man Despenser himself hired. And the
other, the man who killed Mabilla, was built in a more
scrawny manner than a knight, if that woman Joan is to
be believed. It was probably some fellow discovered in
the streets, like the lone bowman sent to kill Ellis.'

'Sir Baldwin, Master Bailiff,' the Coroner called
breathlessly. He had been trying to keep up with them
since seeing them leave the chamber, but their anger had
made their steps fly over the ground.

'Sir John,' Baldwin said coolly. 'How may we serve
you?'

'I think it is unlikely we can do much, except I was not
sure whether I hold any information which could be of
use to you.'

'You did not mention it in there,' Simon said curtly.

'Aye, well, a man may love truth and honour, and yet

choose to keep from accusing a man like Sir Hugh,' Sir John said with a twisted grin.

'You didn't trust us?'

'No, not at first. I do now, though, seeing how you tweaked the tail of Despenser. No, I was just unsure whether you had spoken to Arch.'

'Yes. And got little of any use from him,' Simon admitted.

'Did he tell you about the moon's halo?'

Simon and Baldwin exchanged a blank look.

'I checked with the men. He asserted that he saw a moon with a halo. All others said that the night was black and there was no moon until the middle watches. I asked that guard to the Queen's door, and he said that it was only then that the moon rose, and it did have a halo, just as Arch stated. So he wasn't lying. He was awake through to the middle of the night. Arch even recalled the guard walking the circuit.'

'I do not see how that helps us, my friend,' Baldwin said after a moment's consideration. 'It means we know the assassin must have arrived late into the night, I suppose, but that is all.'

'Why did the guard walk about?' Simon wondered.

'Hmm?'

'Surely all the guards should have kept to their posts, not wandered about like lovers under the stars?'

'Arch said that the Queen's guard was checking because there were rumours of danger,' John shrugged. He left them shortly afterwards, declaring a desire for ale.

Baldwin stood watching him with a frown of concentration marring his features. 'Eleanor was certain that it must be Pilk or Ellis – but either of those two she would have recognised, surely.'

'Yes,' Simon said, frowning. 'Although in the dark . . .'

'We both know that they were all accustomed to candlelight. No, I believe that if it were either of those two, Eleanor and Alicia at least would have recognised him and told us.'

Alicia, Simon thought. 'Alicia never gave us a description of the man, did she? It was only Cecily and Joan and their lady. The Queen and Alicia did not.'

'What of it?'

'When we spoke to Eleanor earlier, you pointed out that the killer must have been aware of the Queen's movements to ambush them all. We spent time thinking of Ellis and Pilk, but what if it wasn't the Despenser's man, but another. Perhaps the Queen had a man come to help her.'

'Which allies does she have here?' Baldwin mused.

'Her Chaplain mentioned one, didn't he? A man-at-arms about the palace, maybe?' Simon stood still, staring up at the grey sky. 'Alicia was not keen to describe the killer . . . and Peter told us she is having an affair with Blaket.'

Baldwin peered at him narrowly. 'What of it?'

'Baldwin, you remember the other day, when we got to the Bishop's palace and the Bishop had Rob serve us in uniform? I didn't recognise him at all at first, even though that was a well-lighted room. There are times when you may not recognise a man, aren't there? When you look at a man in uniform, you may see the uniform, not the man beneath. And since many will always wear the clothes bought for them by their master, if they were to go abroad in different clothes, they might not be recognised.'

'I suppose so. Why – what are you thinking?'

'If the Queen wished a man to do her this favour, she has a limited fund of men from which to draw. Her household is disbanded.'

'True.'

'But there is one man who has been intensely loyal to her. That guard on the door, Blaket. He has been hard to get past, hasn't he? He's been determined to protect his mistress. She has turned his head, perhaps. Or his wallet.'

'He's in the King's pay.'

'Maybe he was, Baldwin. But recall: we met him twice, and did not realise at first that it was the same man, because he was in different places each time. We just thought him a guard by his clothing. Yet if he was not in uniform, would we have recognised him at all?'

'The Queen sees him every day,' Baldwin said. 'He could hardly be unknown to her.'

'No. Nor to most of her ladies,' Simon said. 'But think what descriptions we've had from Eleanor and the others: that the man had the slighter build of one who fights on foot. No great thickened neck like a knight. Like Blaket. And yes, he would be known well enough in daylight – but how many of the ladies had seen him at night, in strange clothes, with a mask covering his features?'

'Why should he try to kill Mabilla?'

'As I said a minute ago, just think how loyal he was to the Queen. When we tried to see her in her chapel, he refused us entry. He was enormously protective of her.'

'True enough – yet I ask you again: why should he kill Mabilla?'

'Because he learned, perhaps, that she was not so loyal to the Queen as he would expect?'

Baldwin looked away. Although he was reluctant to admit it, he wanted to see Despenser accused and convicted. There was something about his swaggering arrogance, his conviction that no matter what, he was safe from any form of justice, that made Baldwin's hackles rise. It was obscene for any man to consider himself above the law. Even the King had his powers restricted by the barony. The law existed to protect all free men from persecution.

'Baldwin, I believe that the Bishop was trying to explain it to us. Perhaps he was telling us the Despenser was innocent of this.'

'And then what? That he was also innocent of ordering the murder of the innkeeper and his wife at the Swan at Chelchede?' Baldwin snapped. 'Simon, you've seen the man, he will take anything he wants and never count the cost to others. All that matters to him is his own intolerable greed.'

'Yes. But Baldwin, are you looking to have him gaoled no matter what? Gaoled for a crime he did not commit?'

'I would see his powers ripped from him, yes,' Baldwin admitted heavily.

'And what happened to the man who said that it was better that ten guilty men go free than even one innocent man be unfairly captured and slain?'

'Ouch! You use my own words against me? Is that kind? Is that fair?'

Simon grinned. The dark mood was leaving his friend. 'So how do we learn what we need to?'

'Do you recall Ellis, just before he died? He told us that the assassin entered by Arch on that part of the wall,' Baldwin said.

'Which was what we thought.'

Baldwin was frowning. 'Yes. Except all the guards were looking for someone climbing *in*. The trick would be to get in past the guards and do so without being seen. What if that was not how he climbed in, but how he intended to get *out*? Perhaps the man was not foolish enough to think that he could get away with climbing in and making his way all over the palace. Easier by far to get in during the day and hide, and then escape that way.'

'But he didn't escape.'

'No. He was stuck in the palace. He died in the King's chamber, if the blood in there was telling us the truth.'

Simon shrugged. 'Perhaps Despenser found his man and slew him himself? He would be one man Jack would trust, surely.'

'Not if he knew Sir Hugh.' Baldwin considered darkly. 'And then, what of the maid?'

Simon shook his head. 'No. It cannot have been Despenser. He would hardly have Jack emasculated and treated in that manner. No, it must have been another, someone who had reason to loathe him.'

'And who sought to . . . Simon, I think I understand at last!'

Chapter Forty

The King sat in his little parlour to the side of his main chamber and waited.

At other times he might have tapped his fingers on the table or the arm of his chair, but not today. Today he felt regally calm. All the tension of the last few days was gone with that confession.

It wasn't what he had wanted, of course. No, he'd wanted to be kept in sublime ignorance of the death, left to assume that the assassin was just another one of those sent to hurt him or his wife. For a while, he had entertained the thought that the man Jack atte Hedge was a murderer sent by the French to kill his wife. There could be no better disincentive for his journey to France than for the French themselves to have had his wife's corpse to point at. Perhaps the French courtiers like that murderous bastard Charles, Count of Valois, had decided that she would serve more use to them dead than alive. After all, if she died and the English King was unable to travel to France for fear of his security, the dukedom would revert to the French Crown, and those who had helped secure it would be able to anticipate a reward.

The knock came and the King motioned to his steward

to open it, and then sat back to consider the man as he walked inside. Such black treachery was repugnant.

'You have betrayed me, my Lord.'

Earl Edmund looked about him with as much dignity as he could muster. 'Your friend Despenser isn't here? Doesn't your little knight want to be here when you try to destroy me?'

'Do not seek to insult my intelligence,' King Edward said with icy calm. 'You have murdered, and sent the evidence here to my court – nay, to my own bloody *room*! You had the effrontery to murder and then confess it to me, your King!'

'And my brother. Yes, I did so. And I would do so again, if I found that the man who was supposed to be my vassal had taken the coin of another. Especially if he was supposed to be my own adviser – *especially* if he was taking Despenser's money to make me look a fool!'

'You need no help, my Lord. You are fully competent to do *that* on your own.'

'My Lord King, I am your loyal and devoted servant. We have the same blood in our veins . . .'

'*No.*'

The denial was so firm that Edmund hesitated. They had the same father, King Edward I, but Edmund was conceived by the King's second wife. 'We are brothers.'

'No longer. You are a fool. You lost me my dukedom, and now I must scrabble for every troop I can find to try to reinvade, or I must bow to the French King and abase myself before him. Me! Your King! All because of your incompetence and wilful foolhardiness. I know how you lost me the war. I know why I have lost Guyenne.'

'My Lord, if Despenser had supplied me with the men promised to us . . .'

'Oh yes, it always comes down to others, does it not? If not Sir Hugh, who would you blame then? Perhaps a French Constable? A Sergeant in your army? You are pathetic, but I have remained loyal to you and the memory of our father all this time. But no more. The gross insult you gave me when you murdered that man – and *had his blasted head delivered to my own hall* . . .' Edward forced himself to sit back again, willing his fingers to release their grip on the arm of the chair, trying to breathe more easily.

'My Lord, I was forced to do that. The man was a black traitor.'

'You think you can murder with impunity?'

That stung. 'You allow your lover to! He slaughters up and down the country and you do nothing! You smile on him, because . . .'

'Yes? Because of what, brother?' the King asked silkily.

Edmund curled his lip. Then he held out his hands, wrists together. 'So, you wish to have me gaoled now? You want to have me taken to the Tower?'

'No. But I will not have your face here in my court. You will go now, Earl. Leave me and do not come back. I will not have flagrant murderers here.'

Edmund made no more defence. He let his hands fall to his sides, and curtly nodded, walking backwards from the room as protocol demanded, and when he was gone, the King let his breath sigh from him.

At least the fool had gone quietly. Now darling Hugh and he would be alone. The King could reign, and rely on his lover without fearing that the jealousy of that half-wit would get in the way.

He stood, and as he did so, he caught sight of the darkened mess on his carpet. An assassin was repellent, but his blood was still more foul. Especially now, some days after the event.

Shouting for his steward, he pointed at it. 'Have that carpet burned.'

Blaket was still smiling after the previous afternoon.

He had met Alicia outside the gate to the Abbey, just a short distance away, but far enough to be free from watchful eyes, and they had made their way over the bridge, past the mill at the Tyburn River, and thence southwards towards Chelchede.

It was cold, and he had pulled off his cloak to offer it to her, but she refused with a pained expression. Still, when they reached the little hovel which he had borrowed for the afternoon, she was happy enough to disrobe, and the pair had made love wildly beside the hearth on a bed of clean straw with rugs and skins laid atop. The memory of those kisses were with him still, along with the scratches on his back from her nails.

When he saw the two men approaching him, he had a premonition of trouble, and when they stopped and fixed him with serious expressions on their faces, he felt his heart begin to thump noisily. He could still remember the pain and anguish on Arch's face after the 'questioning' he had endured.

'You can't go in there, my Lords,' he said. 'The Queen is resting.'

'Why did you do it, Blaket?' Baldwin said.

'Do what?'

'Kill Mabilla.'

Blaket took a deep breath, a diver taking his last before a plunge. 'Yes,' he said.

Simon himself breathed a little more easily now. 'So you admit killing her?'

'Someone had to. She was a danger to my lady the Queen. Our Queen.'

'What made her so dangerous?'

'That I cannot tell you,' he said.

'Cannot or will not?' Simon pressed him.

'He cannot, messieurs,' said the Queen as she pulled open the door.

Simon glanced at Baldwin, and then the two walked past the guard and into the room with the Queen.

'You have been here before, I hear,' she said.

'You have a most devoted guard,' Baldwin smiled. 'He caught us in here.'

'He said that you had been seeking the murderer of that assassin.'

'And of your lady-in-waiting,' Simon said pointedly.

'I know nothing of the death of the assassin. All I do know is, he was sent here to kill me. It was not possible to forgive such an act. It will never be possible.'

'The maid?' Baldwin asked. As he spoke, he saw the blonde woman behind the Queen. It was Alicia, the woman who Peter had said was in love with this guard, Blaket. She sat at a stool with her hands in her lap, listening to every word. 'Mabilla?' Baldwin prompted.

'You ordered her death, Your Majesty?'

The Queen looked at him very directly. 'You think me evil, monsieur? Mabilla was a spy. She watched me all the time – every hour of every day. It would have been pleasant to have ordered her to be removed from my side, but I am much dissipated in my authority of late.'

'Your husband would surely have . . .'

'What? Taken away Mabilla to please *me*? My husband has another lover now. A third person has come between us,' she said bitterly. 'You know this. All know it. And I have to endure the shame.'

'What made it so necessary that she die?'

'She knew that I was trying to write to my brother, the King of France. She watched over me constantly.'

'So why did you order her death?' Baldwin asked. 'She had been watching you for some little while, I suppose. So why have her killed just then?'

'Because she was attempting to have *me* killed. What, you are surprised? You knew that the assassin had been sent to kill me, did you not? How would he have been able to do that, without knowing what I would be doing at different hours of the day? He needed someone to tell him – and Mabilla was the one who did so. She told him all that I was doing – when I went to my chapel, when I would be at prayer, when I returned, when I would be eating, when I would be sleeping, and *where*, too. She had sold me to my executioner.'

'So you ordered Blaket to kill her?'

'Yes. I wanted no more spies in my home. Removing her means no one else will be so keen to commit *petit traison* against me.'

'But what of the assassin?' Baldwin asked.

'Him?' The Queen smiled. 'Ah, for that you must ask my Lord.'

'The King?' Baldwin asked. 'He and Despenser would hardly have a man killed and then make it appear that sodomy was involved, setting the body behind the throne to make it obvious that the dead man was the power behind the King . . .'

Isabella laughed. At first Baldwin thought it was a reaction of horror at the thought of the barbaric treatment of the corpse, but then he realised that it was genuine amusement.

'Monsieur! Monsieur! Did you think that? No! It was merely to say that the man should have no children. He who has dared to try to attack the wife of the King should not be permitted to sire his own children. Any traitor would receive the same punishment.'

Baldwin sighed. That was not a construction he had put on the punishment of the man. Yet it was a normal punishment for the worst traitors, along with hanging and drawing. And yet . . . 'But if, as you allege, Your Majesty, the Despenser killed this man, surely he would not cut off his tarse and thrust it into his mouth? To him, the man was honourable and faithful.'

'You think that there is a limit to that loathsome man's behaviour?'

Baldwin held her gaze for a while, and then nodded. 'I understand. Now – Blaket. What should I do with him?'

The Queen was very calm. 'Monsieur, you could have him arrested. You have his confession, you have my admission of complicity. All you need do is denounce us.'

Baldwin could feel her stillness as she spoke, and he eyed her closely, seeking a clue as to her real feelings. Simon, he saw, was enthralled by her tale. He was looking at her with that contemplative expression which Baldwin knew so well.

And yes, truth be told, Baldwin had a deal of sympathy for her. She had fallen from such power to a position of humble subservience. Her toppling had brought her as low as any poor ward protected by an unjust and unpredictable master. Here she was, a beautiful woman, mother to the King's children, honourable and faithful, and because her husband had discovered he loved another man, she was all but destitute. All her servants had been replaced with those more easily bent to the King's will, her Chaplain even had been removed.

'My lady, I am no judge. I am concerned with the truth, and now I think I know it. I am anxious to see that no man suffers injustice, and I confess, I see injustice here, but only in the actions of others towards you – not from you towards other people. And your guard, I believe, has acted in good faith, if in a deplorable manner.'

'What would you have done?' Blaket said. 'I killed her in order to protect my Lady.'

'Plainly,' Sir Baldwin said. 'And did *she* recognise you?'

'No,' the Queen said. 'I did not.'

But Baldwin had not meant the Queen. Behind her he could see the blonde woman, still watching carefully. Alicia was not eager to see her man punished for protecting the Queen. Perhaps she was in truth an honourable, devoted servant.

In his mind's eye Baldwin saw that little corridor again. The flickering light, the women passing along it from the chapel towards the Queen's chamber, the sudden shock as the man leaped out, his blade flashing, and stabbing Mabilla in the breast while the others all recoiled, screaming, fainting, and one alone being bold enough to move forward. Why? To show her man that he had killed the right woman?

He might never know for certain, but that seemed the most likely tale.

'Your Highness,' he bowed, and he and Simon took their leave.

The King was expecting the second knock, but when the door opened, he found himself confronted by the serious faces of Bishop John of Bath and Wells, and Walter Stapledon, Bishop of Exeter.

'My Lord Bishops – please, enter and take some wine with me,' he said graciously enough.

'I thank you, King Edward. It is good of you to be so kindly towards your humble subjects.'

As humble as two of the richest clerical thieves could be, the King told himself, but he smiled and inclined his head as though he believed the honeyed words. 'And to what do I owe this visit, my Lord Bishops?'

It was Drokensford who spoke. 'My Liege, as you know, it is a matter of great debate among your council as to who should be sent to France to undertake your mission. In an affair of such delicacy and concern, only a most trusted ambassador could be chosen.'

'I know that. We have discussed the topic at such

length, I am grown tired of the whole thing. In God's name! What must I do to protect my Crown? There is no one safe enough.'

'Apart from your wife, of course,' Stapledon reminded him.

'Yes, yes. That is what was concluded.'

'And yet, if you send her there in the guise of a beggar, it will hardly reassure the French King that your intentions towards her are to be kindly upon her return.'

'She is French, and our realm is in a state of suspended war with France,' the King said harshly. 'You expect me to reward the sister of my enemy?'

'My Liege, of course not. But it would not be necessary to reward her, merely to return to her some of the estates and income which are presently denied to her. Elevate her to her correct station before sending her, or the service which she alone can do you might be irreparably damaged before she sails.'

'She is unfaithful to me, her King!'

'There is no evidence of that,' Drokensford said repressively. All knew that his tone implied that there was much fault on the King's part.

'And what if she turns faithless while she is there?'

'Hold back your son,' Stapledon said. 'Keep him safe here, and only when all is agreed do you send him to join her so he may swear fealty to King Charles. And when he goes, I shall go with him as your eyes and ears in the French court.'

'You swear?'

'Yes.'

'Then let it be so!'

Chapter Forty-One

Baldwin left Blaket at the door to the Queen's rooms and stood a moment deep in thought. 'Come with me, old friend,' he said at last, and led Simon back the way which they had taken earlier in the day.

Simon wondered what was making Baldwin frown so. 'Blaket killed Mabilla, then?'

'Apparently so – in order to provide a service to his mistress the Queen, and incidentally, perhaps, to protect his relationship with the Queen's other maid: Alicia. Did you observe how closely that woman watched and listened all through the Queen's speech just now?'

'I only had eyes for the Queen,' Simon admitted. 'But what of it? At last we know who killed the girl.'

'And we know who killed the assassin, Jack.'

'*You* may. I do not.'

'Oh, Simon. It must have been Despenser.'

'Perhaps. Yet Bishop Walter was most insistent. I think he knew something. Perhaps the confessional . . . No matter. I am not convinced it was Sir Hugh.'

'If it were not, then it was surely the only other man who had easy access to that room,' Baldwin said.

'There is only one such man.'

Baldwin nodded. 'And I wish to see him briefly to ask him about that stain on his carpet.'

As they crossed a passage near the King's chamber, they met a couple of servants carrying a rolled rug.

Baldwin stopped them. 'Where did you get that from?'

'The King. He said it has been stained and must be burned.'

'Good fellow! You do not need to do that. Let me buy it from you.'

So saying, he dug in his purse for some coins and pressed them into the men's hands. 'Could you take the thing to the small hall out in the Green Yard?'

The two looked at each other. 'I suppose so.'

'Then do so, and I should be grateful if you could also seek out the Coroner to the household, a knight called John.'

That, it appeared, was still more easy to arrange.

'What are you planning, Baldwin?' Simon asked as they strode forward along the passage to the door to the King's chamber.

'Who is it now?' King Edward demanded.

He had only just disposed of the two Bishops, and now there was another man come to visit him. As the door opened and his steward peeped out, he felt a rising resentment.

If he were at glorious Eltham or Winchester, or up in York, he could have entertained himself happily, traipsing about the land with peasants, helping them with their annual tasks of hedging and ditching, and joining in their little festivities afterwards. There was no one who understood the common people like him.

But no. Here in Thorney Island, he was a prisoner, held here in his cell while those who despised him dropped in to goggle at him and make their demands, while he must sit and nod and make polite conversation until they would leave him and the next ones would appear. He was no better off than Isabella, his Queen. At least she had all semblance of responsibility taken from her. In some ways he would be happy if their positions were reversed, if she were in power and authority, and he was resting in a small, quiet cloister with no one to pester him.

'Who is it now?' he repeated as his servant glanced back at him.

'The Keeper and Bailiff Puttock, my Lord.'

The two rascals entered a moment later, both with their faces to the floor in a wholly respectable display.

'Well?' he demanded of them testily. Where the Bishops had been offered wine and seats, these two could remain standing.

'My Lord, you asked me to tell you when I had successfully concluded my investigations into the murder of the assassin and the lady-in-waiting Mabilla.'

'What of the attempt on my friend's life?'

'That we have resolved,' Baldwin said. 'Your friend is content, I believe, that there will be no more attacks from that quarter.'

The King sat back with some astonishment. 'You are sure of this?'

'Quite certain, my Liege.'

'Then you are to be congratulated, Sir Baldwin. What else?'

'We have investigated the two deaths with all the sagacity at our command. It is certain sure that the assassin died somewhere here in your chambers, my Lord.'

'What?' the King growled. 'You suggest that *I* had some part in the murder?'

'My Lord, of course not. But he was an assassin. If he had been found in your chamber, what could be more natural than that your guards in here, or even your good friend Sir Hugh, should execute him as being a threat to your life?'

'Sir Hugh? No. It was, I believe, one of my guards. Sir Baldwin, you are an astute fellow.'

'I try to use the brains that the good Lord provided for me.'

'And the woman Mabilla?'

Baldwin looked at the King. 'Naturally, the assassin was too fearful to press his attack upon the Queen. The shrieks of the women unsettled him and drove him away. And by accident he happened upon your chamber.'

'Where my men killed him. Then why did none of them tell me this?'

'I should have expected them to have done so. After all, the man did bleed upon your floor-coverings. We noticed that earlier today.'

'So I saw. The good Bailiff could scarce take his eyes from the spot,' the King observed drily.

Simon had the grace to redden. He had thought no one could have seen how his attention was diverted to that patch.

'My Lord, I am sure that if you recall that night, perhaps your men woke you to tell you of an attack thwarted somewhere out in the main hall, and then you went back to sleep. It all appeared as a dream.'

'And if I do not recall such a thing?'

'Then surely the tale I tell did not happen. And another man must be sought, one who had access to your chamber, one who could draw steel in your own room and slay a man.'

'And if that were so?'

'If that were so, my Lord, then it must become known that an assassin entered your chamber. He came so close to finding you, and to executing you in a black, treacherous act. Others in the land might think to themselves that it would be relatively easy to repeat the action of a solitary assassin and try to force their way into your rooms. And perhaps one, or two, or three men might die before the fourth achieved his aim. We do not wish for that. Better by far that we forget the precise location and recall only that the body was discovered in the Great Hall.'

'I can see that you would make a masterful diplomatist, Sir Baldwin.'

'My Liege, I sincerely hope not!' Baldwin said with feeling.

Sir John perched himself on the bench on which the headless body of Piers was resting, arms folded, and peered down at the head, resting on its cheek a few inches away from the torso. He reached over and drew the head down until the stub of ligament and muscle met with those of the torso. It rolled a little, and rested unmatched once more.

'Sir John, I am glad you could come here,' Sir Baldwin said a few moments later, the door rattling on its ancient hinges. He waited until Simon had come in, before slamming the door shut once more. 'What a miserable place this is!'

'I have known worse,' Sir John noted, glancing up at the roof. 'At least it is dry.'

Baldwin did not enlighten him. He had been thinking of the whole of Thorney Island, perhaps extending as far as the city of London itself.

'This man. You know who he was?' Sir John asked. When they shook their heads, he continued, 'Piers de Wrotham. A minor player in this arena, he was a political fellow, who spent his life advising Earl Edmund. However, today the good Earl learned that Piers was receiving instructions from Sir Hugh le Despenser before advising the Earl. Sir Edmund made a gift of his head to the knight, and now he's running from the King's ire. I think he will go into exile in all likelihood.'

'And justice will have been served,' Baldwin said with disgust.

'Do not be angry, Sir Baldwin. I have learned that anger at injustice wins little reward. No, it is better to be resilient in the face of such treatment. We do our jobs, we record our facts, and we try to keep our hearts disconnected from the miserable truth of the mundane nature of the cruelty inflicted upon the men and women of our realm. There are some, like this one here,' he said, looking down at Piers's head once more, 'whose death I cannot mourn, because he was one of those who caused much of the sorrow. But others, others I mourn. The ones who have been mistreated and only seek a little compensation, the ones who've been robbed and seen their livings destroyed by the harsh greed of the barons. There are many who deserve sympathy.'

'Does this Piers not deserve justice?' Simon demanded.

'Aye. But the exile of the killer will be enough. The King may change his mind, I suppose, and allow Earl Edmund to return, but I doubt it. The fellow has lost the Crown its jewel in France. I don't think he'll ever be welcomed back. This was the last sugary coating on the cake of his misdeeds.'

'What of the other deaths?'

'What of them? The innocents will go unavenged, I fear. The assassin – well, I am less concerned about him. But I would like to know the truth of his death. And I would be glad to see the killers of the innkeeper at the Swan brought to justice.'

'They are already at the bar before God and answering for their crimes, I feel sure,' Baldwin said, and told him about the fight between Ellis and the others in the New Palace Yard. 'William Pilk and he were slain. I am sure that one or both were responsible, under Sir Hugh, for the murder of Henry and his wife.'

'What of the killings here? Mabilla and the man?'

Baldwin nodded towards the carpet standing rolled at the wall. 'If you look at that, it has a large bloody mess on it. I think that the assassin died on it. The rug came from the King's own chamber. That was where Jack atte Hedge died.'

'Good God! Why?'

'Jack was told to come and kill the Queen. I am sure that Sir Hugh paid him for that. Sir Hugh also gave him a horse and had a formal agreement with him, an indenture. But he also had a spy in the Queen's cloister. Not only his wife, but a woman who was reporting to him independently of his wife, just in case his amiable, kindly lady might grow fond of the Queen. He obviously feared that she might become disgusted with the task he had given her, that of gaoler. The spy was Mabilla.'

'So the Queen had her killed?'

'In a manner, yes. She told the Despenser that she wanted Mabilla removed. I think she probably made it clear in what way she wanted it to happen. And the Despenser was happy to comply with her demands, and even made the death a demonstration of his power, showing the Queen that whenever he wanted, he could strike at any in Isabella's entourage – including, perhaps, herself.'

'But he appeared quite shocked by the woman's death.'

'He would, though, wouldn't he?' Baldwin said. 'The man is quite a consummate actor.'

'I see,' Sir John said. 'But there are many gaps in your story, Sir Baldwin. If Despenser was to have killed the man, why do so in the King's chamber? Why carry his body to the Great Hall to drop it behind the throne, and why commit that foul mutilation?'

'True enough. But I fear you will have to enquire yourself about those aspects. I am only seeking to tell you the story as I understand it,' Baldwin said.

Sir John nodded thoughtfully. Then he sprang lightly

from the table, and addressed the two. 'I thank you for the tale, in any case. It is quite entertaining.'

'It is the only one you will have on the affair, I think,' Baldwin said.

Later that night, Baldwin was lying back on his bed when Simon challenged him.

'That was a whole cartload of garbage, wasn't it?'

'What was, Simon?'

'The tale you gave to John. There was hardly any truth in it, was there?'

'Simon, look at it this way: we set out to seek a killer, and in the end it became clear that the killer knew his way about the palace, that he was a man who could conceal himself, that he was someone known to Alicia, in all probability, and someone who was removing a woman whom the Queen wanted taken away.'

'Yes.'

'Blaket was plainly the man who killed Mabilla. He confessed as much. Jack was killed in the King's chamber. We know that too. However, Despenser is not so good an actor that he could feign anxiety and rage. He did not know what had happened to his assassin. I am sure of that.'

'But then . . . Oh, in Christ's name, you don't mean—'

'Of course. The King is no fool. He heard about the spying and was none too pleased about it. I dare say he was happy enough to see Mabilla removed. But no matter what, he is a politician too. He was furious to learn that an assassin had been hired to kill his wife. It would ruin any chance of regaining Guyenne.'

'How would he learn of the assassin?'

'Simon, we already know of one double-agent – that man Piers. There are others here who would act in the same manner, finding all they can from one master to sell to another. But let us assume this Piers realised that there was such a plan in motion, and he told the King. Edward saw how much damage this must do, so he himself sought the assassin. He warned a few trusted guards to keep their eyes open. One of them was Blaket. He met Jack and persuaded him to meet with Despenser in a small chamber, near the King's hall. But inside was not Despenser but the King himself. There Jack was murdered, and that obscene mutilation committed.'

'Why that, though? If the King is so fond of other men as you have said, why do that?'

'It was nothing to do with sodomy, Simon. That was a sign of the King's great displeasure at such treason. Castration is common for those who try to commit such offences, as the Queen herself told us.'

'So you mean that Blaket saw all this, and then returned to the Queen's door to kill Mabilla?'

'That was his duty, as he saw it. He loves two ladies, Simon. Alicia with his body, but the Queen with his heart. You saw how devoted he was to her. When she wanted peace, we could approach no further than to him. Passage beyond him would have involved someone's death. Yet he took us to the *King* when he found us in the Queen's rooms.'

'So will you denounce him?'

'What, Blaket or the King? To denounce one means also affirming the guilt of the other. Would you and I live if we succeeded in that, Simon? I do not think so. No. We should consider ourselves fortunate to have escaped this place with our lives.'

'One point, though,' Simon said after a few moments. 'You said that Despenser could not act well, that he wouldn't be able to dissemble in that manner, but you're happy to accuse the King of exactly that. What makes you think that our Liege could do so when Despenser could not?'

'Simon, do you remember the day we first arrived here and saw the roads? I mentioned the King's pastimes, didn't I?'

'Ah – you said that he enjoyed acting!'

'Precisely.'

And that, Baldwin had hoped, would be an end to the matter. He was disgusted with the council of the King, distrusted all those who sought power and advancement from the King, and felt threatened by the King's own most trusted adviser.

There was nothing here for him. He could not alter the decisions being made, because the decisions were made by a few powerful people before ever any meeting was held. Even men whom he had once trusted, like Bishop Walter Stapledon, were proven to be more interested in preserving their own power than in seeing justice done. That might be a harsh view of the Bishop's motives in concealing the indenture, but all Baldwin knew was that the Bishop had held that scrap in trust, and had then passed it on to Despenser, the man whom it accused.

But although Baldwin's own desire was to leave the

city and make his way back to Devon, to his wife and children, at all possible speed, events were shortly to take a turn which he had not predicted.

Chapter Forty-Two

Wednesday after the Feast of the Blessed Virgin Mary[1]

Thorney Island

The Queen was the first to be told of the new proposal –
after Sir Hugh, the Bishops, her son and the King's
ambassadors.

She was startled to receive an invitation to see her
husband. His chambers were so close, and yet she had
grown accustomed to the fact of their separation over the
last months.

'You are sure he wants me?' was her only response to
the request.

The marvellous painted hall in which he waited for her
was a welcoming chamber. The fire in the hearth was
roaring, and although she had left a pleasantly warmed
room behind her, this was so much hotter that Isabella
was forced to shed her cloak.

'My Lord, you asked to see me?' she enquired, giving
him a courtesy and keeping her eyes demurely downcast

---

[1] 6 February 1325

so he might not read the anger in her eyes.

'Lady, I have come to a conclusion.' It sounded as though he had drunk poison, for the words almost choked him. 'Your *brother* has demanded that I should go to him to swear homage for Guyenne and the Duchy. I feel I cannot go at present, not while our countries are at daggers drawn. So I have decided that you shall go in my place.'

'You have?'

'I and the parliament. We are sure that your good offices will aid our negotiations. I wish you to leave within the month.'

'But there is so much to prepare! Surely the Pope could send another to act for you? Would not a Bishop or Archbishop carry more weight than a mere woman?'

'The Pope suggested you,' the King spat.

She looked up then, so that he could read the contempt in her eyes. She had known that all along. It was pathetic of him not to think of the many ways in which a prisoner might learn news of the world. For her part, it was easy. Drokensford kept her well-informed, as always.

'You will go in the first week in March,' the King said, containing his own rage with difficulty. This woman was a she-wolf. Cunning, evil, cruel, she was the embodiment of all that was unnatural in a woman. He could see that she had known about all this beforehand – well, let her think that she had won. When she came back from the French court, when she had done his will over there and won back Guyenne for him, she would return to her prison in England. Not here, though, where she could plot with her friends. Somewhere else, farther away from power. Perhaps in Castle Acre. Norfolk was a county for which she had always asserted a liking. She could go there and fester.

'I suppose I shall be forced to travel with people chosen for me?' she said after a moment.

'I will wish to keep the costs of the embassy at a minimum.'

'Naturally. Yet I would have some men I can trust.'

'You have my word that all will be honourable and trustworthy.'

'Your word? I am reassured.'

He grated his teeth, but swallowed his anger at her sarcasm. 'You wish for a senior man? A Bishop? Earl?'

'Will our son travel with me?'

The King smiled. 'No. He will come later, provided that all the negotiations are successful. I will send him on to you when all the plans have been set out clearly.'

For Sir Hugh, it was the best of all worlds. As he had hoped when he first tried to tempt Earl Edmund into plotting against him, persuading the fool through Piers that Sir Hugh did not want the Queen to leave the country, in reality it was clearly impossible for him to be seen to attempt to prevent her going. The only effective manner of his preserving his power was for the Queen to be apparently supported by him so that the French did not have any more incentive to seek his death.

It would have been best for him to have seen her killed here, but it was not to be.

'My Liege.'

The King took his arm with a smile. 'Come, look at this, Sir Hugh.'

At the window, Sir Hugh looked out. From here they had a view of a magnificent royal barge. 'That is marvellous!'

'Isn't it?'

It was painted in red, with glints of gold where gilt licked the decoration. Cushions were spread about, and Sir Hugh could see that there was a great awning to keep the King and his guests sheltered in the worst of weathers. At the stern was a comfortable-looking seat with padded arms and thick cushions for the King. Beside it, a comfy, but lower chair.

'I had it made for the summer, and wanted to view it beforehand. I hope you and I will be able to use it in the warm months.'

'Yes, I am sure . . .'

'So no more attempts on the Queen's life, Sir Hugh,' the King murmured.

Sir Hugh smiled. 'You need not worry about that.'

'No, I do not – do I?' the King said, but this time – for the first time – Sir Hugh heard that special note in his tone: it was the same tone he had used when pronouncing death on Sir Andrew Harclay; when he told his cousin, Earl Thomas of Lancaster, that he must die; when he spoke to his wife. It was the sort of voice he used for people whom he had once trusted, when he learned of their faithlessness.

There was only one thing for Sir Hugh to do, and he did so hurriedly. Dropping to his knees, he bent his head almost to the floor. 'My Lord, don't blame me! I only sought what I was sure was best for you.'

'Yes – *and* you, eh? No more, Sir Hugh. It is tedious

to have to seek out such men. And they do bleed an inordinate amount.'

Sir Hugh looked up at his lord and lover. 'It was you?'

'So no more, Sir Hugh. I have lost my wife. I would not lose you too.' He paused. 'You must pay. You will buy me a new carpet. My last one was soiled.'

Richard Blaket stood aside as the Queen returned to her chamber, Alicia in attendance. As the Queen entered, Alicia remained outside with him.

'We shall be travelling soon,' she said.

'To Eltham?' Richard asked. He tried to keep the disappointment from his voice, but failed. The guards set about this island were all selected from the area and would not travel with the household when it was moving across the countryside.

'No. We are to go to France. *France!*' She clapped her hands and smiled in delight.

'France?' he said dully. 'How long for?'

'We won't be there all that long,' she said, suddenly quiet as she saw his pain. 'The Queen has to go to discuss things with their King, and then we'll be back.'

He nodded sadly. It was natural that she would be glad to travel to France. It was the centre of culture, of beauty, all that was lovely to a woman.

'You aren't happy?'

'How can I be happy when I'm going to have to wave you goodbye?'

'I will be returning.'

'Yes,' he said. But all he could think of was the long months of loneliness while she was gone.

Chapter Forty-Three

Thursday after the Feast of the Blessed Virgin Mary[1]

Bishop of Exeter's house, Straunde

It was a foul morning. Even as Baldwin and Simon threw their belongings over their mounts and bound them tightly ready for the journey, Rob at Simon's side, swearing as his frozen fingers fumbled with the straps and buckles, a sleeting rain greyed the heavens and Simon had to stop and pull on his broad-brimmed hat to keep the icy chill from seeping down the back of his neck.

'Simon, Sir Baldwin; I wish you God speed,' the Bishop called from the shelter of his doorway. He made the sign of the cross as the three crouched before him. 'Be careful in your journeying, and may you return safely.'

Baldwin and Simon crossed themselves, and Rob hurriedly copied them, before all three mounted their horses and prepared to make their way homewards.

Before they could ride away, though, a messenger clattered through the gateway. 'Sir Baldwin, the King

---

[1] 7 February 1325

wishes to speak with you before you go.'

Baldwin would say nothing as they made their way along Straunde and down King Street, but Simon could see his tension. The knight was wound up like a hempen cord, ready to snap in a moment.

'You had best wait here,' Baldwin said at the gatehouse to the New Palace Yard.

'No. I am coming too,' Simon said.

'You weren't called for.'

'People often forget me. I am too insignificant,' Simon grinned.

In the end Baldwin agreed, but as he passed his reins to Rob, he felt as though his boots were made of lead. He had no idea what the summons presaged, but was convinced that the King must have some reason that would not be to Baldwin's benefit.

The guards stood aside as the two approached, their polearms held upright, and Baldwin and Simon were ushered into the King's chamber by the steward.

'Sir Baldwin. I am glad to see you again.'

'Your Majesty,' Baldwin said, bowing low. He half-expected to be arrested as he stood there.

'You helped my wife a great deal over this strange attempted murder. Do you like her?'

'My Lord? I . . . she is a wonderful lady.'

'But do you *like* her?'

'Me? My Lord, how could I aspire to like her? She is a lady so superior to me, that I would not know what to say to her.'

'You are returning to your homes?'

Baldwin and Simon exchanged confused looks. 'Ah,

yes, my Liege,' Baldwin managed after a short while.

'Good. Well, God speed. I look forward to meeting you both again.'

'Yes, my Liege.'

The King nodded and then astonished both men. He took a purse from his belt and gave it to Baldwin. 'You have been of some service to me and my wife. This will compensate you for the travel and for your efforts when you arrived here.'

'There is no need for this, Your Majesty!' Baldwin gasped as he looked inside.

'I think that there is. Travel is not cheap in my realm, and in any case, this is to compensate you for the return journey.'

'What return?'

'When I send you with my wife to France, Sir Baldwin. You will go with her to protect her on the way. And mind you do protect her – and advise me of any threats to my son when he joins my Queen to pay homage to his uncle.'

Now you can buy any of these other bestselling books by **Michael Jecks** from your bookshop or *direct from his publisher*.

FREE P&P AND UK DELIVERY
(Overseas and Ireland £3.50 per book)

The Abbot's Gibbet	£6.99
The Leper's Return	£6.99
The Mad Monk of Gidleigh	£6.99
The Templar's Penance	£6.99
The Outlaws of Ennor	£6.99
The Tolls of Death	£6.99
The Chapel of Bones	£6.99
The Butcher of St Peter's	£6.99
A Friar's Bloodfeud	£6.99
The Death Ship of Dartmouth	£6.99
The Malice of Unnatural Death	£6.99

TO ORDER SIMPLY CALL THIS NUMBER

01235 400 414

or visit our website: www.headline.co.uk

Prices and availability subject to change without notice.